"A gritty thrill ride. Detective Danny Mangan will take you through the darkest aspects of the human psyche, until you'll be left wondering how the human mind can harbor such darkness."

Officer G. Morrison
National Airport Police Department
Washington, D.C.

www.parkgatepress.com

The Underground Detective

www.dionysusbooks.com

Also by Thomas Laird

Blue Collar and Other Stories (1994)

Cutter (2001)

Season of the Assassin (2003)

Black Dog (2004)

Voices of the Dead (2006)

To Marsha, always. To Kathy and Andy and Anne.

And to Matt Fullerty, who brought back the stuff that dreams are made of.

The Underground Detective

A NOVEL OF CHICAGO STREETS

by

Thomas Laird

Dionysus Books / Parkgate Press

Publishers Online!

For updates and more resources, visit Dionysus Books and Parkgate Press online at

www.dionysusbooks.com
www.parkgatepress.com

Copyright © 2012 Thomas Laird
All Rights Reserved. Permission is granted to copy or reprint portions for any non-commercial use, except that they may not be posted online without permission.

Page layout and cover design by Dionysus Books
Cover photographs courtesy of Flickr and Picasa

ISBN-13: 978-1-937056-60-5

Library of Congress Control Number: 2012935612
Library of Congress Subject Headings:

Chicago (Ill.)--Fiction
Chicago in Fiction
Crime--Fiction
Fiction
Fiction--Psychological aspects
Police--Illinois--Chicago--Fiction
Prostitutes--Crimes against--Fiction
Sex crimes--Fiction

First Edition (worldwide) March 2012
[Parkgate Press: Dionysus Books reference number: 011]

"Every man has some reminiscences which he would not tell to everyone, but only to his friends. He has others which he would not reveal even to his friends, but only to himself, and that in secret. But finally there are still others which a man is even afraid to tell himself, and every decent man has a considerable number of such things stored away. That is, one can even say that the more decent he is, the greater the number of such things in his mind."

Fyodor Dostoyevsky
Notes from Underground (1843)

The Underground Detective

1

You don't know loss until you've got it. So goes the conventional wisdom.

I lost my wife when she took off, about the time our daughter, Kelly, turned four. Mary, my ex-wife, ran out on us in 1973. I came home to marry Mary when my wife was eight months' pregnant. The Army was benevolent enough to let me come back to The World for the nuptials. I was with the Rangers at that time, so it was surprising that they'd let me come home, but as soon as the ceremony and the one-day honeymoon in Oak Lawn, Illinois, were over, I was on a flight back to Southeast Asia.

So Kelly was technically illegitimate for the eight months she was inside my wife. Mary and I had lived together two years prior to our daughter's entry into the world, but I had the feeling we were a terminal couple even before the birthing. I married my wife to give Kelly a name. I didn't want her sharing a "scarlet letter" for the rest of her life. Marriage was the least I could do. But losing Mary hurt more than I thought it would, even if our being together permanently wasn't happening.

I raised Kelly into the teenager she is today. I mean I tried, at least. I suppose you could blame me for her bulimia and her drug habit, but I've already hoisted all the above on my own shoulders. Anybody made parental misfires, it was I. No one else. Mary has been long gone. Kelly barely remembers her mother. She was just four, as I said. Her mom becomes more vague each day.

Kelly is very bright. You couldn't tell by her grades because she skipped school so often that the truant officer and I were on a first name basis. She has been suspended three times from the Catholic high school that I pay major bucks to, and the next time she boogies, she's expelled. I can't blame the school. I try very hard not to be my kid's enabler.

The only reason she's still enrolled at Sacred Heart on the south side is that the truant officer has shown me professional courtesy. At least that's what he calls it, since I'm a Chicago police officer. I've been in Homicide the past five years. My kid's been bulimic and a junkie for the last three years, I estimate. I estimate because Kelly lies so often to me that it's hard to tell how long she's smoked and done uppers and whatever else she's snorted or swallowed. She hasn't injected because I check her arms and legs and all the other usual suspected places. Which really pisses her off. I've taken her in several times for urine drops at our family doctor, but it's my house and my rules, and she can leave any time she wants, I've told her, now that she's seventeen. She's not legal until her next birthday, in August, but I don't explain the letter of the law for her because I really don't want her to leave, but if I ever catch her with tracks I'll arrest her myself, and then she can have the streets and all their shabby splendors.

I've taken her to counseling twice, and she was in out-patient rehab three months ago. But she won't go to a counselor unless I take her there personally. She now weighs about 90 pounds, I guesstimate. I know she's well under the century mark. And I know also that her expulsion from Sacred Heart Academy on the southside is imminent. I know the call is coming from their truant officer at any moment, as I sit here in Homicide, not far from Lake Michigan.

The Rangers liked guys like me. Good students with a couple years at a community college. Good athletes, but shorter (five nine) and with wiry builds. The bigger men made bigger targets, we used to tell each other. Our kind of work required bulldogs, in Vietnam. We had to be tough and we had to persevere, and we did. The War is lost, now that it's 1986. Lost for thirteen years. I don't use the fall of Saigon in 1975 as a terminal date for Vietnam. The peace talks in Paris concluded that sad and lame business, as far as I'm concerned. I returned home in 1972, just a year before Henry Kissinger talked peace in The City of Lights.

One year later, in 1973, my wife left me and my daughter, Kelly. So I know about loss. A lost spouse and a lost war.

And now a daughter who's about to become one of the departed.

"Detective Mangan," the Medical Examiner pronounces.

His name is Harry Morris. I've known him for five years, on the job. He is about fifty, tall and lanky with a shock of chestnut hair always dangling over his brow. It's sometimes distracting, watching him try to tug that hank of unruly hair back away from his forehead.

The survivor was a teenaged female. They've brought her to County Hospital on the west side because she's nineteen and indigent. The copper I talked to, Sergeant Phil Esposito, said he thinks she's a hooker. Phil said he thinks the dead vic was a street denizen, also. Phil is a middle-sized man, about forty-five, with a close-cropped hair cut that is nothing but dark blond stubble. He keeps it short, very GI. He was an MP in the same War I fought.

"It's spooky, Danny," he tells me. His eyes keep looking at the tree, out here in the forest preserve where the two girls were found.

"Why?" I ask the sergeant.

His eyes keep staring at that oak tree where the survivor was bound and gagged with duct tape.

Then he finally looks my way.

"Her hair was snow white. Like the Disney cartoon, *Snow White*. He made her watch the whole thing."

"So we have a witness?"

"No, Danny. Not really. He cut out her tongue, and the poor

broad is catatonic, the ME says, even though he's not a shrink. Her hair was polar bear white, and I never saw this kid even blink once. She's way gone, almost as far away as the dead one. He did things to that one that were highly creative. Things we never saw, even over in the shit."

Esposito took off after he informed me all that.

I lifted the plastic off the victim, and then I saw what Phil was talking about. It might have taken a while to recognize that what was left was human for the poor bastard who stumbled onto the two of them, out here in Evans' Pond.

This preserve is located on the far southwest side. It's on the very edge of the city limits. There are state cops here, too, but it's our jurisdiction, and my case.

Lila arrives just as they remove the corpse. She's been my partner for two years. She's a hard case and ex-military (Air Force), as well. She flew jets and dumped death on the Viet Cong and the NVA. She was shot down twice and was rescued both times, obviously.

Lila is gay. She does not broadcast it because the closet doors have not flown open, yet, in Chicago. The time is coming when it will, I think, but it hasn't arrived, at the moment.

Which matters not at all to me. It would be a true bone of contention for many other police, I'm sure, but I only care about her competence. She's got a shitload of competence and confidence. Her ability and intelligence are sky high. I've never been around a copper who was better at this job, and I trust her in any of the "dark alleys" we've walked down. She has a black belt in karate—I've forgotten what degree it is. But there's nobody in Homicide who'd like to find out if she can handle herself hand-to-hand because I've seen her fuck up several perpetrators who tried to get physical with her. I've never had to intervene for her. I just step the hell back and let her loose. It wasn't pretty, what she did to some of those sorry pricks who provoked her. And they always came at her first. Then they paid for their sins.

Lila is not a large woman, but she would've made a nice Ranger. She's about five-seven and her physique is like sheer tendon—no excess anywhere.

You wouldn't think she was that aggressive when you talked with her in the unmarked car. She likes to talk country western, however, which I detest. The only thing we can converse easily about is baseball. We're both White Sox fans because we're both natives of the southside.

I fill her in about the tongueless survivor. Her eyes widen when I tell her about the kid's newly white locks.

"White?"

"That's what Esposito told me," I tell my partner.

The scene has been scoured, so it's time for us to leave. I look around at the fall foliage and I wonder how anyone could foul this landscape the way it has been soiled. No animal would leave the mess our guy has left.

No animal other than the human variation.

We drive the Eisenhower to Cook County, over on the west side. The traffic is as it usually is, snarled and capable of producing road rage. Lila drives because she can't stand hearing me voice my opinions about the idiots who clog this main artery of the city. She drives the squad as efficiently, I'm certain, as she flew her jets in the War. She glides effortlessly through all the congestion of the prime time Eisenhower Expressway.

It takes an hour to arrive at the hospital. Lila puts the police tag inside our windshield as we park at the entrance to County. We find out at the entry where our survivor's room is. Her name is Helen Gant. She, like the dead vic, is African American. She is nineteen. The murdered girl was about the same age, the ME had informed me, back at Evans' Pond.

We take the elevator up to the fifth floor.

Lila has short auburn hair, but it's not so short that it's what she calls "butch." She keeps it short because she says it's easier to manage in the mornings when we're working days, as we are today. It's near the end of our shift, and I'm getting hungry. We're both in the habit of eating out at fast food places because Lila lives with a non-present roomie and I might as well live alone. Kelly never eats, as far as I can tell. Or she eats when I'm not around, so I don't buy many groceries, and the food I do purchase seems to get eaten only by me.

My partner has very blue eyes. I think she calls them "china blue." I'm not certain what color that is, but her eyes are deeper than sky blue. It's her most outstanding feature. She lives with a female roommate, but I'm not sure they're lovers because she rarely talks about her personal life. She did tell me about her sexual preference, though, because, as she explained, partners needed to be truthful to each other. I told her I didn't care who she was fucking, and she laughed, and that had been the end of the discussion.

We enter Helen Gant's room. A doctor and a nurse are here with her, and now we are, too. We show the doctor our IDs.

"Make it brief. You won't get anything anyway. She's lost a lot of blood, and a tongue, and we're taking her back to surgery in five minutes."

I nod to the physician. Then he and the nurse leave the single room.

"We need to put a guard out there," I tell Lila.

"Yeah, that would be prudent, Danny."

But she's not smiling.

Helen Gant's eyes are closed, now. They've got her hooked up with oxygen, and her mouth is shut and I think they might have the stub of her tongue packed with something to stanch the bleeding if it hasn't all clotted up by now.

The visit here is perfunctory. We knew we couldn't get anything from Helen Gant. We probably never will. We stay a few minutes and Lila writes a few notes in her notebook, and then we head back down to the car.

"He cuts up the other girl and he straps Helen Gant to a tree and rips out her tongue. Helen watches and her afro turns bone white. He leaves us a witness who can't talk and who probably never returns to planet Earth to tell the tale. Even if she can communicate someday, what's your bet, Danny, that this guy will never be identified by Helen

Gant?"

I stare out at the mess of traffic on the Dan Ryan as we head out to Guiseppe's Pizza on the far southwest side. It's Lila's favorite joint. I'll call my daughter when we arrive and ask if she wants some carry out, but I already know Kelly's answer.

The pizza comes quickly, as it always does at Guiseppe's. It never takes more than twenty minutes. It's thin crust. It tastes more like pastry than pizza crust, and the toppings are dynamic, also.

"How's your kid?" Lila asks as she bites into a piece.

The place is typically Italian, with Christmas lights lit through all seasons.

I shrug and take a sip of beer before I eat. I enjoy owning the roof of my mouth, but Lila is always too anxious, and she burns hell out of her mouth every time we come here.

"You're an Air Force Academy grad, but you still don't appreciate what molten pizza does to your palate."

She takes a quick tug at her Diet Coke. Lila doesn't often drink alcohol. She says it's because her dad likes the booze, occasionally, but she never expounds on the subject.

"Army Rangers just have common sense, I guess," she says.

I made the call to Kelly on the pay phone here, and my daughter actually picked up. She sounded sober. I asked her if she went to school today, but I got the sound of silence, just like the song. I asked her if I could bring her anything, but she said she was okay. I wound up mumbling about being home in an hour, but she hung up before I could say goodbye. Lila knew what kind of call it was. I could see it in her blue eyes, but she never said anything to me, she never asked how my kid was. She already knew.

"We have other cases," she said. She was fingering her Coke glass, drawing something in the beads of perspiration on the mug.

"You think we'll come up empty, I take it?"

She smiled at me. She didn't take the bait.

"I know, I know. The fun hasn't even begun…. But it'll be low profile, and you know it."

"Because they're whores," I tell Lila.

"Yes. Because they're whores," she replies.

But there's no smile of recognition on my freckled Irish face. I have hazel eyes. Lila says it's her favorite color, but she doesn't say it with a hint of flirting.

She already knows I'm attracted to her. No one had to tell her. She just knows, and I know she knows, too.

We get the word, later that night, that Helen Gant died. The docs at Emergency thought shock might have caused a fatal seizure. But we've lost our witness, regardless of whatever it was that finished her.

2

I wake up and hear rustling in the living room. I go out into the living room and see what the source of the gentle commotion is. It's Kelly, getting her school stuff pushed into her book bag. It's the same book bag I've inspected over the last six months. Although I haven't found any drugs and even though I haven't caught my daughter with dilated pupils or found her acting spaced way out, I'm still not convinced she's clean.

There's been no odor of weed on her hair or on her clothes, and she doesn't wear any kind of noticeable perfume to mask the rank stink of the smoke from a blunt, but I have difficulty believing she's altogether straight. It isn't the way it is, for junkies or users. They always relapse.

"Would you like to take a look?" she offers.

She'd be a very attractive young woman if she weren't so sickly thin.

"No. I haven't heard from Mr. Baker, lately."

Baker's the truancy guy at Sacred Heart Academy.

"That's because I haven't been truant."

"If I call him, is that what he'll tell me?"

She has her mother's green eyes. She has Mary's face. I see my former wife in my daughter in all the rare moments when I'm allowed to look my kid in the eyes.

"Knock yourself out. Call Mr. Baker."

"What's going on, Kelly?"

"I'm going to school."

"I mean what's going on."

"I just told you, Dad, I'm going—"

"*Tell* me, dammit!"

She smiles delicately, tentatively.

"You're looking for something. You're *always* looking for something. You can't stop being a cop."

"Why'd you stop using?"

I think I've caught her leaning in for a punch. She's off balance and has no retort.

"I told you I—"

"You've told me you were clean before. You lied."

Her pretty but fragile face turns into a frown.

"I'm sorry," I apologize.

"You're not sorry. You just want to catch me doing something so you can feel good about it."

"I'd never feel good about anything like that, Kelly."

"Now who's the liar?"

She grabs hold of her book bag and heads out the door of our southside, brick, three-bedroom home.

I call the head nun, the principal, at Sacred Heart and make an appointment in an hour to see Sr. Rachel. She agrees, and then I head to the shower to take a wash.

Sr. Rachel is a legend at Sacred Heart. She's been there thirty-seven years, and the wear and tear shows only slightly on her face. Her order does not wear a habit. They were liberated, apparently, after Vatican Two.

She is tall. She can face me eye to eye, and she does as she shakes hands with me. We sit in her spartan office, here inside this ancient Catholic girls' school on the southside. The neighborhood is Latino and black, now, as is most of this side of the city. The school and the grounds have been kept up immaculately. Rachel is a proud woman. I can see it in the steely quality of her gaze.

"You want to know what's going on with your daughter, Kelly, I understand from your call."

"Yes."

"You're a policeman, yes?"

"Homicide detective, actually."

I can't help serving one back at her. I'm a product of the Christian Brothers at Trinity High School, on this same side of Chicago.

"Oh?"

"Yes. I'm here because the drums have gone silent, lately."

"Kelly hasn't been truant in a long time."

"I was wondering what brought about the change because she won't confide in me."

"You don't get along?"

"I don't get along with users, dopers, Sister. Even if it's my daughter."

"You never inhaled, I take it."

There's the faintest malevolent grin on her lips, at the moment.

"I've used marijuana, yes. I drank alcohol when I was in the military, yes, but I gave it up after the war. I was hoping my daughter wouldn't have to do the same stupid damn things her father did, but I realize kids experiment. She was beyond 'experiment.'"

"I know. I remember the suspension clearly. She seems to have been able to refrain, the last several months. She hasn't missed school, lately. So where's the *bad* news?"

"You think she's stopped all her crap?"

"I don't know, Detective Mangan. I know she hasn't done anything to stop her from graduating from Sacred Heart next spring. Is that good news to you?"

"If it's true."

"If it's true? Are you questioning my veracity, now?"

She snorts with "now."

"No, Sister, I didn't mean to impugn your....Look, it just happened so quick—"

"She's been talking to Sister Catherine, our school psychologist, who's also a counselor here."

"So why wasn't I informed?"

"Because Kelly explicitly told us that her counseling was to be between herself and Sister Catherine. Even I don't know the specifics, but I know they've been getting together before and after school for several months, now. You mean to tell me that you're just now noticing the change in her behavior, *Detective?*"

I'm positive it'd be my ticket to hell to bitch-slap a nun, but it is my sincere desire to do just that, presently. But I let it go. I'm an adult, I keep telling myself, even though she's talking to me like I'm one of her teenaged charges.

"Yeah, I noticed. But she's seemed straight before, and then she goes under another wave, about the time that I think she's better."

"You need to talk to Sister Catherine."

I find Catherine in the counseling area. She invites me into her office, and then she promptly informs me everything she's said to my daughter is in confidence. She tells me that I need to talk to Kelly about Kelly.

Sister Catherine is in her mid-thirties, it appears. She doesn't wear the penguin uniform, either. She's an attractive woman, except for the stoutness, perhaps. She appears a bit too muscular, not too fat.

This is an interview in which I'm going nowhere, so I surrender and get up to leave.

"You really need to talk to Kelly."

"Why don't you explain that to Kelly, Sister."

I turn and walk out of her cubicle.

Lila and I trace the two kid prosties to the near northside. They worked the Old Town District, which is a rough place for hardened hookers, let alone novices.

The first victim's name was Tracy Amberson. They finally IDed her via her dental work. Luckily for us, she'd had fillings in her teeth, and her dental records told us her name.

Neither girl has parents that anyone can locate. We went back to the high school they'd both dropped out of at sixteen and we got addresses for them, but each girl had been living with an "auntie," a kind soul who'd picked them up off the street. So the information was brief and unhelpful.

We canvas the Old Town area and talk to the working ladies, the sidewalk princesses, who operate in this slum. A few of them remember the faces of the photos we've secured from their high school yearbooks, but no one seems to have been familiar enough with either girl to give us any leads as to who it was who picked them both up and transported them to Evans' Pond and then butchered Tracy Amberson while a tongueless, gagged Helen Gant was forced to watch the slaughter.

Lila walks on the street side of me. We're on Garland Street, walking the hood, coming up empty. It's very un-gentlemanly of me to allow her to walk on the street side, but she's the one who chose the pattern of humping down the street, not I.

This is the best time of fall in the city. It's late October, almost Halloween. It's crisp but not cold, now. The World Series is history, and neither the Cubs nor the Sox have been playing since the beginning of the month, as usual. The Bulls are in pre-season, and the Bears are coming off a World Championship. This is the time of the year when some things seem possible and others seem out of reach.

"What's going on in your skull?" Lila smiles.

"I'm enjoying a walk with a beautiful woman. What could be better than that?"

"Something going on with your kid?"

She knows Kelly's name, but she always refers to her as "your kid."

"Surprisingly, no. She hasn't been expelled, and her hair just smells like hair."

"What about the other thing?"

She's referring to the bulimia.

I shake my head.

"Maybe she'll—"

"Hey. Enjoy the moment. We're going to catch a beast who kills little girls."

"Not-so-little girls," she says, with a suddenly somber look on her face.

"No. They were full-grown. You're right."

She turns and smiles at me. We're both wearing leather jackets. It's in the upper forties and the sun is brilliant, and the wash of pedestrians files by us in both directions. We pass easy loan joints, titty bars and fast food places that murder with lots of fatty calories. This is the city I love. It's like falling in love with a somewhat sympathetic jungle cat. It's beautiful but lethal, too.

"We're not going to get any face time with this guy until he hits someone else, you know," Lila tells me.

I look at her, and then I grin sadly at her.

We catch a break one block before we reach our car. There are a group of three working girls standing in front of Fat Lou's Pawn Shop, here on Garland Street. Fat Lou's doubles as a numbers front, but cops let Lou slide because he's good for street information, from time to time.

Lila approaches them. A female is less intimidating, we both figure. But I figure they don't know Lila.

Two blacks and one Asian. You don't see scores of Asian hookers. Not around here, anyway.

Lila shows the three of them the two photos of our victims. The taller of the two black girls shows emotion when she sees the pictures.

"*That my cousin!*" she blurts. And then there are tears.

We take Halee Maxey downtown with us to interview her. We

sit in the interrogation room on the Homicide Floor, here in the Loop.

Halee is not attractive. She has a jagged scar running along her left side jaw- bone. Somebody cut her deep. It's a thin scar, so my guess is it was a razor that did her.

"You've seen her with Helen Gant?" Lila asks.

Halee sits directly across from the two of us at our rectangular slab of table.

"Yeah. I seen her wid dat bitch. Helen be the one who drag her into the life. I try to tell her to get shut of her, but she doan listen to me."

Tears well and then descend on her face.

"We couldn't find Tracy's family," I say. "Just some woman she lived with on Ardmore Street on the southside."

"Her peoples lives in Mississippi. You doan need to look for them. They drop her like a sacka shit on dem streets. My ma is dead. Doan know no father."

"You ever see them working in Old Town?" Lila asks.

"Yeah. Seen them a few nights back....In fac' I see them get into some man's hooptie."

I can't help my eyes from widening slightly.

"You get a look at him?"

She looks suspiciously at me. I'm the male intruder here, to her.

"Tell him, Halee," Lila says gently.

"Naw. It be dark as my black bottom, that night."

She tries to grin, but then she remembers why she's with us.

"I only see a dark car. Big. Fo' door. Maybe a Chevy, maybe a Ford. Hell, I doan remember."

"What about the john? What about the man?" Lila proceeds.

"Him? He be tall. Taller'n he be."

She nods toward me.

"You remember anything else?" Lila asks.

"Yeah. He wearin' a hoodie. Tryin' to look like he belong on dese streets. But he was white. I saw a little of the side of his face. He was white, all right."

"You didn't notice the plates on his car?" I ask.

"Naw. Why'd I look for some a dat?"

I smile back at her. She seems to soften her glare at me.

17

"You gone arrest me?" she asks me directly.

"We're not Vice," Lila tells her.

But she keeps looking at me, instead.

"You need a ride back, Halee?"

She looks back down at the two photographs of the two dead hookers. Then she looks back up at me.

"Where else I got to go?"

3

When I joined the Rangers—that is, when they accepted me—I thought of the military as a life's career. Then Kelly was conceived and I knew it wasn't going to happen. I served out my tour and arrived home to become a father. The marriage went south, but I don't know what direction Mary headed. Just somewhere far away from me and far away from her very young daughter.

I'd saved up a lot of cash in my two tours in Vietnam. There was nothing to spend money on, for me. I wasn't on drugs or booze, and I didn't do the R and R thing in Japan or anywhere else. So I had it socked away pretty good. It got the two of us a small apartment on the far southwest side while I spent some GI Bill on a community college. I hired a babysitter who conveniently lived in the same three flat with Kelly and me, and then I finished my degree at Loop College, near downtown. From there it was the Police Academy, and after hoofing it in uniform, I graduated to Homicide, a few years ago. Been there since.

Because Kelly saw more of that babysitter than she did of me, and because the majority of time that I spent at home with her she was asleep, we were never very close. It's not that I don't love her because I surely do. We just never seemed to be as close as we should have been. And now, of course, she's like a boarder in the house we finally bought after all those years on the police.

I remember the flight home from Vietnam to marry a very pregnant Mary. I remember the teasing I got from my brothers in arms—but I knew they were all secretly jealous of my temporary trip back to the World.

"When you get back, go to fucking Toronto," Billy James, a staff sergeant whispered to me, the night before I left. We were hunkered in a hootch near a place called Bong Son. It was a tin hut, and the rain was falling softly, making dull thuds against its roof.

Billy was a brother from Des Moines. He was well-educated. Well-spoken. A college graduate who said he just wanted to see the world outside Des Moines, Iowa.

"Go to fucking Toronto, Danny. Take your old lady with the baby inside with you. Don't never come back here."

He whispered in the dark to me while seven other Rangers snored in various degrees of loud.

When I got home, we were married in a civil ceremony. I'm not a practicing Catholic, and Mary called herself an agnostic. Kelly was never officially baptized until I did it when she was just four years old. She's been in Catholic schools since kindergarten. She did well in grade school—good grades, everything. She started off pretty well at Sacred Heart, too, but her troubles with the eating thing and drugs began when she was in the tenth grade.

I suppose it was the people she hung with, but she knows, because she's bright, that she made her own decisions about the things she did, and about the food she didn't eat. The counselors say it's about self-esteem. Kelly was a little pudgy in grammar school, but she took off the excess when she hit the high school. The weight loss apparently wasn't enough, in her eyes, because she gradually stopped eating to the point where it became very noticeable that Kelly wasn't well.

We've been through counseling and rehab repeatedly. I think she might have given up the smoke and the pills when Sacred Heart began a testing policy that randomly checks students. It seems that she wants to get out of school, now, from what Sister Rachel said. I don't know of any other reason she'd clean herself up. As I said, I never saw needle tracks, but she could have shot up where I wouldn't have looked.

She kept telling the counselors that she only did marijuana and a few kinds of pills. I noticed money missing from my wallet a few years ago, when she was a sophomore, but it was chump change, not the kind of money you'd need for the expensive, white girl/white boy suburban shit.

I never ragged her about the missing money. We were on edge with each other often enough as it was. But then the cash wasn't disappearing anymore, about the beginning of her junior year, last year. The only problem that was obvious, last year, was the truancy. I thought she might have a boyfriend, but she'd never say. She didn't say much to me one way or the other until I threatened to throw her out. And then she didn't say anything—it was the look of betrayal in her eyes. The betrayal was coming from me, I mean.

I haven't noticed the odor of pot. I haven't seen the staggering to bed at night with the reek of booze on her breath. Not lately, not this year. Maybe she has turned the corner. To be honest, I was starting not to care. I was certain she was going to land on the street one night, and like her mother, I'd never see her again. But she's still boarding with me. Kelly's probably just biding her time to get out of here, and she's figured the easiest thing to do is just remain until she's eighteen and legal.

Maybe she'll go to college. I have money saved for her schooling, including a college or university. I had a guy in the police tell me about an investment, and I put a good chunk into it, and I've multiplied my investment five times over and then I let it continue to multiple like sex-crazed rabbits. I never touched a penny because that was Kelly's nest egg. Up until now I never thought I'd be able to spend it on her. I still haven't talked about the next level of school to her, and she....She never talks to me about much of anything.

So we'll see. Maybe she'll let me know which way she'll jump, when graduation from Sacred Heart happens, in a few months.

I have a report waiting on my desk when I get to work on Halloween morning. Lila is already in her cubicle, next to mine, reading her copy.

She walks into my tiny office and waves the folder at me. She looks fresh and very pretty, and I again wish there was a chance for me with her. But facts are facts, and I try to resign myself.

"I'm driving," she informs me.

We arrive at Lake Michigan in ten minutes. The scene isn't far from our Loop headquarters. The techs have been out here for a few hours since the body was discovered about one A.M. by an insomniac stroller. He sighted the corpse about twenty yards from the sidewalk he was walking. His dog, a border collie, had sniffed the stiff out before the pedestrian saw the dark hump shape out on the sand.

It's fully light at 8:12 A.M. The techs have laid their yellow tape on the beach because there was nothing to hang their markers onto.

The ME has already left. The crime scene people and their photographer are about to depart. All that remains are Lila and I and the remains.

It's a black female, somewhere between twenty and thirty, I guess, at first appraisal. The ME will be far more specific about her age.

This time the body hasn't been mutilated. Not a mark on her— except for the black and blue bruises around her throat. She was strangled, a tech informed us as he left the beach. Her eyes are wide opened to the point of bugging out. Her tongue lolls out of the left side of her mouth. I'm thinking this guy did her slowly, after he duct taped her hands beneath her as she lay on her back.

The water is only twenty yards behind us. It's gray and cold looking. The sky is blue and serene, but it's chilly here, by the Lake. There is a pier about one hundred yards from us, off to our left.

"I'll be back," I tell Lila. There is one uniform left on the scene, waiting for us to finish.

I don't know why I have to walk out onto that pier, but I have a feeling.

"Danny?" Lila calls at my back. But I'm striding purposefully toward that pile of concrete, so she figures I need a moment alone and she doesn't call my name again.

I reach the pier, and then I walk slowly out to the end of it. It juts out into the water about 200 feet. I look over the edge, and I see the second body floating face down.

I trot back to Lila, and she stands up straight as she replaces the vinyl over the dead girl.

"Call the ME and the crime scene people. Tell them to come back. They missed one."

Lila stares at me, and then she grabs her portable and makes the calls.

"He likes twin killings," I tell her on the ride back.

It took another three hours for them to fish victim number two out of the drink, and then we were on scene with the body for another ninety minutes. We haven't even had time for breakfast, and it's way past lunch. We're headed to an Italian joint in the Loop to combine two meals into one.

Casper's has the red and white checkered tablecloths and the blue and green Christmas lights that are for all seasons. We order pizza because that's what Lila says she's hungry for.

We sit in the dimly lit, unpopulated bistro. They're way past lunch rush and way before the dinner bell strikes. We're alone, with a waitress and a bartender and that's all.

"How's the girl?"

"Ask her. How the hell should I know?"

"Same old."

"Yes."

"Don't get mad, Danny. I'm just trying to be polite."

"I know you are. Sorry."

"So?"

"She seems to want to get the hell out of school. She hasn't blown off classes lately, and I already told you I don't sniff any funny smells on her."

"So it's looking better?" she smiles.

"Can't tell, with her. I told you, she still isn't eating. She's like a sack of parakeet feathers."

"She going to counseling?"

"She's talking to a counselor at school. That's really all I know. And I'm sorry I snapped at you."

I look at her short hair and her perfect, un-made-up face and I want to plant one right on her full, un-colored lips. They do have a color, though. They are a very pale pink, which makes them even more irresistible. But I resist, anyway.

"It's all right. Maybe Kelly's just growing up, coming out of it."

"She's not alone in this thing. I know I have responsibility."

"You might be beating yourself up a little too much and too often, Danny. Even the best families have kids go nuts on them."

The waiter arrives with our soft drinks. Can't have beer until the shift is over. Department policy and our own policy. We never cheat on that rule. Then I don't drink very often as it is. Lila likes to have a pitcher after work before a day off, so I'll join her to be sociable. But I'm just not a juicer. Genetics or whatever the reason really is.

"How's your love life?" I grin at her.

"Getting even, are we?"

"No. Just interested, is all."

"I have no love life. I have a job. About like you. You never date, do you."

I give her my best hard stare, which makes her smile even more broadly. Her teeth are a bit crooked, in spots, but they are very white in spite of their unevenness, and with those delectable, pale pink lips, I have to divert my eyes to the pop mug on the table in front of me.

"I have dated. Once in a while."

"You have to take care of that prostate, Bud."

Lila is very worried about my prostate. She warns me about cancer there, all the time.

"I can always take things into my own hands," I grin back at her.

"You're not the type for self-abuse, partner," she laughs.

"And how do you know?" I laugh back.

"Because you're too goddamned good-looking of an Irishman, that's why."

"Do I turn you on?"

The words flew out of my mouth before I could stop them.

"Sorry."

"About what?" she grins. "We're just screwing around, here, right?"

"Of course."

I try to look as sincere as I can for her. The last thing I want to do is lose Lila. She's the only semblance of a friend I've got. I don't hang around with other cops because it's boring. They always want to talk police talk. It gets old. I've been to cop bars and I've hung with brother officers. You have to play some politics to get a detective's shield. I'm not that dumb; I know how it works and it did. Once I got into Homicide, I quit socializing for the sake of the job. Efficiency is what counts in this division of police work. We may have our politicians and our crooks in the department, and we do, but Homicide is a bit different from the rest of our corps. Dead bodies don't have agendas. They're just dead fucking bodies. We have to find out who caused them all that distress. Which is why I like where I work.

"You're a really half-assed liar, Danny. But I love you for it."

I want to ask her if she has any interest in me at all, but I can't say it. I can't put that kind of tension between us, even if the tension comes from my direction only.

"I wasn't lying. You have grievously hurt my feelings," I tell her with a lame grin on my lips.

"I don't want to lose you as my best friend, Danny."

"Why would you lose me?" I continue, with a full smile, now.

"I have this feeling that you might just disappear on me at any given moment."

Her face goes serious. Her lips are shut. I look at the faint rosy hue on them.

"I'm not going to take off on you or on anyone. People pull that shit with me all the time, but I don't have rabbit in these legs. Trust me."

"But you think I won't be there, eventually. Right?"

"Come on, Lila—"

"I'm serious. You think I'm going to *didi* on you, sooner or later."

Didi is Vietnamese for "leave." She dropped bombs on them. I

25

killed them from the ground. Neither of us likes to talk about the War, so I never bring it up. It's a decade's old news, anyway.

"Don't you?"

I look at her pretty eyes and equally pretty face and I wish everything had been designed differently. Her. Me. The world. My daughter. Mary. Everything.

But it's no use. I don't have an answer for her.

4

Angela Carter was twenty and Khala Gibbons was twenty-one. Angela was the dead woman on the beach and Khala was the floater. Both had been strangled, the Medical Examiner told us, both had been throttled manually. In other words, he used his hands.

There is no semen, no prints. There is evidence that he hurt them both sexually before killing them because there were splinters of wood lodged in each of their vaginas. The doctor thinks he might have used a broom handle, or something similar. The splinters won't offer much in the way of evidence because I think this guy's smart enough to use latex or some kind of glove.

Lila is especially disturbed about the fragments of wood. She's already angry about the deaths of these four women, but the rape is something sensitive to her, naturally. We don't always encounter the sexual angle in the killings we investigate, so that part of the case is a hot spot for Lila.

We go back to Old Town as a starting point. We've gone to the addresses listed for the two new victims, but no one at those listings knows either girl. They were both probably out on the street for a few years, by now. They were homeless and parentless, like the first two.

We find a pair of prostitutes on Manley Road in Old Town standing outside the Apex Theatre. The Apex is an "adult" movie house. Lila walks up to them and shows them the photos of the two newest homicides. They both nod and tell us that they've seen them in the neighborhood, but neither of the hookers knows anything about them personally. They were just two more girls on the street, the short, chubby prostie explains. She's white and her tall thin partner is Hispanic. They don't seem to offer more than a confirmation that they were from around here, as the first murdered pair was.

We decide, after another hour of touring Old Town fruitlessly, to talk to Vice.

Al Parker is the man we contact. He's a tall, bulky black man who played professional football before he tore up his left knee. The knee kept him out of the military, so he decided to hitch up with the police. He's been highly decorated, and he's the bane of pimps in this Area called Old Town. He's famous for making procurers seek a different line of endeavor.

He takes us for a ride to Carlton Boulevard. We park on the street next to a fire hydrant.

"If the Fire Department gets a call here, I'll move," he smiles at Lila, sitting in the front seat next to him. I'm in the back.

"His name is Maurice Devereaux. He claims he's from the Big Sleazy, New Orleans, but he's a piece of shit from the west side. I knew him slightly when I was coming up, on the west side. We both went to Dunbar High School. Maurice was a fair fly back on the football team at Dunbar with me. But that motherfucker turned left, somewhere."

Lila smiles charmingly at Al. I think I feel jealous. Then she turns to me and sticks out her tongue. I can't help but laugh.

"He ought to be making the rounds of his girls any time, now," Parker turns and says directly to me. I'm thinking he's thinking there's something going on between Lila and me. There are numerous other cops who probably have the same suspicion.

"*Fuck 'em*," Lila has pronounced on that very subject.

"It's hard to keep all his players straight. I'm sorry I couldn't make any of those four girls for you. But the faces keep changing about every ten days around here."

He's sitting sideways so he can look at both of us, now. We indeed showed him the pictures of all four women, and I knew as I watched him look them over that he never saw our victims before. These Vice guys tend to have very long memories of their "clients."

It takes another thirty-five minutes before Maurice Devereaux comes sauntering along. The saunter is pimp, all the way, but he doesn't dress the part. There's no Superfly in his apparel. He wears jeans and a leather flight jacket. Except for the strut, he's just another brother from the hood.

Al gets out of our ride and braces him in mid-strut. He takes him by the arm and guides him to our vehicle. Lila gets out of the passenger's side and joins me in the back seat.

Maurice looks like an athlete. He looks like an African warrior— tall, graceful and lean. He's a very handsome young man. He and Al are only in their mid-thirties. Al looks like he's suffered the wounds of sports, but there isn't a mark on the pimp's face.

"What's this all about?" he smiles back at Lila. Lila doesn't return the teeth.

"Oh, shut the fuck up, stupid. You know the fuckin' drill."

He doesn't look over at our driver. He just settles back into his passenger's seat.

"Put your seatbelt on, fuckhead," Al smiles at him. "Don't want no harm comin' your way."

We stop at the Lake. I think Al chose this spot to make Maurice uncomfortable because the breeze off the Lake is very cold, the way the northeast hawk always feels.

"Why can't we go somewhere *inside?*" Devereaux complains as the four of us sit on a bench facing the water. Lila and I both have our collars turned up. If the Vice detective wanted uncomfortable, he's got a complete success. My partner and I are both shivering within seconds.

Al shows him the photos.

"Don't lie. I know they were yours. You lie to me and you know what happens."

"Yeah. I got a good memory."

He rattles off all four of the victims' names. Apparently he's learned not to bullshit Detective Parker.

"They were the ones got found, right?" Devereaux asks.

"They were the ones got found. Yes."

Maurice sits on the far left, and then it's Parker, me and finally Lila. We're both so goddamned cold, we just want this interview over with. If we have to, we'll take this procurer downtown to our own floor and question him.

"So?" Al asks.

"So nothing, Lieutenant. I'm telling you true. I ain't seen these bitches since they got topped. Ain't seen them a week or so before they got tapped. Honest, man. True. They weren't big earners. Not one of them was worth lookin' at. I wouldn't stick my own dick in none of them."

Lila gets up and walks away from us.

Parker slaps Devereaux on the back of his head, and the pimp's noggin flies forward.

"What I do?" he moans.

"You embarrassed the lady, and I take it personal," Parker grins at him.

"I'm sorry, Lady. I mean ma'am."

His shout stops Lila in her tracks. She turns and walks back toward us.

"Apologize," Al instructs Maurice.

"I'm sorry, Lady."

"*Detective*, asshole," Parker commands.

"I'm sorry, Detective, ma'am. Ain't meant no disrespect."

"Good boy....Detective? Any questions for him?"

Lila stops in front of Maurice.

"You ever been ass fucked?" she queries Devereaux.

"What the fuck——"

Lila pops him in the throat, and he grabs at his Adam's apple and goes to the ground.

"You having trouble breathing?"

I'm watching all this as if I'm not part of it. I've learned to let her go when she wants to.

Maurice gags for another few moments, but then he gets back up as if he's going to throw down on her. Lila pops him in the same spot, and down he goes again, clutching his neck.

"Don't get up for a minute, Maurice. Just nod if you know anything we can use to find the guy we're looking for. You know anybody who likes doing threesomes? Sandwiches?"

He looks up at her from his knees.

"I swear...to...God...I don't. I don't know...no one...like that. Not with these...girls."

"You're not going to tell me how ugly they were again, are you, Maurice?"

Al is smiling with pleasure at my partner, now. He's got his arms thrown back over the top of the bench as if he's enjoying a summer's day at the beach. I'm so cold I've lost sensation from the waist down.

"No...I mean, no ma'am."

She helps him up to his feet, and it's pretty certain this interview's over.

I drop Lila off at her apartment complex.

"You want to come in?" she asks me.

"For a minute, sure. I have to check on—"

"Just for a minute, then."

She lives on the third floor of a high rise not far from the Loop. I'm wondering how she can afford the rent even with a roomie.

We take the elevator to the third floor, we disembark, and then she unlocks apartment 307. This is the upper crust neighborhood, and I'm soaking it all in. In all the months we've worked together, this is the first time she's ever invited me inside. I've dropped her off before, but I never made it this far. I figured she didn't want me encountering her roommate.

"You want something to drink?" she asks.

"A diet pop would be good."

She goes to the fridge in her spacious kitchen. This place is more like a suite than an apartment.

"It's a two bedroom. But just one bath, which can be a pain in the ass when she's home."

Her roomie's name is Margaret. She's a flight attendant with United Airlines. I've never seen her, but Lila has only mentioned that God spent way too much time with Margaret. I take that as a compliment, from Lila.

There is a large living room with a three seat sectional couch, a love seat, a recliner with a floor lamp next to it—the lampshade is a tiffany thing. She snapped it on when we came in, and you can see all the reds and greens and browns. For a lampshade made of glass, it almost looks like artwork. Lila and Margaret have expensive tastes. I shop at places that end in "mart."

"You think we ought to talk more with Mister Devereaux?" Lila proffers.

"I think so, but it'll probably wind up being worthless, much like Maurice himself."

"It looked like Al had him frightened," she adds.

She sits on the sofa next to me. The couch is beige, a tasteful light tan. Everything in her place has enough class to make me wonder if Lila has rich parents. But she never talks about her family, either, and I don't bring personal stuff up unless she initiates that kind of conversation.

"How come you never talk about yourself?" I ask her.

"What about me?" she smiles.

Her pink, full lips are doing their magic on me, again.

"Where do you come from? I mean I know you're from the southside because you told me."

"You mean you want the family history?"

"No. Nothing like that. Christ, I don't mean to corner you, Lila."

"I know…. My dad is an attorney. I actually grew up in Hinsdale, but it sounds cooler to say you're from the southside. Sounds tougher, no? Only pussies come from the burbs."

I smile at her, and she shows me those gleaming, crooked teeth.

"My mother is a pediatrician. She works at Christ Hospital in Oak Lawn."

"So why didn't you ever tell me all this?"

"I thought you might think I was bragging on them. I should brag on them, you know. My dad's up for a judge's spot, and my mother's been a respected ob/gynecologist for a long time."

"You have siblings?"

"A brother."

Then she turns her face from mine, so I don't pursue it. But the mention of the brother changed her face dramatically. It's hard to read what's crossing her countenance now.

"You want a rerun with Devereaux?" I ask, changing the subject.

She turns to me and comes right at me and kisses me hard on the mouth. Then she withdraws and we sit together in silence, my unopened can of Diet Coke is sitting on a coaster on her glass, fashionable coffee table.

"Well," is about all I can muster.

"Yeah. Well," she smiles at me. But she doesn't come back for an encore to that shocking kiss.

"You better get back to your kid," she says. Her face has gone sad. It's in her gorgeous blue eyes. I can read *sad* on her, at least.

"I suppose so."

Then I lean in quickly on her and kiss her the same way she did me. This time her arms come around my neck, and then I'm holding her around her waist, and we're straining to get closer than flesh meeting flesh.

I kiss her again before I let her go.

"How advisable is all this?" I ask her, my nose about three inches from the tip of her nose.

"Not very, I guess."

I release her.

"You have me confused," I finally utter.

"Now you know how *I* feel," she says.

5

The day after the encounter with Lila at her apartment, it's as if it never happened. For her, anyway. I get the usual banter and the kidding and the innuendo, but she never says anything about what happened, and I don't bring it up. If she wants to simply forget about it, then I'll have to pretend I've forgotten it, too. But it'll never happen. I won't let go of it.

We spend our days working the two double homicides, but we're reminded by our Captain Jackson that the cases are considered low profile because they are very difficult to solve, and in most instances there is no closure to the murders of prostitutes. They deal with dangerous people who are always shadowy, by nature. Their clients are fairly well versed in concealing themselves. Public embarrassment, if for no other reason, keeps them in those dark corners where they can't be seen. We occasionally catch them, but it's usually because of a dumbass mistake they make. Like leaving semen or fingerprints behind. But if they're going to top a whore, they're usually very careful about leaving calling cards behind them.

The truth is that most police have hardened themselves against feeling sorry for these victims. They figure these women, and sometimes men, are asking for it. They're putting themselves in harm's way, so they decide that their lives are somehow not as worthy as "innocent" vics. It's the way it is, regardless of the media's stories about police impotence in solving these kinds of homicides.

To me, one dead body is worth the same as another stiff—unless it's a child who's been snuffed. Being a father prejudices me against killers who do kids. I know it shouldn't make any difference about their age or their profession, but it simply does. We're all flawed, police included.

We get called onto a case that started out as domestic. The two geezers involved live on the far southwest side. We take the call because the old lady in this white couple, aged 77 (he) and 74 (she), get into a brawl, and the old lady throws a toaster at her husband. The toaster catches the old guy square in the temple, which promptly shatters his skull and causes death to arrive accidentally. It's going to be accidental homicide, Lila and I are certain, once we've interrogated her, but we have to look into any kind of death like this. Something which was not caused naturally, I'm saying.

Catherine Tuohy's reaction to her husband's demise is what keeps us on site longer than we would normally remain.

"Is he dead?" she asks Lila.

Lila nods.

Benjamin Tuohy hasn't moved from where he fell after she clocked him.

"You sure he's dead?" she repeats to me, this time.

"You didn't know he was gone after he lay there for all this time?" I ask her.

"I couldn't be sure. I hit him with the toaster oven and he fell down. But he falls down twice a week, at least. He's getting old, is all."

I'm thinking Alzheimer's, but I'm no doctor. I think we might have to call social services, but Lila's already dialing it in on her phone as she walks out of the kitchen in this modest ranch home on the far southside.

"He's getting old, is all."

There are no tears in her eyes. She jumps out of her kitchen chair just a bit when she hears the ripping sound of the body bag being zipped up, behind her, near the sink. There is a small pool of blood on the white linoleum floor. I see it as the techs lift Benjamin's remains up off the floor and place it gently on the gurney. Then they roll him out of the kitchen.

"He was just getting old," she says.

We have other cases. We keep reminding each other of that fact as we drive back toward Old Town for yet another round of canvassing the streets. We park the car on the street and walk the routes where our four girls trod, night after night. Al Parker got that bit of information for us from the redoubtable Maurice Devereaux.

They inhabited about a square mile of Old Town. We stop at every new group of working girls we encounter. Some of them deny they're working the pavement, but Lila has an intimidating air for those who would be untruthful to her. She gets in their faces if they try bullshitting her, I'm saying. Sometimes I feel like I'm the junior partner, here. I should be jostling these broads, not Lila. I should be intimidating them, instead of my partner. There is no good cop/bad cop deal with us. That crap is for TV, not for Chicago's nasty streets. You can't get anything out of a hoodie by being gentle, nor can you use muscle in place of respect. Most of these denizens of the neighborhood know not to fuck with Homicides because they know most of us don't take money.

We stop in front of Mellman's Deli. Vice gets calls from Mellman's all the time to come shoo the hookers away from their store. Myron Mellman says it gives his customers the wrong idea about his business. He says they'll get the impression the deli is a hangout for whores. So Vice sends uniforms down here to roust them, all the time. Irony is that these girls spend some cash in Myron's place. The food here is notoriously good, and the hos have to eat, like anyone else. So Mellman winds up tossing potential customers away from his doors, but the food's so damn good, they keep returning.

Two Hispanic girls linger near the doorway of the delicatessen. This time I make a move toward them before Lila does. She reaches for my arm, but I'm already in front of them.

"Can we talk, ladies?" I smile the best way I know how to smile at pros.

The grimace seems to work, and they both smile back at me.

"You interested in something special?" the better-looking one of the pair asks.

She was eyeballing Lila, who's now joined our foursome, about ten feet away from Mellman's entrance.

The weather is cold and damp. It reminds me of the scene at the Lake with Al and the procurer. The clouds hang low overhead, and it feels like it could flurry, today. It's November, so it becomes a possibility, even though the forecast didn't mention snow.

I show the pair my shield, and the smiles disappear.

"Shit," the less pretty one says.

"I'm here about these four ladies."

I flash the pictures at them. The photos show the living images of the victims.

"Their names were Helen and Tracy and Angela and Khala. You knew them?"

The better looking of the duo takes the pictures from me and actually studies them.

"Yeah. I saw them around."

Then her partner takes a look, too.

"Yeah," the second prostie chimes in. "I seen them, too. *Son muerto?*"

"That's why we're here," Lila joins in. Her words are pretty well lathered with sarcasm, and the two working girls are aware of it. They may be ignorant, uneducated, but they're not stupid, apparently.

"Anybody ask you two to go off with them for that something special you were talking about?" I ask them.

"You mean a threesome?" the attractive one asks.

"Yes," I answer.

"We get it all the time," the pretty trollop tells me. They're purposefully ignoring Lila, and I know my partner will start to boil shortly. She doesn't enjoy becoming invisible in these kinds of interviews. It's not in her nature to stand in the background.

"From a white guy who wears a hoodie and drives a dark-colored four door ride?" Lila asks.

They snap their eyes toward Lila.

Then their focus goes to the sidewalk, and they suddenly become sullen.

"You know this man?" I inject.

Their eyes are still cast down, as if the principal has caught them smoking in the lavatory.

"Come on. Help us....Please," Lila tells them.

The "please" doesn't sound like her.

"They'll just be four more whores flushed into the big toilet where all the other dead hookers wind up. Is that what you'd like?" my partner asks.

Lila is pissed. She didn't enjoy being put to the side, a moment ago.

"I seen him," the plain one says. "We both did. He tried us about four, five nights ago. Right here, it was. Drives up to that curb in his big shit Ford and asks us do we like sandwiches. We ask him how much he's willing to pay—after we asked him was he a police. He didn't look like a cop, but you never know with these assholes. Well, we just didn't think he was...right. You know. It was nothin' he said or done. He just looked wrong. And out here you got nothin' to go on except this."

She points to her belly.

"Could you describe him?" Lila queries.

"White," the looker smiles.

Her partner smiles.

"You want this to continue downtown?" Lila snaps.

Her grin dissolves. So does the smirk on the face of her not-so-good looking associate.

Lila takes down the information in her notebook. I'm starting to shiver, but my fellow detective, Lila Chapman, doesn't show a quiver. She's as hot as a barrel on a recently discharged .38.

We take the two downtown to see a sketch artist. Neither of them saw or remembered a plate number, which is standard. The only time they'd look at a license is if a john stiffed them of their fee.

We see the artist's rendering of our fellow. He's Caucasian, about six feet one, perhaps 205 pounds. Not muscle-bound, but not flabby, either. They thought he might have gray eyes. The more attractive Hispanic girl remembered his eyes because of their unusual color. The other hooker wasn't as sure about the gray. But I'll take the first one's word. Things that stand out like eye color usually are accurate. Unusual details stick with a witness. The average stuff gets all confused and distorted.

The artist's rendition gets circulated in an all points bulletin. Every squad car receives the image. I don't think it's likely that we'll pick him up on the basis of their description. How many white dudes fit that profile? Thousands? I'm thinking he only wears the hood when he's out looking for prospects. The blue Ford is vague, also. What was the model? The girls couldn't tell. They were out shivering their asses off, looking for a meal ticket at 1:00 A.M. in front of Mellman's. They said he showed up about an hour before they were going to call it quits. Which makes sense, because the streets would be devoid of witnesses at that hour, or almost devoid.

Lila asked them if they saw anybody else out on the sidewalk when he approached them, and they both said the streets were mostly deserted, and that was why they were ready to call it quits for the evening. Early morning, in fact.

"You think he'd be using a borrowed ride?" Lila proposes.

"Might. If he's in the life. If he's a 'citizen,' probably not."

"Why don't we talk with Robbery/Auto Theft and see if they've got anything that resembles our guy's mode of transportation?" she grins.

The list has fifteen vehicles that resemble a blue, four door Ford. We take down the plate numbers and circulate them in conjunction with our artist's drawing of the perpetrator.

All we can do is keep looking in our Area. We both know there's no rule that he's not going to try expanding his AO, area of operations.

It'd be the smart move because he was taking a chance by returning to the turf where he hit first. I have the idea that this guy is clever enough to know that he can't shit where he eats. Location, location, location. Just like the real estate commercials.

I take Lila to Morty's on our dinner break. I'm tired of pizza. Morty's is a regular sit-down deal in the Loop. It's a medium tier restaurant. In other words, you have to use plastic if you're a mere mortal like me, but you don't have to re-mortgage your house to finance Morty's tabs. It's reasonable, but it isn't cheap.

I order a steak. She orders a chef's salad.

"Why can't you order people food?" I smile at her.

She sits across the booth from me. There are no Christmas lights, but the lighting is low and amber-colored and romantic. There is a single white candle enclosed in glass between us.

"Have to watch my girlish figure."

I groan and she laughs at her cornball cliché.

"Nothing wrong with that," I remind her.

She has an athletic frame. She isn't big anywhere, but she's very proportional. Which means very alluring.

"You still feeling hincty about the other night?" she says as she sips her beer. It's after shift, so she's allowed and so am I, but I'm sticking to the Diet Coke.

"As a matter of fact," I reply.

"Don't. It was just a mistake. My mistake. I was just a little weird, and you know how much I like you..."

My heart seems to drop in my chest. It's the part about "liking" me that causes the descent.

"I don't want to screw things up between us, Danny. I don't want to lose you as a partner. I mean on-the-job partner."

My pump has just about hit bottom.

"I don't want to lose you either. As a partner, on the job," I reply.

"Good. Good, because we're right, together. You know?"

I nod as convincingly as I'm able to.

I read the menu, but my eyes can't make sense of the words on the bill of fare.

She takes my right hand away from the menu and she grips it warmly in both of hers.

"You're a really terrible liar, Detective Mangan. And so am I. But you already knew that, didn't you," she whispers.

I drop the menu and take her hands in mine for just a brief moment.

And then the food arrives and we eat in silence until our plates are empty.

6

We cross each other's path occasionally, even if Kelly tries her best to avoid me. I catch her this time at the end of a day's shift in mid-November. In a few weeks it'll be Thanksgiving. We have no relatives to share the holiday with. My parents are both dead. My father passed six years ago, and my mother died four years previous. Both succumbed to cancer. Both were heavy smokers, but Mom was the heavy drinker. She spent the last decade of her life falling off and on the wagon and attending AA meetings when she tumbled off the cart. I loved her dearly, but she was a true rummy and literally could not stop herself from enjoying gin, if there is a way to enjoy that piss. She loved her martinis, and she put herself to sleep most nights with a pitcher of them.

My father threatened to divorce her a few times, but he could never follow through. He loved her, and she loved him right back. But they were World War II products—my dad fought at Anzio—and she worked in a munitions factory, and booze and cigarettes were part of the equipment to stave off the misery of the Depression and WWII.

Mary's people come from northern Ohio. The only time I saw them was at our wedding. Then they headed back to their 700 acre farm in Manchester, Ohio, and I haven't seen or heard from them since. They never communicate with Kelly, either, so I don't miss them even a little bit.

Mary never talks to her daughter, either, which is something I find much more difficult to swallow, but I've learned to live with it, sort of.

Yeah, there are reasons my daughter did (or still does) drugs and reasons why she refuses to eat enough for her to gain any real flesh on her bones and reasons why she's been a sad young woman who has little to do with her father and yet more reasons why her self-esteem is in the mud.

It doesn't make it any easier to live with, knowing why she's unhappy. Sometimes it hits me, in the darkest part of the night, when the sun is still hours from rising. The "dark nights of the soul," somebody called them. I've done my share of the silent weeping. The waterworks just seem to start up on their own, but they end as abruptly as they begin, and fortunately they never start when I'm with other people, Kelly or anybody else.

I've dated a few women over the past years, but none of it ever became serious. My hours are ridiculous, and I just don't have the desire to really get close to another woman. I was never all that close to Mary. There was real heat between us in bed, but that's where the intensity ended. We hardly knew each other, in the beginning, and when we cohabited, we figured out we didn't like each other much. I mean, I loved Mary, and I think she loved me, romantically, but we didn't have a damn thing in common, and it became pretty obvious to both of us *somebody* had to be the one to pack up and depart. So she did the packing and leaving.

It still shocked me when I came home to find a babysitter watching Kelly. The babysitter had no clue that Mary wasn't returning. But I found out when I opened the bedroom closet and saw that all her clothes were gone.

Kelly sits at the kitchen table, and for the first time that I can remember, she's got books spread in front of her. I feel like asking her if she's all right, but I don't do that anymore.

The book she's got is a library copy of the ACT prep.

I stop at the table after I get a Diet Coke from the fridge.

"I thought you already took the ACT," I tell her.

She looks up at me with the same sharp anger her mother would flash my way.

"I'm just interested," I apologize.

"I'm re-taking it in the spring. My math score was too low."

Her ACT was 28, which told me and Sacred Heart that she's been sand-bagging her way through high school with a C+ average when she's a B or an A student inside. Sister Rachel mentioned that her grades had been rising, when I left from our interview. I was so fired up about talking to Sister Catherine that I almost forgot that bit of news.

"Your score was pretty lofty. Why do you need to do it over again?"

She gives me the smile she uses when she knows she's being interrogated by her policeman old man.

"I'm not grilling you, Kelly."

I have frequent urges to embrace my daughter, and I have frequent impulses to slap the shit out of her. But I refrain from both. I don't smack women, and I don't belt males without justifiable cause.

"Sure feels like it, Dad."

"Why are you re-taking it?" I insist.

"I need a higher score to offset my shitty GPA."

Her explanation is so logical that it stifles my impulse to ask her the question again.

"You have a plan?"

"Yes," she says.

The angry smile is withdrawn. She's about to clam up on me.

I sit down across from her at the kitchen table. It is a white, metallic square. It gleams from the overhead fixture because I'm pretty fanatical about cleanliness. It's one of the good habits I retained from the military.

"Why can't I ask you anything, Kelly? Why is it always an intrusion?"

"You can ask me."

"Why are you doing the test again? What's the ultimate purpose? And I don't mean the stuff about offsetting your shitty GPA."

"I want to study nursing at a state school. Maybe go to medical school, if things work out."

I feel a flush at my face.

"What's going on with you? Why all the sudden concern about school?"

"You mean why am I concerned now that it's almost too late?"

She's got the grim grimace of her mother's aimed at me.

"Why is everything I say or ask like a threat to you?"

She has no reply.

"Look. I have money saved for—"

"I don't want a damned dime from you. If I get in, I'm paying my own way. I've got a job lined up for this summer. Sister Catherine helped me find one at the school. I'm trying to find a second job to get the cash together. There are scholarships for kids with single parents, and there are grants for children whose parents are vets—"

"I saved money to put you through! I've got sixty thousand in a savings account for you!"

"I don't want your goddamned blood money! I don't want *anything* from you!"

I feel my hand rise from the table. I feel my arm cocking itself for the blow. I feel the heat for release in my face.

Then she smiles as if she's beaten me at some damned game that I didn't realize we were playing.

I lay my hand back on the table.

"You're right," I tell Kelly. "It was blood money."

She looks at me oddly, as if she didn't expect that response.

Then I get up from the table and march straight out our front door.

"*Dad*—"

But I don't wait for the apology or the curse from her lips. I just keep right on going until I reach the car and the curb.

"You look like a proper ho," I tell Lila.

She doesn't look twenty, but she could pass for twenty-five, which is fourteen years her junior. I'm forty, and she's thirty-nine. We were soldiers once, and a helluva lot younger, then.

Carol Mabry, another Homicide, is in the backseat. We're parked on Grand Avenue, here in the heart of Old Town. Lila and I don't think using decoys will work on our hooded whore-killer, but we figure we have to give it a try.

Carol is younger than Lila, and she looks even younger than her twenty-eight. She's a rising superstar in Homicide—the youngest female detective in our division. She graduated the Academy at twenty-one, and just seven years later she's in the elite corps in the CPD. Quite an accomplishment. And throw in the fact that she's black, which makes her an even rarer commodity in our business.

She's quite the beauty, too. She's gets double-takes every time she walks the halls in the Loop. I'm hoping her obvious charms will not go unnoticed by the asshole we're stalking here in Old Town.

It's starkly cold outside the squad car. The wind, the Hawk, is howling out of the northeast, it's usual direction to blow out of, and it's flurrying lightly. Sort of gets us into the Christmas mode, even if it's a bit early for the holly and the mistletoe sentiments.

"You two hunks of pulchritude ready to take a walk?" I ask both women.

The ebony babe in the back shows me a perfect set of choppers. She's grinning theatrically, just for the two of us.

Her .38 snub-nose is strapped to the small of her back, underneath her red plastic, thigh length coat. It'll be tough to retrieve the piece, but she doesn't want our boy to know she's packing.

Lila has her own .32 snub nose strapped to the back of her upper right thigh. It must be very uncomfortable, and neither girl is going to be capable of doing a fast draw because of the location of their weapons, but they can hardly use a shoulder rig or use an ankle holster if they're going to show a lot of leg to a potential customer.

I'm the one who's doing the real security. I've got my non-department .45 automatic in my shoulder holster, and I've got a pump shotgun on the floor in the backseat. I also have a switchblade in my flight jacket's front left pocket. Guns jam, but switchblades are very effective in close encounters on the street. They are also against department policy, but I figure I'll argue with Internal Affairs *after* I slice this prick wide open. The Rangers taught us how to use knives very effectively and efficiently. We would have all made very professional butchers after the War.

"Ready, Freddy?" I grin at them both.

They nod, but they're not smiling, now. I clutch Lila's hand, here in the front seat of the Ford squad car. Carol can't see my grasp on my partner's hand. No public display of affection, I'm thinking.

They both get out of the car, and the cold wind sweeps inside and overpowers the heater in the vehicle, momentarily. They shut the doors and head down Grand Avenue.

I turn off the engine. Even if it gets cold, I'll be warmer than the girls will be out on that avenue.

They walk about a half block down the street. They stay within my line of vision, but they're not so close that my ride is in their area of operations. They stand outside the Rialto, an adult movie house that sports glaring bright colored lights. No one can miss the two of them while they're in front of this porno parlor. Whores use the lighting to advertise themselves all the time, according to Al Parker, our consultant on this adventure. This is a high traffic avenue, even when the weather is rotten, as it is tonight.

But it's a Saturday night, and nothing much keeps horny pricks from doing their things.

Occasionally, a gust of flurries obscures my sight, here in the ride, but it clears quickly and I can see Lila and Carol doing a little dance in front of the Rialto to try and keep themselves warm. I don't know how they can take more than a half hour or an hour out there in this shit. I'm going to go fetch them in no more than sixty clicks. They can warm back up in here, and then try it for one more round. But two innings is all this game is going to go. They'll both wind up with pneumonia if I don't play umpire and call the contest after two frames.

It's about 11:40 P.M. Prime time if anything's going to happen. The show's still going on inside the Rialto because the perves haven't piled out, yet. I think the next show starts at 12:15 A.M.

A car pulls up to the curb about twenty yards away from Lila and Carol. The guy sits there and lets the engine run, and then finally he shuts off the headlights.

It's a dark blue Ford. Four doors.

He doesn't get out of the vehicle, however, so I don't make a man with a hood. I'm figuring this is too quick, too easy. It's probably some other walking hard-on, not our swinging stiff dick.

The ladies take the cue and walk over to the navy blue ride. I see the window being rolled down on the driver's side. I'm looking for a signal from either of them that I should join the party, but nothing happens.

The lights from that car pop back on, and the blue four door pulls away from the curb and Carol and Lila.

I see Lila shaking her head vigorously so that I'll see there's no sale. They walk back in front of the Rialto and resume their frigid little jig.

I've brought a portable radio with me in case all this goes long, and stakeouts usually become extended. I find a classic rock station. I like classical music for long hauls, but it's hard to find that brand on AM radio.

When I hear "Gimme Shelter" by the Stones, I let it play. I'm in love with their backup singer on that tune, even though I've never seen her. Christ, this lady can sing.

Twenty more minutes go by. The cold must be getting intolerable for the two detectives. I'm not going to let it continue much longer. Maybe real working girls can tolerate this shit, but my two partners aren't going to for much longer. I'm still thinking this guy will move to virgin territories; he's too smart to keep coming back.

A dark green four door pulls up to the curb. He, too, lets his lights linger. He's about thirty yards from Lila and Carol. They're eyeballing him, also, I can see.

Then the lights go out in the front, and the two undercover policewomen head toward the doors of this forest green Ford.

7

I'm watching Lila for an upturned palm, which means I'm out of the car
and running toward her and Carol because there's a bust imminent.
This guy will have to make them an offer, but they've been told not to get
into the car. They're supposed to get him for soliciting, and then we'll
take him downtown for questioning. We're not giving him the chance to
hurt either of the girls or both of them. Once you're moving, anything
can happen.

I call for our three backup squads. They're a half block away, and
I can hear them screeching away from the curbs, just south of me.

Then the green car squeals away from its parking spot, and I see
Carol and Lila lurch backward from the curb, and I watch as the guy in
the four door screams down Grand, right toward the squads. Before my
backups can block him off, he's past them. I do a U turn away from the
sidewalk, and my tires are smoking as I head at the fleeing vehicle. I see
the lights from the squads twirl madly, behind me, as I give chase.

We come to the intersection of Grand and Murray, and the man
in the green ride blows through a red light, and I follow, a quarter block
behind him. The squads are right behind me, and I make the call about
our pursuit so someone ahead can be waiting for him.

He's heading west, toward the worst barrio in the city. He's trying to lose us so he can ditch his car. I'm betting the green four door is stolen and that he's heading toward his own, private ride. He's parked it on the west side because he's either nuts or he's figured there are plenty of alleys to fly down in order to escape us. And he also knows that this side of town isn't a favorite for the uniforms. They come here only when called. Which is why the crime rate soars on the west side.

When we get into the hardest blocks in the city, he wheels left at the corner of 12th and Prairie. He swings to the left so hard that his ride goes up on two wheels on the driver's side. He screeches down the block, and he's got almost a city block in separation from me and the coppers with the strobing blue lights behind me. Two blocks onto Prairie Avenue, and I don't see his taillights anymore. The squads that were supposed to head him off have never shown up to engage, yet.

I jerk to a halt at 14th and Prairie. There's nothing here except a few junkers parked on either side of the street. But no green four door. He's turned into mist.

He figured the streets would be deserted in this kind of weather, and that's why he took a chance on surviving this hood. Whether his real ride is still in place is another question.

I walk back to the squad cars behind me and tell them to search the environs for the green vehicle. I tell them I know he's en route to the car he left planted for his escape route. The uniforms pull their two cars around and begin the pursuit, this time slowly. They turn off their strobes and head down Prairie. At 15th, one turns right and the other goes left. I get back in my unmarked car and head straight up the side street.

When I pass 16th, I see the vacant lot. We used to call them "prairies" when we were kids. We played cowboys and Indians and World War II and Korea on those empty lots overgrown with weeds.

I halt at the side of the open prairie. Even in the dark, I can see the matted down tire tracks. I pull up over the curb and my headlights confirm the depressions in the dying weeds that lead over to an adjacent alley. When I get to the concrete of the alley, I look left and then right. I see a dark shape off to my right, about seventy-five yards down.

I turn off my lights. I should be calling the uniforms, but I feel the force of the moment, and it says I haven't got time to make the call. It's a bad decision, I'm thinking. The first rule is to always call for backup.

Then I see the object looping toward the driver's side of that same green car we've been running toward, and there's a flame that leaves a bright tail behind whatever it is, and then I know what the object is. It's a Molotov cocktail. And the driver's window explodes with a burst of flame and I hit the pavement.

Then I hear him running down the alley, away from me. So I get up and run after him, making a wide arc around the burning green car.

He has a big lead on me, and I was never a great distance runner, but the military made us run marathons. It was part of Ranger training. I wasn't the fastest, but I always finished.

This guy seems to be a distance runner. He has a nice burst, and then, into the next alley, I see the race is lost.

I have to run back to my squad and make the call and hope the uniforms can run him down with their vehicles.

The Fire Department arrives in fifteen minutes. They have the flames extinguished in about forty-five seconds.

I figure he had the Molotov in the trunk for just such an occasion as this. You don't find ready-made explosives lying around in an alley on a cold November night. You don't find *any* crazyass white people running around here most any time of any day in the year. He had an escape plan, and he must have figured on getting rid of the automobile, and that all tells me there's something in the vehicle he doesn't want us to fuck with.

When the fire is completely doused, one of the firemen pries open the trunk with a crowbar. He gags a bit and backs off.

"Smells like burnt chicken. Every goddam time," the fireman tells me.

There are two bodies in the charcoaled trunk. Two females, it appears. They're tied together, and their hands were duct taped behind each of them. There's the same duct tape across their mouths.

The eyes are popped open on both black females, and you can see the look of absolute, sheer terror on those eyes.

He torched them and the car while I was chasing him down the alley. While I was in pursuit, they were being burned alive.

"No way you could have known," Lila tells me again, downtown. "No way."

Carol has already turned in her report to the captain, but we remain in my office.

"They died of asphyxiation," I tell her. "The ME says it could have occurred before he torched the car. He said there might not have been enough air in that trunk. Or it could possibly be carbon monoxide. The look on their eyes? I think the cocktail did it. Those fuckers burn so intensely that it might have sucked the air out of that trunk. The doctor said he'll let us know cause of death as soon as he does."

"You could not have known."

"I know. I know that I could not have known."

"So stop. It's not your fault. He was going for his first foursome. That's why he was cruising and that's why he stopped for us. He must have made us. Maybe I'm too old for the role. Maybe if he hadn't made Carol and me, maybe he wouldn't have stopped and then run—"

"He would've killed them anyway."

"No one found a trace of him on the west side."

"No. No trace. He vanished, like a fucking illusionist."

"Uh uh. He was just headed in another direction, away from us. It's called misdirection, Danny."

"He's very adept at misdirection. Maybe we ought to call him 'The Master Illusionist.' Give him a name the papers'll grab hold of."

"This dick would love the acclaim."

"You think so, Dr. Freud?"

"This was a crowd pleaser, in his head. Like to bet on the psychiatric profile he's going to rate, now that he's a big league series killer?"

"No bet. I should have stopped and tried to put out the fire."

"With what, Danny? Your hands?"

I know she's right, and I know I shouldn't punish myself for what this guy's done, but it's inevitable that at some point you get personally involved in some cases. No matter how detached we're trained to be, these guys can sink the barb right into your guts, into your heart.

Who else but the Bears would have a World Championship deflated by an historical event like the explosion of the Challenger? The day we heard about it, just after the New Year, a deadening thud replaced the celebration that had engulfed Chicago. We were winners of the Super Bowl, we'd bitch slapped New England, but now it was all settled back into perspective by what happened to our astronauts.

Death'll do that to people. It'll remind us all that we're on a very short leash.

A decade and more ago, I was still in a jungle, waiting to return to the World. I was part of this country's most unpopular war and a member of its biggest tragedy—tragedy when it came to waste. A lot of good people died in Vietnam, Americans and Vietnamese. It was unnecessary, the way all wars are at their roots unnecessary.

They say you can't fathom a war until two generations go by after its close. It takes fifty years or so to figure out what really happened.

What really happened? We killed them, big time, and they killed us to a lesser extent, but pretty big time also, and nothing changed. I've heard people talk about the lessons of war. There aren't any we don't already know. What? Don't shoot your bro? Thou shalt not kill? Kind of old sermons, no?

I was in an elite outfit. I was a sniper for a while, and then just a regular grunt who participated in some ventures across borders. All of which I am not at liberty to expound on. I wouldn't go on about my "exploits" if I wanted to, which I don't. There's nothing heroic in what we did. The best thing we did was survive. Not all of us did, of course. That's why there are 58,000 or so heartsick families still grieving their losses in that lost war.

It almost sounds like I'm some Confederate bemoaning the outcome of the Civil War, doesn't it? Well, it was a civil war there, too. Just not ours. No one invited us, really. We crashed that fucking party. Maybe Diehm wanted us there, but they shot his ass, anyway. His own people topped him. They say he was our puppet, but I thought we were the guys who abhorred colonialism and imperialism.

What brought all this on? The loss just keeps happening. The two newest victims, Marla Donald and LaSharon Martin, had no families to speak of. Just like the previous four girls. We've found out that the most recent victims were also whores. Strumpets, hos....Whatever you want to diminish their being with by use of demeaning appellation, they were just human beings. Who the hell gives this guy the okay to pull their plugs?

Who the hell gave us the high sign to terminate all those Vietnamese? Which in turn wasted 58,000 of our finest? (I'm sure there were a great many lumps of flesh on either side who got waxed, but who the hell cares? Good and bad and mediocre, they were still someone's little boy (or girl) at some point in their histories.

I don't usually get caught up in the funk of regret. We were taught to follow orders, in the War, and we did. When they said assassinate, we killed. When they said intercede in a village, we stepped right in. We did what we were told, and most of us never considered the moral weight of our actions.

But we all had doubts from time to time, no matter how patriotic you think you are, and if your brain functions you sometimes have to know that what you're up to is *evil*.

Which is why I became a Homicide. It's cut and dried. Murder is evil. A no-brainer. You don't have to ponder all the possibilities; all you have to do is catch the bastards and let someone else talk about their inhuman behavior.

All you have to do is catch them and hope that justice happens. It's not like that in a war. I never heard any grunt blathering about "ah, the humanity!" We just ate and drank and shit and pissed and humped the landscape and killed some indigenous personnel we were told to kill. Right and wrong didn't come into play very often.

Marla Donald and LaSharon Martin weren't working Old Town. They were working north of the district. He's moved his area of operations slightly north, but far enough away to become more unpredictable.

As unpredictable as he was asphyxiating those two black girls in his trunk.

The car was indeed stolen. Recently. It was green, not blue, but he either got himself a new ride with this car, or the witnesses mistook the color of the vehicle from the beginning of this investigation. I think they probably blew the color of the car. It's hard to tell hue at night, even if the streets are somewhat illuminated.

I don't recall how happy I really was to come home here in 1972. The marriage to Mary wasn't joyous, and this is a hard town, anyway. There are no soft spots that I can think of in Chicago. All of the sides in this burg have reps for being tough and rowdy. There are bad hoods in every direction you head, around here. It's not something relegated to the southside, as some would have you think.

I'm just old enough to remember the stink of the now-closed stockyards. They used to take school children on field trips to the stockyards, but having little guys watch the execution of lambs and calves caused too many traumas. I wonder who the geniuses were who figured watching slaughter could be educational? They probably have PhDs and very fucked up offspring of their own, right now.

There are great museums. There is the Art Institute. There are the Lakeshore and Wrigley and Comiskey. There are the Planetarium and a score of other classy places that dot the landscape in Chicago. It ain't all barrio, of course.

The city I know has blood on the pavement. Comes with the line of work. I don't see a lot of happy faces, old or young. I see faces set in shades of gray—that's rigor mortis taking over. The heat and the color leave the body, the face, and then there's just a waxy impression remaining. I know it sounds depressing and gloomy as hell, but it's the city that I see, in my field of endeavor.

Was I happy to come home in 1972? Of course. But that's only a partial answer. I was happy to leave Vietnam more than I was to return to my life.

I'm only forty. I keep telling myself that. I have half my life yet to live, if statistics don't lie. I can find love and someone *to* love, if my luck doesn't totally remain stagnant. In other words, if things don't stay the way they are.

I have a kid who wants to be somewhere else every time I enter the room. I have a partner who may or may not be bisexual. And she may or may not feel about me the way I feel about her. I have an ex-wife who is somewhere out there in the forest primeval.

And I have six dead bodies that are unaccounted for. *"He tasks me. He heaps me."*

I read that somewhere, but I can't remember where.

Was I happy to come home? There's the question, Hamlet.

8

"Seeing a white boy in my neighborhood after dark is even stranger than seeing a white boy around here in the daylight."

Karen Adams is an RN who lives on the west side. She lives, in fact, on 17th and Stewart, which is just a few blocks removed from the scene of the chase. Karen is a tall African American woman. She's very attractive. And being a registered nurse, I'm wondering why she still lives around here.

"I take care of my mother. She's eighty-six. This is her house. She won't leave it."

We've been scouring these blocks looking for anyone who saw anything unusual on the night we took after the guy in the green car. After two and a half hours of humping the hood, Lila and I came up with a winner on our door-to-door search.

Karen Adams must be six feet tall. She's just about eye-to-eye with me. When I showed her the badge, she let us into her ranch style house. The home is all brick, which means it's been here a long while. Most everything else on the block is sided and pre-fab. Junk, in other words.

We sit on her tan sectional sofa. I'm in the middle and Lila is on my left.

"My mother's at her doctor's office. They have a service that comes pick them up. It's one of those mini buses."

"Did you get a good look at him?" Lila asks.

"It was dark, but our street lamps haven't been shot out on our block, yet," she smiles sadly.

She goes on to give us a description that fits the artist's rendering we already have. It's our fellow, or someone who's a lot like him.

"Did you see the car he drove clearly?" Lila goes on. She continues to scratch notes in her notebook.

"It was a VW Bug, I'm sure. They're hard to mistake."

"Any idea what color?" I ask.

"It was dark. Maybe blue, maybe black. I'm not sure. But I got the plate number."

"You did?" Lila asks.

It seems too good to be true. A Homicide's wet dream. *A license plate number!*

"It read WAGON. That's why I remembered it. That's why I noticed it," the black nurse tells us.

We ask her a few more perfunctory questions, and then we fairly rush out to the squad to get on the radio and try to make the license plates.

The plates lead us to a residence in Highland Park. The car is registered with William Sanderson.

There really aren't residences or houses in Highland Park—there are mostly estates. This is a very wealthy area, one of the richest in the Chicagoland area. You can't hit the affluence meter any higher than around here.

A woman answers the door. I'd expected a butler or a housekeeper, but a well-preserved, sixty-something white woman answers our bell. She is stately and tall, almost a Caucasian version of Karen Adams.

When Lila shows her the ID, a frown takes over her lovely, but ageing face.

"What's this about?" she asks, with a thin smile.

"A homicide investigation, ma'am," I explain.

"Homicide? Oh, my," she says.

She invites us in, and then she leads us to something that looks like a miniature of a library.

"This is the study. I hope it's suitable," she smiles warmly.

We sit on individual, plush leather chairs. They're arranged in a semi-circle. There are shelves of leather bound books behind us, and there is a skylight above us that allows yellow beams to rest upon the carpet beneath us. The rug is a rich amber color. Everything in the place smacks of big cash.

"Why have you come here?" she wants to know.

She has large, white teeth. Perfectly straight, unlike my partner's.

I explain about the license plates.

"They belong to my son, William."

"Is he here, presently?" Lila engages.

"Why, yes. Shall I bring him down?"

I nod, she rises, and then we wait in this lush study.

In less than five she's back.

The kid with her has red hair. Carrot top. He's got freckles, and he's pudgy and he's barely 5'6", I'd estimate.

William Sanderson is also his father's name, we found out. The license plates were in his dad's name because young William is barely sixteen. They bought him a Toyota, and he managed to get it stolen. The Toyota was recovered but demolished, but the license plates were removed from the wreck. The Sandersons hadn't got around to reporting the plates as missing, she informed us.

"We got to sit in a house neither of us'll ever live in," Lila groans as we drive back downtown.

"It was a pretty thought, though, for a little while. Wasn't it?"

She nods at me from the passenger's seat. This time I'm doing the driving.

If it appears too good to be true, then it probably is, the ancient wisdom reads. And it caught us hoping for a big break. The big illumination, the epiphany.

None of which is any closer to happening than it was when the bodies started to pile up. Their six names are on our white board. The names in red are the unsolved list. We have nine names in blood red, to date. Six of them are from this hooded spook who's been toying with us, so far. I don't know if he's taunting us or if he gives a shit who's after him. Either way he pisses me off seriously. Being angry on this job is not being in your happy fucking place. We're supposed to be objective, and most of the time both Lila and I are cool with the notion that some people get away with murder. But resigning myself to anything was never a particular strong suit, in my own professional profile.

I'm starting to itch about this son of a bitch. I'm starting to want him. And I know all that does is make him that much more elusive. Any obsession is a sickness. You don't need a degree in psychology to know all that.

Lila will eventually tell me to cool off. She'll suggest we go out and get drunk. Which we never do. It's just her remedy for me getting strung out and hung up on a case. You do have to let go, occasionally, but it's way too early to think about giving it up. It just seems like some cases are fixes from the beginning. I don't like pre-judging our investigations, but this one seems to have been flying south with the fucking geese from the beginning.

The FBI sticks its ugly federal nose into the six slayings on the third Monday in December. We're right at the Holidays, the jolliest time for murder in the calendar year. No one wants to work Christmas Eve, Christmas Day or News Year's Eve or New Year's Day, but killing doesn't take time off. It's much like the War was. Bombs kept booming at unreasonable hours, and weekends didn't count for jack shit. Bad things just kept on occurring.

But we get no more twin killings involving hookers. Not since those two died in the green car's trunk. It lulls you into a false state of ease, when things go suddenly quiet, and in Chicago we have murders almost round the clock. So many people, so many guns and knives. So many frying pans and meat cleavers and other assorted instruments of mayhem.

The FBI guys are named Travis Rowland and Marty Moriarity. I can't wait to ask Marty about Sherlock and Dr. Watson, but I'll have to bide my time.

Lila gives them both a big smile when they enter my cubicle. Neither of us stands when they enter. There is a well-known sense of adversarial competition between the CPD and the Federal Bureau of Incompetence. We don't like them and they are indifferent toward us. Unless we have information they can use.

Travis is a tall blond young man. Looks like a farmer, but when he talks he sounds very articulate, very well educated. I'm thinking he might be a lawyer. Marty is shorter, more cro magnon. Dark hair. Lots on the back of his hands, but not so much on his prematurely sparse top knot. I could see Marty playing the Wolfman in the remake.

Travis has an eye for Lila. He just about shouts it aloud as he keeps his eyes planted all over her. Marty keeps looking out my window at the skyline of downtown. I have to admit that the tiny view I have is eye-catching. It's a magnificent Loop, after all.

"We want to cooperate with you in any way we can," Travis tells Lila. It's as if I've vacated the room. But now the cro magnon has focused on me.

"When the bullshit is over, let me know what you want," I tell the blond Viking.

"That's a very negative attitude," Travis finally smiles my way. "Highly counterproductive, Detective Mangan."

At least he knows my name.

"That was unnecessarily rude, Danny," Lila erupts, her eyes glaring at mine.

I'm wondering if she's taken a hankering for the taller agent.

"We'll be happy to help," Lila smiles at both feds.

Then they remove themselves and the darkness is gone from my doorway.

"Don't have to incite hostility, Danny."

"Who else is there to incite?"

"Very humorous. Maybe we can use them."

"It doesn't work that way, Lila, and you know it. They attempt to use *us*. That's how they operate."

"Not always," she grins.

"You going to used your feminine wiles on the big goof?"

"He's an attractive big goof. But I had my eye on the ape man. Think he's got a sweater growing on his backside?"

I look out the window and glance at the distant Tribune Building.

"Are you jealous of the bigger one, Danny?"

"Nope. Not me."

"I think you lie, big boy."

"I never lie. Not so's you'd notice."

"I was just trying to appear fraternal. Nothing more. So cool down. Let's go get a beer."

I surprise her and I agree.

We go to the little joint in the Loop that John Belushi made famous on *Saturday Night Live*. The Billygoat. The place notorious for "cheesebugga, no Pepsi, Coke." A lot of the newspaper writers hang here. It's lunch time, and the small bar is packed. We worm our way to the bar because the few tables are taken.

I actually order the "cheesebugga," and after the waiter relays the order at the grill behind the bar, you can hear the cook doing the routine the same way the comedian on the TV does.

The burgers are all right at The Billygoat Tavern, and I don't order a beer, but Lila does. She can drink a few without getting impaired, so I never complain when she takes a belt during our shift. It's never more than one. We've got that rule, but we relax it up, on occasion.

The place is noisy, but the good news is there is no loud music to add to the raucousness. They only stay open until nine at night, and we've been in here after the dinner hour, and it becomes deserted and lonely in here after about seven at night. It's like that "Night Owls" painting, except it's a bar instead of a coffee house/grill.

We have to shout to be heard by each other.

"You're not really jealous."

I look at her and smile.

"You're a big girl. You can decide who you want to lust for," I try to grin.

"You're an idiot, Danny!" she shouts.

I laugh, and then our food and drinks suddenly arrive.

I bite into the burger. It's not bad. It ought to be better for four bucks. Inflation has become a real bitch. I can't afford to eat out as often as I used to.

"Why am I an idiot?" I shout back.

"Because you never really trust anybody, do you."

"I trust you," I tell her in full volume.

The old couple at the table sitting behind us are paying rapt attention at our conversation. I look at the two grayheads, and I can do no other than smile amicably at them. They become self-conscious, and then they glare at their own food.

"No, you don't," she insists, loudly.

I lean over close to her.

"Yes, goddammit, I do! I trust you!"

She kisses me before I can withdraw.

I look at her. I stare into her eyes as intensely as I'm able. Then I kiss her back.

I turn to the oldsters sitting behind us, and I tell them:

"Did you see *that*?" I ask the old man and old woman.

They both nod simultaneously.

Her right nipple sticks out prodigiously. It is pointed and pink. The left nipple is an *inny*. She hovers atop me as we engage for a second go, here at her apartment. It's late in the afternoon, and I thought Kelly might be coming home at any minute, at my house. Lila said her roomie was out of town until next Tuesday, so we opted for Lila's place.

"Do we have any birth control issues?" I ask her suddenly.

"Helluva moment to ask that question," she replies.

Her face is flushed and sweating. I'm covered in lather from the both of us, as well, and as I say, this is the second bout on this afternoon's card.

I've never had anything like this with the girls I've known or with Mary, my ex-wife. I haven't known many women in this way at all, honestly. The ones I made love to were few in number, is what I mean to say. The number of encounters in total would be a much larger digit than the cast of players. I suppose I'm monogamous by nature.

She comes down toward me and rests on top of me, her face flush against my chest.

I kiss the top of her close-cropped head. Her hair is thick enough, however, that you can't see scalp. I'd like to see her with tresses down to her perfect orb of a butt.

"So," is all I can muster.

"Don't talk. Seize the moment. Seize the freaking day, Danny."

"I'd rather seize *you*," I tell her.

"You did a pretty good job of that. Think we both came close to massive coronaries, no?"

She's sitting up, looking down at me with her mystic's eyes.

"Only way to check out, if you have to check out at all."

"Still think this is a mistake?" she demands.

I watch her eyes but they don't blink. Not once.

"I don't care if it's a mistake. As long as we're both making it."

9

On Christmas Eve, I take Kelly to a restaurant on the southwest side, Benedicts. She orders ham and I order turkey, and to my amazement, she eats what's on her plate.

Sr. Catherine has her going, as an out-patient, to St. Mary's Hospital in Oak Lawn for the bulimia. I could never get her to go back to counseling, but this nun has worked the magic. The only reason I know about it is because I get the co-pay bills at the end of the month, and I've been getting them since the end of November.

I don't bring up the out-patient business because she's never discussed her eating disorder with me, not even when I attended the parental gatherings at St. Luke's in Evergreen Park, a few years back.

We don't communicate well, regardless of the subject, so I've pretty much stopped trying.

But she does appear to be just slightly less frail than she was at the beginning of the school year, and the truancy and the drugs (as far as I can tell) have stopped, too. I don't toss her room, anyway, because she's very clever about stashing her stuff.

"You have to work tonight, right?" she asks.

I'm shocked that she initiates the conversation.

"Yeah. I go in at eleven."

"You going to see Lila tonight before you go to work?"

"No. Lila has her own plans before we go on."

"Oh."

She grins just slightly.

"What's so amusing?"

"Nothing."

I don't bite at the ploy.

"Just that I know you have a thing for Lila."

She smirks, just a little.

"And how do you know that?"

"I've seen the way you look at her when she drops you off at the house, sometimes."

Kelly has even been civil to Lila, if not outright friendly.

"Lila is gay," I tell her. My turn to shock.

It doesn't even slow my daughter down.

"That's what women say to keep you at arm's length, Dad. It isn't always true."

"She has a roommate," I tell her.

There is a healthier glow about her color now, too. Maybe she's not just eating *tonight*. Maybe she's finally decided not to puke herself to death to spite me and her AWOL mother.

"That doesn't mean she's a lesbian, Dad."

I haven't heard her say "Dad" much until tonight, either. The notion gets me to thinking *if it sounds too good to be true....*

But I let it go. It's Christmas Eve, for Christ's sake. Neither of us attends church, so—

"I'm going to midnight mass," she says as she picks with a spoon at her orange sherbet.

Benedicts is a mid-scale restaurant. It's a step up from a mom and pop, but it's no chain thing, either. It is tastefully put together, and the interior is all modern and eye pleasing. There are candles lit on all the tables, and the waiters and waitresses all wear white shirts and black bowties.

"You've found the light?" I smile.

"I haven't found anything. But I'm looking," she replies with a sad glance.

"I'm not trying to make fun of you, honey, but shit, all these changes…"

"I have to, Dad. Or I'll die."

She says it straight up, without the melodrama that it sounds like. Because it's true. If she keeps on doing it the old way, she's gone. The doctors told us in the past that she'd play hell on her liver and kidneys and that her heart would finally give out if she kept abusing herself the way she had been.

And I've come to notice that the fridge is emptying out faster than usual, the past few weeks. She's just begun to call off her elongated hunger strike or whatever the bulimia is. I know it's got to do with self-esteem. I know Kelly doesn't like herself, and I know it's more complicated than just a reaction to being a pudgy pre-teenaged girl, at one time. But she's been so secretive about what's going on, and she's been so outright rebellious toward me, the past few years, it's hard to know what's happening with her.

It's an appropriate time to start all over again, I suppose. Christmas, I mean. Maybe that's what Sr. Catherine sold to Kelly, because she's moved her to do things no one else had any success with.

I know enough about psychiatry, however, to understand that nothing happens overnight to cause profound change in human behavior. She seems to take this moment as a cue.

"I can't eat the rest of this sherbet. I think I already ate too much, Dad."

"You did great. Don't worry about it."

She smiles. Then she hands me a card.

I open it. It's plain, no picture or message on the cover. I look inside and it reads: *Merry Christmas. I'm trying.*

I look up at her, and I see her bright, beautiful eyes set in a not-so-haggard face, anymore. I can't say anything for a moment.

"Your presents are under our scrawny-assed tree at home."

"I know," she says. "I saw them there. I'll open them when I get back from midnight mass."

"Why don't you wait until tomorrow morning? We can open them at ten or so, and then I'll take you somewhere that's open, for lunch. It might only be White Castle because nobody much is open on Christmas."

"Take Lila with us. I know she likes you, Dad. More than you think she does."

"Woman's intuition?"

"Yeah. You can call it that."

"I'll drop you off at the church before I go in to work."

"You'll be late, then."

"So I'll be late."

She looks at me quizzically, but then she drops her gaze to the melting orange sherbet, and finally she jabs at the iced sweet stuff with her spoon.

Captain Marshall Clarke is our guy in Homicide. He is one of the first black Homicide commanders in CPD history. He rose through the street and he catapulted over bigotry on the force. Everyone respects him, and the word is that he's always been clean, even when he was in uniform and when he was a lieutenant in Vice.

Lila and I are called onto his carpet on the day after New Year's, January 2, 1987.

He has a very spacious office, compared to our cubicles. It's understandable since he has the responsibilities he owns. Shit flows downhill, and Lila and I are at the bottom of the mountain. So we expect to hear some kind of reprimand for allowing the "Twin Killer," as he is now called in the newspapers, to continue to roam Chicago's mean streets.

Clarke is a medium-sized man, perhaps five feet eight, but he is rather burly. I'd clock him at 205 or so. It's all muscle, though. He must be fifty, but he has the look of a weight lifter or some kind of fitness freak. There's no excess in his poundage.

"So," he begins. "Nothing new on this series fellow."

He isn't smiling. He never does. Marshall Clarke is a very somber-looking man for all seasons.

"No, sir," Lila chimes in.

"I understand," Clarke replies to her. We're both seated on a small two-seater couch against his wall. He also has a nice view of the city, but his is much wider.

"We've circulated the sketch all over northern Illinois," I explain. "We've hit Old Town so often that the hookers make us before we can engage them, and they take off running the other way."

"Understandable. You're doing everything you can do."

He swivels his chair and looks out onto the Lakeshore.

"How many hours you figure you two have clocked on this one case?"

"I don't really know," I answer.

"Probably something close to a couple hundred, so far," Lila estimates.

He turns back toward us.

"I have to ask you to cut back. I don't want your other cases to suffer because you're constantly running after a dead-ender."

"Dead-ender?" I ask.

"You know how hooker cases end up. The Department won't call them low profile, but we all know the truth. The papers are puffing these six murders up, but the readers don't really care, at least not for long, and then the media moves on to something flashier."

"You mean something whiter," Lila tells him.

"As a matter of fact," Clarke smiles.

I can't remember ever seeing his teeth before.

"Sir, that's all bullshit, any way you cut it."

He stares at me, and the smile is gone.

"I know that. You know that. But that's not the way it really works and everybody in Homicide knows it, too."

"The Feds," I say.

"What about them?"

"They're taking this over because it *is* their thing, lately. They get headlines when they solve multiples—they call them 'serial killers,' now—and they don't care about readership. It's about Quantico and profilers and the science behind these mutts who do lots of victims, one after the other."

"That's a very cute soliloquy, Danny. But I don't take orders from the FBI."

I try not to show what I'm thinking. But it appears that he really believes the crap he's just told us.

"So. As I was saying," Clarke says. "You'll have to cut back on the hours you work on the six killings. Am I clear?"

"Perfectly," Lila says.

We turn and walk out the Captain's door.

"Why now?"

She looks at me as we sit in the car. We're parked in the garage at Headquarters in the Loop.

"Because he's right, Danny. You know he's right. The media clowns are only on this one because it involves multiples, and series killings are all the rage on TV and in the movies. Once everyone becomes acquainted with the past histories of these girls, the interest will wane. And he's right about the 'white,' too. If they were white, the news guys would never let go, but with six black whores, give it a month or two, tops. It's reality, partner."

"I never thought I'd hear that out of you, especially you."

"Why? Because I'm a feminist?"

"I didn't know you were a feminist."

"Most gay females are."

"Yeah, but you're bisexual, right?"

"That would explain a few things, now wouldn't it."

She gives me the snide smirk.

I feel my face heating up. I feel very uncomfortable in this territory. A lot of cops are still pissed that females work the streets, as either uniforms or detectives. The old chauvinistic patriarchal atmosphere has not left the building with Elvis, in cop land.

"I want to catch this guy," I rejoin.

"So do I and you know it. And unless Clarke intends to follow us everywhere we go on every shift we work, how's he going to keep tabs on the time we spend on the case?"

She smiles my way. I look all around the garage, but I don't see anyone else. So I move over from the passenger's side and I lay a hot, firm one on her lips.

She responds in kind.

"I don't like sharing," I tell her as we disengage.

"You mean my roomie?" she asks.

"I mean anyone, sitters or pointers."

"That's something for which only time will tell, Danny."

I look over at her. She's been letting her hair grow out, and now it tickles her shoulders. She hasn't let it grow at my suggestion, however.

"You want to get this to another level?" I ask her, looking dead on into her eyes.

"It already is. Or haven't you noticed, dumbass."

She gets out of the squad and walks toward the elevators.

Lila doesn't say anything more about us, the next few days, and I figure I better back off. I can't expect her to get solid with what she must think are demands from me. But I really can't see a threesome working. Not a threesome together all at once. I mean me being with her and she being with another woman when I'm not around. If I were truly a Renaissance Man, maybe I could hack it, but I'm far too square and conservative, when it comes down to relationships. The bit about her being bisexual was a relief at first, but now I don't know if I can live with her part time heterosexuality. Maybe I'm asking too much, but I know I could never switch hit, myself.

Most men look at lesbianism as something indirectly erotic. Guys like to watch women go at each other, romantically, but most straight males have real difficulty watching men grope each other. I'm sure there's something illogical and duplicitous about that attitude, and I don't have anything against homosexuals. I believe in equal rights for everyone. It's just that I'm absolutely Neanderthal when it comes to the woman I intend to spend the rest of my life with.

It'll have to be me and her. No third parties. I never cheated on Mary, and if I wind up with Lila, it'll be the same deal. Like I said, I'm absolutely monogamous. I can't work it any other way.

Maybe I'm archaic. Maybe I am a latent homophobe (but I don't really believe it). I just know that I want Lila all for myself, and I can't see it playing out any other way.

I'll never make any ultimatums for Lila. But I guess I've got one bubbling up inside me. Some day, some time, the pot will probably boil over, and then I'll lose Lila.

Just like I lost the first one.

10

I was with the program. I was a fanatic. I was gung ho, even if I wasn't a Marine. They trained me how to kill for my country and I obliged my nation. I'm not happy about the men I shot and killed, but I'm at least able to say every one of them died at my hands in the heat of combat and in the steam of southeast Asia. It was self- defense. I never went looking for trouble, but I always wound up in the middle of it.

When Clarke tells us to back off on the murders of six people, I smell a rat. The rat doesn't live in our building at Headquarters, either. The rat lives in a more elevated dwelling. Somewhere where the shakers and doers reside.

Everything is political in Chicago. Nothing is untainted by simplicity and logic. Someone wants us to hold back, and it isn't Clarke. Like the military, you take orders from the top. In the police it's the same way. I may have been a bit idealistic about Homicide when I got this job, but I know now that even stiffs suffer the fix.

Blacks used to be victims of the Machine in this town, but now they're evolving into the parts of the device, and soon they'll run the controls. Chicago is becoming a city of color. The Irish are no longer completely in power. Blacks are pushing, and so are Hispanics. Hispanics might someday become the dominant player in this burg, it seems. Their population is beginning to swell. For now, though, the leader in the pack to overthrow my Mick brothers is African Americans.

I never used to care about who ran the show, as long as they let me operate my own way. But that was always a fantasy. You're never in charge of the horse you ride. There are too many variables. The weather, the track, the speed of the horses in your heat. All of the above comes into play, and no matter how fast your animal is, he's prone to all those circumstances around him. And then he might slip and fall, even on a dry track. Maybe there's a gopher hole on that track, and his hoof catches it, and he falls and breaks his leg and you fall with him and get yourself paralyzed and he gets put down.

I'm not a player at the track. But I like to go to Arlington. I think it's less of a fix than the trotters at Hawthorne. I don't bet on the thoroughbreds. I just like to watch them run. When they're not being held back by their jockeys, it's a beautiful sight to behold.

I hate to wax up all metaphoric, but it's the way I see these series murders. It can't have to do with the victims, so it has to have something to do with the Twin Killer, as everyone in the press likes to call this hooded asshole. He has to have some juice if they're calling off the dogs. The only time they talk about manpower hours is when our wages are being negotiated or when they don't like the smell of heat in the air being aimed at the bad guy. This bad guy must have friends.

It's only my personal theory, but *there it is.*

We're going to go with Lila's scenario, however. We'll chase this prick the way we've always pursued him, and we'll hope Clarke doesn't become a dick about us counting the hours we spend doing it. It's pretty hard for him to have an exact accounting of our whereabouts except for the information we give him. Otherwise, he'll have to send a tail after us, and that gets even more expensive.

The story about no one caring about six hookers being slaughtered sounds true enough, but to an honest Homicide, it doesn't matter much who got popped. It matters far more that his killer pays. That may sound cold and inhuman, but the effect is the same no matter what your motivation is: The idea is to catch the perpetrator and get them off the streets forever. The rest is academic.

So do you go after a murderer of a street lowlife any more slowly or less intensely than you do after a high profile perp? I know I don't. Maybe there are detectives who play for the crowd, who lust for the headlines. But I don't think they're all that many like that. It may sound self-serving, but I'm really not in that crew.

It might harken back to my Ranger training. Most of the stuff we did in Vietnam never made it to newsprint. That was the way we planned it. The guys we killed when we were on recon were Viet Cong honchos—they were killers, too. If we splattered their melons with a scope from long distance, anonymously, then that was the way we played it. We didn't leave calling cards, like some of our military brethren. We didn't want them to know who bid them a final farewell. The job was a task, and all you wanted was accomplishment, and we were very efficient at closure.

I've carried that attitude over into my police work. I don't give a shit about medals and commendations. (Mine are stashed in a drawer underneath my underwear, at home. The ones from the War, I mean.) I don't want face time in the papers or on the local news. Let the cowboys on the force have my share of adulation and their own. I just want to eliminate the names in red on our white board in my office. They're the list of the dead who haven't had their murderers brought to justice. Their erasure is the only pleasure I get out of this work. When we blot those names out on that board, it beats my paycheck. It's the only satisfaction that does override the cash I get for doing this work.

Lila and I haven't slept together since the first time we made the earth move. I don't think the earth moved, actually, but I know the mattress and box springs were engaged enthusiastically. I've been looking for a cue from her that she'd enjoy another close encounter, but I haven't been reading any of that from her lately. She comes to work, we ride the streets looking for our hooded fellow and for several other bad guys, and then she drops me off or I take her home, depending on whose turn it is to drive.

It's mid-January, and already I'm starting to think Clarke needn't have worried about the hours we're putting on our top case. It's becoming chillier and chillier—the weather outside and the temperature of our investigation into the Twin Killer.

It's moving toward not moving at all. There have been no similar double slayings, and I'm wondering if our guy hasn't backed off. Or maybe got himself aced. It happens. These people play in dangerous backyards, and maybe some pimp caught up with him and put a few rounds into the top of his head. We get white stiffs collected by the meat wagon all the time. They go into black or mixed hoods and they say the wrong thing or do the inappropriate thing, and they get chilled and slabbed. It does happen.

There is a flurry happening outside our car as we drive back to headquarters. We don't have anything new on our "primary" case, but we did catch two braindeads who killed three people—two on one case and a single on the other. We caught them both because they're stupid and they're stupid because they just had to tell someone else about their own stupidity. Talking delivers more killers than evidence, sometimes. Most killers aren't high IQ motherfuckers. They're just dumb motherfuckers. Lucky for us. Lucky for us that more of them aren't clever, that more of them aren't meticulous planners and connivers.

I look over at Lila, behind the wheel. Her hair is now shoulder length and still descending. I've wanted to run my fingers through those cascading tresses for a couple weeks, now. But I haven't laid a finger on her at all since the night in question.

"You pissed at me?" I finally blurt.

"No? Why would you ask that?"

Her eyes are trained on the street. We're only a few blocks from Headquarters.

"Why would I ask that."

"Sounds like you're pissed at *me*," she retorts. But there is a slight grin on her face.

"You haven't said much of a word to me since the night we were…together."

"You don't have to tiptoe around it, Danny."

She knows I have no talent for subtlety.

"Well?" I ask.

"I thought you wanted to cool it for a while so we could both figure out where we're headed."

"When did I say that?"

"Maybe you didn't say that, but I thought that's what you had in mind."

"I'm for full ahead."

"What if I'm not?" she asks.

I look at her, but her eyes remained focused on the road.

"Okay, then," I tell her.

"Now you are pissed."

"No. Now I know, that's all."

"Danny...."

She turns her face toward me, but I'm the one glaring at the street before us. We're pulling into the parking lot.

"Forget it. I'm all right with it," I tell her when we pull into a space on the lower deck.

"Are you sure?"

"I'm certain," I lie to her.

We seem to be back where we were before things got physical. We joke around the way we always did, and we never bring up what happened in the bedroom or in the squad car when we got things "straight."

But I feel tension every time I see her, now. And she seems just a little too pleasant, every time we're not talking police business.

At home, I'm still watching a slow transformation. Kelly's report card showed four A's and two B's. It's been her best showing in her three and a half years.

I know she's gained weight. She even asked me to take her out to buy new clothes. She wears a uniform that was always too baggy at Sacred Heart, but now she's filling it out nicely. She's showing the same kind of curves that her mother sported, when we were together. Kelly's not getting fat, however. She's made use of the membership I've got at a health club about a mile from the house. She even rides a bike back and forth to add to the physical regimen at the club.

I spent three hundred on her for the clothes, although she tried to argue me into putting some of the stuff back on the racks. I don't think I've bought her new duds since she was a freshman. She never got any taller than she was when she was fourteen, and she unfortunately never gained any weight until the last few weeks. I'm tickled to spend the cash on her. Most of my paycheck lies in the account, after our bills. I've got a pretty decent stash in the bank because I rarely spend anything on either of us. My balance is pretty healthy, then.

She's asked me to go with her to her outpatient treatment, as soon as my schedule allows. I told her I'd make it even if I have to ask for personal time, and her face lit up when she discovered after all this time that I'd do anything for her.

All she had to do was ask.

At least one front of my life has shown some glimmerings of hope. The front with Lila has become extremely dim. She's killing me with kindness. She wants to drive me to work and drop me off all the time, and when we go out for dinner break, she always snatches the tab before I can grab hold of it.

As February arrives, the weather deteriorates. It becomes snowier and colder, and action on the street gets curtailed quite a bit. Homicides are down to a three-year low. We're stuck with the original redliners, as the unsolved cases are called, and nothing new comes onto our white board. It's eerie. It's as if death has blown town and headed for Miami, or toward other warmer climates.

Most of our homicides take place in the heat of summer and early fall. People are out in the hoods, then, and they're pissed because it's hot and sticky. The cold kind of freezes the activity up, quite literally, as it has recently. I'm sure things'll pick up when the spring thaw arrives in March.

You can count on death. Life is iffy, but death is certain. Cheesy but true.

Clarke doesn't pull us in on the carpet, but I know he's been keeping tabs on us via other detectives. There's nothing to call us on because our case against the Twin Killer has gone Arctic. He's not killing, and he hasn't left anything for us to dig up about him.

My thought that he might have been killed doesn't pan out, either. I've checked all the recent killings, and no one even remotely matching his description has popped up onto the screens. It's as if he's submerged, vanished from the surface.

Gone underground.

I remember in college we read *The Odyssey*. I also recall the part where Odysseus (Ulysses) is called to go into the nether world, into hell, to find out about the world of the dead. He has to find out about the underground before he's allowed to surface and return to the land of the living.

So where does the Twin Killer go to hide? Where's he go to wait until the heat is turned down or turned off? He must have a source of income, but he doesn't feel like a shift worker to me. He likes late night activity, and that tells me he can't have a gig that requires getting up at dawn and going off to some factory. It's all supposition, I know, but I have to track him somehow, even if he isn't leaving tracks behind him.

If he's wealthy, that would explain his night life framework. Maybe he doesn't work at all. Which makes him the offspring of somebody powerful, which makes Clarke's little speech about backing off make sense.

But I know it's just my mind exercising itself in lieu of facts, and facts make a case, not imagining.

Lila is closed mouthed about the kind of guy she figures did the six prosties. She doesn't say much. She has always been the non-theoretical detective, between the two of us. She follows the evidence and rarely runs after her intuition. You'd think a woman would be inclined to be bound to intuition, but Lila breaks most everyone's expectations about her to shards.

"We're never going to catch him," I tell her over burgers and fries at an overpriced sports bar on the northside.

"You're just depressed. Stop whining," she smiles.

"I'll stop being depressed when you tell me why you stopped us cold, Lila."

She puts down her half pound burger and shoots a glare right at me.

11

April in Paris it ain't. April in Chicago is more like a climatic tug of war. The winter gives in grudgingly to the spring. The false spring starts in early March, sometimes, and the ice and snow and unbearable hawk cold out of the northeast give way to some southern breezes that merely titillate but do not deliver the relief of April's warming winds.

Our redliners are up to seven, including the killer of the six girls.

It's almost 65 degrees today, on April Fool's Day. It's balmy enough to take a walk to the Lake with Lila on our lunch hour, about 1:15 P.M. We walk to the Lake in under fifteen minutes because our headquarters are that close. As we walk east toward the water, she stops and turns to me.

"You think he's dead?"

"You mean our favorite serial killer?" I try to grin.

"Do you?"

"No. I don't think he's gone anywhere except underground, and only temporarily."

"Why'd he stop?" Lila says, as we begin the trek to the beach. We can see the sand and the Lake, now. It's only a few more blocks. The sun is up in the sky and it's unobstructed by any of the fleecy white clouds that roll slowly overhead.

"Maybe he was bored."

She doesn't respond to my inanity.

"He's not bored," she finally counters.

"No. I don't think so, either. Something came up, maybe. His conscience?"

"He doesn't have one," Lila frowns at me.

"Yeah, I know. It's just that I don't have an explanation for why he's taken a powder. Maybe he fell in love with another series killer and they're off to Canada to make little creeps in their own images."

"Women don't tend to do shit like this," she says.

We're at the entrance to Elm Street Beach. We walk toward the lake water. It's cooler, here, as it always is except in the gooiest days in July and August when there's no place to escape the swelter of the humidity.

We plant ourselves on a bench. Lila bought us two torpedo sandwiches at Luigi's, across the street from HQ, and I bought two cans of Diet Coke from the machine on our floor. I carted the pop and Lila took care of the sandwiches. Not very gentlemanly of me, I know, but Lila carries her own loads and doesn't ask for dispensations, whether it's torpedo sandwiches or our workload.

We eat without talking, but we devour the food quickly because we only have an hour and the trip back to work takes fifteen minutes, just like it did on the way here.

"The Captain has gone quiet, also," Lila says, breaking the silence between us. The beach is sparsely attended. It's way early for the swimmers and the sunbathers, but back on the sidewalk there are the walkers and the joggers and the bicycle riders and the skateboarders. You wouldn't think all this tranquility could be home to the monsters we pursue.

"Yeah, I haven't even seen him, let alone heard from him. But it's understandable. He knows this case has gone static, and maybe he's trying to keep the lull going until everybody loses track of our man."

"Ain't going to happen," she smiles lamely.

"No. It ain't."

"And how's the kid?" she says, aiming her blues at my own eyes.

"The kid is going to graduate with her class. Not with honors, but she had too much ground to make up for all those other years. But she's got everything made up, and I have to say that Sacred Heart bent way back over backwards to help Kelly out. I gotta hand it to them. They went overtime on my kid, and I'm grateful to them. I might have to start going back to church, now."

"Don't get crazy on me, Danny," she laughs.

I look over at her until she stops giggling.

"What do you believe in, Lila?"

"Huh?"

"I mean it. What do you believe in? Anything?"

"Should we take this little interview to the interrogation room?" she laughs again.

"No. I'm serious. What do you believe in? Anything at all? Or are you an atheist?"

"All that sounds more like an accusation."

"Quit answering me like a cop. I'm asking you a serious question. No shit."

"No shit? You really want to know?"

I wait for her to reply.

"There is no God, if that's what you're asking. If there were, how does He stand back and let creatures like the Twin Killer come out of a human womb? Think of all the things that can go wrong in a pregnancy. Think of all the easy resolutions a loving God would be able to create, other than allowing this piece of dirt to breathe. He could've taken care of the problem back in the first trimester, Danny."

"Then we'd be out of a job."

"True. But we could find something else to do besides hunt butchers."

"I couldn't."

"You couldn't do anything besides this?"

"No. I thought about it a lot."

"And you see yourself doing this until retirement."

I watch her eyes. They're dead serious and engaged with mine.

"I love you, Lila. I want to take it to another, higher place."

"You're changing the subject, Danny."

"With me, that subject's never changed."

"You know how I feel about you."

"No, actually I have no idea."

"Come on!"

"I don't, Lila. I can't read you at all."

"You can read anybody on the street, so why can't you see that—"

She breaks off and shifts her gaze to Lake Michigan. The water is a metallic gray-blue. A cloud finally does cover the sun, but just briefly, and then the brilliant light sparkles over the water in front of us. Way out on the horizon, I can see one of those processing plants that cleans the lake water. Its brick front barely darkens the surface of the gray-blue body before us.

"I'm sorry I brought it up again. I'll learn to keep my mouth shut, okay?"

I stand.

"Time to go back," I tell her.

"You can't go back," she grins at me sadly.

Her hair is shoulder length and holding, but it's just the way I always hoped she'd let it grow.

"You in love with that woman you live with?" I ask her, finally. I've never broached that subject with Lila before now.

She looks at me, and her face suddenly colors.

"No. I'm not in love with anybody."

And that answer is the reply I've always feared the most, from Lila.

We've circulated the Twin Killer's mug from the artist to all the hospitals in northern Illinois. Including psychiatric institutions. We've heard nothing for two months.

And on this fifteenth of April, 1987, we get a call from Elgin State—the mental facility, northwest of the city. A doctor named Lawrence Talbot calls me and says he remembers a male patient who fit the description of our fellow. We tell him we'll drive over and have a talk with him.

"Your name sounds familiar," I tell Dr. Talbot.

Lila looks over at me quizzically as we sit on his leather couch in his very simply furnished office.

Talbot smiles.

"I've been hearing that for most of my life. From people old enough to remember *The Wolf Man* movie with Lon Chaney Junior."

Lila is not a horror fan, but I'm a sucker for monster movies, old or new.

"So you saw this man when?" Lila asks.

"About seven weeks ago, but I never connected his face to the circular you gave out until about three days ago. I was reading an article in the *Sun-Times* about how this Twin Killer was still out there, and then it came to me that this man might be the one in the rendering."

"Why was he here?" I ask.

"You know I'm constrained by confidentiality, Detective Mangan."

"I can get a court order," I remind him.

"I'm afraid you'll have to," Dr. Talbot says.

"Can you tell me if it'll be worth my while?"

He looks at me, and then at Lila.

Then he nods gravely.

It's 11:46 A.M. We can be back by late afternoon if we're lucky, if the judge cooperates.

Dr. Talbot says he'll be around until six—later if we'd like him to be.

We're back by 5:16 P.M. Lila did the driving, and the only way we could've gone faster on the expressway was if she'd been piloting one of her combat jets. I was sitting shotgun with white knuckles the whole ride back to Elgin.

It is a well-kept facility. Everything is starkly polished and cleaned. But the colors are muted pastels, no whites. I figure the colors were chosen for their mellowing effect. It mellows me out, anyway. There is no music in the entry. Perhaps they do a soundtrack on the ward. Music also is supposed to have a soothing effect.

We sit back down in Talbot's office after delivering Judge Shanahan's court order.

"He is a very troubled young man."

"His name is?" Lila asks.

"Franklin Toliver," the doctor replies.

"Address?" she queries.

Talbot gives us a number in DesPlaines, Illinois, a rather affluent suburb, in parts, anyway.

"What brought him to mind, other than his physical description?" Lila continues.

"As I said, he's very troubled."

Talbot taps his fingers on his desk top.

"In what way?" I ask.

"He might be schizophrenic. It's hard to say."

"Why is it hard to say, Doctor?" Lila asks.

"He was only here three days. And then he disappeared."

"Disappeared?" I ask him. "Wasn't he constrained?"

"He came in here voluntarily," Talbot tells us.

"But when you heard what he told you—"

He looks right at Lila.

"Detective Chapman, I wish it were an easy thing to figure out if someone was a psychotic killer, but if someone checks themselves in by choice, and he's not in handcuffs when he signs in...."

"I'm sorry, Doctor, I didn't mean to sound rude."

"It's okay," he tells Lila. "I can understand your frustration. If I'd suspected he were the man you're looking for, I'd have been compelled to inform the police. It would've been cut and dried, then, that this man was a danger to everyone around him. But he seemed more dangerous to himself, when I talked to him on those three occasions. And when I was about to ask that he commit himself, he bolted. We have security, of course, but it's not the same level of security we employ for committed, dangerous patients."

"What did he tell you?" I ask.

Talbot drums the copy of the court order with all ten of his fingers. We wait for him to continue.

"He has severe problems in relating to women; that's certain. He has issues with both his parents, but especially with the mother."

"He's how old?" Lila asks Talbot.

"Twenty-seven."

"And he still lives at home?" I ask the psychiatrist.

"On and off, according to Toliver," Talbot responds.

"On and off?" Lila asks again.

Talbot swivels his chair toward my partner.

"The mother throws him out regularly, he said. For smoking marijuana, for drinking binges. He had a history of violence. They threw him out of Western Illinois for assaulting a young woman. The charges were dropped when the young woman didn't testify against him, but the university cashiered him anyway. He was arrested for soliciting prostitutes twice, he told me. He was released on bond both times. There should be police records on all this."

"He mention anything that would lead you to believe he'd have those issues you spoke of with African Americans?" I query.

He drums the folder again.

"Yes. He didn't like blacks or Jews or Hispanics. I found it odd."

"Odd?" Lila asks.

"He comes from an affluent family. He comes from a well-educated background."

"His mother and father are wealthy?" I ask him.

"It's a little deeper than that, even," Talbot answers.

"In what way, exactly," Lila goes on.

"His father, Raymond Toliver, is Lieutenant Governor of the State of Illinois," the doctor explains.

Lila turns to me, but I'm still scanning the psychiatrist as he drums his digits one more time on our court order.

12

We visit the Toliver residence in DesPlaines. The front door has two State Policemen standing in front of it. Lila and I show them our IDs, and the taller cop goes inside the house to announce us.

When he comes back, he motions for us to come inside, and we do. The other State Policeman remains outside, but the cop who beckoned us stays with us.

A woman strides toward the three of us as we stand in the entryway.

"I'm Geraldine Toliver," she says as she extends me a hand. "The Lieutenant Governor is in Springfield, I'm afraid, so you'll have to talk to me."

She shakes hands with Lila, and then our escort turns and walks out the front door.

"We're here about your son," I explain.

"Please come in to the study," she smiles.

She's not much older than I am, perhaps somewhere between forty-five and fifty, I'm guessing. She has chestnut brown hair, she's very tall and erect in stature, and she has a body you'd hook up to a much younger woman than she seems to be.

Lila catches me watching her walk, and she gives me a stagy

frown. I shoot her back a question on my face like, 'What'd I do?' Then the Lieutenant Governor's wife sits on a royal blue couch, and we plant ourselves on another couch of exactly the same color, opposite her. The study is spacious. There are the obligatory bookshelves with hundreds of volumes resting on them. There is a mahogany desk right behind her, and it has a tiffany desk lamp sitting on top of it. There is nothing on the desktop except for the sheen of glaring polish.

"You're here about our son, Franklin."

"Yes."

"He was never committed to that hospital," she offers.

"We're here investigating a series of homicides. We'd like to talk to Franklin," Lila tells her.

Geraldine Toliver sends Lila a cold smile. It seems almost feral, to me. I get a slight shiver down my back. This broad should've been in Homicide. She'd make one helluvan interrogator. She'd compel me to confess in seconds.

"What's that have to do with my son?" she asks.

"We're here to ask him where he was when those killings took place," Lila smiles coldly back at her.

"You think *Franklin* killed several people?" she smiles charmingly, now.

"There were six. You've read about the murders of the six prostitutes?" I ask.

"Of course. It's impossible not to hear about them. They were all black?"

I nod.

"Is Franklin here?"

She stares back at me.

"Franklin has been gone since he checked himself into Elgin."

"He checked himself in, or did you or your husband accompany Franklin?" Lila interjects.

"My son comes and goes as he pleases. He's twenty-seven years old."

"You'd think one of you or both of you would be there if he voluntarily placed himself in a mental hospital," Lila insists.

The Lieutenant Governor's wife appreciates that she's being

grilled about the lack of closeness she displays toward her son.

"Is Franklin an only child?" I ask.

She turns slowly toward me. It looks like a cobra turning toward its victim.

"Yes. He is our only child. I couldn't have any more children after him, according to my doctor."

"How would you describe your relationship with your son?" Lila asks.

She jerks back toward Lila, but my partner doesn't flinch.

"We don't have a relationship. Franklin is merely a boarder here, whenever it suits him. But I can tell you that he's not a murderer."

"The psychiatrist at Elgin begs to differ. He didn't tell us that Franklin confessed, but the doctor had the idea that your son is very troubled. 'Disturbed' was the word he used," Lila tells her.

"The fact that he wound up in the state mental facility tells anyone that much, but it doesn't mean he killed those prostitutes," she shoots back at us.

"No. But we need to talk to Franklin as soon as possible. Does he drive a car?" I ask.

"Yes. A Ford Taurus. It's navy blue. Four doors, I think. I don't remember the license plates, but they're under his father's name."

I look at Lila, and now we're solidly aware why the Captain wanted us to back down. We need to have a talk with our boss ASAP.

"If Franklin contacts you, please let us know."

I hand her my card.

"It's important that he comes in on his own, if possible. If he's not guilty of anything, it helps his case if he comes in on his own accord. Thank you, Mrs. Toliver."

We both stand, she rises, and she guides us out without another word.

"We should've got a search warrant," Lila tells me as she drives us back to the city on the Eisenhower Expressway.

"We'll keep the house under surveillance, if we're allowed."

"*If?*" she asks.

"You don't get the impression that our boss might like to deflect all this away from the Lieutenant Governor?" I ask her.

"Not when the newspapers get a load of who's involved in this thing," she declares.

"You're going to leak it," I tell her.

"You never heard me say that," she smiles.

"Not a good idea, Lila. Not a good career move."

"So we're supposed to back off on a killer with six scalps on his belt just because he's connected?"

"No. We're not going to back off. We just have to play it smart and not go charging in and tell the Captain that we're certain Franklin Toliver is our guy because he may not be. It's true he looks very likely. He fits the description, he fits the psycho profile from the shrink at Elgin, his car is just like the vehicle that was spotted in the vicinity of each of the first two crimes.

"But he wasn't driving a Taurus on the night he torched those two poor broads on the west side. He's not a stupid perp, Lila. He may very well be nuts, but in that case he goes back to Elgin for a long time, which will disappoint the shit out of me because I'd love to have an excuse to shoot him right in the head. We, however, are 'law enforcement,' which simply put means we're garbage men. Woman, excuse me. We pick up the waste and we deliver it to the judicial branch."

"I know how it works, smartass. Thank you very much."

"We have to tread lightly with our commandant. We both know why he tried to leash us on this one. So we play him into a false sense of security. He's looking out for his own ass, and so should we, Lila. I'm not saying we're not pursuing this suspect with all necessary dispatch. I'm saying we tell the Captain that Franklin Toliver is a *person of interest*, and nothing more. I say we fabricate another suspect, highly fictional, that we both figure is a better choice in these six homicides."

"In other words, Danny, in other words we *lie*."

"There you have it, madam."

She shows me her crooked pearlies, and I want to lean toward her and kiss her, but I quickly remember our relationship is only professional, at the moment.

91

We retrieve the license plate number from the DMV. The plates read 11674JM. We circulate the numbers to every police vehicle in northern Illinois. After a half-day with the license number available, we have no sightings.

It appears that the Ford Taurus, the navy blue four-door, has also gone underground.

On the next day, April 23rd, we get a call from our divers that they've just hauled a blue Ford out of the Lake. We rush down to the beach on the far northern perimeter of the city, and we see the tow truck hoisting the vehicle and then hauling it off the beach.

Sergeant Terry Malloy of Auto Theft meets us by the water. The temperatures have chilled back into the forties. The false spring has deserted us once more.

Malloy is a tall man. Thin and wiry, too. He has close-cropped dark brown hair and a mustache. He looks like an actor, not a cop. I can see Lila is slightly smitten with him. He sort of resembles a skinnier Tom Selleck.

"This the ride you've been seeking?" Malloy smiles at Lila.

She smiles back at him, and I feel a slight blush gather on my face.

"Anything inside?" I ask Malloy.

He turns to me and the smile disappears and he's all businesslike, in a jolt.

"Nothing. We turned it inside and out. We'll check it again when we get it into the shop, but it looks clean. If you were looking for blood, the lake probably took care of that. As for your boy, the Lieutenant Gov's bouncing baby, there is no trace."

Word gets around fast. If he knows that Franklin is a connected suspect, then everyone knows. Lila hasn't had time to leak it to the papers yet, I don't think.

We watch as they haul the Taurus toward the parking lot, and then they're out in the street, and Lila and I get back to our car and begin the trip to the impound.

The evidence people scour the Taurus, inside and out, underneath and on the roof—everywhere. They take the vehicle apart, quite literally, and all we're left with is that it's a car registered to Raymond Toliver, second in command to the Governor of the State of Illinois.

We are able to put a pair of detectives on the Toliver home, two days later. Lila has by now leaked word about Franklin Toliver being a "person of interest" in the Twin Killer case, so our Captain doesn't have much choice but to let us watch the house, big shot or not. Raymond Toliver remains in Springfield, and Lila and I prepare to make the multi-hour drive to the State Capitol.

Raymond Toliver fits the same description of his son, except that the father is perhaps thirty pounds heavier and much grayer on the top knot than we're assuming Junior is.

We meet him at his office in Springfield, not far from the State Library. This town is very confusing, and Lila and I get lost three times before we locate Toliver. We arrive twenty-five minutes late for our interview.

He sits behind an oaken desk, immaculately polished, much like the slab in his home back in DesPlaines. There is also a tiffany-style desk lamp sitting on the table's surface, but the light is not lit.

We sit in two straight-backed chairs opposite him.

"You know, of course, what this is about," I tell him.

"Of course. But I know that Franklin is sick, and I know he's *not* a killer. Other than that, I don't know how I can help you."

"We got a court order to talk to his psychiatrist at Elgin," Lila states.

"I'm aware of that."

"Then you know that this doctor thinks Franklin has some severe issues, especially with women and especially with women of color," my partner continues.

"I wasn't aware that he had problems with non-whites, no."

"He never talked about his hatred toward African Americans?" I ask.

"He never went to school with blacks until he went to college, and then it was mostly white students that he encountered. I really don't know why he'd have problems with black women."

Toliver looks the statesman role. He has an elegant quality about him that underscores his being a favorite in the next governor's election in two years. The present big shot has already announced he's getting out of politics after just one tour in the mansion here.

He has odd colored eyes. I'd say they were violet, but I can't be sure in this light. The sun is on the other side of the building, and the room we're in is in shadow. I can't be sure about his eyes, as I say.

He's a good-looking man—as attractive as the guy who did the hookers, I'd say. I can picture the girls sidling right up to that Taurus and looking forward to boinking a guy as handsome as Raymond Toliver. I mean, a guy as handsome as *Franklin* Toliver appears to be, from the artist's version of him. They wouldn't think twice about hopping into that ride. Good-looking young man. Well groomed, like his old man, even with the hoodie hiding his hair. They'd probably just think the young guy was flashing fashion with the hooded sweatshirt. He was being cool, being *fly*. They'd love having the opportunity to screw someone who didn't look like he'd been dragged through the gutters, for once.

"What was your son's relationship with his mother like? I mean, were they close?" I ask.

He stares at me.

"I'm not a doctor. I assume you talked to the physician at Elgin."

"Yes sir. But I'm asking you, if you don't mind."

He looks toward Lila as if he's trying to recruit a confederate. She simply gazes serenely back at him, with no expression on her face at all.

"He did not get on with his mother. I'm sure the analyst brought all that up with you."

"How bad was it?" I continue.

He looks down at the oaken slab. His eyes never come back up.

"Does my son need a lawyer?" he asks us both.

"Your son needs to turn himself in so we can clear all this up."

He looks at me, now.

"Do you have children?" he asks sadly.

"I have a daughter. Yes."

Lila looks over at me.

"He has never given us a moment's rest. Not from the hour he was delivered until right now."

He looks at Lila as if he's asking her to come onto his side, but her non-expression lingers on her pretty face.

"Never. Not from the minute he yelped his first breath," the Lieutenant Governor says.

13

We search in vain for Franklin Toliver. He slipped away from us as easily as he did the security people at Elgin. The vehicle he drove rests in impound, and there is no remnant evidence remaining in the Ford. It has been gone over dozens of times to no purpose.

He's probably grabbed a new ride. He has the funds to pay cash. We accessed his bank account and found that his balance was just over $72,000—mom and pop have been very generous to sonny since he seems to have never have held a job longer than two months. The employment has always been temporary work, fast food and so on. He never finished a college degree, so has no marketable skills.

He was thrown out of Western a long time ago, and he's made no attempt at gaining an education since then. But with a wad sitting in the bank, why worry about making ends meet? He'd always crashed in DesPlaines whenever he needed a place to go, and even though he's supposed to have issues with mommy, she still lets him light in their roost.

We can't freeze his account because we haven't got grounds to officially charge him with anything. He is simply and officially wanted for questioning. However, we can trace his withdrawals from that checking account. He uses checks, so we can be waiting at the twelve branches for him to come get cash. But it's impractical. We can't have cops sitting at twelve different locations six days a week.

Instead, we leave word with the managers at those locations that if Franklin comes calling for his bucks, we're to receive an immediate phone call. His last withdrawal was two weeks ago, and the amount was two thousand. He can submerge for quite a while with that kind of coin, as long as he doesn't have expensive tastes. The average hooker runs you between $25 and $50 bucks for one throw, Al the Vice dick tells us. The expensive hos charge anything you want to pay them, but they're more inclined to do their trade in a Loop hotel where the real money lives. They do guys with corporate plastic—not that they use their cards for the price. I'd imagine they take out cash on the card and then claim it was for "entertainment purposes" for their clients or for themselves. The white collar critter doesn't tend to be dumb enough to leave a paper trail.

Which gives me the epiphany that maybe junior's not cashing his checks anymore. Maybe he's receiving his money from somebody else. Like mommy or daddy. Maybe one of his parents has become a bagman for Franklin. He's been smart before, and why should he go dumb now that we're onto him? He knows that we know about his checking account, so he wouldn't be stupid enough to try and drain the pond there.

Lila and I decide to watch Geraldine Toliver. We figure the Lieutenant Governor's a bit too high profile to be the dropoff guy for his nutjob son. And from the way the father talked about his beloved progeny, I don't think dad wants much to do with Franklin, right about now. I know there are supposed to be "problems" between mother and son, but "problems" has always been a vague area in this case.

Since we don't have his car to run down anymore and since he's backed off from doubling his pleasure with any whores lately, we decide it's all we've got going for ourselves, currently.

We park the car a half block down from the two-acre house in DesPlaines. We don't want the Staties to see us and run our city plates. Officially, we're out of bounds, outside the city limits, but we have the right to park ourselves on public thoroughfares. So we sit and wait.

Lila brings paperbacks with her. She's a big fan of the San Francisco poets, she tells me. Her favorite poet is Lawrence Ferlinghetti.

I've read a few of his things because Lila has offered them to me, and I have to say I think he's a helluva lot funnier than most of the poets I had to read in high school and in college. I despised Robert Frost. I was always hoping he'd enter those snowy woods and stay the fuck in there. Perhaps it was my immaturity, back in high school, but I was never much of a fan of verse.

She reads because it is still daylight. We figure if mommy's going to make a drop for her loving son, it'll be when the banks are open. We could be wrong, of course. She might want to do her deed by darkness, but then it might look a bit stranger for her to be out alone at night. We have to have an excuse lined up for our Captain, in any case. He has not repeated his veiled warning about expending too many man and woman hours on Franklin, but he hasn't told us to charge after Toliver full-blast, either.

The Captain really can't repeat that speech now, of course. Not when it's been made public via the press that Raymond Toliver's son is a person of interest in what has now become a high profile case. The *Sun-Times* has made it a very big deal with the numerous articles about our mysterious underground suspect. The writer's name is Jack Phelan. He's tried to interview both of us at HQ, but we've given him the standard "no comment" routine. His appearance at our place was all for show. Lila's been talking to him via a payphone, I imagine. She wouldn't use her home phone or the one in her office.

"You really think his mother's the candyman, Danny?"

"I don't know. But I'd think his two grand might have dwindled considerably for someone who's being pursued by the FBI and the State Police and the CPD. It must be kind of expensive, moving around every day or two. And his face is plastered everywhere, still, so we can always hope for a sighting of this shitbird."

"You think I was wrong to call Phelan."

"I never heard you say that, Lila."

"Do you think I was wrong?"

I look into her great set of eyes, blue as the bluest sky.

"I would've called him if you hadn't."

She stares out the windshield.

"She's moving," Lila observes.

A tan Mercedes comes rolling out over the crushed gravel driveway. It looks like Geraldine's driving. She turns left onto the side street, and Lila pulls our Ford slowly away from the curb.

The plates match Geraldine's registration. We got a list of their vehicles from DMV.

We follow the Mercedes through DesPlaines as she makes her way to the Stevenson Expressway, and once she exits onto 55 Chicago, we're headed toward the city. The traffic is still light. It won't glom up until around 4:00 P.M. Then rush hour will snarl everything up until well after six. You don't want to be on this expressway during rush unless you enjoy rage.

She keeps heading east, all the way to the Lakeshore Drive North exit. We stay well back from her just in case she's seen *The French Connection* or some other cop flick that suggests everything's a high-speed chase, in our line of work. I prefer low speed pursuits, myself. I'm not a fan of cars or of car races. They're damned dangerous. In fact, I'd choose a firefight back in the War to a haul-ass chase on these city streets. I'd still take my chances with the Viet Cong instead of with Chicago lunatic drivers.

Once we're on Lake Shore, we slow down as we hit the Loop. The curve that comes right after you've left the southside always slows things down to a virtual crawl. Once you get past the near north on the Lake, things open up to about 45 mph. We're at that juncture of the Drive now.

She keeps heading north along the lakeshore.

When we finally get to Tuohy Avenue, she gets off. Then she begins to head west again. (You can't go east unless you want to get wet.) She takes us all the way out to Mannheim Road. We can see jets heading north over our heads because O'Hare isn't far south of here.

Her destination is Rockwood and Wentworth. We're at the very western periphery of the city. We stop the car at the curb about three hundred feet from where she's parked. We're on the east side of the block. Rockwood runs north and south, and we're facing north, as the Mercedes is.

Geraldine gets out of her ride and walks up to a three flat. It's brick and very upscale for the city. This is no blue collar neighborhood.

This is where whites fled in order to avoid the influx of blacks and Hispanics, back in the 1960s. These hoods have remained white and upper middle class in spite of the blockbusters, who operated back when I was in high school, in the middle '60s.

Lila gets out of the car to get the address, and when she does, she hurriedly returns to our car. We call in the address and find out the names of the residents from our address directory downtown.

"Fred Carraway, John Meyers and Victoria Landers. Bottom to top, that's who lives there."

Nothing goes off when we hear those names.

"Does she have a boyfriend?" I proffer.

"Why not a girlfriend, Victoria?" Lila smiles.

We wait for her to come back out. She's in there only twenty minutes. When she gets back into the Mercedes and takes off, we follow her. We figure it might have been an errand, but we'll come back later and check out the three residents.

Geraldine makes two other stops before she makes the long trip back to DesPlaines. Once she returns to the Stevenson West, we cut off at the Loop and return to Headquarters.

Later in the evening we stop at all the places Geraldine Toliver visited. We come up with absolutely nothing. They claim to be friends of the Tolivers, all of them. They knew each other at college or at church or something, but none of them seems to know anything about Franklin. They become sullen, all of them, when we mention her son's name. We're getting nothing from any of the interviewees at all three stops, so we give it up and live to fight another day.

May brings some of the best spring weather we've had in a long time. It's fragrant and soft. The temperatures are in the low seventies, and the humidity is equally comfortable.

Kelly graduates on May 21st. I've already made arrangements to have the day off. I will not miss her big day because my daughter hasn't *had* her share of big days. She's continued to work very hard all year, and she's dragged her grade point average up almost to the "B" level. It's at 2.86, which is a far piece from the 2.1 she was sporting for three years, almost. She was always smart enough to get by with "Cs" even when she was truant and blown out—that's how bright she really is. I have no doubt she'd be hovering in the top ten if she'd ever shown up to school and shown up sober.

Which is all history. The past is prologue, no? That's the positive way to look at it.

That's the way I look at it as I sit with her in group in the outpatient program for eating disorders and addiction at St. Luke's Hospital on the southwest side.

There are four sets of parent(s) and patients. All four patients are females. Kelly is the healthiest looking kid in here. It appears the other three kids have a long road ahead of them.

We finally get around the circle of chairs to Kelly and me. I'm here, like the other parents, to listen and observe. Today it's the kids who get to talk. The therapist is a nice-looking babe named Christine—thirty or so, brunette, dynamically built. Married, according to the rock on her left hand. Christine has an engaging smile. She looks at Kelly and asks her how she'd like to begin today.

"I think I'm still mad at my mother."

The smile leaves my face. It's down to business for my daughter.

"That was a long time ago, wasn't it?" Christine asks.

The other three girls and the three pairs of parents are all watching us. I couldn't tell you what any of them looked like. I have jettisoned my cop's awareness. All I can see is Kelly and the good-looking brunette therapist. No one else is suddenly in the room.

"How could you leave a child as young as I was? I mean, how could you?"

Christine has no reply, and I'm supposed to be listening and observing.

"I could never do that to *her*," Kelly tells her. She's talking only to the therapist, right now.

Kelly begins to cry, but there are no audible clues. She doesn't make any snuffling noises, but the tears meander down her cheeks as if they were involuntarily shed. I feel the pangs of moisture prick at the corners of my own eyes, but I maintain my composure.

"So what happens now?" the therapist asks. "What happens today?"

"I know. I know I have to learn to live with it even though I'm never going to forget it. I can't let her leaving ruin my life. I know all that."

"It's what you do, not what you say, Kelly," Christine answers.

"Yes. I know."

"Knowing and doing are a very different kind of animal from each other," the counselor says gently.

Kelly nods.

"Are you glad your dad is coming to these sessions?"

She nods again, slowly.

"Are you going to try and talk to him more than you have?"

"I haven't talked to him at all....But it's not your fault, Daddy. Any of this. I'm sorry I made it seem like it was. You never left me. Momma did. I'm sorry."

Then I can't hold back, and Christine has the Kleenex box in front of me before I can even ask for it. But then she's probably seen a lot of this.

"What do you want for graduation?" I ask Kelly on the drive back home.

"I've never seen you cry before," she tells me.

"You're mistaken. I had something in my eye."

"In both of them?" she grins.

"If you tell anybody I'll just deny it."

"Tough guy. Airborne. Rangers."

"That's right, little girl. Don't ever forget it."

She looks out the passenger's side window as we head home.

"Are you still mad at Momma, too?" she asks as she watches the dark shapes on the blocks recede behind us.

"Yes," I reply.

She looks at my face as if she's studying it.

"What do you want for graduation?" I repeat.

She watches me a bit longer.

Then she clasps my hand on the steering wheel lightly. Her touch is like a feather. It's barely there.

"I want you to stop being mad at her," Kelly tells me.

14

On graduation night, Lila comes along with me. Since I took the day off, she figured she'd follow her partner's lead. Kelly invited her to the ceremony at Sacred Heart about a month ago on an evening when Lila dropped me home after a day shift.

There are slightly over two hundred graduates in Kelly's class. The gymnasium at Sacred Heart holds a little over a thousand, I'd estimate, but every seat on the bleachers and on the floor is occupied. It's sweltering in here because they have no air conditioning. The school was built when Lincoln was a teenager, I figure, and Catholics are notorious about hanging onto a buck. I never understood why Jews have the reputation of being tight-fisted. The Catholics I've known always had their first dollar in a frame over the mantel.

Lila is excited about being Kelly's guest. I never would have thought she might want to come, even though I know my daughter and my partner like each other. They've never had much time together, but they seem to hit it off every time they're around each other.

The whole deal lasts a little over an hour. Lila is impressed with their dispatch.

"My Academy graduation took three and a half hours."

She graduated from the Air Force Academy in Colorado.

We're filing out of the gym. I have my arm around Kelly, and she's got her arm around my waist, and I'm wondering about when it was that I last even touched my kid. So I squeeze her while I can.

She's put on maybe fifteen pounds, and she looks the best she has since—

I can't recall her looking this good, ever.

Lila takes hold of her from the other side, and we walk toward my car. We're taking Kelly to Donnellen's for a graduation dinner. Kelly asked that a friend of hers come along with us, and he meets us outside, by my ride.

"I'm Mike Carroll," the tall, handsome, athletic-looking young man tells us.

I shake hands with him, and his grip is firm but not overly aggressive. Lila introduces herself, and she shakes with him, also.

Then I look over at Kelly's face, and I see it right away.

Mike Carroll's the reason she's here tonight, with her diploma in hand and fifteen lovely pounds on her newly healthy frame.

I look over at Lila, and she smiles back at me, and she knows now, too.

We visit some people who knew Franklin Toliver. We begin with the dean at Western Illinois University in Macomb. It takes us a few hours to get there from the city, but I figure we have to know this goof to find him. Hunters have to understand the kind of animal they're stalking. It's not a luck thing, tracking somebody down. It's about preparation.

The dean's name is Bob Milton. He's in charge of discipline. In other words, he's the man who threw Franklin out of school.

"If I could've had him jailed, I would've."

He looks almost angry as he says it.

Milton is nearing retirement, I'd suppose. Must be in his middle sixties at least. He's probably had a tummy full of puerile college boys and frat rats.

"Why wasn't he sent up for the thing with the young lady?" Lila asks him.

"She didn't want to get into a trial. She didn't want the trauma. It's not an unusual way for young women to go. They've already been abused, and they don't want a defense lawyer to do it again in a courtroom. And we know who Franklin's father is."

"Yes, we do," I confess.

"He'd had scrapes with women before. I even had a complaint from a teaching assistant he had in an English course. He kept bothering her about going out with him. And then she began to receive strange phone calls. We presumed it was Franklin, but the calls were all made from various payphones off campus, so we couldn't prove anything—the police, I mean. They tried to trace the calls on her line, and the caller was running all over Macomb. He knew what he was doing."

"How were you able to can him, then?" Lila asks.

"His grades were dismal. There were several complaints from his resident advisors. It finally accumulated enough for us to get rid of him."

The graying man looks somberly at both of us.

"Do you really think he's a murderer?" he asks us.

"We intend to find out," is all I can respond.

We take lunch in one of the campus bar and grills—O'Flannagan's. I don't know anything about this university and neither does Lila, but we're hungry after the multiple hour drive and O'Flannagan's is packed, which suggests to me that somebody must like what they're selling.

"I think Kelly applied here," I tell Lila over the roar of Def Leppard on the jukebox.

"What?" she squints at me. So I repeat what I said.

"Oh," she replies. "I thought she wanted to be a nurse or a doctor."

"She applied at a few places. She wants to do it all on her own, but I think I have her softened up to let me help her. I've been saving for her college ever since I was in the Army."

"I've seen you two. Before and after. That's what it looks like. Before and after. It's amazing."

"I always loved her. I'm glad she's finally letting me."

Lila grasps my left hand. We're sitting at the bar because there were no tables available and we still have a long drive back to the city to look forward to. I actually do look forward to the trip back because it allows me to be alone with her. Other than on the job, there doesn't seem to be any other excuse to see her. I don't ask her anywhere on our off hours because I can't bear the awkwardness of hearing a polite refusal from her.

I'm certain it is my male ego at work, but I can't understand how she can blow so hot and cold. The few times we were together felt like the beginning of something with her, and they wound up being terminal—or at least it feels that way, sometimes.

In the War, I was used to reading people. The men I was with in the Rangers. The enemy we sought. The brass we took shit from. The indigenous personnel in all the tiny hamlets and villages we humped through. All those human beings had a "tell," just like in poker. There was something about their faces or their body language that betrayed what they were really thinking. It was part of my job to be able to read the trail on their faces.

But with Lila, it's hard or impossible. I've almost stopped trying to decipher her moods or her state of mind. Either she's too good at concealment or I'm losing my touch.

Our food finally arrives. Two cheeseburgers. Burgers are usually a reliable choice in a bar and grill. I take a bite, and it is better than edible.

Then I put my sandwich back on the plate. The music has ceased for a moment, so I turn to my partner.

"I'm in love with you," I tell her.

She looks at me carefully, and then she places her own burger back on the plate next to her fries.

"I'm in love with you, too, Danny, and I'm not happy about it at all."

We head back to the city, and it's uncomfortably quiet in the car as Lila drives us, so I put the radio on to an FM station that's coming in, all this way from Chicago. It's a rock station, and Lila doesn't protest my selection.

"Why are you not happy about it?"

"Because it'll screw things up."

"Screw what things up?" I ask.

"Our professional relationship, for one. My career, for another."

"You're aiming higher?" I ask.

"Yeah. Aren't you?" she asks me back.

"No. I figure on being in Homicide until I retire or hit a slab. I like the work. I thought you did, too."

"I do. But I want to move up in the Department."

"You want to be the first female Commander, huh?" I smile.

"Yes," she replies, with a dead serious stare.

"I'm not being a smartass, Lila. I don't have problems with a woman—"

"You don't? You really don't, Danny?"

"No, I really do not."

She looks at me suspiciously.

"What makes you think I've got anything against—"

"Mary, for starters."

I look over at her, but I haven't got any answers.

"Look, Danny. I want something without the baggage."

"You mean Kelly?"

"I do *not* mean the kid."

"Then why can't you ever say her name?"

"I say her name."

She reddens slightly at the cheekbones.

"No, as a matter of public record, you always call her 'the kid.'"

"It's a term of affection."

"What the hell is this baggage? You mean Mary, again?"

"Yes. That's exactly what I mean."

"What about her? She left me a long time ago. It's over."

"Is it, Danny? Is it really?"

Then I remember Kelly asking me to forgive her mother, and I go quiet.

"Nothing left to say?" she asks.

I look out the windshield at the highway. We're about an hour away from the Loop, depending on traffic, as always.

I turn the radio off and close my eyes.

"Okay, then," she says. I can see the anger burning in there. This time I can read her perfectly, but I turn away and close my eyes and listen to the tires humming on the blacktop.

I'm alone in my office in the HQ by the Lake. She offered to drop me home, but I told her I had paperwork to do. So she took off without another word. We spent the last fifty minutes of the ride back from the university in total silence. I think my going quiet on her was what pissed her off the most. Lila, like most women, like most human beings, has a real problem with indifference.

And indifferent is the last thing I am about her. I don't know why I clammed up. I guess I was angry, too. Angry that she had me so well-pegged. I have not gotten rid of my anger at my wife's desertion. I have never let go of it, and now I have Lila and Kelly both on my ass about my pent-up emotion aimed at my one-time wife.

I don't take betrayal well. Not in my personal life or anywhere else. One thing I could count on in Vietnam was the men I fought with. It was the only thing you could count on. Without the surrounding grunts to look after your ass, you were lost.

In romantic relationships betrayal is commonplace. In the military it means either a brutal confrontation in which someone's ass is in a world of hurt, or it means death to the betrayer. There is no civility involved in dealing with backstabbing motherfuckers. You beat them bad enough to be hospitalized or you save the medics the trouble of patching them back up. I was never put in such a situation in southeast Asia, but as soon as I got home, damn near, she simply walked, on me.

I know I should be able to distinguish between battle and life in The World, but to me some virtues and vices are universal. Some shit you simply do not do, especially to those who care about you.

Mary crossed the line, and the line distinguishes what is and is not forgivable.

I try to occupy myself with work, with the jackets I've read over and over about each homicide Lila and I are involved with. But I can't concentrate.

"*I love you, too, Danny, and I'm not happy about it at all.*"

Or something close to that.

I should be celebrating. Lila admitted she loves me. Sort of. At least she said the words.

But there's always a goddamned "but." There's always a fucking "however." That exclusive word that negates every other damn thing you just heard. What she said ought to be a cause for joy, for celebration. But I don't feel like popping the bubbly. All I feel is dead empty because she says I'm carrying weight around over my ex-wife, and that weight will always come between us.

Not to mention her career aspirations. I don't begrudge her a life above where we are now. It'd be great if she rose to Commander.

Great for her, I suppose, because if she did start to elevate, I'd be left down here. And dating or bedding your partner is an official no-no in the CPD. If anyone even catches the drift that we're a couple or that we've been coupling, they'll separate us.

And a partner is all she is, right now. Lila is stubborn. I read that much about her, for sure. Once she gets a notion in her head, she's not likely to let go of it very easily. She can be like a little badger on pet theories. I've seen her that way before.

She thinks I'm hung up about Mary cutting Kelly and me loose, and the sad fact is that she's absolutely dead on right about it.

June first, and here I am. Sitting in the waiting room. No one else is here. Two o'clock in the afternoon on my one day off this week. Franklin Toliver runs loose like a mad hound of hell in the streets, and I'm here in a waiting room. Waiting. Which is what these places are for, of course.

Lila is God knows where on her free day. I never talk to her on the phone, lately. We only see each other on the job, and we don't breach personal shit, anymore.

Kelly has her college choices narrowed to three: Northern Illinois at DeKalb, Illinois State University in Normal, and Western Illinois in Macomb. All three are public universities. We can afford them—I can afford them, I mean—but Kelly has insisted on taking the Federal Loan, if not the private loan. I'll take care of what the feds don't pay. My nest egg is now in six digits. The market has been very kind.

She wants to get a bachelor's degree as well as her nursing certificate, the RN.

I actually see Mike Carroll at the house, now. They must have been seeing each other outside our home, because the night of graduation was the first time I ever laid eyes on him. It must be going pretty seriously between Kelly and him because she says they plan on going to the same school together, in the fall. Mike graduated from a public high school, not far from Sacred Heart.

I'm ruminating, I suppose you'd call it. My mind wanders, here in this waiting room.

Then the receptionist gets a buzz at her phone. The fifty-something blonde smiles up at me.

"Dr. Fernandez will see you now," she beams at me.

I rise from my chair and I put the unread sports magazine back on the table.

Then I head toward the Department psychiatrist's office.

15

The other people who encountered Franklin didn't like him much,
either. There were no true girlfriends. He was good looking enough
to date frequently in high school and at college, but no one wanted a
second taste. Franklin is beginning to fit a true Quantico version of
"sociopath." He's a loner, he has trouble making lasting relationships, he's
white, he's the right age but on the younger side of the spectrum, and he
has no noticeable conscience, according to those who know him at all.

The mother and father have refused to grant us an interview
unless we have some kind of legal justification to "invade our privacy."
Franklin is still wanted for questioning, officially, but nothing more. Our
hands are tied, and the Captain informs me that the Lieutenant
Governor's attorneys are very high powered. In other words, he won't
fuck with them until there's an arrest warrant for the younger Toliver.

As far as we know, he hasn't broken any laws—unless we pick
him up for dumping his car in the Lake, and I doubt we could prove it
was Franklin who did that little trick. He doesn't leave witnesses or
evidence. Leaving Elgin when he was voluntary was not illegal, either, so
we can't nab him for going AWOL out of the nuthouse.

We will inevitably catch up with this little prick. He can't stay below the radar for much longer because too many agencies are looking for him. But I hope we get him before the FBI or the Staties do. They'll have to turn him over to us because all of the murders were done in our province, in Chicago. I don't want anyone else talking to him first. I know it sounds like bureaucratic bullshit, but I want a throw at Franklin without anyone else muddying his water.

Dr. Fernandez is Dr. Arlene Fernandez, and I think she's the singularly most beautiful Hispanic woman I have ever encountered. I don't know why she inherited "Arlene," but she looks very much the Latina. Brown eyes, tawny colored skin, including her face. Full, exotic lips, with just a slight touch of pink lipstick. I'm happy I showed up to see her, after all.

This is my second trip. I'm scheduled to see her once a week until she tells me otherwise, and since the department picks up the tab because she works for the CPD, I'm not worried about her bill. Psychiatrists are a luxury, in my salary bracket.

There is no couch in her office. I'm almost disappointed. In the movies there's always a leather couch. In here it's just a simple but comfortable cushioned straight-backed chair. I can rest my head against the back, because the back goes up higher than my head by about a foot. It's a recliner for a giant, except it doesn't recline.

"How are you?" she begins.

I grin at her and she grins back.

"I take it you're still in pursuit of the main event," she smiles slyly.

"Yes. We are still hacking away."

I've already told her about Lila because what I say in here, she repeatedly underscores, is in strictest confidence and the Department can't use it against me.

"How about the personal front?"

She uses military jargon frequently, which leads me to believe she might have been GI at one point in her life. It's one way to get the school bills paid.

"Same, also."

She nods.

"Things are moving along with your daughter?"

"Yeah. She's settled on Northern Illinois since her boyfriend got a partial ride there for baseball."

She knows about Kelly's ongoing battle with bulimia and addiction, and she was genuinely pleased to hear about the help they gave her at Sacred Heart and she very much liked hearing I'm going to counseling with my daughter.

My time here is cloudier, though. She wants to talk about things outside the realm of Kelly and Lila, the only two people I really have in my life. (And I'm not at all sure where Lila is, currently, in my little sphere of existence.)

"You are angry with Mary. It's understandable. What you do with that anger is very important. We've already discussed that it'll probably never vanish, Danny. Forgiveness may sound easy from a pulpit or an analyst's office, but it is very difficult to deal with in the real world where people hurt bad when other people disrupt their lives, the way your wife did your world and Kelly's world."

I sit and watch her.

"Do you have stress over what happened in Vietnam?"

"You mean to me or toward the general situation?" I ask her.

"Both," she replies, her hands clasped on top of her blond-colored desk. Her fingernails are the same pink rose color that she sports on her lush lips.

"I'm not sure what you want me to say," I tell her.

"Do you feel guilt at what you did there?"

"Yes. Sometimes."

"But not always?"

"I killed people in self-defense. I never scoped anyone who wasn't trying to kill me and the people around me."

"But just the act of killing didn't disturb you?"

"No. It was what I was trained to do. It's what the military trains everyone to do. Kill, that is. We were not a fraternal order, Doctor. We didn't sandbag rivers during the flood. That's the Red Cross, not us."

I smile to show her I'm not venting at her.

"I was a Marine," she grins. "*Semper fi.*"

114

"They paid your way through school?"

"After I got out, they helped, yes. God bless the GI bill," she smiles again.

"You go to Vietnam?" I ask.

"No, it was slightly before my time."

She looks like she's somewhere in her mid to late thirties. She's ripe, a flat-out beautiful woman. Not wearing a ring, either.

"Back to you, Danny."

"Back to me. Yes, I killed people, and I sometimes regret killing in general, but I honestly didn't lose any sleep killing VC honchos who killed quite a number of the guys I served with. I didn't walk away from Vietnam with any recurring nightmares. I know you folks like to talk about dreams."

"I'm not a Freudian, but dreams are important. What do you dream about?"

"I had a dream last night. I was a kid on the southside again, and I was running after the ice cream guy, you know the guy in the truck with the little musical jingle. He wouldn't stop for me even though my old man gave me a dollar and I was supposed to buy ice cream for everybody in the family."

"Sounds very metaphorical, Danny," she laughs out loud.

"I actually had that dream, Doctor. I wouldn't lie to you."

"I know you wouldn't."

She folds her hands on the table like a well-mannered school child. It is probably apparent to her that I'm attracted to her, and she is likely aware that I'm trying to tell her shit that'll please her in her official capacity as my therapist/analyst.

"Tell me what you experienced. Tell me what you remember."

She's got me cornered. There's forty-five minutes remaining in the session, and I've got no place where I can escape. I can't lie to her because she reads me as well as Lila does.

Dr. Fernandez is no dummy. She's heard cops try to evade her before, and as I said, I have this pressing desire to please her. And ravish her, too. I'm sure she's aware of the heat I'm throwing her way, and I'm sure she's used to that kind of male reaction to her presence.

I tell her that I joined the Rangers for the challenge. If I was going to be in the Army, I didn't want it to be the four year hitch and then back to civilian life and the usual run of the mill time spent doing my duty. I wanted to see if I could *endure*, and I figured joining the most elite corps in the Army would let me find out if there was anything about me that was out of the ordinary.

My size is average. I'm not very tall and I'm not particularly the most muscular specimen anyone has ever seen. I'm just ordinary. But I kept believing there was something extraordinary in me even though people couldn't spot it on my exterior. Heart, is what I was thinking about. If I couldn't beat them in size and bulk, I could outlast them in perseverance.

Ranger training was all about outlasting the enemy. The legend is that the corps started with Roger's Rangers in the French and Indian Wars, but the reality is a lot more contemporary. There was Darby's Rangers in World War II—they were the guys who breached the Germans' defenses at Normandy in 1944. And their exploits continued in Korea. So heritage and history have a lot to do with why I signed up for Ranger training.

It was as difficult as the media had written it was. Most of the men who signed up with me bailed out before it was over. I hold nothing against them. Everybody wanted to give it up at one point or other. I lasted. I took it. And I finally got through it. I think the training I received is part of the reason I rose through the ranks so quickly, here in the CPD. Discipline was not lacking, where I've been. We never lost our sense of purpose in-country, either. Most of us didn't do dope or do it very often. Most of us kept our GI haircuts and most of us didn't disrespect our country, even though we had suspicions that Vietnam was a bullshit beef with very suspect motivations at its core. We were Americans. We were Rangers. But we didn't need any fucking country western anthems to keep us on task. We didn't need public approval, either. We carried out our orders and killed the enemy.

Our only flaw was the trust we put in other people, back home, to do the right thing before they sent us into the shit.

So I tell Dr. Fernandez all of the above and she listens intently.

I really didn't have very many night sweats. I know that a lot of ex-grunts do and did, but I wasn't one of them. I have the occasional nightmare, but nightmares are not exclusive to Vietnam vets. And I haven't had a single urge to go up to a high place and start wasting a big number of civilians. I've had no compulsion to waste any politicians who are too dumb to deserve to live.

It was our War, for better or worse, and I suppose God will be the only legitimate judge for the things I've done. As I said, I'm not a practicing Catholic, but I don't have any roiling regrets about my trigger time in-country. Fuck it and there it is.

"I want to continue seeing you once a week, Danny."

"Do you date your nutty patients? Ever? Any exceptions?"

She smiles winningly. I'm not sorry I made the half-joke.

"Next week? Right?" she aims the same warmth at me.

I want to sigh brokenheartedly, but I just get up and leave with a shit-eaten grin, instead.

In the third week of June the real heat begins—temperature-wise, I mean. The mercury soars into the mid-nineties. What had been a mild late spring emerges as a brutal early summer. With the heat comes murder, and a few of them are black hookers. But the MO is different, totally, and none of the new victims on our white board are twin-killings. Nobody was made to witness their partner's demise and then killed or left insane, the way one of the girls was in the initial case we think Franklin Toliver was responsible for.

Homicide is all about endurance. If you have a low tolerance for frustration, then our department in the CPD is not for you. Go teach school or milk the stock market for millions. You don't want my job. The irritation factor is sky high. Our clients can't speak for themselves, so there's always that extra challenge for our branch of the law.

Lila treats me like a partner but not as a lover or a friend, and it's making me very disturbed. I talk to Fernandez about it, and she says I have to talk it out with Lila, but then I start to notice Dr. Fernandez's magnificent breasts. Or I'll scope her exquisite booty, whenever she stands and turns around, which is painfully rare in our sessions. I know I'm being a chauvinistic pig, and I know Lila would ream me for all the

117

above, but my shrink is too well gifted by God for me not to notice. I try to keep things professional when I see the doc, but I spend way too much of the hour fantasizing about seeing her without her doctor's "suit" on. She dresses in these severe unisex outfits that drive me wild with desire. I don't know if I can continue with her, and I know the issue is *mine*, not hers. It's not her fault that she is one of the most beautiful women I've ever seen in my life—and no exaggeration.

If she wound up as Lila's secret lover, I'd be fucking devastated.

But I will try to keep it in my pants, figuratively, from now on, when I see her.

Lila comes into my office.

"Still love me?" she asks.

But there's no smirk on her face.

"Yeah, as a matter of fact," I tell her.

"Let's take an early lunch."

We drive over to her apartment.

"Is there any chance your roomie—"

"She moved out last night," Lila says as we park in her complex's lot.

We walk up to the entry. Lila slides her ID card into the slot, and the door opens. We take the elevator up to her floor.

She opens her door, and we're inside. The door to the roomie's bedroom is opened, and I can see into it. The shades in there are opened, and the sunlight fills the unoccupied bedroom.

"What happened to all the career business and the 'it'll get in the way of our partnership' stuff?" I ask as we sit on her couch.

Apparently most of the furniture belongs to Lila because all the living room chairs and couches are still here.

"I haven't had a woman as a lover in eighteen months, and my roommate was never one of them. She had more boyfriends than a mutt has fleas, Danny."

"You still didn't answer my questions."

"I don't know. Why does every damn thing have to have a reason?"

"Why all of this? So abruptly? Can you see why I'm asking?"

She stands before me.

"All my life I heard people asking me why I was going to the Academy. Then why was I going to fly jets in combat. Why was I going to kill innocent babies in that goddamned useless war. All these damned questions, Danny. Then I meet you. I'm just fresh out of a relationship with some woman who winds up being stupider than Reagan's astrologer, and I see you and the seesaw begins again. I've been attracted to men and women, boys and girls, all my life, but I never had a relationship with a female until my mid-twenties. I thought that that one was it, the permanent happening in my life. But I was wrong. As usual. I always make shitty personal calls.

"And then you come along and stir the pot and I don't know my ass from my left nipple and I tell myself I'll go slow, real slow. And then you and I go to bed, and I want the white picket fence fantasy bred into all good American little girls, only I tell myself it'll all go bad the next time some attractive member of my own sex flaunts it in my face.

"Believe it or not, Danny, I was kinda thinking of you, about all this. I knew how Mary fucked you all up, and I swore I'd never do anything like that to you. I couldn't bear it if I hurt you that way. *Now* do you understand?"

She bends down and kisses me.

"I'm really not the bitch you think I am. Am I, Danny? Tell me. Please?"

She starts to cry, and then I get up off the couch and take hold of her. I guide her out the door, and I head us back to the parking lot below.

"Name your poison. I'm buying you the most disgustingly overpriced lunch in the Loop," I tell her as we walk out into the lot.

Before she can get in behind the wheel, I hold her tightly and I kiss each wet eye.

119

16

It's the age of "The Evil Empire." There's a Commie in every bush. Santa Claus is a Red. Ernest Hemingway leaned toward Pink and the Loyalists and toward his drinking buddy Fidel Castro, *El Commandante*. We're going to build weapons out of *Star Wars*, killer satellites, to zap our greatest enemies, the Russians.

That was why we were in Vietnam in the '60s and '70s, no? To stop the cascading drop of the dominoes. We were the Dutch boys with the fingers in all those Asian dikes. We were the forerunners of a technological, bloodless war—at least no blood so's you'd notice. Hellfire would rein on The Evil Empire and Democracy would reign a thousand years. Sounds sort of like The Third Reich, doesn't it?

Fifty-eight thousand and more of us died, along with a lot more Vietnamese, to stop the new Huns, the new Barbarians. Trouble was, I could never really tell if I were the solution or part of the problem. Things were confusing, in spite of my resolve to get the job done—which we did, mostly.

And we still lost that obscene war. We still came home in disgrace.

However, attitudes, like waistlines, are constantly changing. First we're hawk, and then we're dove. It's hard to tell the players without a scorecard. In Vietnam, the bad guys didn't always display their colors, like the black knights who opposed Camelot. There was no blue and gray. They didn't sport swastikas or wear red stars on their caps. The Chinese Army wore uniforms, and the NVA could be spotted, sort of, on occasion. Otherwise it was a turkey shoot minus the fucking turkeys. You couldn't always be certain you were popping a VC honcho or operative or whether you were tearing up indigenous personnel by mistake. We took our best shots, but it was very possible innocent bystanders went down, instead, sometimes. Collateral casualties mar every fun fucking loving war.

It's becoming the age of cybernetics, the papers and all the media have announced numerous times. Computers are taking over. The Selectric II I use at work for my paper reports is a mastodon, a furry relic, I'm informed. We're into the age of ether. All data will be carried electronically.

I like my IBM. I know it'll be easier to print out corrected copy via a keyboard hooked to a computer, but I'll miss the directness of my written tasks as they still remain direct, today. I'll miss the fucking clacking. I'll miss White Out or those little tabs you stick in the carriage or the "X" button that deletes mistakes on my Selectric II.

Adapt or die, motherfucker. It was the same law of Darwin in the jungle, too. Adapt or perish. You swim with the tide or it washes over you.

You listen to your Captain telling you to back off the perpetrator of six homicides (that we're aware of) or you get taken off the case altogether.

Or Franklin Toliver becomes the fucking Invisible Man, and you just hope you won't be bagging and tagging new duos from the hood, black girls who were supplying the world's oldest service—to the worst possible service-ee, our boy Franklin.

Prostitutes are engaged in the most dangerous profession in the world, next to combat grunts and harried husbands. Whores get killed off in the thousands across the nation every year, but it's difficult to post an exact number on their fates because many of them die or disappear and they're never reported as MIA, missing in action.

You must excuse all the military terms used above, but it is a lot like combat duty, if you're a lady of the pavement. They get slashed and they get shot and they get dismembered and even burned alive. I'd say they earn combat pay. I know they've chosen an immoral and unpleasant way of making a living, but if you ever saw where some of these girls, and young men, came from, you might not be as harsh in your judgment toward their demises.

They had it coming. Right? They asked for it because they chose to put themselves in harm's way. Correct?

Since when do any of us good Jews or Christians or Moslems or Buddhists get to pass judgment on our other fellow travelers in this life? The book says, "Judge not, lest ye be judged," or something close to that. You wouldn't think you'd be hearing bible text from a non-participant like me, now would you?

But I've begun to participate, after all. I told Kelly I'd start going to mass with her, and I have. We go to the Sunday eight o'clock at St. Mark's Church in Oak Lawn on the southwest side. I've been to four in a row, now, and it's late July. I can't say I've heard every word of every homily, but I try to listen to what's going on. Just remembering when to stand and when to sit and when to kneel tasks me a little bit. As I say, it's been a long time. I don't remember many of the prayers except the Our Father and the Hail Mary and the Glory Be. The prayer to St. Michael about fucking the devil up is a little sketchy in my memory, but it's starting to come back, as is the confession thing. I haven't been to formal confession since they made us all go, back in high school. So I've got a lot to confess, and I figure this Saturday may as well become a point of departure for me, spiritually speaking.

The spiritual element is something I've ignored greatly throughout most of my life. I might've whispered a few Hail Marys out in the jungle after blowing someone's brains out upon the departure away from the ambush site, but I don't count any of that as spiritual. If praying to get away with killing someone, in a war or anywhere else, is considered religious, then I'd rather join a fucking voodoo cult. You can't really believe any loving God listens to some asshole praying to get away with homicide, can you? Well, if you can, you ought to join Psy Ops, those crazy bastards who work with the CIA or whatever letters they're sporting currently.

I never thought I'd go back to the Church, and who knows? It may not take, eventually. But I've actually enjoyed being with my daughter at mass. We go out for breakfast after the eight o'clock, and the last three Sundays, here in July, we've met up with Lila at a restaurant. Lila and Kelly alternate on choosing where we eat. I just like being with them both.

They're beginning to sound like two close girlfriends. Kelly shows unreal excitement in her eyes when she talks about going off to Northern in August (with her boyfriend, Michael. She doesn't call him Mike, as I do) and when she talks about nursing and about maybe going all the way for an MD, someday. I don't think I've ever been happier than I am when I just sit and listen to the two of them.

Lila is a professional listener. She has that talent in an interrogation room. Which is why I let her handle the bulk of the interviews we conduct for the CPD. She really hears people. She doesn't listen sideways, as some cops do. As a lot of civilians do, as well. She actually connects up to the person, whether they're lying or telling gospel. Lila has a bullshit meter in her head. She knows liars immediately.

Kelly hasn't lied to me that I know of since she sobered up and started eating her way back to health.

My daughter is truly blooming before my eyes, and it's very difficult not to water-up when I realize her transformation. It really is like a rose, when they bloom and their gorgeous petals open up and flourish. There has never been an event in my life that resembles her metamorphosis, except maybe her birth, which I missed because of a war. Kelly was as near death as any wounded GI I've ever witnessed on the battlefield. I've seen men literally gasp their last. I've seen the bulb turn off behind their eyes.

I always expected the worst-case scenario phone call telling me that my daughter was found dead in some alley or on some street. That's how junkies die, and Kelly was a junkie for a few years.

Something or someone saved her. Maybe it was Sr. Catherine or maybe it was Mike Carroll. But I think it was a combination of the above—and I think my daughter had more than a little to do with it, herself.

Any drug counselor, and I've known several outstanding therapists, will tell you that no one ever goes straight unless they make up their own minds that they're going to. No program, no guru, no priest or nun or reverend or rabbi or mullah can help you be free of that mountain of a monkey on your back. You are the only person who can deliver yourself, ultimately.

Kelly dragged Kelly back from the edge of the abyss. I felt impotent to help her, most of the time. You can't lock them up or bitch them out of it. It has to come from within. There has to be sufficient character to pull this kind of miracle off.

Kelly saved Kelly. Nobody else. The word "proud" is far too insufficient to express how I feel about her. She's not all the way out of the woods, yet. Life is never that facile. There'll be tests, hurdles, the usual.

But for now, I'm watching Kelly grow, instead of doing the other thing, and I'll try to be happy for her and for me, and I'll try not to listen for footsteps coming up behind us.

Franklin Toliver has had several sightings, but none of them have been confirmed. None of the girls came from money, and no self-respecting charitable organization or church is willing to pop for reward money. Rich kids have that advantage when they get waxed or snatched. Someone is always willing to put up cash in exchange for justice. Jefferson's words about equality were, after all, nothing but idealistic. All men are not created equal, politically or any other damn way. If you were ever in a men's shower room, you already knew *that*.

So just to screw my theory, the *Chicago Sun-Times* ponies up ten thousand bucks for anyone who comes up with evidence or *whatever* that helps catch the killer or killers of the six girls. Some columnist named Jimmy Malone comes up with a personal crusade to collect even more than the cash the paper's going to provide, and by the third week in July, the amount has doubled to twenty grand.

Funny how some people believe that bill of goods about equality that Jefferson tried to sell.

Anyway, we've received a number of calls on Franklin because the *Sun-Times* has let it slip that he's a "person of interest." They're really taking their balls in hand to mess with a politician's son that way, but they do have the truth to back them up—Franklin *is* a person of interest.

I can see the hairs on our Captain's neck standing on end when he reads about the Lieutenant Governor's son in the paper. I wonder if our boss is one of Toliver's bag men? Maybe he's just a loyal voter. Or maybe I'm wrong about our honcho. Perhaps the shit is simply cascading on him from above.

Whatever might be the case, we're getting calls. But we haven't nabbed that hooded son of a bitch, yet.

Lila and I get called to a part of the city where homicides are very infrequent. You don't find stiffs on the Gold Coast unless they're dead from natural causes, most of the time. And you don't find celebrity's spouses shot and raped in these high rises where security is part of the attraction.

There is a doorman and there are security guards who sweep all thirty floors constantly, looking out for thieves and muggers. They don't usually have to look out for murderers and rapists. That's not the type who frequents this high rise of condos on Michigan Avenue. This is truly the high rent district in the Loop.

The celebrity is Bill O'Connor. He is the popular talk show host whose program is syndicated in a hundred and fifty markets in North America. He has his own magazine, a la *People*, but his mag is called BO, a little play on initials for body odor. The magazine caters to movie stars and TV celebrities and the rich and idle of the world. But it ranks second in circulation to the above-mentioned *People*. It has made O'Connor a very rich schlockmeister. His word is solicited by all kinds of people in order for them to consider themselves "stars."

We arrive at 3:42 A.M. Lila and I have the third shift, the graveyard watch, this week. Only Captains are pretty much assured of working solely days. Most killings happen on off hours, anyway. People never seem to be able to get themselves butchered at reasonable hours. It's a downside of Homicide.

The ME is still on hand. This time it's Dr. Garrison. He's young for this job—maybe forty. He's also a looker, and it doesn't slip by my partner, who seems to fawn on him just noticeably.

But she finds out the facts, so far. Rape is obvious, but more specifically it's sodomy. And there is semen in none of her orifices.

"He spent some time with her," Garrison tells us both. "He lingered."

"How much linger?" I ask.

"Can't tell until the tests come through, but I'd say he was up here at least a few hours. Looks like he had a couple of drinks. There's an empty tumbler in the sink with some scotch on the bottom. He had a least one, but the bottle on the counter is half-empty. Maybe somebody else drank the better part of it. We'll never know. But I'm betting he took his time."

The body is hung by its heels from the light fixture in the spacious living room. The fixture is an expensive piece of electrical art. Probably a multi-thousand dollar chandelier. It shows the construction values in this condo that the weight didn't pull the lights down out of the ceiling, but Mrs. Sharon O'Connor looks like she might have tipped the scales at barely one hundred pounds. She might be five feet two. The weight she did have was nicely distributed. She's naked, so we see all her charms.

The only thing not so charming is her slit throat.

"How long you think it'll be before we get the call?" Lila asks me, back in my cubicle.

"You're trying to say this is a high profile killing?" I grin.

"There were already thirty reporters downstairs."

I nod. I know. We both waded through them with several perfunctory "no comments."

"The first guy we look at is Bill," she says.

"Doesn't look good. He has an alibi."

"I know. But it's almost always the old man. Lousy marriage, she ate crackers in bed."

"She could've eaten all the crackers she wanted, if I'd had a shot at her. Before the slit throat, of course."

Lila groans.

"You don't seem to be as sympathetic towards Sharon O'Connor as you were toward our departed working girls, Danny."

"She'll get plenty of sympathy elsewhere. All I want is the sweet human being who relieved her of her life."

"That much, you're democratic about. But it usually is someone they knew."

"There was no forced entry. Was that your first clue, Holmes?"

Lila doesn't like it when I make Holmes jokes with her. She's not crazy about Dr. Watson, either.

"So, as usual, how the hell did he gain entry? She let him in or he had a way in, past a doorman and three security guys who check those floors every twenty-five minutes. How'd he avoid all that surveillance?"

"Maybe, I'm just guessing, maybe someone helped him avoid detection."

I smile broadly at her.

"I hate it when you're smug."

"I know," I grin just as widely.

"I really hate smug, Danny. I really do."

17

We continue to receive messages concerning the whereabouts of our number one prospect for the Twin Killings. All of them turn up nothing. Franklin is either very clever or very dead, I'm thinking. He cannot remain out of view for long unless he's fled the country, but we have contacted the Royal Canadian Mounted Police and the Mexican *rurales*, the *policia* south of the border. And for good measure we contacted Interpol, as well. The alert is far reaching enough that Franklin will not be able to transport his sorry ass very easily. Someone will see him, and then Lila and I will be there.

Bill O'Connor comes downtown voluntarily, accompanied by his attorney. O'Connor is a good-looking Mick, sandy-haired and six feet four. He played guard in football at the University of Notre Dame. He's around my age, and his personal info says that he was rejected by the Marines because of two bad knees, courtesy of the Golden Dome.

His lawyer is Patrick Callahan, a not nearly so attractive Harp. He's five-seven and pudgy and balding , and he reminds me of Cervantes'

Sancho Panza, Don Quixote's beer-barrel buddy.

Callahan doesn't say anything because O'Connor does all the talking, once Lila asks him to go over his alibi for the night his wife Sharon was raped and murdered and hung from the ceiling.

"I was working with my two assistants, Denise Wyrick and Don Carmon. You have their statements, right?"

Lila nods at him.

"You were with them until 1:47 A.M. Is that correct?" she asks the talk show host.

"Yes, that's right."

"Isn't that awfully late to be working?"

He smiles at Lila. I sit next to my partner, and I am ignored.

So I smile at Callahan, the mouthpiece, and he squirms visibly and trains his eyes on my partner.

"Not when you've got a magazine to put to bed by the morning in question," he tells her.

"Okay. Now. What was your relationship with Sharon like? Were you deeply in love?"

"Yes."

He casts his eyes down onto the table, and for the first time since he arrived I don't see impatience on his friendly face. This guy is America's sweetheart. He's got answers for everybody, whether it's your soured relationship or your psychotic thirteen year old, Bill knows the cure or he'll damn well bring on an "expert" who does know the solution.

"I loved Sharon very much."

"That's not what some of your other staffers told us. They said there were problems, that Sharon was talking about a divorce," Lila insists.

Now O'Connor looks to me as if I'm going to rise to his defense simply because I'm his "bro." But I watch him carefully, and I show no signs of empathy, and he shifts his gaze back to this bitch who's antagonizing him.

"Was there talk of a split, Mr. O'Connor?" she goes on.

"Yes. But only because I'd been spending too much time on the magazine, and we'd settled that problem. I was delegating more authority to my senior editor so I'd have more time for Sharon."

"There are no children. Is that right?"

"Sharon couldn't have children, but we were thinking about adoption."

"Where is this headed, Detective?" Callahan finally interjects. "Because it seems you're beginning to head far afield."

"I'm trying to find out if your client was on amicable terms with Mrs. O'Connor."

"Asked and answered, Detective. Can we get this headed toward some kind of conclusion? Mr. O'Connor has been through enough, don't you think?"

"We have to ask this stuff," I tell the attorney. "A man of your experience knows the drill. Right, Counselor?"

He finally peers over at me, and then he shuts up.

"I know this is painful, sir, but we have to eliminate any of the possibilities left on the board," Lila tells O'Connor. She sounds less aggressive, this time. She knows his alibi is fairly strong.

Which doesn't mean he didn't kill his wife or have Sharon O'Connor killed. We don't know how solid an alibi from two employees really is, but we'll bring them both around and find out soon.

"I think that's all, then," she tells the lawyer and his client.

They stand up and depart hurriedly. I'm sure O'Connor has business to attend to.

"He almost pissed himself, he was in such a rush to get out of here," Lila says to me as I buy her a Diet Coke at the machine down the hall from our cubicles. I pop for a Diet for me, too.

We walk back to my mini office and we sit inside. Lila gazes out at the skyline, but I'm peering out into the hall at nothing.

"If he were guilty, I think he would've put on a much better show for us," she claims.

"Yeah. You'd think an actor like O'Connor could put on the despondent husband for us, but he just seemed a little too detached. His sense of theatre is really horseshit. I was expecting Olivier decrying the death of Desdemona in *Othello*. Sumshit like that."

Lila laughs. We haven't had much to giggle about, lately. Franklin still lurks out there in some dark hole and now a rapist/murderer has styled and profiled himself into a major media clusterfuck. They're camped out on the first floor in the lobby, waiting for us to tell them "no comment" for the sixth time today. I'm afraid I'll find one leaning over the stall in the john while I'm making a major transaction.

"You don't like Bill O'Connor?" I ask her.

"You mean perpetrator-wise or TV personality-wise?"

"Perp, naturally."

"I think he sucks big time for either," she says, deadpan.

I have to hustle to make Kelly's last therapy session at the hospital. It's like a second graduation for her, she said.

The head shrink's name is Marion Quillian. She's the head of the Eating Disorders Department. She's fairly young—perhaps in her early forties, like me. She must have been a nova to take over her department at such a young age. She has prematurely silver hair, but it looks good on her. She is leaning toward voluptuous, and maybe she's packing a few extra pounds, but she has a nice glow of aliveness about her.

"You should be very proud, Mr. Mangan."

I guess no one told her I'm a cop, and I'm not about to.

"I am very proud of Kelly," I say, and I look at my girl and I squeeze her hand.

"I'd like Kelly to come in every few months and have a chat with me, just to see how she's progressing."

Kelly nods at the shrink. She knows the war's never totally over when it comes to addiction. It's always an ongoing battle. Booze or drugs or bulimia—whatever kind of destructive behavior you're hooked to, you have to constantly sharpen the blade. It's always trying to find a way back in.

"I think you've come a long way, a very long way. If I weren't a scientist, I'd think it was a miracle. And I never talk about miracles. It was hard work, yes, but the manner in which you took all this on is nothing short of…well, it's remarkable. You both have a lot to be proud of."

131

She stands and shakes my daughter's hand, and then she comes around her desk toward Kelly and gives her a for-real embrace. I think I see tears in her doctor's eyes. I never saw a doctor cry before. I've seen medics weep in the field, but never have I seen this kind of emotion from a medical person back in The World.

We meet Lila for breakfast on this second Sunday in August. It's torrid outside. Burning. Throw in a jungle setting, and this is the climate we endured in Vietnam. Maybe the heat is not quite as intense, but it's fucking boiling out there.

We've had our share of domestic killings, lately, but Lila and I have cleaned those cases relatively quickly. When you're enraged, you don't think much about covering your tracks and your ass. And someone always talks. Always. Those cases are the infamous "slam dunks." We get many more of those than we do homicides like the Twin Killings and Sharon O'Connor.

We eat at Bob Evans. Lila insists they have the best pancakes, and Kelly loves blueberry pancakes with whipped cream.

I'm not worried that she'll gain a lot of weight that she'll want to dump by purging because I've seen her exercise regimen. Kelly never eats between meals, and she's got a solid metabolism. She's an eighteen year old kid. She ought to.

You can see by the rose blush on her cheeks that she's come back from the near-dead.

I always found *The Odyssey* an interesting story, even when I read it first in my junior year in high school. I liked the story about Odysseus' descent into Hades, into the Land of the Dead. He was to learn the things in the world of the dead so that he might rise back to the world of the living.

My daughter has made that journey. I made it in Vietnam, and I'm still trying to emerge into that light, all the way. I haven't pulled myself above the surface yet, but I think I'm making progress. My daughter has literally been reborn. It almost makes me believe in the Resurrection. Why Christ would be so special always gave me doubt about the Easter story.

And this is nowhere near Easter. This is the doggest-assed dog day in August, in the heat of what has been an unbearably tropical summer in Chicago. Tempers have been flaring in every neighborhood. Loving spouses have been slaughtering each other with frying pans and cocktail tables. It's almost as if a mad dog epidemic has seized the city, the last couple months.

Lila and I are trying to keep the lid on the pressure cooker, but we can't be successful all the time. People get away with murder. They get away with shit, and shit really does happen. We try to minimize their successes at the "perfect crime" and our batting average ain't bad.

And then my daughter comes back from the other side. She blooms like that rose I was talking about, and my entire existence suddenly has meaning—almost.

If Lila would get it straight where we're headed, then I think I could bear most anything.

But things are definitely improved in my family of two.

Her mother, of course, never sent a message or a card. She hasn't sent Kelly anything since she left. I wonder how much my kid can remember about Mary. It can't be much. Other than that her mother deserted her when Kelly needed her the most.

I'm trying to get rid of all that bile by talking to Dr. Fernandez, but like all things in the head, the big one, I mean, it goes slowly.

The pancakes come, and I partake in our overdose of syrup and sugar. I can only manage to clean half of my plate, but Kelly and Lila both make clean sweeps of their meals.

We make time for the interviews with the three roving security men and time for the doorman. We have no reason to ask the four of them for semen samples, and as of now we have no reason to suspect any of them. The security guys do not work together, so there's no way to find out where they were at the time of the slaying—except for the security cameras at the end of each hallway. Going by the ME's time of death, after we look at the tape, all three security guys were elsewhere when the throat-slitting occurred. The doctor can be relatively certain of the time because of body temperature, which can be determined by a rectal thermometer. The human body cools off predictably after death has swarmed over the corpse.

So O'Connor was with his flunkies and the four men in charge of the high rise are all accounted for. So who the hell remains?

The doorman didn't see anyone other than residents enter the building, but that doesn't mean someone couldn't slip by him when he was out to take a piss or a smoke. The front door greeter doesn't take his breaks on a regular schedule so that someone casing the building can establish a routine.

It's certain that someone did get into Sharon O'Connor's place. There were bruises that indicated a struggle, but the fight might have occurred just before her demise. She could have known her killer and let him in. The sex—at least some of it—might have been consensual. The sodomy was not. There were tears in the anus. The oral business was probably part of the beating she took. There were bruises and lacerations on her face, as well.

Only the vaginal sex showed no necessary signs of physical distress.

Maybe it started off as rough love, and then maybe it got way out of hand.

There are no maybes that Sharon's dead.

We printed the entire condo. We fingerprinted the hallway, as well. We'll see if we come up with anything interesting, but prints have to have a match in somebody's system, so if our man was neither military or a convict, he'll be next to impossible to locate.

The media and the hierarchy will not allow us to push Sharon O'Connor's case aside. If it hadn't been for the newspaper, the Twin Killings might have been shoved to the bottom of the stack. Six black prosties still do not equal one glamorous white celebrity's wife. It's a good thing the *Sun-Times* has turned up the heat on our original case, or those six young women might just as well have been sucked to the bottom of Lake Michigan, as if they'd never been a part of this planet in the first place.

18

His name is Wade Andrews. He says he is Angela Carter's grandfather. Angela was in the second pair of victims in Old Town. He walks into my office on a late July afternoon. He tells me his name and why he's here, and then I buzz Lila to come on in over here. She responds quickly, and there are three of us in my small space. I have Wade sit down, and Lila stands in front of the shut office door.

"I'm from Tennessee. Place called Donaldson. It's just a farm town, and I been farmin' since...since I can remember."

He has a soft southern accent. And it's enriched by his roots, by his race.

"My son, Darius, had this little girl. I didn't know her at all because I cain't afford trips anywheres. Darius, he come to Chicago when he twenty-seven. Give up farming wid me. Said he had to have somethin' better."

Wade must be near sixty, but he's robust and erect. The farm hasn't stooped him, and his hair is lightly peppered with silver. His teeth are white and perfect, and he looks like he would've made an excellent athlete in any sport you might choose.

"He didn't las' long in Chicago. He get himself shot eighteen year ago. They sent his body back home to me when I found out he been shot. It's about drugs, the po-lice tells me. A man called me on the telephone. He said he was wid you, *ho*-micide."

There is no sadness in his eyes. I look over to Lila, but she's watching Andrews.

"I come up here because Darius tole me he had a little girl when he first come here. The gal he had her wid and him never got married, but Darius say it was the gal who didn't want none of him. She was a prostitute, but my son didn't know that when they made that chile. He wanta do the right thing, but this woman ran off after the chile was born. All Darius knew was that she name the chile Angela. He say she called her her little angel and that was why she call her Angela.

"Darius never saw much of his baby, but he caught up with Monique—that was her name—and he give her some monies for Angela, from time to time.

"But when the girl turn about two, Darius say, he never see either of them again. I come here to see her grave because she be my blood. They say that County bury her. Is that right?"

"Yes, sir," I answer. "Would you like us to drive you out there?"

"I got to git back on the evenin' bus. I really cain't afford this trip, but this girl was my blood, and my son try to do the right thing by her and by her momma, but this Monique is a whoor. I'm sorry to use that language, ma'am, but what is is."

Lila smiles at him. She puts her hand on his shoulder as he remains seated.

"You did a good thing," she tells Andrews.

I get up, and we head out and then downstairs toward the car.

The cemetery is on the southwest side. Cook County pops for the indigent who get planted here. It's reminiscent of a town's boot hill, almost, even though most of these victims of murder and mayhem weren't gunslingers. Most of them were simply too poor to be buried at their own expense.

Her name and date of birth and death are all that are inscribed on Angela Carter's small stone. Carter, apparently, was her mother's surname. There's no mention of Darius or Wade's side of the family, because it really wasn't a family.

It makes it difficult for me to understand why Wade Andrews came all this way to honor a woman he never knew. I understand that she was his blood—if in fact Angela really was sired by Darius. In Monique's line of work, it's anybody's guess who the real father was. She might have told Darius he was, but that's a lot to take on faith. The word of a hooker, I mean.

But Darius believed her, it seems. Maybe his timing was absolutely right to be Angela's father, but what really matters now is that Wade Andrews believed that she was his grandchild, his blood granddaughter. He came all this way to visit a stranger, so I have to be in awe of his faith, his loyalty, to what is largely belief, not knowledge.

He stands in front of the meager stone and clasps his hands and lowers his head, and he prays. So I join in. I cross myself, say an internal Our Father and a Hail Mary and a Glory Be, and then I thank God that I'm not praying over Kelly's grave. It could've easily been her, but not at this cemetery. I have life insurance on my daughter, and a formal funeral would've been taken care of.

Tears sting my eyes, and I feel a trickle leaking down my left cheek. I look over at Lila, but she's watching Wade pray. I haven't been found out; I haven't been caught in the act of sentiment or emotion or grief or fear or joy that it's not my own blood that I might have been called to make a similar trip.

I'm lucky. Wade's unfortunate, unfortunate that his son and granddaughter are both dead as a result of mindless violence.

Things have just changed. I've seen all six bodies of the Twin Killings. I've seen all the CPD photographs of the slain women. But now, just now, there has finally been a *face* attached to one of the six dead women.

I give Wade the two twenties I've got left in my wallet. Lila gives him fifty out of her own cash. He tries very hard to refuse us, here at the Greyhound Terminal in Downtown, but I take him by the shoulders and I face him eye to eye.

"I will arrest you if you don't take this money, Wade."

He looks at me as if he wonders if I'm for real, and then I smile at him, and he grins nervously. I'm sure he has had bad experiences with white cops before.

"Y'all is very kind," he says. He casts his eyes on his shoes.

I take hold of his shoulders one more time.

"I've been a policeman a long time, Wade. I've been on Homicide for a long bit, too, and I want you to know that I've never seen anyone do what you've done. I don't know you hardly even a little, but I know you're one of the finest men I ever met. I'm proud to have known you, sir."

I shake his hand. Then the door to his bus swooshes open, and he and the other travelers board, and Wade Andrews heads back to Tennessee.

We go to Waukegan to interview a possible sighting of Franklin Toliver. It seems that even the suburbs have their working girls, so the old notion that you move to the burbs to escape the corruption of the big city seems to be negated in this trip north.

Her name is Patsy Jankowski. She's in her late twenties, and she lives in a condo on Percy Boulevard in this middle-classed neighborhood. The reason we know she's a hooker is because she tells us up front when we begin our conversation.

She's tall, maybe five ten, and she has a little extra heft to her, and her trade has perhaps made her appear about ten years senior to her real age (the age she gave us), but she's not unattractive. Her makeup is slightly garish, but that's typical to the prosties I've encountered on the job—the living ones, I mean.

Her condo is modest but well kept. She has a roommate, she's told Lila. (Lila asks the initial questions to put her at her ease. Lila is less threatening, my partner and I think. Patsy's furniture looks Mart-bought, nothing expensive, but solid and durable stuff. A couch, a loveseat, a couple chairs and a dinette set.

The roommate also runs the area with her. The roomie is two years younger and better looking, Patsy smiles. The reason we're here is because she thinks she bumped into Franklin just two nights ago, out on the pavement.

"A guy pulls up in a Camaro. Brand new. Black. Real street machine. So it gets our interest right away."

She told Lila that her roommate/partner, her name is Rosalie, won't talk to cops unless it's by strict copper invitation.

"You get the plates?" Lila asks.

"We're not *cops*," Patsy grins.

"Okay, what else?" Lila goes on.

"What happened?" I join in.

Patsy looks at me with a sort of come on glance that Lila notices, and I can see my partner flinch just slightly.

"Well, we're here, so I guess either he wasn't the guy you're looking for or we were lucky he didn't take both of us on. I think he mighta got spooked when Tony came peddling up to us."

"Tony?" Lila queries.

"Our man, you know?"

"You mean your pimp," Lila says.

There's an edge to her tone, and I'm thinking this interrogation might go south in a hurry. Usually Lila is very calm and cool about asking questions.

"Yeah. That, too," Patsy tells her with a slight frown.

"Okay. Okay, so what happened?" I continue.

"I'm right up in the driver's window, so I get a good look at this john. And then I remember the story in the papers about the black girls, and then it all clicks, so I stand up straight and I look back at Tony and Rosalie, and when I do, this dude peels away from the curb. And that's it."

"You sure it was the man in the drawing? You sure it was Franklin Toliver?" Lila asks her.

"I was two fucking inches from his nose. I could smell the son of a bitch's after fucking shave."

I might have to referee this, if things keep going as they are. So I

139

call a halt to our little talk. I give Patsy my card and Lila gives her one, too, but she dumps Lila's unceremoniously on her coffee table but holds mine between a finger and a thumb. She holds it aloft so I can see she's got it firmly in hand.

I'm thinking it's too bad she's a pro.

And then I see Lila giving me the evil eye, and I get us the hell out of there.

"How many black Camaros are there in the city and suburbs?" I ask.

I receive no answer from my partner, seated on the passenger's side.

"You can't be pissed at this woman," I finally utter.

"Pissed? I'm not pissed."

"Then, what's wrong, Lila?"

"Nothing. Nothing's wrong."

One thing I'll hand to my ex, Mary. She never pulled the "nothing's wrong" bullshit on me. She was *happy* to inform me exactly what it was that she was irate at me about.

"Please don't do that," I tell Lila.

"Do what?"

"Shit, I surrender."

She glares over at me.

"I've never seen you do that with a woman we've talked to," Lila says.

"Do what?"

"Fawn all over her the way you did."

"Christ, you did all the talking!"

"It's not just words, Danny, it's the way you looked at that bitch."

"Are you telling me you're jealous of *Patsy*, for Jesus' sake?"

She sits there, aiming warheads out the windshield.

"I guess I should feel flattered," I finally retort.

"*Flattered?*" she demands.

"I never saw you jealous of anybody before, so I guess I must be special."

"You're special, all right."

"I got eyes for nobody but you, baby," I grin at her.

She looks over with her eyes slitted, as if she's about to strike.

"I mean it," I tell her.

Her eyes widen a bit.

"Move in with me. Kelly's going to school and the house will be empty and I can't stand not being with you anymore."

Her face softens.

"Is that a for real offer?" she asks.

"It is absolutely dead on for real."

She looks back out into traffic.

"I'll think about it."

With her reply, my heart drops toward the bottom of my insides.

She gets over the crap with Patsy in about two hours, I estimate. After we go to Freddy's Bistro on Waveland Avenue by Wrigley Field, her demeanor softens and she's back to normal. But she won't discuss my offer to have her cohabitate with me and I don't bring it up again.

We sit in Freddy's, which has a 1950s atmosphere inside, replete with James Dean and Elvis and Marilyn Monroe posters to waiters with doowop hairdos and waitresses with beehives. There's an actual 1957 Chevy sitting smack in the middle of the spacious dining room, and the wait staff approaches you on roller skates, like a Saturday night drive-in.

I'm drinking a Diet Coke—one of the few non-'50s things they allow in Freddy's. Sign of the times, like computers and guys who are in touch with their inner child.

Lila opts for a strawberry shake. It's so thick that she has to use a spoon to dislodge it out of the glass.

"Where are we?" I ask.

She stops spooning the shake and looks up at me.

"You mean on the case or something else?"

"I mean on the case. We're on the clock, remember?"

"Sometimes it's hard to tell, with you, Danny."

She takes another go at her thick shake.

"Where do we go?" I ask her again.

"He's headed north, if it's really Toliver. He's gone to white meat, too, it appears."

"We can ask for a shift of concentration of squad coverage to the far northside. We can ask for the suburban cops to step up the surveillance, also."

I really want to ask her again to move in with me, but I can't risk it. With Lila, you get your answer when *she's* ready. I don't feel like pressing my luck.

"I think Franklin's been getting help from his mommy," she counters. "I think that line about Franklin and her having issues was bogus. I think it was done intentionally, to throw us off the scent. I don't think he's left the area. I don't think he *didi*-ed on us, Danny. I think he's stayed very close to home."

19

We'd love to search the Toliver home in DesPlaines, but until we get something evidentiary that will grant us a warrant, all we can do is have a squad or two cruise by the house that Mrs. Toliver supposedly inhabits alone. The DesPlaines P.D. has been very cooperative, but since there are already State Police assigned to her, they can't justify the expenditure of more coppers. The Staties patrol the outside of the home, not the inside, unless she calls for help, so Franklin could be inside without their knowledge. The State Police don't always cooperate with city investigations, however. But you'd think in the case of murder they'd let us know if Franklin were lurking around. Most cops draw the line with murder. It's not like junior might have some outstanding traffic warrants. I feel fairly confident that their loyalty to the Lieutenant Governor doesn't extend *that* far. Not with all the publicity going on from the *Sun-Times.*

Lila and I take a drive past the place once or twice a week, just to let our presence be felt and observed. The Staties might have some of their own plain clothes detectives chasing down Franklin, for all we know. As I said, they don't necessarily share the wealth when it comes to intelligence. We seem to have to all fend for ourselves, from law enforcement agency to law enforcement agency. Politics doesn't end at the State Capitol or the Nation's Capitol.

I'm getting anxious about the death of Sharon O'Connor, also. Nothing's coming up. No one's talking, except the media, of course. O'Connor's show has gone into hiatus and reruns, and I'm told someone else is running his magazine while Bill himself has gone into seclusion in their Michigan Avenue high rise.

We're investigating a shooting on the far southside, a drive-by. A fourteen- year-old black girl has been shot in an apparent gang-related killing. We have these things weekly and in multiples. Lila and I could be kept busy by drive-bys and nothing else if our load weren't divided up among all the other Homicides in our division. They try to spread out these kinds of murders because they frequently go unsolved.

But today we have a witness. Brenda Fairchild's grandmother, Marguerite Fairchild, witnessed the homicide from their front porch. She watched her granddaughter collapse on the front sidewalk.

Brenda's head was literally exploded by an automatic pistol of some sort. The ME is finishing up with her out on the sidewalk. We're standing on the porch talking to Marguerite Fairchild, and she's got plenty to tell us.

"I don't give no good goddamn what they say about talking to the po-lice. I don't give no good goddamn if they come back and do me, too."

She's not mournful. She's *enraged*. Infuriated. Take your pick of wrathful synonyms. She tells us the make and model of the car—it's an '82 Chevy, four door. Green. Whitewalls. Dent on the left rear quarter panel. She got the license number, also. ZD 1345. Illinois plates. We immediately call in the plates, and within ten minutes we have an ID. It's Arthur Remington's ride. He is a known felon. He's blown probation, and he's a chieftain of the Rubios, one of the worst bunch of gangbangers in this Area. The cops in the Gang Unit all know him. They've liked him for several murders they could never prove.

Now's our chance. We thank Mrs. Fairchild and give her our condolences for her loss. When they zip up Brenda's body bag, she says to no one in particular:

"*I don't give a good goddamn anymore.*"

Arthur Remington decides he won't come out of his house on 121st and Lawn Avenue. It's about two miles from the shooting. There are patrol cars on either end of the block. There are eight squads parked two abreast in the street, blocking traffic and serving as a shield for us. There are probably twenty officers here already. Several are stationed out back of Arthur's crib, in the alley. There are houses on either side of him, and we've escorted the inhabitants out of the line of fire. Cops are inside those two houses now also, with rifles pointed at Remington's windows. He's in a box, and he doesn't seem to have any hostages to negotiate with.

There were three of his partners in the '82 Chevy that now sits directly in front of his residence. Marguerite didn't identify them, but she knew Arthur from around the hood. She'd seem him terrorize the neighbors and her, often enough. We're assuming all four of them are inside. I don't think they've had time to boogie and disperse. We were on them just minutes after the call came in.

The SWATs are on the way, but I'd rather diffuse the situation before there's a major firefight here. So I yell out to him. The windows are opened. He must not be able to afford air conditioning on his gangbanger's salary.

"Arthur Remington! Come out of the house with your hands in the air. Come on out now!"

We don't hear anything. Lila and I are crouched behind the rear end of a patrol car, out in the street. It's hot and sweltering. It's mid-August, the real dogassed portion of a Chicago summer. I literally feel scorched all over. Even the vehicle we're behind gives off heat.

"Remington! Come on out now!"

We hear the pop and then the boom of the window on the passenger's side of the car we're behind. Glass flies everywhere, and we all duck. A cop in the house to the left of Remington's fires from his window with a short burst. Then there's a volley of gunfire from the front windows streaming out at Lila and me and the half dozen other patrolmen hunching behind the cars. Our strobes are all lit and they're dancing in circles while the sun blazes down on us unmercifully.

I've got the shotgun from our vehicle. It's a 12 gauge pump. I jerk up and fire four times, and the blasts blow the three front windows into the house. I see the blinds jump backwards from the pellets, and then I hear a scream.

But the scream is not from Remington or his bros—

It's from Lila. She's down, and there's blood pumping out of her neck.

We're en route to St. Luke's. It's the closest hospital.

I'm in the ambulance with Lila. They've wadded up her wound and they've got her hooked up to oxygen. She looks gray, and I'm very frightened. The male technician tells her she's going to be fine.

"What's her name?" he whispers to me. I tell him.

"Lila. You hear me, Lila? Hang on. We'll be there in a couple minutes and you're gonna be fine. Lila?"

She blinks a few tears at us.

We arrive at St. Luke's in eighteen minutes. Even with the flashing lights, traffic doesn't allow us to get here any faster. I feel nausea coming on, but I fight it off.

I've seen guys die of neck wounds in the field, but I've never seen a cop hit. Most of the time, we never even have to draw our weapons. I picked Lila's .38 special off the street after she went down. I put it in our car before I left with the ambulance.

They get her on a gurney quickly. She's gone from gray to white, and I tell myself I don't have time to get sick. I run into Emergency with her, but once they get her in a room, they kick me out.

Three hours into surgery, and still no word. I sit in the waiting room. I don't smoke, never have, and I don't chew. Tobacco was almost universal in Vietnam. Everyone used, almost. Nicotine is notorious for its calming effect, or so say the addicts. I don't like smoke, can't stand the stink. Someday someone's going to outlaw the stench in all public places. Lots of cops smoke, and Lila does, too. When I'm not around her. I can smell it on her clothing frequently. She knows I don't have the habit, so she doesn't light up when I'm with her.

Four hours go by, and I'm frantic. I go to the nurse at the desk, and she must see the terror in my eyes, and she says she'll check into it right now. A few minutes later, when she returns to the nurses' station, she tells me.

"They're just finishing up. Someone will be out to see you shortly."

She's an older nurse. Must be approaching retirement. Her eyes look tired. Perhaps it's near the end of her shift. Or maybe she's tired of checking on shot-up cops. Or shot up or hurting people in general.

A man in blue hospital garb with a hat and a mask which dangles over his chest approaches me.

"Are you the officer with Lila?" he asks.

He's an Indian. Very dark, very handsome. But no accent other than American.

I nod.

"The bullet nicked an artery in her neck, but we closed it off nicely. She lost a lot of blood, I'm afraid. They tell me you stanched the wound out on the street until the paramedics arrived."

I nod again. I want to shake him and get him to tell me if—

"You probably saved her life. What is your name, sir?"

"Daniel Mangan."

He shakes my hand.

"I expect Lila to be fine very soon. She has a very strong heart. But I think you saved her for me. She was almost very low on oil," he smiles.

He tells me I can see her in a few hours when she comes fully out of the anesthesia. He shakes my hand, smiles, and then he turns and walks away.

She's still extremely pale, as you would expect. They have her hooked up to a few bags of various fluids.

I was no medic. I was a trigger man in the war. I opened holes in people; I didn't close them. I know enough about first aid from Ranger training to be aware that you apply direct pressure to wounds. Bleeding leads to shock and shock leads to eternity, our instructor informed us. I'm glad I remembered his words.

It's 10:37 P.M. I called Kelly and told her what happened. She wanted to rush down here, but I told her to wait until Lila was able to have visitors, and she didn't argue with me.

"Are you okay, Daddy?" she asked. Her voice broke. She's never talked to me about the dangers of being a policeman, and I never brought the subject up. As I said, we usually arrive after the damage has been done, and it's rare that we have to resort to violence. But shit does happen. This was our turn.

I ask her if she'll be all right by herself. Our neighborhood is fairly solid, but so was Sharon O'Connor's area before someone dispatched her.

She says not to worry, but I'm thinking of sending a patrol car out to our block. Then I dismiss the thought and tell myself to stop thinking paranoid.

I tell her I'll be home as soon as I can.

Lila blinks at midnight, right on the stroke because I look at my watch when she does.

"Lila?"

Her eyes slit open a bit wider.

"Lila? Can you hear me?"

"Of course," she hoarsely mutters.

I stand up and grip her hand firmly, but I don't squeeze. She's got tubes running all over her and her bed. She has at least two drips dripping into her.

"Don't talk. Just relax. You want the nurse?" I ask her.

She shakes her head gently.

"Where are we?" she whispers so low I have to bend toward her to pick it up.

"St. Luke's."

"What happened, Danny?" she whispers again. It takes great effort to manage the question.

"You got hit," I tell her.

"Yeah?" she smiles wearily. "No shit?"

"No shit. Purple heart land."

"I'm really...pooped."

I have to laugh, and then she squeezes my hand so hard that it frightens me, at first.

"You have to go slow, Lila."

She barely nods.

"Don't talk anymore. I'm going to go tell the nurse you're awake."

I walk out of the room to the nurses' station. We're in a private room, now, and so the nurse isn't the same one who checked on her status for me. This one's younger and chubbier, but not at all worn-out, and she's a lot more upbeat, too.

She comes into Lila's room herself, and I watch her check my partner out.

The nurse finally turns to me.

"You need to go home and rest or you'll be bunking in one of our facilities yourself."

She smiles warmly. She's Hispanic. Her brown eyes are all lit up in concern for me, so I don't argue. I walk over to Lila and tell her I'll be back in the morning.

Then I bend over and kiss her softly on the lips. The nurse gives me a knowing grin.

"Professional courtesy. I understand," she smiles.

I take off toward the elevators.

Lila gets a three-week vacation, minimum, the doctor told me when I returned the next day. Kelly came with me, and both of them wept together. And then Lila made Kelly cut it out, and then I started bawling briefly, so I stepped out into the hall to contain the damage.

You take US 38 from the city to get to Northern. There are lots of Chicago kids at this university, so the road is packed. We drive up early, about 6:30 A.M., to avoid the crush that the college warned parents would happen if we waited until the afternoon. We arrive in ninety minutes, and a slight stream of cars and U Hauls are already forming on the campus.

It's a big school—over 20,000 students. When school's in session, the population of DeKalb doubles, or so goes the legend.

I think Kelly is anxious about the move. She's never really been out of my house before. At least not for any length of time, not even when she took off on me a few times, temporarily. The most she was gone was a few days, and I always tracked her down at one of her few friend's houses. She hasn't bolted on me for about two years, now. In the last six months, she's a brand new person.

Mike Carroll will be here a little after noon, she informed me. His parents aren't early risers and they're always late wherever they go. And they don't much care for Kelly, my daughter enlightened me, earlier. They know about her past, and they're not the most forgiving people. But Mike has been working on them, she said, and they're slowly coming around. They'd better, Kelly said, because Mike doesn't give a shit what they think.

They're also wary of the fact that I'm a cop, and like a lot of citizens in Chicago, they think we're all on the take. I laughed when Kelly told me the above.

She lives in a dorm called Grant Towers. They're out in the middle of a cornfield. It looks like the whole university sprouted up with the corn.

It takes two hours to unpack her. She's on the third floor, so we take a slow elevator up with her several bags and cartons of belongings. I'm hanging around to take her to lunch at one of the fast food joints on the main drag of US 38. Then I'm going to get back to St. Luke's and see Lila. She was supposed to accompany us on Kelly's move to Northern, but she's not nearly recovered enough, yet.

I sit on the bottom bunk that Kelly has commandeered.

"It's a big room," I tell her.

"It's beautiful. I love it."

Then I'm holding her tightly. I look down at her wet face.

"You're only sixty miles from me. I'll be here so much you'll want me to stay the hell home."

"Never happen, Daddy."

"You'll get all caught up in this campus life. But hell, enjoy it, because working really sucks."

She laughs and hugs me again. I put my fingers through her hair as she presses her face against my chest, and it occurs to me.

This is loss. It's happening to me again.

20

I haven't worked without a partner since I became a Homicide. She's going to need three weeks after she gets out of the hospital, minimum, and that makes six weeks total before there's a chance I get Lila back as my partner.

I go over to the hospital during visiting hours in the evening whether I'm on shift or not. Kelly calls her on the phone in the evenings, as well, and Lila converses with her as long as she feels up to it, but Kelly knows enough to keep it short.

Watching Lila has become my chief preoccupation and duty. She was standing right next to me when she took the bullet, but I never heard the one that got her, and I'm not going to ask her if she heard it. In Vietnam, that was the legend: you never heard the one that got you. Fortunately, this one didn't kill her, but I'm wondering if she's going to become gun shy now that she's been wounded in action.

She never got hit in Vietnam. Of course she was several thousand feet up when she dropped explosives on the enemy in the war, but it still takes balls to risk your ass up in a jet while the gunners on the surface are doing their best to splatter you all over the sky. A lot of pilots took the heat in southeast Asia. Some were recovered; some wound up in the

Hanoi Hilton and shitholes just like it. Some wound up MIA. It was bad on the ground with our guys, but Lila had it bad, too.

This time it just seems more extraordinary, being in a firefight on the city streets. The streets are supposed to be places where kids play ball or draw chalk figures on the sidewalks, or where old guys take walks with those three-pronged canes on sunny afternoons, or where mothers cart home groceries in two-wheelers from the local supermarket.

It isn't supposed to be the scene of a nineteenth century Dodge City shootout between Wyatt Earp and Doc Holliday and Johnny Ringo and the fucking Clanton Brothers. This is the end of the twentieth century. We're supposed to be civilized, here in The World.

The only thing missing is the triple canopy jungle, a place where the sunlight isn't allowed because of the thick vegetation cover overhead. There should be tigers and pythons and all those things indigenous to the rain forest. This is my home town, not fucking Laos or Thailand or Vietnam. This is The World that I flew the Freedom Bird to return to.

You have to think Lila might be a little skittish to go back out on the street. When she saw enemy flack, it must have seemed surreal, up in the clouds. She must have wondered who the hell was *that* pissed at her. She never took fire on the ground, the way we did. She was in a jet, going hundreds of miles per hour, an almost impossible object to hit unless they got lucky, down below.

Now it all had to seem much more *intentional*, what with those pricks in that house on the southside trading fire with us, out on the street. I'm saying it's not exactly what she's used to, even though she's a full, blooded combat vet. There's something about being a grunt out in the field that is unlike any other profession in the military. We didn't always go hand to hand, but a firefight is as close as you can get. You see the product of your destruction. It's up close and personal. You see bodies become jellied masses of goo. You see their brain matter spitting behind their skulls, and it's no movie. This is the real thing, bodies broken, exploded, fragmented, torn and mutilated beyond recognition. And sometimes you are the cause of all of the above.

As I say, I'm more or less familiar with such scenarios, but Lila was too far away to see the result of the death she dropped, the napalm, the high explosives, the white phosphorus, the saturation bombs. With

153

grunts, it's in living color and close-up. Which makes me wonder if she wants to go back for a rerun when she recuperates.

I've got a lot of time to ponder all the above because I'm alone during my shifts, now that we're at the tail end of August. My only amusement outside of work is deciding how much time I'll worry about whether the Bears can repeat a Superbowl Championship. The Cubs and the White Sox and the Blackhawks have shown no signs of life, lately, but the Bulls might actually win something before we're all dead.

Kelly is on campus. I call her frequently, and she sounds generally happy to hear from me. That kind of feeling from her is something relatively new for me, so I don't take it for granted. There were a number of years when we didn't communicate at all, unless absolutely necessary, and even then our talk was usually unpleasant. Sr. Catherine has phoned my daughter a few times, over the summer and even more recently since Kelly got to Northern Illinois University. It's nice to see that my kid wasn't just a case to the nun. They actually became friends, I've been informed by my nurse-to-be.

Other than the calls and the wondering about all those Chicago sports seasons, I'm alone.

Which is what takes me to a breeder of border collies. I saw this breed of dogs on PBS, and the show stuck it deep into me. I had to have one. So I called a local vet and asked if he knew where I might buy a pooch. He sent me to a residence not far from where we live. The guy's name is Markey, Bill Markey, and he breeds the canines for fun and profit. He works as a stockbroker downtown, and he lives in a non-descript brick ranch, about six miles from me. He keeps the dogs in the basement, but he tells me he never keeps them very long because border collies are a hot item, at the moment.

Bill's about sixty, I figure. He tells me he's a widower with three grown kids, all out of the house. I tell him I know all about it, but that I'm missing just one offspring, myself.

He shows me the litter. They're twelve weeks old, ready to go, but there are only two left, a male and a female. I'd love to buy them both, but I can imagine the problems with a male and a female when they reach whatever the age is that mating takes over. So I take the boy. I'm going to call him Sonny, after Sonny Corleone in *The Godfather*, one of my all-time favorite movies.

Sonny has a black and white face, and he has black and white interspersed all over him. Just like a patrol car, I'm thinking. He's had his shots, but I'll need to take him to the vet for checkups regularly, and then Bill suggests I have him fixed.

My knees start to come together. I can't bear to think about sterilizing Sonny.

"Would you consider mating him, in a few years?" I ask the sixty-year-old breeder.

"Sure. Just give me a call."

"Can I get one of his pups for stud service?" I smile.

"Absolutely. That's standard."

I take Sonny home. He comes with a collar and a leash, and he has his tag for his vaccinations. He's housebroken, also, Bill told me. He warned me, though, that border collies aren't always good house pets and that sometimes they can become hyper-active.

When he gets home, the first thing he does is yank himself out of his collar and run down the street, away from me.

There goes two hundred and twenty-five bucks, I'm thinking. I run down the sidewalk after him, but he's gone. I feel like bawling the way I did when Lila got clipped. Instead, I go back to my front porch and sit on the steps in this soupy August evening, and I wait and watch it get dark. I think about calling somebody, but the dog's collar is still attached to the leash Bill gave me. It'd be almost comical except that I really wanted to take Sonny home with me.

Maybe it's a message from God, it occurs to me. Maybe I'm supposed to be alone. It does seem to follow a pattern, after all.

Then after about ninety minutes of feeling my ass go to sleep on the stoop, here trots Sonny from down the block. I'm not sure it's him at first, so I just sit there. But he saunters right up to me and starts slobbering all over me with his tongue.

"You took the tour, huh? You little jerk."

He doesn't take offense at the "little jerk," so I slip the collar back over his head, and I walk him into my house.

I've got a fenced in yard, a six-footer, and I've got about a third-acre lot, pretty big for a city dwelling. I'm worried that Sonny might be a digger, but after three days with me, he's king of the yard, and he becomes very territorial. He's pissed up every square foot of the chainlink to show the other mutts in the hood he's the man. He isn't much of a barker, but he cuts loose if anyone approaches the house, front or back. Sonny's my new security system.

He stays outside during the day. There are two maple trees in the back, so he has plenty of shade from the heat, but I never leave him out at night. If I'm working second or third, I leave him in the basement. Border collies are escape artists, Bill told me, so I have to make sure there's no way he can bolt on another tour of the area. He'd have to be able to open the door, but the fucker doesn't have thumbs, so I feel confident he'll be there when I get back home.

There is still no record of Franklin Toliver tapping his bank account, so I'm thinking that Lila was right. He's within the house or he's within close range of the house. He has to be a nocturnal creature by now. His face has been too well circulated for him to bop down the pavement during the light hours. No, he's more like a vampire—night time's the right time.

The Vice guy, Al, has circulated his picture to all the pimps in his area, and Vice has spread the photo all over the city. If he does show a hair on his booty to a working girl, we hope they're going to cooperate and drop a dime on Franklin. After all the publicity, you'd think they'd want him out of the way as much as we do. He's cutting down on business, Al informs me. The girls are becoming very wary about getting into some dude's ride and going anywhere remote with him. They'd rather do a standup in an alley, but a lot of johns aren't up for quick pops like that. The girls tell them to go fuck themselves, so business has gone into a mini-recession, the Vice copper explained to me on the phone.

I don't expect Franklin to return to his former hunting ground, and we did have that call from Waukegan identifying Toliver, but this guy might be thinking what I'm thinking. Isn't that the idea in a battle? To think as your opponent thinks? We'll have to see, if and when he pops up. Because where Franklin is is a bad place. I don't mean his mother's house. I mean his state of mind. It could very well be that he has the urge to kill very badly by now but he doesn't have the opportunity. Again, the pressure cooker's lid has to blow when the heat builds too high. The lid will fly explosively, and somebody's bound to get really fucked up.

Bill O'Connor throws a first class funeral for his wife, Sharon. It's no pauper's grave for *her*, pardner. They go out to Woodland Springs, in suburban Oak Forest. The media is denied access inside the cemetery, but I'm not, when I show the badge. A cop's shield is still pretty much "open Sesame." We get in where others do not tread, even at fancy night clubs and trendy joints that have lines outside with ex-NFL players holding ropes to keep the petty middle classers out.

There are more than two hundred attendees standing here at gravesite. There are thousands of dollars of cut flowers stationed all around the grave. A Protestant minister does the service. It is brief and eloquent, especially since he probably never met the dearly departed.

I come to see the audience, the mourners. Frequently, a killer will want a last taste of the misery he's caused and he'll show up at the funeral. I have a photographer standing back in the trees about a hundred feet from us taking photos of everyone in attendance. I come personally, though, to take a look at the faces.

This time, I can't make any connection to any of the people here. It's not that I can make them as the perp just by sight, but there are occasions when gut instinct can prove helpful on a murder case. It's not extra sensory perception. It's nothing supernatural. But it has to do with body language, the way people pose themselves, sometimes.

Today nothing helpful occurs to me.

Until at the end, when I look squarely at the grieving husband himself. The problem is that there *is* no grief on his face. He holds himself as if he's attending some kind of photo op. His face is blank, without emotion of any kind.

Some people display their grief in a host of different ways. Some cry, some become hysterical, and some freeze like Bambi in the headlights. There's nothing but detached calm in Bill O'Connor's demeanor. He's either too good an actor, or he just doesn't give a shit that his wife's been brutally slain.

The other alternate is that he's delighting in the moment. Perhaps he's happy she's out of the way. Maybe this is where he knew long ago the road would end for her.

He has an iron clad alibi. His staffers were with him during and long after the time of death. Their testimony to the cops who interviewed the two of them had no inconsistencies. They were right in sync with each other.

They're all very good. Too good. The tracks are hidden too well. There are no cracks in the structure; everything's neat and tidy.

I wish Lila were healthy enough to be here for me to bounce all this stuff off her to see what her reactions are.

I can see O'Connor doing Sharon or having her done. It wasn't one of the three security men. We have their whereabouts established on video, and we've checked to make certain that the tapes have not been tampered with.

Then it's got to be the doorman. He's the only one left. He must have seen someone unusual come through that door in time to meet up, fatally, with Sharon O'Connor. Did Bill the Magnate of Television and Master of the Printed Slick Word have his old lady whacked? Did his two staffers lie about their boss's whereabouts? They've been properly questioned once, but I think I'll have to take a run at all of them— doorman, staffers and Big Boy Bill—all by my lonesome.

I spend my off time checking on Lila. She's got two more weeks in the hospital and then three more at home. When I'm not phoning my daughter in DeKalb, I'm spending quality time with my Lassie (Sonny) Come Home.

He hasn't tried to take off on me again, yet. I'm almost tempted to take him out front and let him off the leash and see if he has any rabbit in his legs, but I'm too attached to him by now to give it a test.

The *Sun-Times* has deemed it fit to publish my photograph and Lila's in their newspaper. It isn't ordinary for cops to receive such publicity, but it isn't worth the effort to go after them for pasting my mug in their paper. They're just trying to keep the hookers' murders alive in print, and it's still selling copy. They've just taken the personal approach to the case. They've done biographies of all six of the women who were killed, presumably by Franklin Toliver or by person or persons unknown. They've done pieces on Lila and me.

Somehow they've got wind that I received the Bronze and Silver Star and four Purple Hearts, and all the detectives at work have been calling me "Superstar" until I want to douse all their lights. It's all good-natured, I suppose, but what I did in the War is between me and the Department shrink. I've never told Kelly or Lila about the medals I have stowed in a suitcase in my closet in the bedroom, but now she'll know, if she reads the paper. And I know she reads the *Times* and the *Tribune*.

When I receive a phone call from my daughter regarding all of the above, I know I've finally hit it, big time.

21

The doorman at O'Connor's swank roost's name is Frank Swanson. He's been at the entrance of the place for eighteen years. When I bring him into Homicide, he is naturally very nervous about my star treatment toward him.

Frank is pushing seventy. He looks as if retirement has passed him by without his consent. So I think it's about money. It must have been significant cash if he's willing to hide evidence in a murder rap against his boss. Or, as I said, it could be a conspiracy, on O'Connor's part. Whichever way it plays out, Frank Swanson's in the shit if I've deduced all this correctly—there's just no other way I can figure that a person known or unknown got past the doorman.

Unless Frank was goofing off, asleep or drunk, or both.

We sit in my office. I don't want to talk to him in the interrogation room because I want this to be more like Pearl Harbor, a sneak attack. He's facing the window behind me, and he's staring out into the Loop. He's basically bald, with a red fringe along the perimeter of his dome. The hair is scruffy, and he needs a haircut. I'm big about hair because I've retained something close to a GI cut ever since I returned to The World. Kelly and Lila both rib me about its shortness, but I feel like a slob when it grows out too long.

You'd think a guy who works the door at a hot stuff high rise on Michigan Avenue would be more alert when it comes to his grooming. He's growing a bit of a stubble with his beard, also.

"How you doing, Frank?" I ask.

"Not bad. Not bad," he mumbles.

"You feeling okay?"

"Oh, I'm good, thanks."

"You need coffee or a pop?"

"No. I'm fine."

"You look a little pale, Frank."

He shoots me a look that acknowledges that I'm fucking with him.

"I just don't know why I'm here."

"You're here regarding the Sharon O'Connor murder."

"I figured it'd have to be about her, but they already questioned me, more than once."

"Loose ends, you know? It's all very routine stuff, Frank. I thought you'd rather come down here to talk than do it at your job, no?"

"Yeah. I guess."

"No. I don't think you killed Mrs. O'Connor," I smile broadly at the old guy.

He returns the smile rather weakly. I'm wondering if he really is sick. But we go on to the end.

"What can I tell you I haven't already, Detective Mangan?"

"Were you sick the night Mrs. O'Connor was killed, Frank?"

"No. I was okay, that night."

"You drink, Frank?"

"Socially."

He winces with "socially," just slightly.

"You drink heavier, sometimes?"

He watches me carefully.

"You mean like New Year's Eve and stuff?"

"I mean maybe more often than that."

He looks back out the window, averting my gaze.

"Frank. Look at me, Frank. Were you drunk that night?"

"I wasn't—I wasn't drunk. I'd had a few at my lunch break."

"Who watches the door when you take your breaks?"

"Nobody."

Swanson squirms in his chair, across from me.

"So anyone could just walk right in?"

"No. I lock the door and they have to ring the bell that gets me in the little break room I have off the lobby."

"You ever forget to lock that door? Or maybe forget about answering the bell?"

"No. Not once. Not ever. I'd get canned."

"You need this job, Frank?"

He starts to avoid my eyes by glancing side to side. It's as if he feels trapped and he's looking for a way out of my office.

"You sure I can't get you something to drink, Frank? Anything?"

"I could use coffee."

"How do you take it?"

"Black," he replies.

"Sugar?"

He shakes his head as if I've knocked him down and picked him back up again so I can knock him down again. I'm not enjoying myself at all, but I can't let him off the hook now.

I go to the break room to get his coffee. It's just down the hall. I wait a few beats at the coffee maker, and then I walk back slowly to my office.

He's standing by my window. The windows don't open in this building because we have climate control. I'm wondering if he was thinking about taking a nosedive out of here.

But then he returns to his chair and sits down.

I hand him the paper cup of black coffee, and he sips at it.

"So you weren't loaded on the night Mrs. O'Connor had her throat slit."

He grimaces as he tries to take another sip.

"He hung her upside down, like you would if you slaughtered a pig."

"Oh my—"

"That wasn't in the papers, Frank. You never saw the body, did you."

"No. I never."

"It was pretty terrible. You fight in Korea?"

"No. I had flat feet and high blood pressure. I still do."

"You got a shitty job for a guy with flat feet," I tell him.

"I get to sit down when it's slow, and I got medication for the BP."

"That's good. You take a rest the night she got killed? You sit down for a while?"

"I probably—"

"You maybe could've nodded off? Just for a minute. Just for a minute?" I grin.

His forehead is beading with moisture. I don't have any hot white lights on him, just a couple of fluorescents, on the ceiling. My desk lamp is unlit.

"No. I would've remembered crapping out. I don't do that."

"They pay you medical insurance on this job?"

"No. I've got Medicare, though."

"Doesn't pay all the bills, though, right?"

"Sometimes."

I watch him sipping his coffee carefully. Our brew is extraordinarily hot. It's scalding. We all make jokes about dumping a cup on our crotches and suing the Department, but no one has ever given it a shot.

"How many medications do you take, Frank?"

"I don't see—"

"You don't have to see, Frank. How many medications?"

He looks up at the ceiling, up at my lights.

"Uh, five. Yeah, five."

"All those for high blood pressure?"

"I take something for the gout, too."

"What kinds of meds?"

"Something to control my blood pressure. Some stuff to help the blood flow. Like that."

"How much does Medicare cover?"

"Maybe half."

"So how much do you have to pay monthly, Frank?"

"Detective—"

"How much?"

"Maybe a hundred, a hundred and a half."

"That sounds like a big bite. Especially on your salary."

He nods.

"They big tippers at your place?" I ask him.

"Some of them. Not all of them."

He tries to sip his coffee, again. It's still too hot, so he can only get a taste. Otherwise he'll fry his upper lip.

"How about Bill O'Connor?"

Now he has a look of recognition in his eyes. He knows where I'm going.

"He's a very generous man."

"How generous?" I ask Swanson.

He ponders the latest question.

"Maybe a hundred on the Holidays. A fifty, here or there."

"It's not like he can't afford it, right?"

He grins sheepishly.

"No. He can afford it all right."

"You know what happens when guys withhold evidence, Frank?"

He doesn't answer.

"They go to jail. And if you go to court and perjure yourself....Shit, now you're talking about getting in the shit very big time."

"I didn't withhold anything, Detective."

"I know. I heard you. But I'm just saying. What do you owe Bill O'Connor, anyway? Is he worth jail time?"

"I didn't withhold anything, Detective, I swear to God, I didn't."

"I believe you, Frank. I just want you to know the score on this thing. I find out you weren't totally forthright and honest and up front, I have to come after you. And the guy I should be harassing doesn't give a shit if you take the fall instead of him. I know you didn't have anything to do with Sharon's death. Not directly. But if you lied for O'Connor or for someone who works for O'Connor, it's almost like you helped cut her throat yourself. Now maybe that sounds a little dramatic or melodramatic, but that's the way it is. Because if you're helping somebody out on this thing, if you even looked the other way or something, you're an accessory to murder, and that is some serious shit you don't ever want to wade into, Frank."

He puts the cup back onto my desk.

"I think I might need a lawyer," he says. His eyes twitch just visibly.

"Nah, you don't. We're all done. Unless you got something else you want to tell me."

I hand him my card.

"You ever read *Crime and Punishment*, Frank?"

"No. I never."

"It's about a kid, a college punk, who axe murders this old pawnbroker and her half-sister. He's looking good for the deed, too. No witnesses, none of the fancy evidence shit we use today. I mean this kid is *free*. Except for one item. You know what screws him, finally, Frank?"

He shakes his head. His forehead is really wet, now.

"His conscience. Just his own conscience. Ain't that a bitch, Frank? Ain't it?"

I laugh, and then I rise. I motion to the door.

"You're outta here, partner," I tell him.

He gets up and slowly shuffles to the door.

"You know, Frank," I add just as he's about to depart. "You know, a guy like O'Connor could afford to buy you, he could afford to pay for a hit on the old lady. Easy. Just as easy, he could afford to get rid of loose ends, say, if he got nervous about those loose ends."

Swanson turns and looks at me. I'm not smiling anymore. He has his eyes wide open, just before he turns and walks away.

I read a lot in Vietnam, whenever I had the opportunity. Whenever I had R and R lined up, I just stayed on base. I was sending money back home from the War, and I didn't spend cash on booze or broads or drugs. We could get good stuff in-country, when we weren't out on ops or crossing borders we weren't supposed to cross. I read Dostoevsky and Tolstoy and

Flaubert and a lot of American authors I avoided reading when I was in school. I even read Shakespeare and Milton. But most of all I kept rereading *The Odyssey*. I read *about* Homer's epic, also. I read how it was done orally, at first, because there was no recorded writing until later. The story was told and retold over and over so often that these "bards" memorized every line.

If it hadn't been for writing, though, we never would have seen *The Odyssey* or *The Iliad* or a lot of other classic stuff.

Yeah, all the literature I've been exposed to was read largely on my own. Boredom started me reading, but it became fascinating, later on, especially when I was in combat. Fascinating because the writing, the words, was so very different from my landscape, from my personal environment, when I was in combat.

There was savagery in those stories, but it was framed in poetry. There was no such poetry in the experiences I had. I guess war is a typical topic in literature. It's got that grandiose conflict in it that is the stuff of storytelling. But I never had time to notice the sweep and grandeur of the terror I was living in a battle or in a firefight. There was only an immense desire for survival, nothing more. Politics and poetry were nowhere present, nor was drama or insight or irony—any of those literary terms they teach you in a classroom.

The Odyssey struck me differently than any war story or war novel I've ever come across. Odysseus knew firsthand about death because the gods stuck death in his face and those gods wouldn't let him look away. They kept messing with him for twenty years until they let him go home, and then there was more killing to deal with. It never stopped. Only the prophesy of that blind guy, Tiresias, told Odysseus that he would croak peacefully, that he'd go out like a gentle tide when he was very, very old.

I don't know if I'll go gently into that splendid evening. I survived two tours in Vietnam, with a few nicks to remind me of my time there. So I came back home to continue to deal with the Reaper. My job is to catch those people who would bring death on before its natural approach. Like Homer's guy, it looks like God or the gods of Odysseus are sticking it in my face and they simply won't let me look the other way.

22

The workload is catching up to me. I never realized how much Lila took off my shoulders until I had to handle all the details by myself. She was far better at getting written reports on paper than I am, and I used to rely heavily on her to help me do my own paperwork.

But the biggest burden is still Franklin Toliver. He won't go away even though there have been no new sightings of him in weeks—maybe it's months, by now.

It's late September, but the heat holds on, climate-wise, I mean. This summer won't surrender. On and on it goes, and when the humidity lingers with the high temperatures, the murder toll rises. We know that the full moon is a legend, but the heat is truly a decent predictor of human behavior when it comes to offing your fellow man. The domestics pile up high when it's this hot. Even air conditioning doesn't put a dent on the mayhem. The gangs are out on the streets along with pissed off husbands and wives, angry brothers and sisters, really hacked boyfriends and girlfriends. The slightest provocation sets them off.

Add that list of potential homicides to the real ones we're already dealing with. Summer is our busy season, like Christmas is for the retailers. *We be murders.* Except that we don't discount our goodies, in the

Homicide Division. Life comes at one set rate, pretty much. At least it does in my eyes.

It seems remote, by now, that there's any chance Franklin has shacked up in his mommy's house. The State cops would not have let it happen. Their reputation is pretty solid when it comes to being uncorrupted. There are crooked five-ohs wherever you look, but the State Police are regarded as pretty much on the up and up. We're the ones with the rep for taking money to look the other way. There's a well-known story about why bars stay open in Chicago. The Captain gets his, the Lieutenant gets his, and the Sergeant in the bar's Area gets his—they all get theirs or the tavern gets closed. There's truth to the fable because I've seen the scenario unfold before my very eyes. A lot of cops *are* taking money. The story from *Serpico*, the book and the flick, is not fictional throughout the nation. It makes this job even more difficult when the public doesn't trust you, and finding killers who plan their crimes is made much more unlikely when nobody talks to you because they're not sure if you're connected or not.

I truly believe the reason that Jesus Christ got whacked on Calvary was because he was not connected. If he'd run with a crew, no one could've touched Him. You cannot fuck with made men unless you yourself have a death wish. Jesus was just a carpenter from Nazareth. He didn't even have a union behind him, so who spoke for Him in front of Pontius Pilate? Nobody piped up, as I recall the story. They sat back and asked for the life of that asshole thief, instead. And Christ winds up getting literally nailed, and look how jolly the world is today. If He really delivered us from sin, you have to wonder what deliverance really is.

I get all these fever-y little thoughts when I think about Toliver still being out on the streets. I feel helpless, even with all the resources the CPD has. We're actually sharing information with the FBI, on this case, and it has still got us exactly nowhere.

And I keep rattling the same cages over and over with no apparent results. I call the Lieutenant Governor about twice a week to see if he's made any contact, and I get his assistant, a snotty little punk who came from the Chicago Machine politics. I'd like to talk to him face to face, someday, but it's probably better that I don't. He's *connected*, you understand. He's not in the Mob, at least not in the Sicilian crew. He's in the post-Boss gang that has ruled Chicago politics as well as a good chunk of the funny business occurring in the State Capitol. So he gets to be snotty with Homicide detectives, like me.

Nothing on the Sharon O'Connor front, either. I've closed several slammer homicides in the last couple weeks, but a stiff could've closed those cases. All of them were domestics, all had witnesses who were tickled to death to send Uncle Artie or Whoever to the slammer for popping Aunt Fucking Frieda over the nob with a skillet or a ball bat. Real Sherlock Holmes stuff.

I'm visiting Lila several times a week. She doesn't need my help. She pretty much is getting ready to come back to work, or at least she seems ready physically. Mentally, I'm not so sure.

I'm sitting on her couch at her apartment. The extra room is still unoccupied since the flight attendant exited. Lila's lived alone now for a while.

"When's he going to release you?" I ask her.

"Maybe in a couple weeks," she says.

She's cut her hair short again and she's lost a lot of weight and she wasn't heavy in the first place.

"Maybe?" I ask.

"I still don't have much endurance, Danny. The blood loss took a lot out of me."

"Yeah, I'm sure it did."

"Thanks for the backup," she snorts.

"I didn't mean it that way. I know you were hurting. I just miss you, is all."

"How can you miss me? You're over here two or three times a week."

"I miss you on the job. Things are piling up."

"They always do in the heat, Daniel."

She rarely calls me that. No one does, except for Lila when she's poking at me.

Her apartment is the usual military immaculate. She's got the energy to keep it spotless, it appears. I know she can't pay for a maid on a detective's pay. My place is not nearly as GI as hers. I'll bet she does the corners with a toothbrush.

"I just miss you. If I'm coming over too much, then I'll stop."

She frowns. It makes her pale face look even whiter. There is not much color at her cheeks—or anywhere else. Only her gorgeous eyes remain as alive as I remembered them.

"Don't talk like that. You know I want you to come over here. Christ, you're talking like a jilted high school kid."

"I feel jilted."

She doesn't answer.

"I can't talk about that, right now, Danny."

She means my offer to have her move in with me.

"Let's talk about Kelly," she says. Suddenly, a slight blush appears at her cheeks.

"She's fighting with Mike," I reply.

"You didn't think they'd be happy forever after, did you?"

"I was hoping. She has some endless happiness coming to her."

"It doesn't work that way, does it?"

"No. It doesn't."

We sit in silence. She's in her recliner, across from me, and white light is pouring in from her western-facing windows. She has central air, of course, but you can feel how torrid it must be outside just by seeing the color of the sunlight.

"Anything new on the big two fronts?" she asks.

"Toliver is still subterranean. I think O'Connor did his wife or paid someone to do her. I think the doorman was crapped out and the hitter got inside when he was z-ing, or I think old Frank Swanson was paid off to keep his mouth shut. I think the latter scenario is much more likely. Frank needs the money and Frank is rightly frightened of Bill O'Connor."

"What's his motive?" Lila asks. She's perked up, now that I'm talking about work.

"What are the usuals? I'm thinking he took out a big policy, but so what? He's fucking rich anyway. He's worth a half billion, our people tell me. You know, our bean counters. Then there's the other woman."

"Is there another?" she asks. She's sitting up straight, now.

"I don't know, but I'm making inquiries. It's tough to get intell on him because he makes all his employees sign no-disclosure documents, and Mr. O'Connor has only the best attorneys."

"Of course. So?"

"So I'm going to find out, but like I say, it might come hard, digging into his personal life. He hasn't got where he is by being lazy about his private shit. The papers would love to catch big Bill with his peepee in the wrong outlet. They haven't yet. Not even the rag mags and the scandal sheets. He's sued those guys three times and walked away with millions. They don't want to fuck with big Bill because he sues and wins. There are other clowns out there who love the pub no matter what it's saying or smearing them with."

"He's not like all the others, though."

"No, Lila. He's what they used to call discreet. Maybe it's because he's a Catholic, like me. And Irish and old fucking fashioned."

"I wonder if he had a pre-nuptial agreement with Sharon," she ponders.

"He did. I checked with his lawyers, and they were very insulted-sounding when I asked them."

"What did she have?"

"Nothing. She was blue collar. She worked as an office assistant for him when he began to get lucky and made his big breakout on the tube."

Lila pulls the recliner back so that her legs are elevated. She leans back and clasps her fingers together.

"Are you tired? I'll go, if you're pooped."

"I'm pooped, but don't go."

"All right, but let me know when you've had enough of me."

"You really won't let anyone close. Don't you know that, Danny? Your daughter knows it. Even though you're getting better, you still won't really open up. And that's what scares me about you, about us. Haven't you figured that out, yet?"

"I told you I loved you. That isn't *open*, for crissake?"

"I know you love me. But you won't let me get close. You didn't let Mary get close, either, did—"

171

"I don't want to go there, Lila....I better get going. I have to go on shift at six tonight."

She watches me rise.

"Okay. But what about O'Connor? What's his motive? No monetary gain, so why would he zip her? He could divorce Sharon and she winds up with shit. Why kill her?"

"Maybe he thought she needed killing. Maybe she was cheating on him. Maybe she wouldn't leave big Bill, and her lover boy aced her. *Crime of passion.* You know, they still do happen."

"Yeah, I guess they do."

"I gotta go."

"I'll see you later. Tell Kelly not to go nuts over a fight with her guy. It'll pass."

"You think?"

"They always do," Lila insists.

"Not with me. People usually tend to stay pissed at me. I'll talk to you later."

She leans back in her chair. Her face has gone pale again. I open the door and I'm out in the hall.

Lila's not going to be back for another month to six weeks. Her doctor doesn't like something about her blood count. And hearing that news from her on the phone makes me frightened for her. I thought she'd be back at work with me in just a few weeks, and now it looks more like months, or even longer than that.

So my Captain lends me a partner, temporarily. His name is Justin Grant. Justin is a tall black officer who's been in Homicide just six months. But he's known as a dude on the fast track.

"You have trouble partnering with a black man?"

I look at him in the locker room, standing next to me as I'm dressing to go on shift. I wear a navy sport coat a lot of the time, but I wear jeans coming to and leaving from work. I don't wear a tie unless there's a directive from the boss, and he's usually laid back about our attire. I only wear the tie when I go to court, pretty much.

"You have trouble with a cracker?" I counter.

He smiles.

"It pays to ask questions first," he beams. His teeth are gleaming white, long, and perfect. I wouldn't want the fucker to bite me.

"I got no Aryan tear drops on my cheeks. I fought with lots of African Americans, in the day. Some of my best friends aren't black. And some of my best friends aren't white or Hispanic, either. In fact, I'm just pretty fucking short on friends."

He laughs again, good-naturedly. I'm softening on Justin, I think. I don't blame him for sizing me up. There aren't many black Homicides, and there's the usual reason for that fact, too.

"I think we can get along," Justin smiles again.

He's dressed in beautiful threads. Sharkskin suit, white shirt, gray, striped tie. Very professional-looking.

"Franklin Toliver is our main entrée, no?" he asks.

"And Bill O'Connor," I add.

"You mean whoever did his wife?"

I look at him and wait.

"You think—"

"Could possibly be."

This time *I* smile back at Justin Grant. He's a handsome young man in his early thirties. I'm sure that women find him very attractive. I'll bet Lila would be interested in him, even though she's ten years older than he is. Any woman would find him appealing, I'd guess. He has a natural charm about him, after we got through the initial racial introductions.

"Justin?"

"Yes?"

"Do people who murder other people really irritate you? Do they really piss you off?"

"Without a doubt, they do."

"Welcome to Homicide."

23

We invite Mr. William O'Connor and his attorneys (two) downtown for an informal chat. Surprisingly, he agrees, and we meet in an interrogation room down the hall because my tiny office won't accommodate all five of us—Justin is with me now, too, naturally.

The attorneys position themselves on either flank of big Bill, who's sporting a canary yellow blazer and an aqua blue silk tie. The lawyers are dressed in more mute colors, brown and navy. They don't say anything after I thank O'Connor personally for his time.

"It's no problem. Anything I can do to help."

He beams as if he's come from a million dollar signing for an autobiography to be published by Doubleday—which he indeed has just accomplished a few hours ago, Justin informs me. The Doubleday people came to Chicago to ink him, which is an unusual setup in publishing, according to my new partner. Usually the deals are done in NYC.

"I've talked to Frank Swanson," I tell him.

He looks at me quizzically.

"Your doorman. Frank? Remember him?"

"Oh! Sure, I had a brain lock there for a moment. I'm not very good with names."

Justin sits at the end of the rectangular table, opposite from me. That way, we have *them* flanked. Justin was not in the military. He came to the police directly from college at DePaul University in the Loop. I'm wondering if he's a Catholic, coming out of that Jesuit institution.

"I have to believe the person who murdered your wife made entry through the front door, by Frank Swanson, because all the other exits were locked and there was no sign of forced entry anywhere in your building."

"You think he was somewhere other than where he was supposed to be on the night Sharon got…killed?"

"The guy got in somewhere, unless he's a tenant, and we checked the occupants thoroughly and everyone is accounted for on the night in question. So unless this killer dropped onto your roof and somehow climbed down into your window, it's hard to see where else he came in. And your windows don't open, correct?"

"They don't, no."

Justin looks over to me. I can see him staring at me out of the corner of my eye, but I keep my gaze on O'Connor. The sandy-haired, handsome TV icon is unflappable. He's calm and sure. He never averts his eyes from mine when I'm asking him a question.

"Did you and your wife have a happy marriage?" I ask, suddenly.

It takes big Bill slightly off guard.

But the mouthpiece in brown, on his right, answers.

"Do I sense an accusation lurking in there, Detective Mangan?"

He's the older of the two attorneys. He's got a shaved topknot and he's wearing thick glasses. He looks like a lawyer, I'm thinking. He's got that bulldog presence about him.

"We're trying to eliminate possibilities, Counselor," Justin adds.

I look at my younger partner and I smile at him.

"Like he said," I say. "Did you have a happy marriage?"

"It wasn't all shits and grins, if that's what you mean."

He's trying to make me think he's confiding in me because everything sounded rosy in media accounts of his relationship with Sharon. He wants me to think he's being genuine, no bullshit, with me. Then I'll believe whatever real bullshit he has stored up for me, later.

"You have fights?" I ask.

"Occasionally. Nothing drawn out. We never had any great number of battles. Typical marital stuff, I'd suppose you'd say."

"You never became physical in any of these quarrels?"

"There is a faint odor here, Detective," the attorney in navy blue pipes in.

"I'm not accusing your client of anything, sir. I just want to know if there was any problem or problems from either side of the marriage."

The guy in blue backs off and sits back in his chair.

"You ever have an affair, Mr. O'Connor?" I query.

Bill simply smiles. He's had tougher interviews with Barbara Walters and the babe on NBC, probably.

"Never. Not once. I was faithful to Sharon."

I like the way he uses her name, to personalize her. He doesn't just call her his "wife." He calls her by name. Killers like to de-personalize their victims. They sometimes even refer to their vics as "it." The hardcore murderers, the series killers, make very spooky interviews, and I'm not getting that kind of vibe from Bill O'Connor.

"Did Sharon ever have an affair or affairs that you knew about?"

He looks at me, but his smirk is gone. He flushes angrily.

"None that I knew of."

Now he's gone and done it. He lets his eyes dart away from me, and I know he's lying.

"Could she have had something romantic going and you weren't aware of it?" Justin throws in.

"I don't think so," he says softly.

But his face is still flushed. And Justin has an arrogant grin on his dark, African face, and it further accentuates his bright white teeth. It almost looks like a snarl that he's throwing big Bill's way.

"Did you have her watched?" Justin continues.

"This is becoming outrageous," the shyster in brown says as he gets to his feet.

"Sit down, Ben," O'Connor tells him. And Ben obeys.

"We need to know if there was anyone with a real motive to kill your wife and with a real reason to do it in such a violent manner," I tell O'Connor. "My partner is trying to ask if it's possible that Sharon could've had a lover who might have been jealous of your relationship, that maybe someone might have been angry enough at your wife to kill her."

"I can't imagine that to be true. We loved each other very much."

There's just enough of a twitch to suggest he's lying to me again. I'm beginning to think Sharon had a fella. If it's true, there are very good odds she had no idea how volcanic her lover was. The ME suggested that at least some of the sex wasn't consensual, and the brutality of it didn't look anything like "rough love." The sodomy was something not even an animal would do to another animal. It was meant to torture, to be cruel, to hurt, and to punish.

I'm again wondering if the man before me has that kind of sadism in him. It's very difficult to gauge what people really have inside them.

"If the killer knew your wife, then is it fair to say you were completely unaware of him?"

"My wife never cheated on me, to my knowledge."

This time his eyes meet mine directly. He's either summoning the focus to convince me, or he's being honest. Hard call. The guy's a fucking TV actor, after all.

"I hope you understand that this unpleasantness was necessary, Mr. O'Connor. We really appreciate your time and your patience."

I stand up and so does Justin. Then the three of them rise and leave the interrogation room.

"We're nowhere," I tell Justin.

We're seated at a booth at McDonald's on Fullerton and Grand on the north side. We've been called for yet another domestic. This time a man's daughter has stuck the old man with a screwdriver. The daughter is sixteen and claims her father was molesting her. The girl seems righteous, but we interviewed her brother and the mother, and they both told us it was about the daughter's running around with the local *Diablos*, an Hispanic gang. The girl and all her family are Mexican-Americans. They speak very little English, but I find out that Justin Grant is fluent in Spanish.

"I lived in Mexico for two summers while I was going to DePaul.

Spanish was my minor."

"What was your major?" I ask him.

He sips at his Coke. I'm drinking a Diet. We've finished our Big Macs, and we're trying to digest all the animal fat.

"Religious studies. I was going to be a priest. In fact I was headed to the seminary, and then I fell away from the Church."

"Can I ask why you fell away?"

He gives me a toothsome grin.

"I noticed women. I was a slow starter. In high school I played basketball, but I didn't go out with girls. My moms thought I was gay."

The teeth remain on his face. I'm sure the ladies love his pearlies.

"I'll bet she's relieved," I remark.

"You cannot imagine. Being black and gay is almost a death sentence, in my neighborhood."

"You seeing anyone currently?"

"I'm seeing a few women, yes."

The grin fades, and I can see he doesn't want to delve any further into his private life.

"I'm in love with someone, and it's headed straight to hell."

I try to look like I'm cracking wise, but I don't think I'm being very convincing by the look Justin shoots back at me.

"That serious?"

"Yeah, that serious," I tell my temporary partner.

"I'm not ready to latch onto anyone just yet."

"You're young. Go for it."

"I want to have a family, but not yet....You have kids?"

"A daughter."

"Wife?"

I hesitate, and I look down at my cup of Diet Coke.

"Had one, once upon a time."

"I take it you're no longer together and that your new love is another lady?"

"Yes."

"So we're getting to know each other," he smiles radiantly once more.

I drive up on a weekend in late September to see Kelly. I asked Lila to come along, but she's down with the flu, now. Her recovery has been thrown yet another roadblock. She's really ill, but she's able to take care of herself, she claims, and since it's some kind of virus, the only cure is a lot of sack time.

The drive to DeKalb takes about an hour and a half, depending, as always, upon the traffic. It's a Saturday, so the flow is pretty smooth. I arrive at her dorm around eleven A.M. She's waiting for me at the entrance.

It's becoming more like fall, finally. The temperature will only hit 65, this afternoon, according to the weatherman on CBS. I watched the news before I left home. I let Sonny the border collie out in the backyard and gave him plenty of water and food. I expect to be home by early evening, so he should be fine by himself in that fenced-in yard until I get back. I don't go on shift with Justin until 4:00 P.M. on Sunday.

She looks thin, this time. I can't tell how many pounds she dropped, but I know she's thinner since I saw her last.

"Would you like an early lunch?" I ask her after I give her a peck on her left cheek.

"Sure," she says, and she gets into my car and we drive toward town.

"What's going on with Michael?"

"Nothing," she replies.

There's no avoidance in her tone. But there's no invitation to continue my line of questioning, either. I've already vowed not to interrogate my daughter in the few hours we have together today.

We're sitting inside a campus favorite called Patsy's. They serve lousy pizza but passable sandwiches, Kelly has informed me on the way over.

"How are you?" I ask because I can't think of where else to begin.

"You can see," she says, and she lowers her eyes.

179

We ordered our food at the entrance, and they bring it out to the tables. It's dimly lit in here. Kelly says Patsy's is a big date place on campus.

The tables are heavy and wooden, and if you were to rub your hands across the surface you'd acquire a bunch of splinters. It's artsy fartsy folksy in here, I suppose you'd say.

"Are you purging, Honey?"

I've never called her Honey before, and she jerks her head up at me.

"No. I'm not."

"I know you don't like to talk about it, but you can understand why I'm asking, no?"

"I know you worry about me, Daddy. It's okay."

"You going to let me in on it?"

She looks at me sadly. Then the tears filter slowly down her cheeks.

"I don't know if I like it here."

"Is this because of Mike?"

"Maybe. But I don't know if I picked the right place to come to school."

"You can always transfer. You didn't take a blood oath to come here, Kelly."

She smiles briefly, and her tears cease.

"I wouldn't want you to bail out just because you weren't getting along with your boyfriend, Honey. There must be ten thousand guys on this campus."

Her face goes solemn again. This is the countenance that reminds me of her mother, Mary.

"I just feel lonely, here. People seem so…detached, I guess."

"You think you've given anybody but Mike a fair shot, around here?"

She grins sheepishly.

"I guess not."

"Tell you what. Give it 'til the semester. Christmas. If you still feel the way you do, we'll sign you up somewhere else. Sound fair?"

"I think so."

"You want to come home on weekends, remember you haven't been exiled to this place."

She grins again.

"Maybe it might help to see Sr. Catherine again."

"I talk to her on the phone at least twice a week, Dad. And I haven't been purging. I've been running three miles every morning, but I haven't been eating very much."

"One last question and I'll shut up."

"And I haven't been drinking or doing anything *recreational*, either. You never stop being a cop, do you."

24

I'm sitting with Detective Justin Grant at Fatso's Bar on Cermak Road. Justin doesn't drink at all, and I'm on my usual diet pop. We take our lunch break here because it's a popular bar and grill, the food is medium expensive and it's very good.

Fatso, the owner, is really Pete Fordacci, and Pete weighs about 120 pounds and goes six foot one. Hence "Fatso."

We sit in a booth. We both ordered the tenderloins "as big as your head."

"Which head?" I ask the waitress. She's young and a bit pudgy, but very nice, and she even laughs at the same joke/question I ask her every time I order the pork tenderloin. I leave her a fifteen percent tip, so she puts up with me.

She trots off to put in the order after bringing Justin an iced tea and me my Diet Coke.

"That stuff's going to kill you," Justin pronounces, pointing at my drink.

"So will that limey drink you're drinking."

"Tea is a natural diuretic," my partner informs me.

A guy walks up to our booth. He's someone I've never seen in the flesh before, but I've seen his picture in all the papers. His name is Fast Tony Vronski, and he rules the 23rd Ward, the fattest property on the southside, and he's one of Hizzoner's most powerful ward bosses. He is second in command to the mayor, in clout. Fast Tony is also a big shot in Democratic politics, and the Democrats own Chicago and Cook County and most of northern Illinois, where most of the state's population resides.

"Can I join you gents for a minute?" Tony asks me. He doesn't look directly at Justin.

He motions for me to scoot over, so I do before I think about what I'm allowing to happen. Maybe it's the good manners my mom taught me, but I probably should've told him to get the fuck out of my face.

He sits down, anyway.

Now he looks over at Justin.

"Do you mind if I have a moment alone with Detective Mangan?" he asks Grant.

"He's my partner. He isn't going anywhere," I tell Vronski. I'm looking him directly in his brown eyes.

The Polish population of Chicago was said to be larger than that of Warsaw, Poland, at one time. I don't know if it's accurate, but it's a nice fable even if it's bullshit.

"I'll be happy to——"

"Sit down, Justin. Please. I insist," I tell him, and I motion for him to remain.

Grant sits back down.

"All right," Vronski smiles. "We'll play your rules, Mangan."

"*Detective* Mangan," I correct him.

"You aren't much for the amenities, are you," Fast Tony grins.

"Is there something you wanted, Alderman?" I go on.

We have only the half hour for lunch here, and Laughing Boy is throwing us off the trough, and I'm becoming unhappy. I know he's a fixer and a wheeler and a dealer, but I didn't think I'd ever see him darkening the table where I ate.

"I just wanted to see how your investigation on those dead girls was going."

"It isn't going. We have only the one guy as a blue ribbon candidate, but his daddy is in Springfield. I take it you know him?"

Tony grins widely.

"Oh, you think I'm here to lean on you. Is that it, Mangan?"

I forgo correcting him again. He wouldn't get it, anyway.

"What is it you want? I'm not in your ward, so I can't vote for you."

"I'm not here for your vote. I'm here to see if justice is being done or if you're just going through the motions with this thing."

"I don't do things for effect, Alderman."

Justin is smiling slightly, but he puts his hand over his lower face to hide his amusement.

"You think I'm some clown you can blow off, Mangan?"

"Look, either get to it, or we have to eat and go back to work."

He looks at me, and then he tries to soften his gaze. He's going to become my doting uncle, now. I can feel it coming.

"Ray Toliver is one of the finest men in this state. *In this country.* I don't give a shit if you think you know me. I'm telling you. If that kid drags his father down, the State of Illinois is the party that loses. Not the Democrats or the fucking Republicans, those fucking hillbillies from south of I-80. The whole goddamn state loses if Ray goes under with his crazy goddamned son. Do you follow?"

"I'm a little confused. Do you want us to nail his kid, or do you want us to pretend he never existed? What is it you want? Why don't you cut the fucking dance and just say it?"

"I would never intrude on a police investigation. Never. I want justice done, *without* Raymond Toliver going down the shithole with his piece of shit son."

The way he glares at me, I understand how this prick rose to power. He makes Machiavelli look like a friendly statesman.

"We don't have anything on the burner regarding Toliver Senior. In fact, I rather liked the man when I met him."

Justin is hiding behind his right hand again.

The girl arrives with our lunch.

"You know which way shit flows, don't you son?"

"Aren't you a little young to be my dad?" I ask him.

His face sours.

"You think you're fucking untouchable because you're a Homicide? Is that it?"

"No, no. I know what you're capable of."

"And you got these big balls. Right? War hero. Big Army Ranger. Yeah, I read the papers, too. You think your buddies in the media can save you, once the crap storm starts?"

"Are you threatening me, Alderman?"

He stops abruptly. Suddenly his express loses steam. He tries to come on as my best friend again.

"You thinking about a higher pay grade, Detective Mangan?"

"Oh, I'd love it."

"They tell me you're on the fast track. I know your Captain very well."

"Really."

"Yeah, really. And he knows the facts of fucking life."

"He does?"

"Don't play dumb with me, Mangan. I'm not amused."

"I still haven't grasped exactly what it is you want."

"I want you to catch that little prick in a hurry or find someone else to lean on. You're taking his old man down with him. Do you understand?"

"You think we're dragging our asses on this one?"

"I want results, Detective. Just like the rest of the city. I want justice for those dead girls, no matter what they did with their lives."

Justin's hand comes off his lips. I can see his eyes boring in on Vronski. So I try to end this little joust before my new partner wades into the offal.

"That's what we want, too, Alderman. And I have no desire to cause the Lieutenant Governor any problems. I'm not political, Mr. Vronski. But if you think I'm not the man for this case, maybe you really should talk to the mayor, and then he can talk to the Commander and then he—"

"All right. I'm done. You heard what I said. Ray Toliver doesn't deserve to get pulled under along with that miserable son of a bitch he sired. I'm done, then. You two officers have a nice lunch."

He rises from the table. I notice now that his white hair is razor cut. Had to be a stylist. He's short in stature—maybe five feet six. And he's a wiry little shit. He's maybe fifteen years my senior, but he looks tanned and healthy. I'm sure the tan came from one of our local beaches, not the Cayman Islands or Bermuda.

He walks away, and within ten feet of us, he's waving at someone else and smiling, and he goes to some other guy's table and begins glad-handing another possible voter.

After Fatso's, Justin and I drive back to Headquarters. We're in city traffic, so it takes the better part of a half hour to go just a few miles. We get halted by every stoplight.

"That was really brave, the way you talked to that guy. Not very bright, but brave," Justin tells me.

"What's he gonna do? Not invite me to his birthday party?"

"You know what he can do."

I look over to him, and I grin.

"You start worrying about what these kind of weasels can do to you, and you might as well resign right away. Once they start telling me to lay off someone in a homicide investigation, then you can occupy my spot on your way to the top, Detective Grant."

"I'm just saying you could've been more tactical in the way you talked to him. That's all I'm saying."

The blocks crawl by as we approach yet another red light on Monroe Street. It's an overcast day, so it's becoming more like fall as the days recede.

"If you wanted a politician for a partner, you came to the wrong address, Justin."

"I'm not saying that, either. I just don't think you need to antagonize people who can do you great harm."

I look over at him again. He's doing the driving. That's what junior partners are for.

"Look, Danny. You got a rep. It came out in big bold print in that article the guy in the *Times* wrote. Vronski isn't going to mess with someone in the spotlight, and you're there, now. He might come back at you when you're not in the limelight anymore. That's all I'm saying. You have to look out for yourself."

I find it strange that I'm getting the brunt of these words of wisdom. Surviving used to be *all* that I cared about. Getting home. Getting back to my life and back to The World. And now I'm being re-educated by Justin Grant, a Homicide for just six months.

"Thanks, Justin. I appreciate your concern for my welfare."

"He didn't tell you to lay off Franklin Toliver. He asked you to be gentle with *Raymond* Toliver."

"I know, Justin. I was right there. With you."

"Look, Danny, I don't mean to tell you your job. I just don't want to see you throw your life away on account of that cracker, Vronski."

I look at Justin carefully. He looks back at me, and then his eyes go to the landscape sweeping past him on the driver's side window.

"I shouldn't have called him that. I'm really not a racist."

"I never thought you were," I tell him.

He looks back out at the road and we come upon yet another red light. I'm wondering if we'll ever arrive at Headquarters.

"Just look out for your own self," he says, finally.

And then the light turns green.

Lila has overcome the flu, but her blood count remains a problem. The doctor has her on vitamins and an iron rich diet. She's been warned to stop smoking altogether, also.

"I can't drink any alcohol. They don't want my blood any thinner," she tells me at her place when I visit on a Friday night.

"You can live without it. You don't drink much, anyhow," I tell her.

She sits in her recliner and I'm back on her couch again, as if I'm her audience. I sure don't feel like her lover anymore, and I'm wondering if I'm even her friend, lately.

"Danny?"

"Yeah?"

"I think it would be better if we weren't partners, anymore."

I sit there, stunned. She's sitting on that recliner with a red, white and blue afghan thrown over her from the waist down.

"What in Christ's name brought all this on?"

She sits up and drops her feet to the floor.

"I've been thinking about all this for a long time. I've got nothing to do lately but sit around and think about things. I think it would be better for both of us if we stopped seeing so much of each other."

Again, I'm baffled. I didn't see any of this coming on.

"Did I do something to you, Lila?"

"No. It isn't that. Look. I love you, but I think we need some time and distance, and I think it would be better for us on the job if we worked with other people. You get along with this guy Justin, don't you?"

"Yeah, but I get along with you much better. At least I thought I did."

"I don't want you pissed at me. I really do love you, and if we're going to have a relationship some—"

"*If?*"

She watches me, but she doesn't start up again. She sits there looking at me as if she's convincing me telepathically.

"What do you mean, if?" I ask again.

"You know the chance we were taking by getting involved when we were partners."

"*Were?* I never thought we stopped being together."

"You're making this—"

I get up from her couch.

"Okay. I'll request that Justin sticks with me as my permanent partner. All you have to do is put it in writing, whenever you come back."

I head toward the door, and I'm waiting for her to stop me, to call out my name, but the door is closed behind me, and I'm headed out of here.

25

October is the finest month of the twelve. It usually offers the best weather, up until Halloween. The cold usually triumphs over an Indian summer by the time the Day of the Dead arrives. *Dia del muerto.* All Saints is November one, I think I remember. Since I'm becoming a practicing Catholic again, even though Kelly's not with me at mass anymore because she's at school, I ought to remember Holy Days. At Trinity High School, where I went, we celebrated all the Holy Days, and we had at least one mass per month that was an all-school celebration of the Eucharist. You didn't get out of church, even if you weren't a Catholic or even if you didn't practice the faith but paid the tuition. It was what they called mandatory.

On the first Sunday in October, my aloneness really sets in on me. Kelly's at Northern until the Thanksgiving break. (A makeup with Michael seems to be in the offing, the last time I talked to her—last Wednesday, I think.) I haven't heard from Lila since I walked out of her apartment. And our two major redline cases remain in scarlet.

Justin is doing fine as a partner. We get on well, but it's not the same without Lila. It never will be the same without her. I should call her on the phone and at least make the attempt to clear the air between us, but that would feel like capitulation to me, somehow, and I still can't think what I did to bring all that on, with her.

Women are mysteries beyond my grasp, even though I've heard their cryptic qualities stated better than I just did. I couldn't follow why Mary dumped me and Kelly. I never abused my ex physically or mentally or psychologically, that I can recall. We never had any drop down brawls of the verbal/oral kind when we were together. Our fights were more of the silent, brooding type. She sometimes wouldn't talk to me for days.

I'm still seeing Dr. Fernandez. I'm not on a first name basis with her—I'd love to call her Arlene sometime soon, but I know it's all very professional with her as far as I'm concerned. And I'm still in love with Lila and probably always will be.

I still love Mary. I never stopped. I don't stop caring about people, but some of them have no problem cutting me out of their concerns, Mary being the number one culprit, here. It's beyond my ken why human beings can simply stop loving someone once the process begins, but apparently a lot of folks have no difficulty turning their emotions on and off.

Dr. Fernandez looks her beautiful best again today. Regardless of how I feel for Lila, I really want to make contact with the doc's pink lips. I'd like to feel my hands on her shoulders, on the small of her back. I'd like to break up that authoritarian gaze she aims at me and replace it with some really nasty, get-down desire.

I sit in the same straight-backed chair I always do when I keep my appointments with her. She sits behind her desk, not six feet away from me, but she might as well be in the Ukraine, as far as my getting any closer to her goes. I suppose I'm transferring all my lust at my therapist because Lila won't have anything to do with me.

I've told Dr. Fernandez about Lila because what I say to her stays in confidence. She can suggest that the Department put me on leave for health reasons, and she can also suggest that they can me, outright, if she thinks I'm unfit. There is a whole list of steps to get me thrown off the force, however. It's not as easy as you might think. I do have some rights. And I don't think she thinks I'm some kind of menace to myself or to the people of the City of Chicago, though.

"How are you doing, Detective Mangan?"

She won't call me Danny. It's all very above board, in here.

"I'm as deep in the shit as I've ever been."

I explain to her about what happened with Lila.

"And why do you think she wants to discontinue your professional relationship as well as your personal relationship?"

It hurts just to hear her say it out loud.

"She told me I was never open, with her. I guess that would be why."

"*Are* you open with her, Detective?"

"I'm more open than I am with anyone else, I suppose."

"Why would she think you're withholding on her, then?"

I have to avert my eyes from the psychiatrist.

"Do you look away when you're talking to her, too?" she asks.

"I'm sorry. I guess I do, sometimes."

She looks at her perfectly painted fingernails. This time they're colored a deep red, and it contrasts with the slight blush of her lips.

"We need to talk about your mother and father."

"I've been through all that before with you, haven't I?"

"You don't like to talk about either one."

"No. I don't."

"Is it because of your mother's alcoholism, Danny?"

She shocks me with the use of my given name. I watch her intently.

"I guess that has something to do with it."

"You guess?"

"Okay, it has a lot to do with it."

"How can it hurt to bring all this out since it's been so long since they both passed away?"

"I don't like to dwell."

"You do like to carry burdens on yourself."

"I don't know what you—"

"Yes, you do. You're a tough guy, aren't you. Dependent on no one. Then you began to depend on Mary and she left you, just like both your parents did. They died on you. Now your daughter has gone off to begin her life and you feel a sense of betrayal even though you understand

191

that all children have to leave their parents eventually. And Lila has betrayed you by refusing to enter into any kind of serious relationship. She wouldn't move in with you.

"And I'm doing way too much talking, Danny, but it gets very frustrating to watch you evade me, every time you come in here. Are you afraid that all this is a sign of weakness, the therapy, I mean?"

"My parents didn't believe in taking your problems to anyone else, not the personal kind, anyway."

"Yeah? Well that was then and this is now, no? And since when did you do as your mother and father did? Did they want you to join the Army?"

"They wanted me to go to college right out of high school."

"So you joined up when no one else was enlisting. You didn't wait for the draft. You hauled ass into the recruiter all on your own and then you joined up with the most elite fighting force you could sign up with. Isn't that right?"

"You want me to say that I did all that to spite my parents?"

"Didn't you?"

"I joined the Rangers because I wanted to see what I really had. I told you all that before."

"You had a death wish. Don't you still?"

"Are you kidding? I don't want to die."

"I know. I just said it to see how you'd react. Sorry."

"So you're pushing my buttons to see what turns on."

She smiles. She watches me with a slight grin.

"I don't know how else to move you to react. React with any kind of emotion. You're the stoic's stoic, Detective. Lila's right: You never let your guard down. You didn't come from abusive parents. They were simply frail and human, and so are you, but you're damned if you'll let anyone know it. It's your little secret. You're not *perfect*. Welcome to the human race. You're not some super-warrior. That's only what they trained you to be, and you weren't going to let them down. They made you a killer, but you doubted the reasons for the killing and kept your feelings suppressed. You kept them hidden, and you're still doing it, Danny, even with the people you care deeply about."

I smile back at her.

192

"I thought you were supposed to ask me how *I* felt about this and that. You know, you do the asking and I do the bringing up out of the depths of my soul."

"I gave you the 'B' version. If I waited for you to tell me, we'd both be senior citizens by the time you confessed what's going on inside you."

"I confess I'd like to know if you're married."

"No."

"Seeing anyone?"

"Let's get back to you."

"How about I change therapists so I can start seeing you up close and personal?"

"That's very tempting, but sorry, I don't go out with men who're on the rebound."

"Can't get anything past this goal keeper."

"You want Lila back?"

The smirk leaves my lips.

"You know I do."

"You going to stop hitting on me?"

"When have I ever done that before?"

She stares at me insistently.

"Who says it'd be on the rebound?"

"I do. You love Lila. Or were you lying to me?"

"I never—"

"I know, Danny. You never do anything that weak."

"Tell me how you really feel about me."

"You don't want to know, do you?"

"Sure. Fire away."

"We talk in strict confidence in this room. Does that include what I say to you?"

"Now you got me all worked up."

"You're an attractive man. But you're hooked on Lila and you're transferring all that emotion onto me. It's common for patients to do that with their therapists, especially if the psychologist is of the opposite gender."

"So I'm typical, then?"

"Only with this supposed lust you have for your doctor."

"I'm striking out here, ain't I."

She nods and smiles.

"I gave it a shot."

She laughs and keeps her eyes trained on mine. She won't waver.

"Tell me about your mom."

So I tell her how she embarrassed me when I tried to bring friends home. I tell Dr. Fernandez how my school friends could smell the vodka on her even though vodka used to be called the businessman's booze because it wasn't supposed to leave an odor on you. I tell her how my friends would watch her stagger—only slightly—around the house. And then I explain how I just stopped having my buddies and girlfriends into the house altogether.

She nods as if she really understands me.

"What about your father?"

I explain about his experience in World War II, how I grew up thinking I could never be that brave. I tell her how I was terrified that I was a coward and that I could never match up to him. He got to fight in a "Good War," and I was stuck with Vietnam.

She nods again as I unload all this old baggage I've been saving up for forty years.

And then I tell her I loved both of my parents. I never held anything against them. My mother had a weakness, sure, but she never missed making a dinner or keeping my clothes clean. She loved me completely. She never held back. It was just that she couldn't stop with her addiction.

And then my daughter comes along, and it's as if I passed something terrible on to Kelly, something I never really had to deal with. I drank, but I didn't have to, the way my mother did. Yet whatever Kelly's addictions are and were, I have to look to myself as their source.

"That's not necessarily true or fair," Fernandez interrupts me. "People are equipped with free will. They make their own choices. Good parents have screwed up offspring, and it works in reverse, sometimes."

"If it's mine, I can bear it."

"What if it isn't your fault? None of it. What if Mary chose to leave you, all on her own? What if Kelly began purging at her own desire?

What if Lila left because there was something inside her, all her very own, that decided to head out away from you? Why does it always have to land on you, Danny? Why are you always your own worst punching bag?"

I look down at my hands, resting on the arms of this straight back chair. I don't have any witty comeback.

"So I guess I'm free, then. Right?"

"You tell me, Detective. You tell me. Who the hell's ever free?"

"I thought you said it wasn't necessarily my fault."

"It wasn't. It isn't. Sometimes it absolutely is your own doing. Sometimes you do get the primate on your own shoulders. And sometimes you have to know when to unload. When it's time to forgive yourself."

I look at her eyes. They're too gentle for the tough woman who's been telling me to take it easy on myself, sometimes. They're too understanding to be the eyes of the consummate professional who turned my puerile come-on to her aside with the ease that a world class matador would sidestep a killer bull.

"It is time to give yourself a break, isn't it?"

She tells me all that as I keep boring in on her brown, Latina eyes.

"Who did Franklin Toliver hang with in high school or college?" Justin muses as we finish up with yet another drive-by slaying on the near northside. This time it's a ten year old African American boy. I can see a stab register on Justin's face as he looks at the dead boy lying on the sidewalk at Ardmore and Durham Avenues. It's gang-related. It almost always is. But this time we don't have any willing witnesses who are ready to talk to us. Everyone around here is deaf and dumb by choice.

We walk back to our car. Justin asks the same question again about Franklin, the phantom of Old Town. The murderer of six women. Jack the Ripper, who only rips some of his victims. Others he simply strangles or incinerates.

"He had no one. He was always a loner," I tell my new full time partner.

Apparently Lila has called the Captain and made her wishes formal.

"He didn't hang with anyone," I repeat.

"He must have someone he confides in. Someone he'd go to in desperation."

"Only mommy. But the shrink said he had problems with her, too. I think his old man would drop a dime, himself, if Franklin showed up in Springfield."

"So if he doesn't hang with his mother or father, he has to be holing up somewhere, and he can't be going to the grocery store or the laundromat on his own, so that leaves a girlfriend or a boyfriend."

"I'd figure a female, if he's living with anyone. A moll, like in the gangster movies," I smile at Grant.

"Who'd know about a woman in sonny's life?" Justin poses.

"The shrink in Elgin, maybe?" I reply.

26

D r. Lawrence Talbot meets Justin and me at the front door of
Admissions. I'm still expecting him to turn into the Wolfman at the
full moon, but he won't go along with my fantasy. He's a mere mortal
with an MD in Psychiatry, but he has no fangs and no facial hair.

He takes us down the hall past the front desk toward his office.
He opens the door, and then he shuts it behind the two of us. We sit in
two high backed chairs opposite his desk. He must have dragged the
second chair in just to accommodate both of us.

I introduce Justin Grant to Dr. Talbot.

"No offense, but your previous partner was a little better
looking," the shrink grins.

Justin takes the crack for what it is, but I find myself coloring
slightly at the cheeks. Talbot notices my blush, but he keeps on going.

"He didn't have any close friends, male or female, or so Franklin
told me."

I suppose I could've conducted this interview over the phone, but
I hate telephone conversations because you can't see the face of the
person you're talking to. You can't read them, in other words. There is

197

no body language to observe, no *tell,* on their faces. Even though I have no reason to doubt Dr. Talbot's veracity, everyone tends to lie or withhold things, at least some of the time. It's harder for them to fool you if you're looking right at them. There's nowhere to hide. You can't roll your eyes or hold the phone away from your ear, pretending to listen to my questions. I'm right in front of you, daring you to try and escape my glance.

Talbot seems not to be holding back. Why would he? Unless the Lieutenant Governor or Fast Tony Vronski had a talk with him before we arrived. Anything is possible, so that's why we took the ride to Elgin.

"He did talk about one particular young woman he knew at the university, however," Talbot recalls.

"You mean at Western?" I ask.

"Yes. I don't think he went to college anywhere else, did he?"

"No. Only at Macomb," Justin adds.

"Her name was...Let me look it up."

He grabs hold of a manila-colored file on his desktop.

"Her name was Jennifer O'Brien. He knew her from a class he took his second year. He only lasted three semesters at Western Illinois before they threw him out."

"Yeah, I talked to the dean who tossed him."

"What was so special about Jennifer O'Brien?" Justin asks.

Talbot peruses his file, and then he closes it and places it on his desk.

"Have you ever read William Faulkner?" he asks us both.

"I read him a bit, when I was in the war."

"The Vietnam War?" he queries me.

I hesitate because I've learned not to bring up that war unless I know exactly whom I'm talking to.

"That was the only war I had," I tell the doctor.

He smiles, but it's a reassuring smile. I don't think he's going to spit at me or call me a baby killer.

"Did you read *The Sound and the Fury?*" he goes on.

"As a matter of fact, yes," I answer.

Justin looks over at me and he grins.

"Well, I actually *did* read it, dammit."

The two men laugh. But it isn't a laugh that's poking fun at me, the poor, illiterate ex-grunt. They just didn't expect a Homicide to have read Faulkner. I'm wondering what my partner has read, now.

"There's a character named Quentin Compson. Do you recall him and his sister, Candace? Caddy, they called her?"

I nod.

"*All women are bitches....*But I think it was his brother, Jason, who said that. Quentin asked, 'Did you ever have a sister?' Maybe he said that other stuff, too. I don't remember. It was hard to read that novel, but I remember I liked it a lot."

"Yes," Talbot says. "But it comes to mind because that was the way Franklin looked at most women—*bitches*. And it wasn't just that he had a demeaning attitude toward females. He was way beyond demeaning. And then you throw color into the mix. He railed about women of color, especially African American women. He told me they were all whores. He threw in Hispanics in that rant, also.

"It brings Jennifer to mind because she was the only girl or female he never lumped into his frenetic little cauldron of hatred. He told me how much he admired her. It seems he went out with Ms. O'Brien several times, but their relationship was specifically platonic. They were merely good friends, according to Toliver. Hearing him talk about her as he did made me think of multiple personality disorders, because Franklin never had positive things to say about anything feminine—other than Jennifer O'Brien. She was the sole recipient of his admiration for anything female."

"What was unique about her?" I ask.

"He had no sexual designs on her, but from what he told me she was a beautiful young woman."

"How can he hold that kind of view about a woman when everything else in him is hateful toward the fairer sex?" Justin asks.

"The only predictable thing about Franklin Toliver is his unpredictability. Perhaps he made this young woman up. Maybe she was all fantasy, but if she was a chimera of his imagination, she was a very powerful concoction, indeed. He made me believe she was real. And I'm pretty used to listening to patients fabricate, pretty used to hearing them lie to me. I don't think he made up Jennifer. She was the one pure female he'd ever encountered, in *his* mind."

"Could she be a replacement for Franklin's mother?" Justin proffers.

"I don't think so," Talbot grins. "Franklin related several Oedipal episodes he'd dreamed or fantasized about his mother, and they were all uniformly ugly scenarios. He wanted his mother dead. I don't know how else to put it. On the one hand he loved his mother unconditionally, but he also despised her for her sex.

"You can see why I was so upset when he bolted from these walls. Toliver is a very emotionally and psychologically disturbed young man. He should be institutionalized."

"We'd love to accommodate you on that one, Dr. Talbot, but we're having a little difficulty locating this guy," Justin smiles.

Talbot doesn't return the smile.

"You both already know very well how dangerous he is."

He looks out the window in his office, behind us.

"He isn't going to stop killing women, you know," he tells us.

His face has gone solemn and worried.

"He's probably just begun. And you know about these series murderers. They tend to get better at it, if someone doesn't stop them."

He averts his gaze once more out at the grounds of the Elgin State Mental Facility. It's as if he's expecting someone to arrive here, and he doesn't want to miss their arrival.

Jennifer O'Brien graduated from Western Illinois University just last spring. We go to the registrar to find out her address. Her latest residence was with her parents in Orland Park, a southwestern suburb of Chicago. We've got another long ride ahead of us, but Justin calls her parents' telephone just to make sure Jennifer will be there to meet us. Justin nods in affirmation after he makes the call on the phone in the unmarked Ford.

We should make Orland Park in around three hours.

Jennifer is at home when we arrive at her parents' ranch house at 149th and Highland Avenue. It's a modest home in a middle middle-class neighborhood. The people who reside here are working class. They're likely people employed as middle management in someone else's company. I don't see doctors and lawyers living here. These are more pale-blue collar type of folks, and you can tell by the brand of cars parked on the streets and in the driveways.

Jennifer's mother answers the door. We know who it is because she tells us her name is Evelyn O'Brien, Jennifer's mom.

"Come on in," she tells us warily. I don't think she's wary because Justin is black. I think it's because we announced we were both Homicides when my partner made the phone call, three hours ago. Justin said she sounded very anxious when he talked to her.

We enter the house. The living room is small but well kept. The furniture is functional, utilitarian. Not like the stuff I've seen in fancier neighborhoods around Chicago. She sits us down on a three-seat sofa. It's cream colored and it looks relatively new. There is a mahogany coffee table in front of us at our feet, and there are two stuffed chairs opposite us. There's no TV in the living room, and I find that a bit unusual.

"I'll get Jennifer. She just got home from school. She teaches at the middle school, here in Orland Park. And she's engaged. Going to be married next August. Well, I'll just...."

And she leaves us.

It takes about ten minutes before her daughter descends the staircase leading to the upstairs bedrooms. At least I presume bedrooms are what's upstairs. The ranch is actually a split-level. It's deceptive from the way it appears on the outside. The lower level, where we are, is slightly dug into the property.

She appears, and I see that Talbot had it right. At least he had Franklin's description of her right on the money. She's beyond pretty. She's a beautiful woman, and there's no exaggeration in that description. She has an extraordinary presence about her, and I'm thinking her fiancé is one lucky bastard. Few men wind up with someone who exudes...serenity, I guess you'd say. Yes, 'serene' is the exact word.

Jennifer O'Brien has an aura about her that makes you feel at ease with yourself immediately, no matter what toil and travail might be bubbling below your own surface. When this young woman enters a room, it's almost as if a hush comes along with her. You can't be raucous or violent in her presence. She has a calming influence upon whatever or whoever is near her.

I can imagine she casts a spell over her students, too.

She smiles and sits opposite us on one of the sturdy stuffed chairs. There's no pretense in her. She doesn't seem capable of one false word or move, and she hasn't even opened her mouth, yet. And a pretty set of peach colored lips they are, also. I'd like to see the man who convinced her to marry him. I'd like to know what kind of magic influence he must be able to cast toward Jennifer O'Brien.

"You're here about Franklin Toliver," she says as she settles in. Her mother didn't come into the living room with her. It's just the three of us, and there's no sign of her father.

"Yes," Justin says. "As your mother likely told you, we'd like to know about your relationship with him at college, a few years ago."

"He was a few years ahead of me, but they kicked him out his sophomore year. I was just a freshman. It took me five years to get through because I had a double major."

She makes me melt, just listening to her softly muted, hypnotic voice. She sounds like a soprano, but there's no sharp, high-pitched edge to her voice. She speaks in a voice that you're compelled to listen to—every syllable of every utterance. Jennifer is the complete package. I'm getting the idea why Franklin placed her on a pedestal. I see why she came off so differently from any other girl he ever knew.

"You think Franklin's a murderer?"

I look at her vivacious mouth, and I have the urge to kiss her, and I wonder how Franklin could control himself when he was with her. But she seems, somehow, unapproachable, as well. This woman is a puzzle to me, so perhaps that's how Toliver saw her, too. Elevated. Aloof. Goddess-like. But who the hell knows what was going on in that crazy bastard's head. Maybe she was a younger version of some idealized mother he never had. Maybe.

"He's a person of interest," I tell her. I dread repeating that line to everyone we interview, but it's all we've got to say, officially, about our most likely suspect. Hell, he's not our most likely perp—he's *it*. If someone else really did those women, then we really are chasing a spook, not a human prey.

"I only knew him briefly."

"Were you very close?" Justin asks her. She crosses her long, lithe legs and I have a tremendous desire to groan, but I somehow control myself.

What kind of genes produced this offspring? I'd love to get a look at her old man.

"We were friends. Nothing more."

"Did Franklin confide in you?" Justin continues.

I can see my partner is properly impressed by Jennifer. He's got a frozen grin on his face that tells me he's struggling not to be intimidated by the hoodoo Ms. O'Brien seems to spread as she enters a room.

"Yes. I think so. But he was a very private person. Anyone could tell he was troubled. But if I thought he was capable of doing all those terrible things you think he did, I would've contacted you long ago."

"We're not here to make you feel accountable for anything he might have done, and we still have nothing to formally charge him with. We just want to bring him in for questioning."

She looks at me and smiles, and I can feel a little quivering going on somewhere way deep inside me. I have the urge to call this off before I start slobbering all over myself. Whatever she has is powerful shit. It's like being in a room with one of those for-real faith healers. She has that kind of charisma.

"You think he did those terrible things, don't you, Detective...ah Detective, what's your name?"

"Mangan. I'm sorry. This is Detective Grant. That was very rude of us."

"Don't apologize....You think he did all those awful things, don't you."

I watch her eyes. They're green, sort of emerald-colored. Quintessentially Irish, they appear. Her hair is red, true red, and she has light freckles dotting her pale, fragile complexion.

"Tell me the things Franklin Toliver told you, Jennifer. Tell me why he picked you to talk to. You were special to him, weren't you," I tell her.

She smiles. Then the look fades and her face darkens.

"He was like looking into a dark corner in your bedroom. He was like looking into a dark corner when you were afraid and you didn't know what was in the room with you when the lights were all out. He was like that moving thing that you just barely notice out of the corner of your eye, but you can't quite make out exactly who or what the moving entity really is.

"I never knew Franklin. Not the way he wanted me to know him.

"He frightened me, Detective Mangan. He frightened me terribly, but he never once laid a hand on me."

She smiles at me strangely, and the hair on the back of my neck stands up as if a chill breeze has just crept up behind me and grazed me from behind.

27

I'd like to meet her fiancé. I really would. I'd like to see him melt before her gaze, the way everyone else seems to.

"Have you heard anything from Franklin Toliver since your college years?" I ask her.

She finally seems taken off guard.

"No.... Why would I want to talk to Franklin?"

The calming smile reappears on her lips and face, just as if it were all conjured for Justin Grant and me.

"I was thinking it'd be more likely he would want to contact you, since he thought so highly of you."

"That's very flattering," she smiles warmly at me. "But I don't think he'd even remember me, after all these years."

"I think he'd remember you," Justin adds. "You're apparently the only young woman he *didn't* abuse, one way or another, all the way from high school through the university."

"I can't believe I'm all that special in his life," she insists.

Modesty doesn't play as well, with her. In my experience, really beautiful women and extraordinarily handsome men are well aware what they look like. How they hide that self-knowledge is another thing, however. Some aren't able to come off as anything but arrogant about their physical attractiveness, and others seem at ease with the fact that God spent way too much time with them.

I think she's lying, and I think Franklin has been hanging onto his past association with her. At least he's been trying to, I have to believe, unless he's even a crazier son of a bitch than we think he is. I can't see how you'd cut this young woman adrift from your dinghy unless she insisted on it, and I get the impression she doesn't really believe Toliver is capable of what we think he's capable of.

"Withholding information in a possible homicide case is a bad thing to become involved with, Jennifer. You're a teacher. You're going to be married. You don't want any clouds over all that. Now I ask you again. Has Franklin Toliver contacted you since you went to school together?"

It really bothers me to cause her to switch her amicable attitude toward me and replace it with the attitude she now aims my way. It's the first time she's flashed hostility at either of us, but it's a subtle shade of animosity. I think it's difficult for her to flash negativity at most anyone. It's the teacher in her, especially the teacher and caretaker of young children in her. They are inclined to keep it light, keep it happy, almost all of the time. Otherwise you'd have a herd of weeping little shits on your hands. And I think she shows that same upbeat face toward most of the folks she comes in contact with.

"Tell me, Jennifer. We have a pretty fair idea that your old schoolmate has murdered at least six women."

Justin is watching her intently. I turn to him, but his eyes never leave Jennifer O'Brien.

For the first time since we laid eyes on her, Jennifer appears anxious. There's none of her original cool remaining. She fidgets. She squirms just noticeably.

"You're not the person we came to grill or make feel bad," I tell her. I don't want her clamming up and lawyering up or whatever she figures she's supposed to do from watching all those TV cop shows.

"We're not here to make you uncomfortable," Justin reassures her. "We're here to find out where Franklin Toliver is so we can find out if he really is the man who killed the six women. If we catch him, it'll either exonerate him or stop the slayings. It's win/win, Jennifer."

She becomes noticeably more ill at ease when Justin talks to her. I noticed how she backed off, just barely, when I introduced him to her. I thought it might just be shyness.

"What brought you two together at Western?" I ask her. "Just the class you were in?"

She shifts her eyes toward me, once more, and I think I have a subtle odor in my nostrils.

"I hope you haven't forgotten my original question. We'll get back to it in a second, but what was it that helped you hit it off so well with Franklin that he's kept you in mind all these years later?"

She's decided to withdraw from the field. It's in her body language. She uncrosses her legs and settles back against the sofa on which she's perched. She even looks like a bird ready to take flight. There's a hawk approaching, she figures, and Jennifer is now a bird of prey trying to escape a predator—and I'm the predator.

"You can talk to us here or talk to us downtown."

I hate the bad cop scene, but she doesn't leave me much choice.

"He said he was in love with me. I told him I didn't feel the same way, but I wanted to be friends, and he couldn't live with those limitations, he said, back at school. And then he got thrown out, and I thought it was the end of it. But six months after they'd expelled him at Macomb, I started getting phone calls.

"We used to talk for hours. I enjoyed the conversations. We looked at things...similarly, I guess you'd say."

"What kinds of things do you mean?" I ask her.

She shifts her eyes just momentarily at Justin, and then she darts her gaze back at me. She seems to have trouble looking at my partner, at least for any length of time.

"You have a variety of kids at the school where you teach?" I ask her.

"Variety?" she repeats.

"I mean racially," I answer.

This is a far southwestern suburb, Orland Park. There aren't many African Americans in the vicinity, yet. This is where whites headed when the blockbusting began, almost twenty-five years ago. The white population of Chicago moved to the burbs, west and south and north.

"Racially?" she parrots.

She's not going to make it easy on me.

"Do you have any African American students in your class? What grade do you teach?"

"I teach the fifth grade at Henry Harrison Middle School. And we have Hispanic and Asian—"

"Do you teach any black children, Jennifer?"

Her eyes smolder at me as if she figures she's finally snared into answering.

"No. Not this year. But we do have black children at our school, yes."

"But *you* don't have any."

"I already told you. No."

The friendly love goddess has turned into a stonewalling adversary, I'm thinking. I look over at Justin, but he's still watching her while she shoots lasers my way.

"Has that man contacted you lately?" I finally throw her way.

She looks as though she'd like to come off that couch at me. That's the way I read her. I can see her tightening in her upper body. I can see the flush of anger in her cheeks, in the jut of her magnificent jaw.

"He has. He's never stopped."

"Do you know where he is, now?" Justin engages.

She avoids looking at my partner. She figures there's no advantage in trying to seem indifferent toward Justin, any longer.

"No. He never says. I think he's been moving about because he knows all of you want to get hold of him. He says it doesn't matter what the truth is. You've already made up your minds he's responsible for what happened."

"What does he tell you about that?" Justin asks her.

She finally eyes my partner.

"He says you're going to get him because he's white and they were all black. He says anybody knows he wouldn't dirty himself with people like them."

Justin smiles, now that she's exposing her colors, as it were.

208

"He's never told you where he is or where he's headed."

"No. And I've never asked."

"You remember what I told you about holding back information," I warn her.

"I have a fine memory, Detective Mangan. I think I've talked to you both enough. If you need to talk to me again, I want a lawyer to be there when you do."

I stand. Justin gets up, as well.

"Maybe you'd like to see the crime photos, Jennifer. Maybe Franklin's not the good guy you think he is or that he says he is. After you've seen the photos, maybe when your nightmares stop, maybe you'll have a different take on Toliver."

"If he calls, we'd like you to let us know. I mean if he calls again."

We turn and head toward the door. She stands and quietly watches us go, but she doesn't throw any friendly salutations our way on our way out.

"Such a pretty girl. You think she's a racist, right?" Justin says as I head us back north on Mannheim Road—they call it LaGrange Road, here in the south suburbs.

"What do you suppose caused her to be a soulful best friend of Franklin's?"

"Hard to believe, anyway."

"Why? Because she's so damned good looking? What makes you think assholes *look* like assholes?"

"Yes, I know, Danny. It just seems—"

"A pity. I'll go along with that."

He watches the park district woods go by as we head back toward Headquarters. We'll catch 55 to Chicago to go back to work.

"We need to have her phone tapped," I tell Justin.

"She's smart. She won't say anything to him that we can use."

"We can hope to get his number and location, if he's dumb enough to talk long enough for us to trace the call."

"When has a movie dick ever successfully traced a call and caught a guy as a result of the trace? I've never seen it once."

"Yeah? Well, we have to hope he does something really stupid some time very soon or we'll both be doing traffic in the Loop with the old guys waiting on retirement, and that can't be the fast lane you were hoping to be tooling down, no?"

He grins at me and then turns back toward the scenery that's receding behind the Ford I'm driving.

I arrange a wiretap with my Captain and with the Cook County District Attorney's Office, and the County Prosecutor gets a judge to sign off on the tap. It'll be up and running in eighteen hours. Cook County knows Franklin is high profile, and even though Cook County is heavily Democratic, as is the Lieutenant Governor, there doesn't seem to be any opposition, lately, to our playing tag with Franklin Toliver. I think even Fast Tony Vronski wants this little problem to just disappear.

But I don't trust that slimy prick Vronski as far as I could throw his Olds 98. He's still a snake in the elephant grass, as far as I can figure it.

I drive by Bill O'Connor's high-rise with and without Justin as often as I can, and I make my presence obvious to my favorite doorman, there. I make sure I slow down so Mr. Swanson can be certain it really is me, and I sometimes smile and wave at him.

Even amateur sleuths understand that the more time that goes by after a homicide, the harder it becomes to apprehend the suspect or suspects. Most killers aren't like John Dillinger or Baby Face Nelson— they don't leave calling cards or other signature remnants that shout out whose work the slayings were. Dillinger killed cops, so everyone from the Chicago Outfit to the FBI lusted for his blood, and eventually that blood lust was sated.

We're after the murderer of six black hookers, and even though the media has helped fuel the fire for justice, it really would have expedited things if Franklin had whacked a cop. Then all bets are off, all the hounds are unleashed, and politics can't intrude on an investigation into the killing of a police officer.

They were just whores, the lowest feeders on the food chain. And color them black to make them even more disposable. No matter how much righteous indignation the *Times* can drum up with their reward money, the facts still remain:

Nobody really gives a shit about six dead nigger prostitutes.

Ugly word, nigger? Sure. But it's the word used, still, by a good-sized chunk of the Caucasian population. Maybe they don't use it out in the open as often—Archie Bunker on the TV show made it painfully public that it was uncool to call blacks by that coinage, along with coon, spearchucker and so on. But the word remains, and so does the sentiment. Race is a very big issue in Chicago, and it's a very big deal everywhere. I can't think of a color-blind society anywhere on Earth. Some places are more liberal than others, but Chicago is a very segregated city. Neighborhoods have very well defined color boundaries, and anybody who claims that their hood is racially diverse and color-blind is probably stretching the truth.

Racism was dominant in Vietnam, too. We looked at them as gooks, and they hated us right back as white outlanders—even though a lot of American GIs came in assorted flavors and ethnic backgrounds.

There are all kinds of roadblocks cluttering our way, on this case. Maybe when Justin entered the fray I became even more aware of how nasty this color business can be. I fought with a whole lot of brothers in Vietnam. There were American Indians and Hispanics and Asian brothers in arms, as well. We really did try to look out for each other's asses. We really did claim we'd all go down together. At least in the Rangers things were that way. There was a team concept, and ego was left out of it, in the field, especially.

But I'm certain we all had that ingrown notion that we really weren't all the same on the inside, somewhere deep in the fabric. It's too deeply instilled in most of us. *This* separates me from you. *That* keeps us distinct from each other. Like that Frost poem about walls. There has to be something to keep us all at arm's length from each other. There is something fearful about allowing the other guy or woman to encroach on our sacred private property.

In spite of all of the above, or maybe because of it, I'm going to catch that son of a bitch, Franklin Toliver.

And I'm going to throw in whoever it was that put out Sharon O'Connor's headlights, as well.

28

Lila stops by my office on her first day back to work, two weeks
before Christmas. Justin is in his own cubicle, three doors down.
He's calling about the phone tap to see if there were any positives from
Franklin. I have my doubts we'll catch him this way because I know
Jennifer O'Brien has already called him on an outside line, probably at a
booth, and she's warned him away. So we'll have to start tailing her,
Justin and I agreed.

"You look good," I tell her as she stands in the doorway. "Got
time to talk?"

She enters my office and sits down at the lone chair opposite me.

"Do you feel all right, really?"

She grins slyly at me.

"I'm out of sick leave."

"Come on!"

"No. I feel okay. I just get tired easily, so I can only work half
shifts until the doctor signs off that I'm fit."

Her paleness is evident. The white is whiter than usual. She looks
anemic, but I'm no MD.

"How's Kelly?"

"Getting over the boyfriend, but doing a lot better than she was two months ago."

"Yeah. I talked to her last night."

"Then why'd you ask?" I smile.

She returns the gesture, and I recall again why I've been in love with her for as long as I have.

"Just to hear you say it, Danny."

I want to tell her that I still want her back as a partner and that I still want her to move in with me, but the words simply won't get started.

"What's going on with the Toliver case?"

I inform her where we are.

"At least it's the first decent lead you've had in months, no?"

"It was your case, too, Lila."

She sends her glance down at the table in front of us.

"Well, yeah, but not anymore," she concludes.

"Yes. Not anymore."

"What about the O'Connor thing?" she wants to know.

"Dead in the water. I think the doorman let the killer in or he was drunk and asleep when the guy made entry. Either way, he's fucked if he tells me either of the above, so he's not talking, and right now I have no evidence that this guy let the boogey man in the house, so we're waiting."

"Hurry up and wait. Just like the military."

I nod at her, but what I really want to do is kiss her. *All over her face.*

"I missed you. I still do," I finally blurt.

"I missed you, too."

I notice the past tense in her reply, and my heart sinks again, the way it always does when she puts me to the side.

"I better boogey," she says, and she rises out of the chair with a noticeable effort.

"You're not really out of sick days," I say to her.

"Not really."

"Then you look like you need a nap."

"I'll learn to doze on the job," she smiles with a strained effort.

"You wouldn't know how to do that."

"You think?"

"I know."

"I'll see you around, Danny."

"I still want you back."

"You mean as your partner?"

"I mean every way you got."

She gives me an intense stare, but then she smiles again and walks out my door.

Justin and I have arranged with the Cook County Police and with the Sheriff's Office and with the Orland Park PD to keep tabs on Jennifer O'Brien. Regular tabs. There's no money to watch her all three shifts on a twenty-four hour basis just because I think she's still in touch with Toliver, but there's enough suspicion about her to keep an eye on her at night. During the day, she's a teacher at that grade school, and I've already contacted her principal, a guy named Elroy, and he's agreed to call me if she ever takes a personal day or if she calls in sick. I'm also planning on checking in with Jennifer's fiancé. I called the mother, and she told me his name was Rick Carlisle, and she even sprung for a phone number. I could hear the concern in both the principal's voice and Mrs. O'Brien's tone when I talked to them both.

But I didn't intimate that there was any problem when I talked to the two. I just told them it was routine follow up. They still sounded wary, the way I would if I were them.

Jennifer has shown no inclination to go out at night—except with Rick Carlisle, on the weekends and once or twice during the week. I'm wondering if Carlisle knows about the other man in his future bride's life. I wonder if he knows his fiancée's attitude toward non-whites. Maybe he feels the same way.

I'll have to ask him, straight up.

Kelly comes back from Northern Illinois University at the end of the second week of December. She's just finished final exams for the semester, and she looks haggard, all tuckered out. Her weight looks as if it's stabilized since I saw her last at Thanksgiving, but she appears weary.

"You feeling all right?" I ask her as we drive toward Franco's Pizza on the Friday she's come home.

"I just need to vegetate for the three weeks off."

She smiles, and I begin to think that maybe she's gotten over Michael.

"I've gotten over Michael," she says when I hit the first red light.

"You don't need to—"

"I know you want to know, and I'm glad you care about me, Dad."

I can remember the silent little person I had to deal with during those years of booze, drugs and bulimia. She doesn't sound like that young woman at all, and this time my major pump swells and rises in my chest. This has the chance to be the first happy Christmas in my recent memory. I can't recall looking forward to the Holidays in so long that....

In so long that there *is* no recollection of a happy Yuletide in my head. It's always been just another day or two—Christmas and New Year's. Just two days that everybody else got off and went to exotic places like Vail, Colorado, or some other resort, say, in a tropical clime. The Holidays were just notches on the calendar. They were just red Xs when I was in Vietnam. Two more days I was short, once I got past both of them on the calendar.

I've always dreaded holidays of any kind. I must have looked forward to them when I was in school, but as an adult, I don't remember getting all wound up with anticipation about them.

"Are you going to stay at Northern, Kelly?"

She looks over at me and smiles and nods.

"You getting on better, lately?"

She nods again.

"Well?"

"It's not a boyfriend, but I've been going out with a few guys I've met in the dorm and in class. It's that I'm starting to settle in, I guess. I like the teachers and I like my classes. Mostly I think it's because Michael was why I went to this school, Dad. It really boiled down to him, and I think I depended on him to make me happy. And then when it went bad....

"Sr. Catherine talked to me about depending upon other people for my happiness. She said I'd have to learn to live alone, for a time in my life. She told me most people can't be happy unless their time is filled with another person's presence, and she said that putting my happiness in someone else's hands would make me a lifetime dependent. You know what she means?"

I look at my daughter, and I remember the hard years we just came out of. I remember those years and the years on top of them that were spent trying to get over the loss of her mother, Mary.

Life has not been especially kind to me, over the last ten years or so. I haven't been crippled or killed, like a number of my brothers in arms were, and I've never starved or suffered privation. Maybe just those weeks of training I survived and my trigger time in the jungle in Asia. But I came out of all that in one physical piece, so I could be far worse off.

The thing is, I can't recall a time when I had cause to celebrate. I never knew joy, but I knew plenty of other people who did, and I felt cheated, frankly. I understand that a great many fellow human beings suffer far more than I have or ever will, but somehow that knowledge gives me no comfort.

I suppose I'm greedy. I want to be in love and have that object of my affection love me the same way with the same, equal energy. I want my daughter to love her father the way children love their old men.

Oh, and throw in justice, when it comes to the product of work that I do.

"You sure you're okay? We can look at other schools over your break. I'll take some time and go around with you."

"No, Dad. I'm going to stay. I actually like it there, now."

We arrive at yet another red light. Franco's is in Evergreen Park, not far from where we live.

It's flurrying outside, but nothing's sticking to the ground. We haven't had a measurable snowfall this winter, yet, but winter doesn't officially begin for a few days.

"You sure?"

She nods her head and smiles. The light turns green, and I press the gas gently. I'm not really in a hurry to get anywhere. It seems like a long time since we've been together, but it was just Thanksgiving. We went out to a restaurant, as usual, because I have no clue how to do a turkey. And neither of us has any family, and Lila was with her own people on that day.

"How is Lila?" Kelly asks.

She makes me wonder if she's a mind reader. She's done this to me lots of times. She'll bring up someone I'm thinking about, right at the very moment.

"She's back to work, but only part time until she feels full strength."

"She's not your partner, anymore?"

I look over at my tired-out kid. The crap life's thrown at her in her nineteen years, she ought to be a little worn thin.

"No. She's partnered to Brian Anderson, now."

"Who's he?"

"Younger than I am. In his early thirties. About Justin's age."

I've introduced Kelly to Justin Grant, and she took to him immediately. She thinks he's very handsome, she told me. I'm gratified to see that my daughter doesn't have difficulty with Justin's color. I've never heard Kelly talk the hate talk that they are prone to, on the streets. She was saved from that set of problems, at least. She never heard the hate talk from me, I know. I have enough problems without that shit in my repertoire.

"You're really sure you want to stay where you are?"

"I want to go into medicine. After four years, I want to apply at the University of Chicago, if my grades are good enough. If they're not, I'll stick with nursing."

"Hell, you got a plan."

We hit another red. Maybe we'll be eating pizza before the dawn breaks, this way.

"I got a plan, Dad, yes," she giggles at me.

"You want to go to school until you're an old lady."

"I'd be in my late twenties, maybe thirty."

"And you'd be in debt up to your fanny."

"I'll try and get grants. Maybe scholarships. My dad is a single parent," she reminds me.

"And I'll put my ass in hock up to my nostrils to get you through, if that's what you really want."

She reaches across at me and extends her hand. I take her left with my right and give it a hard squeeze. Then we release, and Franco's sign is lit, just ahead on the right. The snow is coming down a little harder, now.

"I'm sorry," she says, when I pull to a stop in the parking lot.

"Sorry about what?"

"All the years I wasted, hating you."

"I never hated you. Not once," I tell her.

"I know. That's why I'm so sorry, Dad."

She comes across the seat and hugs me. And then she springs toward the passenger's door and gets out into the parking lot.

I don't know what to get Kelly for Christmas. I usually just got her clothes that she took back to exchange for what she really wanted. This time I figure the gift has to be more special.

Christmas morning we're going to the eight o'clock. Then we're headed off to one of the few eateries that's open on Christmas. I tell her we'll open gifts when we get back from lunch or brunch or whatever this meal will be.

We walk out the house and find that there's a light dusting of snow on the ground, but there's not enough to screw up the roads. The sun is out, but it's brisk and cold.

She sees the Chevy Impala sitting out at the curb, but she doesn't act surprised. Until I hold out the keys in front of me.

There's a question on her face.

"Merry Christmas," I tell her.

"Daddy!"

"Don't get too excited. It's used. But the mileage is great, and I got hooked up to the car via Auto Theft/Robbery. It's a great deal, and like I said, low miles. It's a nice ride, no?"

She rushes me and gives me a crushing embrace. Tears stream down her face.

"Now I won't have to make all those pain in the ass rides to take you home, and now you can come home whenever you feel like it."

She continues the bear hug.

"You like that shade of red?"

It's a cherry colored two-door, an '84. New set of tires.

"I love it."

"Good, because you're driving."

29

The new FBI agents look very much unlike the first two boobs we encountered, Lila and I, when we began the Twin Killer case. The older of the two is named Jeffrey Mason. He has silver and black hair, and although he must be closing in on retirement, he has icy, intelligent blue eyes that tell me he's nobody's fool.

The other agent's name is Bill Munson. He's perhaps forty-five, but he's just as intense-looking as his partner. Munson is semi-bald, with that wisp of hair he combs over the top of his head to make him appear as if he's still got fur on his dome.

The Captain has arranged this meeting for us at FBI headquarters, about a mile from CPD's home base.

Mason talks first after Justin and I are seated in their spacious interview room on the second floor in the Federal Building.

"We're involved in the investigation of hate crimes," he tells us.

We're seated opposite each other—FBI on the window side and Justin and I are across from the two special agents. I'd almost think it was done intentionally, to keep the light in our eyes and at their backs, but the Captain told me to set aside our grievances against the Bureau for one day because they had some goodies for us.

Munson remains mute, his hands folded on the table like a school kid's.

"You're interested in Franklin Toliver for the so-called 'Twin Killings.' Right?"

I smile and nod. I'm trying to be cooperative.

"Toliver has been associated with the Aryan Nation for the last four years."

"The neo Nazis?" Justin asks.

Both of the FBI guys' last names begin with an "M." I'm thinking of calling them after the famous candies with that same letter doubled up—M and Ms.

"Yes. The Aryan Nation. Toliver is on their rolls, but we only just associated him with the guy you're looking for."

"I thought you were looking for him, too," I tell them both.

"We are," Munson finally joins in. "But the Area Director has made it clear we are to cooperate with the Chicago Police Department. He's very adamant that we do so."

"Why the big change of heart?" I smile.

"We don't have the time or the inclination to address that issue," Mason replies. He's giving me his very best steely glare.

"Okay. What's going on?"

They both look back at me.

"We picked up information on Toliver during a phone call to the local commandant of the Aryan Nation. The commandant's name is Larry Pickett. It seems that Pickett recruited Toliver, four years ago, and they're very tight."

"And we're hearing all this just now, but there's nothing political going on with Franklin Toliver's daddy? Is that what we're supposed to swallow?" I ask Mason.

He ignores me.

"We have a phone number for Toliver. At least the phone he used to contact Pickett."

"And you didn't race over and cuff Toliver? Why?"

Munson clears his throat.

"We have his apartment under surveillance. We're trying to

gather information on the hierarchy of the Aryan Nation, and we didn't want to disturb an ongoing investigation," he tells Justin and me.

"In other words," my partner says, "you don't like Toliver as your primary, but you think he can help you develop a case against Pickett."

"We did. But we realize that Toliver poses too much of a threat against the public, and the murders fall under your jurisdiction," Mason explains.

"I think you're both full of shit," I tell the two FBI guys.

Mason and Munson, the M and M twins, sit quietly, patiently.

"I think someone has yanked your leashes and told you to hand Toliver over after all this time because somebody wants Franklin to go away and disappear and stop getting his famous last name in the papers so that daddy can make his run for governor—or maybe someone likes Raymond Toliver for VP material in the Presidential election. Could that be a possibility?

"You boys are very fortunate that Franklin has gone dormant with regard to killing people-- as far as we know, anyway. Because if you've been holding back from us all these months, the way I suspect you have, your asses'll be candidates for the deep fryer. Shame on you. Shame on all of you."

He slides the manila file over to Justin. Then we both rise and leave.

We set up surveillance on the apartment from which Franklin made the call to Larry Pickett. There has been no one in or out of here for these two days in January. It's mid-month and frigid. The only good news is that it's been dry.

Kelly's back at second semester classes. My dog Sonny is chewing the shit out of anything he can get his teeth on because his one-year choppers are coming in, and he's become a major pain in the ass, so I've had to keep him in a metal kennel when he's indoors and I'm not home. Otherwise it's like termites going through the furniture and the curtains. The vet says it'll halt once the teeth really come in. But I had to lock him up in that kennel, and it damn near breaks my heart to see him cooped up that way. I keep telling myself it's just temporary.

Lila is the veritable passing ship in my life at Headquarters. I see her in the halls infrequently, and since she doesn't call me at all, I don't phone her, either. I can't remember when I ever had a love life, after high school.

The apartment building is on the far southwest side, just barely within city boundaries. It's fortunate, because otherwise we'd have to be sharing the detail with a number of other agencies and police forces. This is our territory, however, and we're handling it. And this time there's somebody here all three shifts and every day. Apparently our honchos downtown have decided we've fucked with Franklin long enough.

Justin and I are on third shift. I don't mind midnights now that Kelly is out of the house, but I never liked being out on the street at night when she was home alone. Sonny can take care of himself, but there is no really secure neighborhood in Chicago. Bad things happened in Old Town and on the Gold Coast. Those two hoods are as diverse as you can get, but people got whacked in both locations. There really is no safe haven in this world, let alone in this city. Point your finger in any direction, and evil lives there.

I sleep every chance I get when I have to watch a site. Justin's on and I'm off. That way we both get a chance to be alert when something happens. We both try to gut it out at the same time, we both get tired, and when you're fatigued, you make mistakes. Vince Lombardi said, "Fatigue makes cowards of us all." The Rangers lived by those words, and that was why we never got more than three or four hours sleep at any one time, because if you learn to combat weariness, you learn how to handle guerilla warfare. There are no hours, in combat. You have to react when you'd rather be crapped out, and you have to learn, also, how to not give in to absolute fatigue.

It's three forty-two A.M. We're the only car parked in front of 12347 South Westmore. The apartment is part of a three flat. These residences are very old but very well kept up. This is one of the few all-white neighborhoods left on the southwest side. Hoods are either well integrated or black, in this vicinity. These few square blocks are the exception.

At three fifty-six, a car pulls up and parks about fifty feet in front of us. Justin nudges me, but I'm not asleep anyway. Sometimes I can't conk, even though I keep my eyes shut.

Justin slumps down behind the wheel.

I have my eyes just over the dashboard, and I see it's a dark sedan, but I can't see the make or the plates. When the driver gets out, we both see he's the right height and the right build. He's not wearing a hood, but it's too dark to see what color his hair is. It is only apparent that he's a white male and that the body size fits our bill.

When he heads right toward the apartment building we're watching, Justin calls for backup. He tells them it's a priority and to haul ass here.

Then we get up and slowly and quietly get out of the unmarked ride. We don't shut the doors because he's not inside the entry yet.

When we get to the door, he's already inside and on his way up. The top apartment on floor three is where Toliver made the call.

The second entry inside the outer door is locked. I have a pick with me.

"Highly illegal," Justin says with a smirk.

"Yes. It certainly is. Want to wait for backup and a battering ram?"

He shakes his head.

"So," I say, and I proceed to insert the needle nose of the pick. I have it opened in less than a minute.

"It was still opened when we arrived, right?" I look at my partner.

"How many years for B and E?" he asks, deadpan.

We walk softly and slowly up the three flights of steps. There is carpeting on the stairs, so our footfalls are muffled. I don't hear any screeching of tires outside, so I figure we can't wait. We've waited long enough on this guy. It's time to meet Franklin Toliver face to face.

So I kick open the heavy wooden door with a well-practiced heel that has blown open other entries many times before. The blow from my foot sends the door inward with a boom. And when we rush through the portal, I see the gun.

I have my .38 raised as I enter the apartment, and Justin is one stride behind me. I see the orange flame spit at us both as I step inside, and I feel my own hand rise as if by itself, and then I've loosed two

225

rounds right at the source of the orange blast, and now I hear a scream from in front of me, and then I hear a thump on the floor.

Only three shots have rung out—two were mine. Justin never got off a shot that I heard. I see a body slumped before me. He's not moving, and it's so dark in here I can't see his face.

"Justin?" I say as I turn back toward the doorway.

Justin doesn't answer because he's sprawled back out onto the landing.

The suspect's name is Marvin Gillespie. He's a member of the Aryan Nation, also. The apartment was being shared by Gillespie and Toliver, but the man I shot won't be talking for a few hours, at least. I caught him in the chest and in the face, but he's expected to live.

Justin Grant, my partner of these few months, died on the way to St. Helen's Hospital in the Loop. I took the ride with him, but he was never conscious. He barely had a pulse when they put him on board the ambulance. He never spoke. He never opened his eyes. The shot that killed my partner blasted right through his heart. Gillespie turned out to be a marksman. It'll only took him one bullet to kill Franklin. If this were the war, that would equal maximum efficiency.

I should be grieving for Justin, but all I feel is numb. It happened so fast that I suppose it hasn't really registered, at the moment. But I dealt with death for two tours in Vietnam. Guys went down around me, and I had to swallow the grief because we had to survive—*I* had to go on. There was no community in death. The man on the ground was gone. You had to leave him to death and keep going or soon you'd join him. It really was a simple matter of survival.

This is not Vietnam and it's not a war. This is The World. My partner has been murdered and Marvin Gillespie will be executed by the State of Illinois for killing a policeman. I should feel *differently*. All deaths are not equal. *This is The World!*, I keep telling myself. This is not some fucking rainforest, and I should feel grief, I should feel loss.

Justin and I were almost friends. We never had time to get all the way there. I should be struggling with my emotions, feeling the stings of tears in my eyes.

But there is nothing. *Nihil. Nada.* Just a vast suction. Just a vacuum. Nothing and nothing and nothing.

I sat at the hospital for two hours after the ER doctor confirmed that Justin really was gone. The ER physician wanted to take a look at me because he told me I might be in shock or ready to enter into it. I convinced him I was all right. I lied effectively to him, and he let me be. So I sat in the waiting room alone until dawn was just a rumor off to the east, out the window and behind the plate glass that I sat in front of.

I'm able to talk to Marvin Gillespie the next afternoon, with the permission of his surgeon and attending physician, Dr. Phillips.

The Captain sent Sergeant Granger to be with me. When I went into Headquarters the following morning, he gave me the lecture that there would be an investigation into the shootings. I'd be talked to by the Internal Affairs people, which is SOP after all discharges of our weapons in the line of duty.

Granger is an old hand. He's an outrageously handsome man. He'd be a duplicate of Paul Newman, the actor—if Granger had a helluva lot more hair. He's divorced, I understand, and quite the lady killer, mop or no mop. More importantly, he's here to make sure I'm all right and that I don't throw any more slugs into Gillespie. The Captain suggested someone else talk to this wounded member of the Aryan Nation, but I apparently convinced him that I was the right interrogator and that it was all business, nothing personal.

He sent Granger anyway, just in case.

Gillespie is covered with tubes, but I'm amazed at how good his color is. *He looks too damned good.*

He has just the faintest of sneers on his lips as we enter the private room. There are two uniforms on the door. Granger has his eyes trained onto me. I can feel them piercing my back.

Dr. Eunice Phillips waits for us, next to Gillespie's bed.

"You only have five minutes, and I mean five minutes," she tells us. Then she leaves the room, and Marvin's sneer leaves his face.

"*Doctor?*" he whines as she leaves. But Phillips keeps on going.

"I'm glad you can talk, Marvin. This won't take even the five minutes. You've got this one shot. If you cooperate, maybe they won't execute you, but since you killed a cop, who knows?

"You can locate Franklin Toliver for us and *maybe* catch a break from the judge for your help in clearing up six homicides, or you can pull the trigger on yourself if you don't help us. Because if you stand mute, you piece of shit motherfucker, it's a death sentence for absolutely goddam sure. You read me, asshole?"

There's no defiant leer coming from Gillespie now. He was shocked that Dr. Phillips left him to us, it appears.

"Where is Franklin Toliver?" I ask him.

He looks at Granger with an appeal on his visage. Granger looks out the window behind his hospital bed and refuses to engage with Gillespie.

"Last time. Last chance," I tell Marvin.

"*Where is Franklin Toliver?*"

30

I get off the desk one week later. Before that happened, my release
after Internal Affairs cleared the shoot, I attended Justin Grant's
funeral. His entire family showed, and the family included over one
hundred members. His mother and father and two brothers and three
sisters survive him. There were dozens of other relatives in attendance,
also. The Chicago Police Department does put on an impressive
ceremony. There were a few hundred brother cops there, too, and the
bagpipers played "Amazing Grace," and the color guard sent up several
volleys in Justin Grant's memory.

I guess I'm still in a state of numbness. I went to Dr. Fernandez
the day before the funeral, and she told me I was probably suffering from
delayed shock. She said it would hit me hard some time soon. She also
reminded me about Vietnam and the delayed stress syndrome, which I
haven't experienced to date. The doc told me that just because I hadn't
gone through it didn't mean I wouldn't, eventually.

Then there's the part about feeling guilty that Justin got it and I
didn't. There is always natural relief when you survive and other people
don't, but there is a tendency to blame yourself for the other guy's death.

I could've waited for backup. But we'd still be the ones standing in front of the door Marvin Gillespie was hiding behind. Maybe all those extra troops might have dissuaded Gillespie from bearing down on us, but there's no way of knowing.

The Department has declared it a righteous shoot—my plugging the Aryan Nation asshole.

And Justin's still dead, and replaying it over and over won't change the outcome, and it will not relieve my guilt: My partner was shot and killed.

That makes one Wounded in Action and one Killed in Action, as far as partnering with me goes. I'll be the guy everyone shies away from, now. I don't blame them. What happened to Justin is every cop's spouse's nightmare.

We were all in dress blues for the funeral. The sky was cloudy when it began, and only when everyone in attendance was ready to disperse and depart, it began to snow.

Gillespie told Granger and me that Franklin Toliver only lived in one spot for a few days, and then he moved on. He said that Franklin was becoming a little frazzled by his gypsy-like existence, and he said that Toliver even talked about killing himself. Marvin said he was mostly annoyed that there was all this commotion about the killings of "six nigger sluts." He said he'd like to do six more, but that the heat was too high. Toliver claimed he was waiting until he became a cold case or until the police thought he'd been killed or died from natural causes.

Marvin told Granger and me that Franklin was obsessed with Jack the Ripper, but he didn't enjoy using a knife all that much, not like the famous Brit murderer enjoyed slicing his victims. He said he preferred strangulation because it was slower, and then he said you were able to watch the process of death at your leisure. Stabbing proved too traumatic to his first victims, Marvin said. Toliver wanted to spend some time with them in their last agonies.

I remember I was thinking, while I was listening to Gillespie, the great pleasure it would give me to wrap all those tubes around Marvin's throat and to watch his wattage dim in front of my eyes.

There was no forwarding address. He swore that Toliver never told him where he was going next.

But there was one piece of information that widened my eyes a bit. Marvin talked about the Aryan Nation's walk in Marquette Park, which was coming up on Washington's Birthday, February 22nd. Gillespie swore that Toliver told him he'd be there for the walk, that he wouldn't miss it even if every fucking cop in the city were there.

I believed Marvin Gillespie, but it seemed to be a boast, on Toliver's part, because lots of policemen would be there to keep the peace. You could always expect protesters from the Holocaust Movement, a Jewish survivor organization, to have a heavy presence wherever the Aryan Nation appeared in public. There would be words between the two groups, and frequently it got worse than merely words. People got arrested from both sides, and it was a busy day in whichever Area the Aryans darkened with their presence.

Washington's Birthday is still a few weeks away, and I can't wait for that date to continue going after Franklin. I've stopped blaming myself for Justin's death, at least for now, because I was there, I saw the man who pulled the trigger. And I know why we were at that third floor apartment in the first place. It was to find Franklin Toliver. He's the man who started all these gears in motion, killing six prostitutes, six *human beings*, for better or worse, and starting this whole series of tragedies. It was Franklin who began all this, but I'll be the one who ends it.

I've decided to kill him, if I can.

I still keep tabs on Swanson and on Bill O'Connor. Nothing new turns up. The magic act of getting inside the building to slice open Sharon O'Connor is still unsolved and no closer to resolution than it was the moment we arrived on scene to view her body dangling from the ceiling. No one's talking, Swanson foremost in the mutes associated with this murder.

Big Bill goes on with his syndicated empire, the TV show and the glossy, slick magazine, *BO*. He hasn't missed a beat. There is still no real evidence that there were marital difficulties from either party, and I can establish no new leads into the private love life of Sharon O'Connor. There is of course someone who knows what the story is in this homicide, and if there's one person, it's likely there are others who know who Sharon O'Connor saw last before she wound up at the business end of a rope.

I'm going to lean again on Swanson because he's most vulnerable. I know it sounds unjust and unfair, but O'Connor has too many fine attorneys to shield him from me and my questions. If I don't have a warrant or a reasonable excuse, I can't haul him down here again. He'd claim harassment, and he'd be correct in his claim. My hands are tied with big Bill, unless someone comes forth with an interesting story.

And no one has. Yet.

Lila sticks her head in my doorway.

"Busy?" she asks.

"No. Come on in."

Her face is flush with healthy color. The transformation is remarkable. She's been revitalized, damn near reborn.

"You're looking really good," I tell her.

"Wish I could say the same for you, Danny."

"Thanks for your input," I smile.

She sits down opposite me and looks right at me.

"How's life with Detective Anderson?"

She hesitates. She looks out the window behind me, and then she shifts her gaze quickly back at me.

"Okay."

"Just okay?" I smile.

"He doesn't much like being partnered with a woman, but he tolerates it."

"I'm betting you could kick his ass in a duke out."

She grins.

"I don't hit fellow coppers."

"That's a fine attitude, Lila."

Her hair is shorn close, once again. Her lips are unblemished with artificial color. She's a natural, and she always will be, and it's why I'm nuts about her and always will be, too.

"I was saying. You look bad, Danny. You look gray."

"I got to take care of two jobs with only these two hands."

"You should take time off. I mean, after losing Justin the way you did. That's gotta be difficult."

"It is. But I've lost people before."

I watch her eyes, and they turn sad and morose.

"Yeah, I know. I deserved that."

"Not your fault, Lila."

She looks at me carefully.

"You still seeing the shrink?"

"Yeah. She's a babe, too."

"Is she doing you any good?"

"Someone to talk to, I guess."

Her eyes meet my desk, briefly.

"Maybe you need to take leave. They usually offer extra vacation after something like this."

"I almost lost *you*. Remember? Oh yeah, I forgot. I did lose you, didn't I."

She rises.

"You really ought to take some time off, Danny. You look tired. You look more than tired, and it scares me. And you have to stay healthy for Kelly, you know?"

"Kelly's tough. She survived all those years without me. She can stand on her own."

She glares at me angrily. Her cheeks are crimson. I've never seen this kind of fine anger on her, before.

"Nobody's that tough, Danny. Not you and not me. She needs you now, especially now when you're finally getting things right about each other. You going to throw that away chasing this asshole and all those other assholes? Are they really worth losing your kid a second time? She's all you've got. You better get your head out of your ass."

Lila turns and bolts out of my cubicle.

I haven't been to confession since I was at Trinity High School, back on the southside. I've sloughed off going to mass after Christmas, and I told myself it was because I was busy with my caseload. I'm sure it has something to do with what happened to Justin Grant, however. Violence usually helps to shake anyone's faith.

The first man I killed happened my third week in combat. It was during a firefight near Quang Tri, I think it was, some obscure hamlet in the boonies. We were on a search and destroy mission, and I was deep into the bush waiting for a VC patrol that we knew had been operating out of Quang Tri.

He stepped out of the underbrush into a small clearing, and he became a clean target with a quarter moon's light illuminating the area. I was waiting for him and his platoon, and they showed up as expected, and I gave him a single tap to the forehead from my starlight-scoped rifle, and I sent the back of his skull into the underbrush behind him, and he jerked back like a rag doll on a string.

There was no drama. There was no theatrical tension or storyline. I simply blew his brains out, his platoon retreated back into the jungle, and that was the extent of the night's encounter in Quang Tri.

I have a number of other war stories that I will share with no one, not even a priest. It was the war, and I have to endure the memories.

But I'm here to talk to Fr. Mark, anyway. It's almost Lent, so I'm supposed to go to confession anyway. It's a Saturday evening, and Washington's Birthday is only several days away, and we haven't heard anything new on Toliver's whereabouts, and the surveillance with Jennifer O'Brien has proved fruitless, so far.

If he doesn't show as promised at the rally, we're in the shit. At least I am. And I know that Franklin knows we've talked to Marvin Gillespie. He's aware that Marvin has likely tried to use him as leverage to avoid the hangman. I still have the gut instinct that Franklin will try to fox all of us and show up. I'm betting he'll come in disguise.

Unless he really has a death wish. In which case I hope I'm the cop standing close enough to put one shot, one tap, into his brain pan.

I take my turn in the old-fashioned confession booth. We're

separated by a screen, and you can only faintly make out the outline of the priest's face, on the other side.

"Bless me Father, for I have sinned."

He asks me the last time I went to confession, and I start doing a tap dance. I can't remember when it was, and then I tell him about going at Trinity, a thousand years ago. He laughs gently and tells me to go on.

I tell him I feel bad about the way I talked to Lila the last time we were in my office together. I tell him I should not have blamed her for pulling back from me, that she had every right to decide that I wasn't right for her. I tell the priest that I don't blame her for not loving me, that I'm extremely difficult to love. Case in point being my daughter Kelly. I explain how distant and detached I used to be to her, and he replies that it seems I'm trying to fix that problem if I'm here telling him all about it. I explain that things are better with my daughter now, and he tells me I'm doing all that I can if I'm trying to put our relationship back the way it should be.

"I'm a police officer."

"I know," Fr. Mark says. "I've seen your picture in the paper."

He must have excellent vision through this screen separating us.

"I'm hunting the man who killed six prostitutes. As well as a few other murderers, too."

"I understand."

"I want to kill the man who murdered those women."

"That's not your job, is it."

"No, Father, it's not my job, but my partner was killed during the investigation of this guy."

"So you blame Franklin Toliver—isn't that his name?—for the death of your fellow policeman."

"I blame myself, too."

"Because you're alive and he's dead."

"Yes. And I know I shouldn't think that way."

"It wasn't your fault, was it?"

"I guess not."

"The other man pulled the trigger, didn't he?"

"Yes. He did."

"Killing Toliver won't bring your partner back, and you already knew that."

"I know."

"You have a daughter. She needs you. Why would you jeopardize both your lives for a murderer?"

"I was trained to kill my enemies, Father."

"The war is over."

"I know."

"It doesn't sound like you know."

"I'm not a murderer. I was a soldier, then."

"You're a policeman now. And you're someone's father. Don't be an idiot. Don't throw your life away, Detective Mangan."

"I know you're right, Father."

"Damn right I'm right. Say ten Hail Marys and ten Our Fathers and ten Glory Be's and stop acting like a jackass, Danny."

He slams the screen shut, and it appears that confession's over.

31

Washington's Birthday approaches—it's the fifth of February, today. We have made no new inroads toward Franklin Toliver through Jennifer O'Brien. Our visit to her house must have put both of them on high alert, and none of her incoming phone calls has been suspicious.

I get a call from the DesPlaines PD. They say to rush over to the Toliver residence, but they won't tell me what's going on over the phone. So I check out with the Captain, who raises his eyebrows dramatically when I tell him where I'm headed.

Lieutenant Bill Bartell of the DesPlaines police meets me at the door of the Lieutenant Governor's home. The State Police are milling about out front—there must be ten of them, this time. They don't even look my way, and I don't recognize any of them.

Bartell escorts me into the house, but Mrs. Toliver is nowhere to be seen. He directs us both up the staircase that starts just a few feet from the entryway. We head up a flight, and then turn right, and he stops us at the first door in the hallway.

"It's Mrs. Toliver's bedroom," Bartell explains.

The door is open, and there are photographers and assorted crime scene specialists packing the bedroom. Bartell walks us right past them all until we reach a huge walk-in closet. The accordion doors are opened. I walk closer.

Mrs. Raymond Toliver is hanging by the neck, inside. She's used a wide belt to dangle herself from a hook in the closet. Her feet are barely off the ground. She was shorter than I thought she was, after meeting her the first time. If she'd used her tiptoes, she might not have got the job done.

Her arms dangle loosely. There are no bruises, no signs of a struggle. She is wearing only a light green nightgown, which appears to be silk or something like silk. Her eyes are bugged open, and her tongue bulges and lolls out of the left corner of her mouth. There is a wet spot beneath her, and I can smell the strong stench of urine.

"We're thinking straight suicide, but we'll do an autopsy, of course, and then we'll be more sure. We'll also run toxicology, see if she was on something. But it doesn't look suspicious, at this point. I'm pretty sure it's suicide," Bartell tells me.

"Note?" I ask.

Bartell is middle aged, perhaps fifty. He has the look of an ex-military. Short- cropped hair, what's left of it. Tall, maybe six-two. Probably hits the scales at 215, and he looks like he cares about his body. No excess blubber that I can tell, even though he's wearing a leather jacket that goes thigh length. He appears to be some kind of ex-athlete. He has the prominent jaw minus the jowls. No turkey neck, yet. Wide shoulders, and not much bulge in the middle.

"We haven't found one."

"Was she seeing a doctor?" I ask.

"We have to find that out, too. We'll apprise you of everything as soon as we know."

"I appreciate it, Lieutenant."

"This has got to be more bad luck for Raymond Toliver," he says with a sigh.

"It's been running bad for him. Yes," I concur.

"You ever met him?" he asks me.

I look over at the grotesque thing his pretty wife has become.

"Yeah, I did, but just briefly. We mostly talked about his son."

"Yes. His son. Some guys just seem to find the shit, no?"

There's no grin of pleasure on Bartell's face. He appears genuinely saddened by the death here and by the business with Franklin Toliver that is yet unfinished.

I'm thinking about my own happy life story, but I'm not going to share it with this DesPlaines policeman.

"Bad luck and worse," I finally reply.

We turn from the suspended body just as the morgue people bring on the body bag. I flinch just slightly when I hear them tear it open.

I'm supposed to drive up to DeKalb to see Kelly on Sunday. The Washington's Birthday Aryan Nation rally is scheduled for the holiday on Tuesday. So I can only spend a few hours with her because I have a lot to do to prepare for that get-together in Marquette Park. It's a long shot that Franklin will show up because the police presence will be suffocating. Even if Toliver weren't suspected of wanting to attend, the place'd be crawling with coppers. He really has to be nuts if he shows his sorry ass, but then he's the guy who did six prostitutes in the whores' own backyard. No one can say Franklin's timid about taking chances, and since we have no idea where else he might be, the holiday assembly in the park is our best shot at him. He might just be thinking what I'm thinking: *He can't be that stupid.* Whatever. I'll be there with a host of other assorted five-ohs, including the Federal Bureau of Investigation. They've been sharing information with us, lately, but they'd still like to make the headlines by grabbing Franklin at a high profile event.

I've been worrying about shooting this piece of shit. When I said I'd do him instead of arresting him, I really meant it. And I still might clock him if the opportunity shows up.

The priest was right, however. I'm not a murderer, even though I suppose I was an assassin in Vietnam, if you don't buy the "soldier at war" theory. My killings were all pretty much premeditated in the War, but I also knew the enemy was fully prepared to unload one into me without provocation, as well. It was our job to kill each other, and no one made any fucking bones about it on either side, back then. It was why we were there.

Now I'm a cop. I'm not an executioner. I know I'm sworn to uphold the law, not abuse it for my own personal satisfaction.

More importantly, I care what Kelly would think if she found out I took that law into my own hands. I couldn't face her. I don't want my daughter to be ashamed of me—which is why I've turned down money before I entered Homicide. When I was a patrolman and a green detective, I was offered cash a number of times. I worked with guys who took bucks for favors. I know coppers who have private stashes to put their kids through college, or they have an outside "income" to support their mistresses or summer homes on some fucking lake in Wisconsin or Michigan. I'm not a rat. As long as it didn't affect a case I was working, I kept the "blue silence." If they'd ever asked to buy off a criminal, I would've found a fed or a newspaper guy and I would've squealed like a rat in a trap, and I wouldn't have cared. I can't overcome all the corruption in this city, and it's damn near hopeless. But I can deal with my own white board. I'm not fucking Batman; I'm no caped crusader. I can only handle what's on my own, personal plate. I know it sounds like copping out, like rationalization, but there it is.

I'll never be accused of being a saint. My feet are pretty firmly planted down here in the mud.

Frank Swanson is waiting at my cubicle door.

It's 9:45 P.M. on the Saturday night before the Washington Day fiasco.

"You need to talk, Frank?"

It's six below outside, and there's sweat on his upper lip even though he's holding his ankle-length overcoat over his right arm.

I motion for him to come inside, and he does. He sits down in the chair across from my desk without asking first.

"She had a boyfriend. Her husband knew about it. He never stopped her from seeing this guy. She told me all about it because she paid me to let him in all the time when Bill wasn't around, and that was most of the time."

"Slow down, Frank."

"Can I have something to drink?"

"You mean soda pop?"

"Anything," he answers. "My mouth is so damn dry it hurts to talk."

I walk to the door and then down the hallway. I stop by Sergeant Bill Terrio's cubicle.

"I need a witness to something," I tell Terrio. Bill's been a Homicide for twenty years. He's a gangly-looking veteran of Korea, the war before mine. He's got longer than GI hair, and he looks perpetually unshaven. You might call him swarthy—it's the Eye-tie in him.

He comes back down the hall with me after I buy Swanson a Seven Up from the machine.

When we get back to my office, Frank is still where he was.

"This is Sergeant Terrio. We're going to take a walk to an interrogation room, Frank. It'll be much more comfortable there, okay?"

He gets up from his seat, and then he swoons, and I have to prop him up, momentarily.

"You all right, Frank?" I ask.

Terrio has him by the other forearm.

"I'm gonna lose my fucking job," he tells me, mournfully, as if he's lost a family member.

"You can sell your story to the rag mags and make a million, and then fuck big Bill," the Sergeant smiles at him.

Frank looks over at the Sergeant, and then he regains his legs, and we walk down the hall to the interview room.

I pop open the Seven Up for Swanson. He sips at it slowly, and gradually his paleness passes.

"What was her boyfriend's name?" I ask.

Terrio has paused outside to begin the tape machine inside here. The microphone sits in front of Swanson. He stares at it.

"We have to record this," I tell him.

He nods. Then he watches the Sergeant sit down on the far end of the rectangular table. I'm opposite Swanson.

"Kirk Radley. And this guy is a loser. I could never believe she'd have anything to do with a bum like him."

"Why's he a bum?" I ask.

"He's a small time cocaine peddler. But his clientele are all from the Gold Coast. All the celebs use him because he's not running with the Italians or with any other crew. He does business with them all, so he's just a middleman. So at least they're not buying direct from the Outfit or anybody like that. You understand?"

"He's not as unwashed?" Terrio smiles.

Swanson remembers the Sergeant's heritage, and he blushes a little.

"No offense, Sergeant," Frank apologizes.

"No offense taken. I'm not even Sicilian, so what can I say?" Terrio grins.

"You let Radley in the night Sharon was murdered?" I ask.

"He comes in at least four, five times a week. He comes in late, like he did, so the other residents never get a gander at him. He's smart about going unseen, seeing the trade he's in."

"So he came in that night?" I ask again.

"She paid me to look for him. She paid me two hundred a month to keep my mouth shut. And he pays me, too. He says if I ever told anybody about him coming to see Sharon....He says he knows where I live. He says he'd cut me, Detective Mangan. He'd find me asleep and he'd slit me from my balls to my chin. That's the words he used.

"I knew he was wrong. I knew something like this was gonna happen. I haven't seen him since that night. I don't know how he got out. I might have been in the john."

"Might have been asleep?" I ask.

He looks at both of us sheepishly.

"I'll lose my job. I'm seventy years old and I got no pension. I only got the government insurance for all the shit I have to take for my blood pressure. You know what I'm saying?"

"You're already in for withholding, Frank," Terrio informs him.

"That guy threatened to fucking *kill* me," he pleads to me.

"I think I might be able to help you out, but I can't promise anything," I reply.

Swanson leans back hard against his chair.

"He said he'd cut me open like a fucking fish and gut me if I ever told anybody he was up there with her."

"We'll put people on you, Frank. He won't get close. He won't know you talked to us until it's too late," I soothe him.

"This guy is a fuckin' loon, Detective Mangan. He's the kind of asshole who uses his own product. You understand? His eyes get as big as saucers, every time I let the son of a bitch in. I think he likes threatening me, fuckin' with me. He's smart, though. He knows the security guys' routine, in the building. He knows where they are and when. None of them ever asked me who he was. He went into her place and out of it, like clockwork. I'm the only one who knew.

"O'Connor couldn't.....She used to tell me things about him. Embarrassed the hell out of me. Christ she showed me a tattoo on her right tit when I walked her to the elevator. Almost made me shit.

"O'Connor can't, you know."

"Can't what?" I ask.

"He couldn't *do* her, you know? He couldn't...*get it up*. She told me this shit when she came home one night, all blown out. She was addicted, Detective. She was using coke as a backup. She was snorting heroin, too, I think."

"She told you?"

He looks at me, then at Terrio.

"She'd been off everything for a few months. He sent her to some joint out in Arizona for rehab. She was clean, the night she...died."

That was why the tox tests were negative. She must have been off dope for a long time.

"Why'd she keep seeing Radley if she was off the shit?" I ask.

"She liked bad boys, I guess. I don't know. Her marriage was just for show. He's too busy to care what she does, and I guess he's had this problem for a coupla years. It gets lonely, wouldn't you think?"

He sips again at his Seven Up.

"I woulda told you at first, but this guy....You don't *know* this guy. When he looks at you, your skin shrivels up and tries to crawl off into a corner. I never seen eyes like his, and when he's flyin'? Shit. He's a scary son of a bitch, Detective. I mean fucking frightening. He said he was gonna slit me open like—"

"A fish. I caught that."

"You know where he hangs?" Terrio asks.

"Like I said, he's got clients on the Gold Coast. He's a delivery boy, but he's still a fucking nightmare," Swanson laments.

32

Tomorrow is the Aryan Hatefest in Marquette Park. They're going to get the frigid tundra reception from Mother Nature. It's supposed to top out at zero, with flurries intermittent. With any luck, these neo-assholes will get frostbite on their dicks, and then they won't be able to create any new Hitler Youth. One can always hope.

The Zionists will be there, as well, and they promise to be even more violent than the Aryans. They've got a lot more to be pissed off about than these morphs with the swastikas.

Today, however, Sergeant Terrio and I are more concerned with Kirk Radley.

"You ever read *To Kill a Mockingbird?*" I ask my guinea partner-for-a-day.

"Maybe in high school or sumshit. I can't remember."

I smile and let it go as we get into Terrio's unmarked vehicle. There are three squads headed out with us.

We get a fix on Radley's whereabouts from the DEA and from our own Narcotics squad. They both know him, and they've both allowed him to rattle around selling his death to the elite of Michigan Avenue and the Gold Coast because they'd very much like to know who his suppliers are. Thus he was able to be there the night Mrs. O'Connor met the Light, or whatever Death really is.

He has an apartment on Grand Canal, on the near northside. It's a fairly dumpy hood, but it makes good cover for Radley and people like him because he fits right into this over-ripe environment. It's a high crime area, and there is more than enough illegal drug usage around these parts. But Radley, according to our informant, Swanson, doesn't deal with these locals. He takes his trade over by Lake Michigan, where they can afford coke, the white boy's blow of choice.

It's three A.M. The best time to bust in for a collar is very early morning. We try to catch them in a daze, just after the evening's binge is beginning to peter down to paralysis. Then you don't have to get involved in as many firefights as you would if you tried to take them around lunch or dinnertime.

We pull up to his apartment building first. The squads are right behind us, but they've left all their lights off.

Terrio deploys two uniforms out back, near the alley. The other patrolmen will accompany Bill and me up the stairs. Radley's on the third floor, so it's highly unlikely he'll try to jump out his front windows. He tries to fly, it's two broken legs, and he won't be hard to catch up with.

Terrio picks the entry lock. We don't have a search warrant, and the pick is illegal, but someone will testify that the door was open when we arrived. A uniform props it open with a newspaper, just to make it look believable.

I'm thinking about how Lila took one in the neck. I'm remembering how Justin flopped back and died with the single shot that Marvin threw at him. I don't think I've ever really been afraid to get into a gunfight, but it's not as if I look forward to them. I've just never really worried about getting shot. It never occurs to me that I'll be killed. I know men get wasted all the time in these things, but I solemnly believe this is not how I'll check out, when the time comes. I have this very clear notion that I won't be let off the hook at a young age. God, in His ultimate joker-dom, somehow intends to dangle me out here as long as He can. I'm not going to get any early out.

We reach the third floor door. Two of the uniforms have brought up the swinging sledge. We move down out of their way, and they start their rocking back and forth motion with the sledge, and then they finally shoot it toward the door, and on the first blow the entry explodes inward, and we're rushing through the doorway, weapons extended.

The lights are all off. We swivel in every direction, but no one is shouting "Clear!" like the cops in the movies do. If he's here, he's already heard us come in.

The bedroom door is down a hall to the left.

The door is unlocked. Terrio turns the handle, but he stands to the side. A gunshot blasts through the middle panel, and then the Sergeant rips the door wide open. Another round pops through the entryway, and then we rush Radley.

He's up on the bed, standing, buck-naked. When he sees the four of us aiming at his noggin, he immediately drops the piece onto the mattress.

"Jesus Christ! I thought you were a bunch of coons come to rob me!"

The black patrolman next to me looks at me and smiles.

"I have no idea what you're talking about."

He smiles at Terrio, and then at me. We have him in the same room where I questioned the doorman, with Bill Terrio.

"We have a witness that has you in the building at the time of the murder. You have any other clients in that building where Sharon O'Connor lived?"

"I wasn't there."

"You know the jury's going to love the old guy who barely makes ends meet by working for the rich and famous. Then they're going to get to know *you* real well over the course of the trial, Kirk."

He's watching me with a slight sneer on his lips. It's his street look, his badass persona.

"We already found the knife you used on her. Clean it any way you try, there's almost always a trace left over. And then it's weasel on a stick for you, motherfucker," Terrio grins.

"You confess, you might get life. You never know. You make the

Prosecutor work, he will stick his weewer in every single one of your orifices. You'll be one unhappy bitch when he gets through with you, *Kirky*."

"You don't have a thing. I want a lawyer."

"We already made the call. Since you're indigent—now there's a fucking laugh—we'll have to get you a grab-bag guy. You know, a PD. They love feeding swine to the grinder. No, Kirk, you'd be lots better off confessing."

He's starting to squirm. Twenty years ago, we might have used a telephone book off his head before his attorney arrived. If you hit them just right, they don't leave much of a mark or a bruise. The sound is scarier than how much it hurts. I've seen really brutal interrogations in Vietnam and in Laos and Cambodia, but I never engaged in that kind of thing on the job. For one thing it's not me, and for another you can lose your job with the new attitude toward police brutality.

So we have to use psych ops to get them to own up. And when that doesn't work, they lawyer up and it's up to the Prosecutor to unhinge them in court.

"I'll wait for my lawyer," he repeats.

Party's over. Too bad there's no telephone book handy. Be nice to offer him a parting shot.

At dawn, I'm still in the office.

Lila walks in.

"I'm back."

"Back where?" I ask. I'm tired and woozy, and I have to get a couple hours sleep before we go to Marquette Park for all the fun and frolic. Especially if Franklin Toliver actually appears.

"Back with you. Didn't the Captain tell you? Anderson left Homicide, and he's going into Tactical/Gangs again."

"I haven't seen the Captain." Then I see the memo stuck to the upper left of my desk.

"You never read memos," she smiles.

"It's a flaw. I admit it."

"Aren't we due to go to that Aryan thing this afternoon?" she asks.

"The Captain?"

"Yeah. He filled me in."

"It's today. Yes."

"You look shitty. You need to go rest for a few."

"Really? You think?"

She smiles sadly at me, this time.

"You could've hooked on with somebody else if you wanted to, Lila."

"I guess. I didn't want to."

"Why not?"

"Because we work well together. How's that?"

"Not good enough."

Her hair has grown back to her shoulders. Her eyes remain as blue as an October's fair sky, and her color is back to full and blooming. I'm in love with her all over again, and this time I can barely restrain my urge to jump across the desk and lay one on her lips.

"I want you back, Danny. But you have to go slow."

"You want me back as a partner, you mean?"

"You going to pull it all out of me?"

"I just want to know what the hell's going on inside you, this time."

She glances over my head at the serene and cold February sky.

"I love you."

"You do?"

"Yes. I do."

"And you figured that out when?"

"I always knew. I told you before. I just couldn't commit."

"But now you can?" I ask.

"Why are you making this so hard?"

I look at her pale pink lips, her best feature. I like the rest of her a whole helluva lot, too, but her lips are perhaps the most sensual detail in a sensual package.

"Maybe I'm a little bewildered. You know, Lila, that I was ready to make things permanent for us, but that's not how it's supposed to work. Don't you watch those afternoon talk shows?"

"I don't watch television."

"I'm an eighties guy. I'm supposed to get in touch with my inner feelings and I'm supposed to be open with you about how I feel, and I have. But you, being the woman in this partnership, are supposed to really be the relationship person of the two of us. *I'm* supposed to be the hard case that you have to labor to win over.

"You've never been married and then fucked over. I should be the one who's wary about solidifying our deal. See, you should be the heartbroken one who thought it was all over between us when you got shot and then sidled up to a new partner."

"All right. Okay. Are you through?"

"Yeah. I got all that spleen out. And the bitch of this is that I love you more than I did before you boogied on me."

"You do?"

A smile spreads over her face.

"You didn't think there was no price of readmission, did you?"

I get up and walk over to her.

"We've got a few hours before we go out to the park to meet Franklin."

I bend over and kiss her.

"I love you, Lila. I never stopped loving you, and I'm never going to stop loving you, either."

I bend and kiss her again, and she stands and hugs me.

"My place is closer," she says, looking right into and through me.

Her nipples are pink and taut. This would be a great shot in an R rated soft porno, but I don't think I'm aroused as much as I am overwhelmed with her. I don't know where to begin. It's as if I'm a sixteen-year-old kid in the backseat at a drive-in with not the slightest idea what comes next. It's what some of these goofy Catholics call "born again virginity." The idea is asinine, but it almost captures where I am, right now.

She puts her fingers through my short, stubbly hair. It's difficult to explain how much *affection* is worth. I had plenty of sexual arousal with Mary, and with a few other women I've been with. The two encounters with Lila were plenty exciting, but what distinguishes our lovemaking is the way she simply touches me. And I don't mean the usual sexual touching or the penetration itself—all of which are very cool, don't get me wrong. But what stays with me more than anything else is the love I see in Lila's eyes, and the slight grazing of her fingertips against my hair and my flesh. She does everything else very well, of course, and there's no doubt she's the most energetic and enthusiastic lover I've ever had or ever will have. There can be no doubt she's got no equal, at least not in my life or in my future life.

It's tough to call it by a name. I feel safe with her. Comforted, with her. Sheltered, with Lila. It's not because she's a cop or a black belt or because she was a fighter Ace in the Vietnam War. It's not because she took a bullet that could've got me, back out there in the street with that gangbanger.

I really have never felt this deeply about anyone. I thought I did with Mary. I still do love her even though I shouldn't. I just can't shake what I felt about my ex-wife.

If Lila leaves again, I know I'll never recover from this one. This is for all time, and there's no coming off the mat if she takes off on me like Mary did. I may have some resiliency. I was trained to keep fighting until there was no breath left in my lungs and no beat in my heart and no wave in my brain. I shouldn't be thinking about losing Lila. I should instead be relishing and living in the moment.

What happened to Justin can happen to me, and now I don't feel so goddamned invincible. There could very well be a bullet with my initials carved in its tip. I don't own any damn ghost shirt that makes me invisible to my enemies.

And in just a few hours, all this wonderful heat and pink-nippled flesh will be replaced by a much more stark scene in Marquette Park. The torrid pleasure will become iciness. I shouldn't be thinking about any of that now.

So I look down into her eyes and I kiss her as intensely as I know how to, and she thrusts her tongue into my lips just as we thrust ourselves against each other below. I'm as deep into Lila as I can be. I don't want to move because I know I'll climax way too soon because there's too much intensity, too much fire inside both of us.

She pants and moans, and I see surprise on her face, and then I see it again, and then once more. I can't contain, so it begins, a lengthy and slow draining of everything I've stored up for all these months, all these years, and everything wells and ebbs and wells and ebbs, and my release is explosive and long. Lila moans again, and then I see her finishing in her eyes again, and she smiles and laughs in joy and I'm still flowing into her and it won't seem to stop.

When it's finally done, I have to lie by her side in exhaustion.

"*Ready for round two?*" she giggles.

"You've murdered me. You're under arrest."

She turns over onto me and licks the sweat from my chest down to my groin, and then she takes me and starts it all up, one more time.

33

After we share a shower, we have to get ready to go to work. The march, the rally, whatever this thing is, begins at 1:30 P.M. The days are still short and will be until spring elongates the sunlight, but there will be no illumination on this gathering. The clouds are thick and bulbous and snow-bearing. It's better suited for a funeral in Moscow, outside.

We drive to the southwest side and Marquette Park. I used to play softball here when I was in high school, but the racial intolerance has been high in this neighborhood since I can remember. Blacks didn't tarry around these blocks twenty years ago, but the city is in flux, things keep changing, and Hispanics and African Americans have made inroads into this vicinity. Soon, most whites will have fled to the monochrome far suburbs, if they can afford the migration.

The anti-Semitic thing is more insidious, of course, because there's no way some of these mutants can spot a Jew simply by sight. That doesn't stop bigots, however. They have a nose for intolerance the way a hound has a snout for the kill.

We arrive just fifteen minutes before the Aryan Nation begins its walk through the park, which will then be followed by their high muckety's address to his people. He better keep it quick, or all his apostles will remain frozen in place. The Hawk is booming in out of the northeast, and the flurries have already stormed the storm troopers and all the rest of us, as well.

There are literally hordes of police here. State, Federal, County and City. I can't imagine how any uprising will get started with all the firepower in attendance.

The Zionist Movement is well represented. And their ultra conservative brothers, the Hasidic Jews are among us, also. You can tell them by their hats and long side locks and by their traditional garb. There must be a few dozen of the Hasidim awaiting the speech from the Aryan president, Elroy Carpenter. Here's a motherfucker who embraces "teeth optional." Elroy is dressed in his SS uniform with the skull and cross on his left armband. There is a blown up poster of Adolph Hitler near the podium where the address will be given. Some of the flurries have already obliterated the poster.

"Can we go home, back to my nice, comfortable bed?" Lila smiles coyly at me.

"Don't get me crazy."

"He hasn't got the balls to show up here, Danny. Look at all the po-lice."

"Marvin said he was going to show anyway. And Marvin would've showed if I hadn't shot the sorry son of a bitch. I should've put one in his head, but then he wouldn't have directed us here, no?"

"You see anybody who even remotely resembles Franklin?" she asks.

The Aryans are walking past us now, and they will traverse the entire park on the concrete path that circles this recreation area. The Zionists follow the Aryans, and then all the cops are right behind both of them. It'll take a good hour to get around the entire park, I figure. Then the speech could go on for—who the hell knows how long. It's going to be a miserable afternoon, any way you cut it.

At least I can walk with Lila, right behind the suits, the FBI guys. I can't remember when we spent this much time together, period. It's been a long time since she was shot and since she got a new partner. Now she's back, but I'm still afraid that this is a dream that's going to turn into a nightmare when I wake up and find she's gone again.

I spent most of my adult life waiting for those footsteps to creep up behind me. Dr. Fernandez says I have a few paranoid tendencies, but she thought it was typical of an ex-combat soldier to be suspicious of everyone and everything around him. I just have to really come to terms with the cease fire, the beautiful Latina shrink explained to me.

She wants us to work on my relationship with Mary. She said I have to formally get over my ex-wife before I can move on to anyone—like Lila. Fernandez told me that I've got to learn to trust people more. I asked her if she was going to stand behind me and let me fall into her arms, and she thought that crack was very amusing but not likely to happen.

"I'm dying," Lila says. She's clenching her sides, even though she's wearing a thigh length leather coat and a scarf and a knitted hat and gloves. I'm wearing my own black leather coat and gloves and a knitted watch hat, and my teeth are chattering already, too. The Hawk is at his most brutal in January and February in Chicago. He floats in on ice wings and spreads his chill to anybody dumb enough to be outside in this shit.

We're halfway around the park, now. I can faintly hear the chants of the Aryans, the guys in the SS and Gestapo outfits that they rented from some Halloween outfitter, probably. Unless they had relatives from the Old Country. But you'd think they'd be smart enough to ditch those unis after WWII was lost. Unless, of course, they were headed for South America or Central America, where they're kind of lax about immigration.

The Zionists are shouting now, too, and they're chanting something right back at the neos, but the wind is blowing at our backs and I can't make out the words.

The hour finally passes, and we're back at the podium. No sign of Franklin Toliver, and I don't think there will be, today.

Elroy jumps up on his platform and does the perfunctory "Sieg heil!" and his followers respond in kind.

The Zionists and the Hasidim begin shouting at them in Yiddish or in Hebrew—I have no idea which. But they're not crying out, "Let's be friends!" That much I'm sure about.

"You think we could skip the speech?" Lila says to me. We're standing at the rear of the assembly of friends and foes and cops.

"You really uncomfortable?" I ask.

She gives me a look.

"Give it just five more minutes. Let's take a look around, and then we'll get out of here."

She nods and clutches herself.

I tend to forget she's only been back full time for just a little while after being wounded.

We walk from the left rear of them all toward the other flank. I see Aryans in uniform, but I don't see anyone who's the right height. They're either much taller than Franklin, or they're short and toad-sized. Some of them are shaven bald and look like ex-cons. The Aryans are still big, in the joint. Some have the tattooed tear- drops atop a cheek to designate their loyalties to the Brotherhood. These guys are scarier than the little shit freaks who want to belong to something because they're nothing without numbers behind them.

We finally approach the Hasidim. The beards and the long locks. The gabardines and the hats. Most of them wear glasses. Most look rather scholarly because most of them *are*.

As we approach the far edge of the crowd, one of the ultra conservative Jews looks toward me, just briefly. He's dressed as his brethren Hasidim are, but as we get closer, my eyes wander down to his feet.

He's wearing black running shoes.

I stop in my tracks and force myself to look at the speaker, and he's in mid-rant. Lila looks over to me.

I whisper straight ahead and don't turn to her.

"The guy on the end is wearing running shoes. Black running shoes," I tell Lila.

"Is that Kosher?" she grins.

I unzip my jacket and reach for my .38 police special, and I palm it and take it out and drop my hand with the gun at the side. Lila goes inside her coat, then, and removes her .38 snubnose. She also lets her hand with the weapon drop to her side.

We begin to move toward the far flank where the guy with the sneakers was standing.

He's not standing there anymore. We keep moving in his direction, and when we get to where he was, I see a man walking quickly across the softball diamonds. He's making a beeline to the parking lot.

"Go back and get help," I tell Lila.

"I'm not going anywhere."

"Lila, goddammit! Don't let him get away again!"

She stops abruptly, and then she heads back to the crowd of believers and policemen.

I keep going after the Hasidim with the tennis shoes. He's got a half block lead on me, so I break into a run. He looks over his shoulder quickly, sees me pursuing him, and he breaks into a sprint, as well.

"*Nah, not this time, motherfucker!*" I'm thinking to myself. I'm not going to expend any air by calling out to him. The cavalry will soon be following us, but he could get to his ride and be out of here before I can catch up. The parking lot is only a block ahead of him, so I have to cut the distance between us. I might be able to nail him from here, but a .38 is not exactly a sniper rifle, and when you're running and bouncing, the odds are horseshit that I'll plant one in him.

And it might not be Franklin. Who knows? Maybe this Hasidim has outstanding warrants on him. Maybe he's not who I think he is, and then if I pop him, I'll be in a world of dung.

I'm getting closer. He's not doing very well in all his bulky clothing, but he doesn't stop to throw off any of the dead weight he's wearing. He knows he's got to reach that lot.

I hear some noise behind us, and I know it must be Lila and her new friends. Some of them will be on foot, and the rest will be in their cars, racing to block off that distant lot.

It's a quarter block from the parking area—he's at that juncture, but I'm a football field away from him. It's difficult getting traction in leather shoes out here on the half inch of newly fallen snow, but I'm managing to move closer.

My heart is thumping. I can feel the pounding of it on my temples, too. I'm breathing out of my nose so I don't get winded. As I said before, I'm not a great sprinter, but I'm used to finishing the run regardless of how far it is I have to go.

Now I'm about a hundred feet behind him, but he's approaching his ride, but he hasn't bee-lined toward any particular car yet.

"Stop!" I yell out. He keeps in stride.

This is where I blow it out, all the stops. I'm in a dead sprint behind him. I'm begging God that I don't fall. Not now, not after I've cut it to twenty feet.

He slips, goes down, and takes a header just five feet before the lot begins.

And then I'm on him. I'm over him. He's trying to get up, but I shove the barrel in his back.

"Turn over slowly."

I still have the snout in his back.

"Keep your arms at your sides and keep your hands wide open. Do it!"

He turns over the way I tell him to, and then he lies flat on his backside. It looks like he's about to make an angel in the snow.

Lila and the troops are about one hundred yards away from us. I hear the shriek of sirens out in the street.

"Put your hands underneath you," I tell him. He wedges both hands at the small of his back. I stand over him with the pistol pointed at his nose, and with my left hand I pat him down. No hard objects. No weapons.

I reach down and take hold of his beard, and I pull it off. I tear off his hat and throw his glasses on the snow.

"You shouldn't have worn the Nikes, Franklin," I tell him.

The CPD coppers make the official arrest, and they handcuff Franklin Toliver and haul him into a cruiser and take off for downtown. He points out his car for us before they drive away. It's a non-descript Chevy Chevette. Green. One of his favorite colors.

The crime scene specialists arrive in fifteen minutes, and they pop Franklin's trunk, and lo and behold, they find a hunting knife wrapped in a blanket. They find a sawed-off shotgun in the trunk, as well, and they find rolls of duct tape. The specialists seem optimistic that the knife and the tape were used in the six murders, but there's no telling until they do a full evaluation.

He's off the streets, finally, I'm thinking. Lila gives me a hug in spite of all the witnesses to her gesture of endearment.

But I don't kiss her. That'd be begging for it, I figure. I'm not much for public displays of affection, anyway. I like loving when it is specifically one on one.

He's cuffed to the ring on the table, and he's wearing leg irons as well, when Lila and I interview him for the first time, two days later. He has not requested an attorney, but a judge will supply him with one anyway, eventually.

"Your mother hung herself," I tell him.

He looks at me as if I'd uttered something in Pakistani.

"Did you read about it in the papers?"

He remains silent.

"Your father's career is in the shit," I tell him.

He looks at me with a passive stare.

He's a handsome young man. He favors Raymond, his father.

"And the topper is that you slaughtered six women."

Still no response.

"It won't look good for you in court if you don't show remorse, Franklin."

"Really?"

He looks bemused.

"Yeah. They'll oven roast you for sure if you give them this silent shit. Judges don't like it when you do the psychotic act. Mostly they figure you'd be better off dead."

"Is that right?"

He's trying to get a rise out of me, but that's not how this works. He's the one facing the hangman, the executioner, not me.

Lila watches him intently, but Franklin won't lift his gaze from me.

"Would you like to confess? Or would you rather let the jury hear

259

how there was a blood remnant that matches Khala Gibbons'? It's so hard to tidy up after you cut someone all up, Franklin. And the fibers from the duct tape? It's amazing what the FBI lab can do to match the tape to the stuff we found on all of the women."

He smiles faintly, as if he's bored.

"Doesn't matter? Is that the way it is?"

The smile becomes broader, much more pleased with itself.

"I'll be there. Right at the end, right at lights out, Franklin. I'll be there when you head toward the underworld, my man. You ever read Homer?"

His face goes sober, but he doesn't say anything.

"You're one of those few people, Franklin, that when you die, everybody thinks the world is just slightly better, then. We'll be talking again soon, partner. Have a sparkling afternoon, motherfucker."

34

It takes a large sized U-Haul truck to get Lila moved in on the weekend after Franklin goes into the slammer. We get about six cops who are willing to help us move Lila in, and Kelly comes home from Northern to join forces with the rest of us. It takes about seven hours to get her stuff inside my house, and then another four, after our copper friends leave, for Lila and Kelly and I to get her stuff arranged as she likes it. What had been a rather Spartan dwelling for my daughter and me now appears a little over-choked. Some of this stuff will have to be discarded, and we'll need to buy some new stuff to make the house ours instead of just mine and Kelly's.

Lila is subletting her apartment to a pal of hers that she's known for a long time. Her girlfriend—she says it was strictly platonic—has been after Lila to let her move in after the flight attendant left. Now her buddy wants the whole thing for herself.

It will be very different for me to cohabitate with someone other than my daughter. It used to be like living alone when Kelly was going through all her "issues." Only recently has it felt like I was sharing the house with my kid, and now I've got something very different going.

I want to marry Lila. I know that her bi-sexuality makes that idea a bit chancey. It could be that she'll find another woman that she finds desirable, but if she does consent to marriage, it'll have to be strictly monogamous—just the two of us. That's one line that stays in the sand. It's not negotiable. I know it's the Eighties and that I should be more open-minded, but I'll never be adaptable to any threesome. It just isn't in my repertoire.

The subject of marriage has never come up, but I get the idea that our relationship is definitely long term. She's never given me cause to think this is all just temporary. Christ, the Saturday we moved her in was the second longest day next to D-Day, and I'm not fired up about moving her out, someday.

I'm remembering what my shrink keeps telling me about living in the present instead of dwelling on past rejections and betrayals I've experienced. Lila is not Mary, not even a little bit like my ex-wife. I cannot become paranoid about our life together. I have to give it a chance, learn to trust that she'll be there every day and that I won't find all her clothes and furniture gone, some night when I come home.

The cops who moved her in are all aware that this arrangement is strictly against Department policy. We're not supposed to have a partnership in and out of the work place. We'll be separated as work partners if they ever find out. The guys who helped us move are all reliable, so again I'll have to put my trust in someone besides myself.

The first night we're in bed at our house, we have to curb our enthusiasm because Kelly's staying here until tomorrow, Sunday, afternoon. She doesn't need to get an earful of any cooperate howling coming out of either of us. So we have to go slowly and calmly, and I rather like it. Starting on Sunday night, we can go back to our previous primate behavior, which I thoroughly enjoy, also. For the sake of the kid, we'll keep it down to a low growl, tonight.

We interview Franklin again on Monday morning. He has not shaven, and his face is beginning to resemble that of the Hasidim he posed as, back in Marquette Park.

Lila is seated at the far left of the rectangular slab, and I'm directly opposite Toliver. They're videotaping the proceedings. Franklin peers up at the camera lens in the corner off to my right.

"You still haven't hired a lawyer?" I ask him.

He grins at me with his best nutsy grin.

"Your father is hiring one, I've heard, however. We could postpone this talk until he's available, Franklin."

"I don't mind talking to you. I mean, I don't mind talking to *her*."

"You remember me from the time you had the two girls in the trunk, don't you, Franklin," Lila tells him.

He smiles widely at her.

"That was the time you Molotov-ed the car and fried those last two women. I'm sure you recall, don't you?"

"I'm sorry. You have me confused with someone else."

"Come on, Franklin. They already have you, with the knife and the duct tape. Why don't you just confess and save the State of Illinois a few million bucks? That way you can go make new friends in the joint. You know, those guys you like so well with the teardrop tattoos?"

"They're not my friends. I don't have any friends."

"That's a shame," I tell him.

I watch him closely, but he won't make eye contact with me.

"Were there others, Franklin? It doesn't matter now if you tell me. They can only execute you once. You might as well tell me who else you did. Maybe they have families who'd like to be put at peace. I don't figure we've got you down for everything you've done. You want to tell us how many others there were?"

He looks at me with an entirely blank expression. His eyes are dead, lifeless. The pupils are large and black, like those belonging to a shark. The famous dolls' eyes. He's a predator. He has the look of a hunter. It takes you in and sizes you up. He's calculating what it takes to drain the sap and substance out of you. He's like a butcher eyeing a steer before he cuts its throat.

He's figuring what he'd do to the body once the killing's accomplished.

His hands are shackled to the ring on the table, and his ankle chains are hooked to a ring on the floor. He still seems dangerous, lethal.

"There were no others. You've got the wrong man. I've never hurt anyone."

I smile at him, and it begins to agitate him.

"Franklin. Franklin. What interests me is why you have this thing for black women. I know you were interested in some white meat after you did the six black hookers, but that was probably just because the black meat was getting a little too difficult to get close to. You knew we'd see a pattern, and you're not dumb enough to overplay your hand, right?"

He watches me with his still, dark eyes.

"But if you'd had a choice, you'd still be killing nigger whores, right?"

The word "nigger" makes his face tighten. His eyes narrow upon mine.

"That's what you call them, isn't it, Franklin? *Niggers?*"

He shrugs and sneers.

"What'd they do to piss you off like this? Some black kid steal your fucking lunch money? They have any black kids in those DesPlaines schools?"

"I grew up in the city."

"You have African Americans in your grade schools? High school?"

He looks down at Lila and grins. Then he turns back to me.

"I don't remember. It was so long ago."

"What, they kicked your ass out on the playground? Is that it? Some little pickaninny popped you upside the head and you took it out on those poor, lame women?"

"I didn't kill anyone. You've got the wrong man."

"We'll do the research. We'll find out eventually why you did what you did. But it doesn't really matter. You killed them, and that's that. Why you did it is what they call academic. See, it's for my own edification and education, Franklin. Usually we look for motive before we catch them. Sometimes it helps apprehending asswipes like you. Not always, but sometimes. I just like to understand what went into your skull and made you snuff all those girls.

"Was it because they were prostitutes?"

He shrugs again and sends his eyes against a spot on the wall behind me. I know this interview will be pointless. I know he'll never admit what he did. He won't confess. He'll take it to court with the finest defense attorney his father can afford, and then he'll hope that twelve honest peers will find him innocent of all the charges. And he might get himself acquitted. It happens, despite all the evidence the prosecution can muster, it happens. It's true that you never know what a jury's going to do.

That's why we go after a confession, even knowing that Franklin hasn't got it in him to admit what he did.

The new term is "sociopath." But it's just an academic term for "asshole." Because sociopaths, like assholes, are what they are because they're unaware of what they are, and they do what they do just because they do it.

No, Franklin will never confess. He'll stonewall us, and he'll remain mute in the courtroom. He'll let his lawyer do the pleading, and he believes he's too clever to meet the executioner, the hangman.

I have to go after him, though. I can't just let it be up to the judicial branch. If I can get him to confess, then he'll die in prison or rot there until he does die. If I leave it up to blind justice... As I said, you never know what a jury'll do.

I look at him, suddenly, and I know what he's up to. He'll go for an insanity plea. He's been to Elgin, and perhaps he rather enjoyed it, telling Dr. Talbot all about his mommy and how he hated her and how she hated him right back. And now he can tell Talbot about all his guilt now that he's provoked mommy to string herself up in the closet. He can affect a pose about how sad all this makes him, how he's getting a raw deal because no one has ever taken the time to understand him—except for Jennifer O'Brien, who also betrayed him eventually by getting married to some other man. I'm sure he'll parade out his pathology, and he'll let them dope him up with anti-depressants and other wonder drugs. They'll find the cause of his psychoses, and some fine day—

He'll get sprung from the mental hospital, and then he can go right back and do his thing, but this time he'll make no mistakes like the Aryan Nation parade and the black gym shoes, because Franklin Toliver is too clever not to learn from his mistakes.

"No, Franklin. I don't think you're crazy. I think you're evil."

Lila looks over at me. I can see her concerned look out of the

265

corner of my eye.

"If you had anything of value inside you, you'd tell me what you did, but since you don't, you won't. Good luck at the trial, nickeldick."

"What was that all about?" she asks me as we work the vending machines in the hall outside our offices.

"He's going to cop insanity. That's what I'd do if I was his high-priced mouthpiece."

"But he won't get it, will he?"

"Did you like his crazy show? The stares and the glares? Maybe he'll eat his fucking sport coat for the judge and the jury, or maybe he'll eat one of the jury people."

"They couldn't be that lame. Everything he did was premeditated, and premeditation is—"

"The mark of a functioning mind. Crazy dudes don't pre-think. They act on impulse, right? We should talk to Fernandez and ask her what chance she thinks he has."

"What good would that do, Danny?"

"None, I suppose. It'll be up to those twelve fine citizens. We have blood, we have a knife and we have duct tape. You think that'll be enough? We'll never get a confession. I should've shot him when he ran."

"You couldn't be sure it was him, Danny. Cut it out."

"Details, details. The devil's always in the details."

"He's not going to get away with it. Our prosecutor is really good. He's the first string. The newspapers made sure we wouldn't be throwing any bench-rider at Franklin."

"His father is the Lieutenant Governor of our fair state. You think he might know a really good criminal lawyer?"

She frowns instead of answering me.

The attorney's name is Mick Kelly. He's the second coming of Clarence Darrow, according to the *Sun-Times*. The *Tribune* calls him a "great white shark." I've seen Kelly in court, and he is very good. He doesn't always win, but I'd want him defending me if I whacked six women, or just one. He's very passionate with his defense. I've literally seen him cause male jurors to weep. Kelly does win lots more than he loses.

I thought about going at Toliver one more time, but now that he's got a lawyer, he'll be clammed up until the trial begins. Kelly will do all the talking from here on out.

Kirk Radley will not benefit from such an illustrious attorney as Franklin Toliver has hired. Radley has got himself a second tier ambulance chaser. It appears that Kirk has squandered most of his profit on very slow racehorses and on a real lack of talent at high stakes poker.

But his attorney, Kell Skarsland, has convinced him to confess to killing Sharon, and their angle will be irresistible compulsion. In other words, Kirk was temporarily insane when he gutted and hung Mrs. O'Connor from her chandelier. I don't like Radley's chances, but those dozen jurors are an unpredictable lot. They are what the scientists call "variables." You never know what they'll do or what they'll believe. That's why ambulance chasers make the big bucks, if they're exceptional litigators.

In March, I'm settling into domesticity. Lila has arranged the house and gotten rid of the clutter. Our home looks just like that—a home, not a house.

She has breached the topic of the parameters of our relationship. Lila says she knows I can't live with the idea of her being with another woman (or man), and that's the way she wants it, too. But she doesn't get into marriage, and I'm not going to try and rush her. She's not the type you try to coerce or push along. She'll let me know when she wants to make it formal, and I'm just happy that everything's turned around the way it has.

I never believed in second chances. First chances are rare enough, but getting a second shot never seems to happen, at least to me. Mary never came back and asked to start over.

I never got a second shot at a target in the war. The VC and the NVA were hard enough to hit with the first shot. You weren't likely to get an encore to put them away.

When Lila quit the partnership, I tried to resign myself to living without her, permanently. But she re-entered. She came back. Only that collie, Lassie, ever came back, that I can remember.

I'm not much of a believer in miracles. That's why I had such trouble going back to the church. You are supposed to truly believe that Jesus Christ came back from the dead, that he offers us eternal life, and all the rest. Just the magic act of being reanimated and having that boulder turned aside and the burial ground being empty is cause for some healthy skepticism. You're asked to believe without seeing. "Act as if ye had faith."

I find the above very difficult to do. Yet I'm trying. I'm trying to put aside what Dr. Fernandez calls my "cynicism" when it comes to believing in other people. I always seem to need evidence. It's the cop in me, I guess.

Faith? It's like sticking your toe out over the abyss and believing, having faith, that if you step out there into space, you won't plummet to the bottom.

35

"*S*urprise!*"

I sit up in a jolt. The first thing I reach for is my Smith & Wesson, but it's locked in the nightstand where it's always been since Kelly was old enough to crawl.

Speaking of Kelly, she's standing alongside the bed with Lila, and the both of them are holding a cake with a single lit candle.

"You don't need to shoot us, Danny. It's only your birthday!"

Lila laughs and gives me a "*Whoo whoo!*"

"What the hell is *this?* I thought you were at school," I tell my daughter.

"I drove up for your birthday, Dad. Whatta you suppose?" she giggles. "It's Sunday, but I have to go back tonight to study for a test."

"Pretty soon you'll be fifty, big boy," Lila cracks.

I'm sitting up, rubbing my eyes.

"I got most of a decade before that happens."

"And it's a fine thing, Danny. I don't want to wake up next to a geezer any time soon."

She bends over and kisses me, and she slips me just a hint of tongue.

"The full production will come later this evening."

I blush, but I can't help laughing at her. Then Kelly bends over and plants one on my left cheek.

"Get up, birthday boy. I've got reservations at The Saville."

"*Where?*" I ask Lila.

"You heard me. Nothing's too good for the birthday boy."

"Jesus, are we going to have to take out another freaking mortgage?"

"It's on me, slick. Get a shower. We're on our way in twenty minutes."

"What the hell time is it?" I ask, and then I peer over at the digital clock on the nightstand. It's 8:46 A.M.

The Saville is prime time in the Loop. They don't serve breakfast—it's called "brunch." And it begins at 9:00 and goes until 11:00. They only offer brunch on the weekends, and it goes for $39.95 per person. I want to turn us around and head us for Mac Land, but Lila is having none of it.

"Shoot the moon, big boy. You nailed Franklin Toliver and Kirk Radley, pretty much without my help, and both of them one after the other. They're going to make you a sergeant, my love."

"You'll pass the test before I do. You're the Air Force Academy brainiac."

The Saville is as advertised. I was required to wear a shirt and tie in here, and that is definitely not something I'm used to. The booths are plush and fancy. They're all purple. But Lila corrects me and tells me it's more like lavender.

"My parents took me here for my Academy graduation present. They can afford this joint on a regular basis."

I look around at the swells inside here—the guys in the sport coats or the Ivy League Sunday morning attire or whatever it is. I start to feel a bit uncomfortable.

Then a waiter arrives with a tiny cake with a single candle lit atop it, and then a host of other waiters circle around him and us in our lavender booth.

"Oh, shit," I mutter.

"Oh *yeah*," Kelly laughs.

There is glee in Lila's face as the waiters sing "Happy Birthday" to me. All the big deals turn and look at us, and some of them even smile and join in.

Lila had to reserve the booth two weeks in advance, and she tells me she's lucky there were any seats left. This place is perpetually sold out, and usually you have to make arrangements two or more months in advance.

"We lucked out. And the manager is a buddy of my old man's."

Lila's father, the lawyer, that is.

They bring us a fruit bowl—each of us gets our own bowl. It's loaded with fruits I can't even identify. Lila explains that there are peaches, mangos, kiwis, oranges, apples and several other goodies even she doesn't know. Everything tastes delicious, so I'm not going to ask for an itemized list.

Then you get a Belgian waffle. At least that's what Lila recommends, so we all go for it. The waffle comes with syrup or blueberry topping. They lay a pound of butter on the table when the waffles arrive. They bring out a platter of sausage patties and bacon, and each of us gets a sixteen ounce glass of fresh-squeezed orange juice—pulpless and seedless, of course.

"Happy birthday, Love," Lila toasts with her juice.

"Happy birthday, Dad," Kelly joins in, her glass hoisted.

I never celebrate my birthday. I mean never. I must have had parties when I was a kid, but I can't recall them. Just vaguely, maybe. Christmas and Easter used to be a family meal with either of my parents' relatives, but everyone's dead, by now. And Kelly and I didn't do holidays or special days when she was going through her stuff.

This is unique, and not because of the expensive bistro we're at. The Saville is classy, all right, but it's the two people with me who've made this day unlike any other day.

I think I feel a few pangs at my eyes, but I ride it out. This day doesn't include sorrow or any of its cousins. No melancholy. No regrets, if only for a day.

Who knows? There might be a lot more days like this. But I can't let myself walk that way, yet. I just have to live in the present, the way the Department psychiatrist has been urging me to live.

My birthday fell on the Ides of March. The fifteenth. A week later, on the twenty-third, the trial of Franklin Toliver began. The jury selection took a full five days, which isn't all that long for a big time criminal trial. This case was so well publicized that it could've been difficult to find twelve unbiased jurors, but Mick Kelly, the defense attorney, and Chad Steinback, the Prosecutor, are very professional lawyers, and neither is into stalling tactics. They're both pretty aggressive and both like to get the case to the jury as fast as possible because they understand lawyers who work slowly are like pitchers in baseball who dawdle. You lose the jurors by going slowly, just the way a hurler has his defense fall asleep behind him if he dances on the mound and puts everyone around him night-night.

On the following Monday, the actual trial begins, and the defense has copped for insanity. Kelly says his boy is a genuine loon and that he is not a candidate for death or life—the usual penalties for a capital crime. For multiple homicides, it tends to swing toward execution.

I don't pretend to be a seer or a prophet, but I figured it'd be the smartest move for Franklin. He's such an unlikeable fuck that Mick would never let him speak in open court if he could avoid it. Even if he really weren't guilty, most juries would want to throttle this prick themselves. I'm saying Toliver doesn't have refined people skills. Kelly knows that, you can bet, and if he pleads insanity, he can trot out shrinks and counselors who'll all swear that Franklin Toliver would give *Freud* fucking nightmares.

The Prosecutor will try to show that Franklin knew the difference between right and wrong and that he intentionally and deliberately planned to murder his six victims. I'm certain that Kelly will bring up the victims' backgrounds, which really has no bearing on the case, and Steinback will protest that he is trying to diminish the lives of the murdered women. He'll say Kelly is playing the race card in reverse, and Mick will vehemently deny all of the above.

Lawyers like to plant seeds. Even if things said in court are overruled by the judge, the jury has already heard the testimony, and just because the testimony has been stricken from the record, the twelve honest souls have heard it and likely will remember it.

I've been present at a number of murder trials. Most of them are cut and dried. Most of the time a guilty verdict is obvious, and it takes place. Quickly. The Perry Mason stuff, the Hollywood trials, is far more dramatic and far more full of suspense and theatrics than the real kind of law that I've witnessed. It's a grind to the end, and some litigators are more flamboyant than others. But this isn't a college or high school debate. They're deciding life and death, so the atmosphere is pretty much deadly serious and somber.

On the fifth day of the trial, Dr. Talbot from the Elgin State Mental Hospital is called to the stand. He's a defense witness, which surprises me a little since he's the guy who first put me onto Franklin.

He explains his credentials at Kelly's request. He tells us he's a Princeton University M.D. He tells us his experience in the field, and then the defense goes at it.

"In Mr. Toliver's stay at Elgin, did you find him to be a danger to the people around him?" Kelly asks.

"He really wasn't there long enough for me to give an adequate appraisal of his 'danger' to society, but he was a very troubled young man."

"From your interviews with Toliver, did you sense underlying issues that might cause you to push for commitment to Elgin?"

"He's leading, Your Honor," Steinback protests. "He's asking the doctor to project an answer. Mr. Toliver left the hospital after three days. As Dr. Talbot already said, there was no way to make a viable diagnosis on Mr. Toliver after such a short stay at the institution."

"I agree, Mr. Kelly," Judge Maury Birnbaum says.

Kelly turns and smiles at Steinback.

Chad Steinback is an ex-guard on the basketball team at Northwestern in Evanston. He's six four and still lanky, at fifty, with no paunch and no excess weight and a head full of salt and pepper hair.

Kelly presses on about what Toliver related to the shrink about his relationship with his late mother. Talbot confirms that Mrs. Toliver abused Franklin physically by beating him when he was a small child, all the way up through adolescence. When Franklin became taller than his mother, the doctor says, the mother could no longer beat Franklin, but Franklin admitted striking her on more than one occasion. The fights ceased when Raymond Toliver intervened one time when the younger Toliver was sixteen. Raymond apparently popped young Franklin straight in the teeth, which caused subsequent orthodontia to the tune of three thousand bucks.

After that violent outburst, there was no further history, since Franklin blew the coop at Elgin.

On cross, Steinback establishes that Franklin appeared in command of his emotions. Talbot tries again to explain that a three-day stay is no indicator of madness or any other mental instability, but that Toliver seemed a likely candidate for in-depth therapy of at least six months.

"But what you're really saying is that you don't really know if Franklin Toliver is dangerously insane. You're saying that you didn't have enough time to formulate a valid diagnosis. Is that fair to say, Dr. Talbot?"

Talbot hesitates. He stares over at Franklin Toliver and Mick Kelly.

"Yes. That's fair to say."

He says it so softly that Steinback insists he speak up.

So he says it again. This time, a little louder.

My turn in court won't happen for a while, yet, Steinback informs me after court is adjourned on the first day. We're standing outside the courtroom, and all of the witnesses and other audience members have meandered past us, by now.

"He's not going to get off by being nuts, is he?" I finally ask Chad

Steinback.

"I shouldn't think so, but you know the deal with juries, Danny."

"But he won't get off. Not this guy."

"I'll do everything I can to prevent it.... What's troubling you?"

We're alone in the outer hall. We can hear the voices of people on the floor below us. The stairs are right in front of us.

"It took a long time to locate this piece of crap."

"I understand, Danny."

"He's not like any of the other perps I've cuffed. This guy is special."

"Because he killed in multiples?" Steinback asks.

"I've caught a few of those before.... No, this guy is different."

"Why?"

"Because he enjoys what he does. And I'm starting to think the race business is a front. I think he would've become equal opportunity for his next victims. And there would've been more if his face wasn't plastered all over the state and if his daddy wasn't as high profile as he is."

"I'm going to try my best to see he doesn't get a vacation at the hospital, Danny. That's the best I can promise."

"He got out of Elgin the one time, already."

"Even if they think he's crazy, the next time the security will be a lot tighter."

"Don't give him the chance to find out, Mr. Steinback. Don't give him the opportunity."

The Prosecutor looks at me directly. There's no evasiveness in his eyes.

"I know you'll do your best. I've seen you work plenty. I don't mean to sound disrespectful, so don't get me wrong. It's just that this guy thinks he's smarter than you or me or the judge. He thinks he can play *anyone*.

"You think he'll put Franklin on the stand?"

"I don't think so. Franklin doesn't come off as Mister Wonderful, as you are already aware, Danny."

"This guy, Kelly. You've gone against him before?"

"Yes. Several times."

"You've beat him?"

"A majority of the time, as a matter of fact. But he's as good as it gets. Don't underestimate him, because I won't."

"That's what I was afraid you were going to say," I tell him.

36

Mick Kelly keeps trotting out his crew of psychoanalysts who concur with Franklin's plea of insanity, and Steinback does a fine job of refuting them all. If I were on the jury, I'd hang Franklin this afternoon, but then I'm probably prejudiced.

Kelly decides to pull out all the stops on the fifth day into his defense. He calls his client, Franklin Toliver, to the stand.

Toliver has always been lead into the court in cuffs and ankle shackles, but the Deputies have unlocked him to sit at the defense table with his attorney. Four Deputies are always within a few feet of Franklin, however, even when he rises and heads for the witness chair.

The flag of the United States is in front of the flag of Illinois, right behind him. The Lieutenant Governor has chosen not to attend his son's trial. It's understandable, and at least the old man hired Kelly, one of the best criminal attorneys in Chicago and in the state.

They swear Toliver in. He's wearing a tan suit, a white shirt, and a power black, silk tie. He appears to be an up and coming young businessman who got lost in the courthouse and wound up on trial for his life. Very good staging from Mick Kelly. Dancers would call it

277

choreographing, I suppose.

Mick approaches Toliver. The five women and seven men in the jury have their eyes planted on the both of them. The courtroom is standing room only, and no one's moving a muscle—there really is a hush, just like in *Perry Mason* or *The Defenders*. Those two TV shows would be kind of dated, at least in my daughter Kelly's mind, but they were the lawyer shows I watched as a kid. *The Defenders* was a much superior show and by far more realistic to the courtrooms I've experienced.

"Did you kill Helen Gant and Tracy Anderson and Angela Carter and Khala Gibbons and Marla Donald and Lasharon Martin?"

"I don't know," Franklin answers, deadpan serious.

"You don't know?" Kelly asks. His voice is attempting "incredulous."

"I mean, I don't remember."

"You have no memory of killing all six of these women?"

"It seems, sometimes, like it happened in a dream, but I can't actually say I remember killing anybody."

"You expect the jury to believe you have no recollection of the murders? The prosecution has proved the knife they found in your trunk was indeed the weapon that was used on at least one of the victims. They have fibers that they've tied conclusively to the duct tape also found in your car. And you still can't recall killing any one of these women?"

"Why is Mr. Kelly doing my job, Your Honor?" Steinback asks as he stands.

The gallery and the jury engage in some muffled laughter.

The judge hammers just once with his gavel.

"It seems that you're covering old ground, Mr. Kelly."

"I'm trying to show the jury that my client really does not have any recollection of committing the crimes he's been accused of. We're not arguing that Mr. Toliver didn't do these killings. What we're saying is that he was not in command of his faculties during the course of the six slayings."

"That's about the worst scenario I've heard since daytime television, Your Honor."

There's more laughter, and then the judge slams the gavel one more time.

"Let's keep it somewhat relevant, okay?" the judge suggests.

Kelly returns his glance to Toliver.

"Do you think you know the difference between right and wrong, Franklin?"

"Yes. I think I do."

"Is killing six women wrong?"

"Killing anyone is wrong, yes."

"Do you have any guilt about what you did?"

"I don't remember harming anyone."

"Here we go again, Your Honor," Steinback interjects.

"I apologize.... Franklin, did you feel bad about the death of your mother?"

"Yes. I did. I mean I do."

"Irrelevant," Steinback protests.

"Yes, it is, Mr. Kelly."

"Your Honor, I'm trying to show my client's state of mind. You heard him tell us, just now, rather indecisively, that he felt bad about his mother's suicide. If Franklin is ambivalent about his feelings toward his own mother—"

"Please, Your Honor! We've already heard about Franklin's inability to love, his inability to respond emotionally as a sane person would. These are simply stalling tactics to mislead the jurors into thinking Mr. Kelly's client is deranged, that he has no grasp of reality."

"I agree, sir. Get on with it and knock off the sidetracking, Counselor."

Kelly gestures theatrically to the jury, as if he has been frustrated in his sincere attempts to display the febrile mind of Franklin Toliver.

"My mother," Franklin says softly.

"What, sir?" the judge asks him.

"*My mother was the most miserable animal that ever crawled on earth. My mother*—"

"Restrain your client, Mr. Kelly."

"My mother was the most miserable *bitch* who ever wormed her way—"

"Mr. Toliver! You will be quiet or you will be removed from this courtroom!"

"She was insane. You have no idea what it was like, living in that house—"

"Sit down, Mr. Toliver!"

The Deputies are converging on the witness box.

Suddenly Franklin throws his arms toward the ceiling and he lets out a lupine howl that causes several of the females in the jury and several more women in the audience to burst out with screams of their own.

Toliver hurls himself toward the judge, and two of the Deputies grab him about the throat and shoulders and haul him back into the witness box. They can't seem to subdue him down into his chair, so I trot toward the scene up front. I motion for Lila to stay seated. She doesn't need this kind of exercise.

As I approach the witness chair, Franklin has managed to throw off both Deputies. The other cops assigned to Franklin are circling the judge, who's standing off in a corner, as far away as he can get from Toliver.

Franklin explodes toward me, as if he was waiting his chance to get at me. He tries to grab me by the throat, but I kick him in the left shin, and he flops quickly. With a remarkable recovery, he gets to his knees and tries to throw his arms about my legs. Instead, he gets my left knee in his nose. I see the blood gout from his nostrils, and I'm pretty sure I've broken his beak. He looks amazed as he wipes the blood from his chin, and he tries to get to his feet, just as the first two deputies jump him, and finally they take him to the floor and throw his irons back on as they were, before he was unleashed in here.

The courtroom, however, is still bedlam. I search out the face of his defense attorney, Mick Kelly, and instead of seeing any form of joy for a scene he helped to concoct, I see genuine horror on Kelly's visage.

This has all been the creation of the man they're pulling to his feet, right now. There's no smile of joy or victory on Franklin's bloody puss. But he glares directly at me, and he keeps his eyes firmly on mine as the cops drag him out of the courtroom.

"They'll never buy that bullshit," I tell Chad Steinback as we have coffee in the cafeteria downstairs from the courtroom.

"I'll bet you a 'C' note they do," the Prosecutor glumly replies.

"How can they *not* know all that was theater?" I ask.

"You saw Kelly," Lila says. She's sitting with us at the table. The cafeteria is virtually empty. Everyone's gone, by now. It's 5:00 P.M. Business is concluded, but the café stays open until 8:00 P.M.

"What about it?" I ask her.

"She's right," Steinback adds. "He wasn't in on it. He's not that good an actor. Nobody is. This was all Franklin. He just won his Emmy and his Oscar, all in one performance. It was a beaut. He scared the shit out of me, too. I think it was the howl. He probably listened to the wolves out at Brookfield Zoo before laying it on us, here. Lon Chaney Junior would've been proud, Danny. I thought fucking hair was going to sprout from his cheeks.

"I prosecuted a swinging dick who thought he was a vampire, once. Drained all his female victims of their blood over the course of a few days. Bled them to death and then sold their blood to vampire cults. Franklin is definitely more fucked up than the vampire guy."

"You think he's crazy now, too?" I ask.

"Doesn't matter what I think or you think or Lila thinks. Even the judge probably knows Franklin's a performance artist. It only matters what those twelve honest citizens think. You two take a gander at them while you, Danny, were busting Franklin's face?"

Neither of us answers because we both know he's right.

"I don't like our chances at all. We have him cold on the evidence, but they really bought Mr. Toliver's grand production. All he needed was lions, tigers and bears. Dorothy and Toto weren't necessary.

"They think he's nuts. Certifiable. Looney. Insane. Totally fucked up. And speaking of totally fucked, that's *us*, by the way."

Closing arguments are finished three days later, and on April 28, 1987, Franklin Toliver is found innocent on account of mental incapacity— insanity—and he is remanded to the Elgin State Mental Facility in Elgin, Illinois.

I go to Steinback's table after the court is cleared. Lila is with me. Steinback's female assistant is the last to leave before we join the

Prosecutor.

"We lose. I can't believe it, but we lose," Steinback pronounces.

"He's not free, Chad. He's going to a hospital," I say. "This time under highest security."

It's like a lame apology, and the three of us know it.

"No, he's not at liberty to dismember anyone. At least for a while. I don't know about you, Danny, or you, Lila, but I'm not going to be able to sleep sound and comfortable for a long, long time."

He snaps his briefcase shut, and then he smiles painfully at both of us, and Chad Steinback departs.

The *Sun-Times* and the *Tribune* both bemoan the verdict of insanity, but there's nothing to be done by us, anymore. Franklin's in the laughing academy instead of death row, and everyone is taking this one as a defeat. Even though we've got Toliver off the white board (and Sharon O'Connor's killer, too), it doesn't seem like anything good has just occurred. It seems like a miscarriage of justice.

Murderers *do* get away with it. It does happen. Sometimes we never even apprehend them at all. It is rare, however. And even though it doesn't occur very often, it doesn't make Lila or me feel any happier about the outcome.

Perhaps I should've let him knock me down and put me on the floor, and then I could've been justified in breaking his neck. It's a move I've accomplished more than once in Vietnam. I could've snapped his neck easily, but I would've had to been in a jeopardized position. I simply reacted and stopped him before he could get me in a compromised spot. I simply became defensive. I didn't have time to do anything else.

The two of us get to accompany Franklin Toliver on his brief trip from County Jail to Elgin. He is again shackled heavily, his cuffed hands ringed to a chain around his waist, and his ankles bound close together with irons so that he has to shuffle like some dude on a chain gang.

We get him into a van. There are two County Deputies in the back with us, and Toliver, for the ride out west and north.

We pull out of the underground lot, and I see the sunlight pour through the windshield. There is a chain link divide between us and the van's driver, another County cop. Toliver has been chained yet again to a ring in the floor of the vehicle.

He sits between the two County men, and Lila and I are on the opposite side.

"Detective Mangan," Toliver smiles. His nose has been reset. He has a shiner under his left eye.

I look at him but I don't respond.

"See what you did?" he points to his black eye.

"Shut the fuck up or we'll have an accident. My billy might slip into your other eye, Franklin," the County cop on his left warns him.

"It's okay. Let him talk," I wave. The County guy nods in affirmation. It's up to me.

"Broke it clean. You know I never meant to hurt you. Right?"

I don't answer. We've got a forty-five minute trip. We might as well be entertained by the newly-deemed crazy fucker. "The Wolf Man," the *Trib* christened him because of his magna performance in court.

"You are one lovely woman, Ma'am," he says to Lila.

Lila doesn't rise to him. Her face is expressionless.

"Don't go there, Franklin. Then it'll get ugly," the same County cop tells him.

"I didn't mean anything."

The cop throws a quick elbow into Franklin's left side ribcage. The air *oofs* out of him.

"*Oooops*," the County guy smiles.

Franklin gasps for air, but he recovers quickly enough.

"Love tap, motherfucker," the cop explains.

"*He* hits harder," Toliver tries to grin and gestures toward me.

"You don't want to irritate the lady," I say. "She's the *real* killer in here."

Franklin peers over at Lila, and Lila beams right at him. Her smile is wide and brilliant.

37

In June, the newspapers play up Frank Swanson's firing at the high rise downtown. Frank has sold his story to *The Tattletale*, a rag mag, for six figures, and big Bill is suing Swanson and the magazine for libel.

The tale of Sharon's nasty relationship with Kirk Radley is in there, and so is the stuff about Bill O'Connor not being able to get a rise on demand, as it were. All of this lovely, sordid crap appears in the June edition, and the legit newspapers have a field day with the libel suit. O'Connor has gone to reruns on his TV show, so we'll see in the fall if he's going to air his grievances.

Me? I'm kind of glad to see O'Connor get it in the neck. I remember his empty face when we interviewed him about his wife's murder. It was as if we were talking about some stranger that had been sliced open and hung upside down in his living room. He seemed as if there were no connection between him and Sharon.

Which was why I wanted the killer to be O'Connor, at first. There would have been some kind of satisfaction putting that blowhard in a hole for the rest of his life. But Kirk took his place. One scumwad for another. At least we caught the feces that really killed her.

It just seems as if justice swerved around Bill O'Connor. Maybe his magazine, *BO*, is appropriately titled, after all.

Lila wants to paint the inside of our house. She asked me how long it's been since it was painted inside.

"Never. Since I've lived here."

"Jesus! And how long is *that?*" she replies.

"Nine years?" I guess.

"That cinches it."

Some men would think Lila was being pushy, and they'd be right. But I like her swagger around the house. She's moved in completely, by now. She's a resident, a member, of this household. Before, it was Kelly and me, and then Sonny the border collie. Now Lila is a shareholder in our enterprise. She belongs here. She fits.

And it fills up a big hole in my life, the one that Mary left, all those years before.

She wants to do our bedroom in pale yellow. I like pale yellow, too. She wants to do the kitchen in baby blue. I go along with that choice, also.

"Do you really like those colors, or are you just placating me, Danny?"

"I really like them."

"You're sure?"

She has her interrogator's glare aimed at me at the moment. Her hair has grown out long again, this time down to her shoulders. And she knows long hair puts me into heat. She's been using a very muted red lipstick that has made her face seem healthier, more vibrant, and she's been using a few other cosmetics just to brighten what is already a glow that has brought happiness my way, for once.

I'm trying to follow Fernandez's advice not to look for the leaden cloud somewhere, and sometimes it's a struggle.

We're both going to take next week off to get this painting done. She says she's tired of the look, in here. She's putting her own signature on the joint, and I'm all for it.

"What do you think about marriage?" she asks as we put the second coat of yellow on the bedroom walls, one week later. There are plastic sheets covering everything we couldn't move out of here. And everything's moved out, away from the walls. There are two ladders, here, but we've already done the ceiling in white, and first.

"I like the idea, if you mean you and me."

She makes a fart sound with her lips.

"You know I mean you and me."

"Then we'd have to break up the partner thing," I remind her.

"I can live with that," she says. She's got her pensive look on her full-bloom beautiful face.

"I don't know if *I* can," I tell her.

She stops rolling yellow on her wall, momentarily.

"You don't?"

"I like having you there with me all day, and then having you here at night, too. And I never get tired of you, the way you get tired of me."

"Who gets tired of you?"

"I can see it when you look up into the air, sometimes. It's like telling me to shut the hell up."

"Sometimes you do go on, Danny."

"I know. But I never get sick of listening to you even when you're spreading the bullshit upon the waters."

"What bullshit? What waters?"

I dip my two fingers into the paint pan, and then I flick a few drops that land squarely on her left breast side, on top of her Cubs' tee shirt.

"That's my good tee, dammit."

"Cub fan. Heresy," I tease her.

"I'd miss you, too, Danny. But I want to get married. Don't you?"

I drop my roller into the pan.

"Jesus Christ, Lila. I've wanted to ask you to marry me since I first laid eyes on you."

"Really?"

"Yes, really. Don't you ever listen to me? I've done every

goddam thing except have it printed in the headlines or put up on a banner behind a goddam airplane. Can't you read me at all?"

"Apparently not."

"You read everybody else like a first grade primer. Why not me?"

"I don't know. You're difficult to pierce, for me."

"I feel special."

"Good. You are."

"We better stop the love fest and finish the walls," I tell her.

"Not until you ask me, officially."

"Here and now?"

She nods, and her long hair flaps behind her head.

"You want me on my knees?" I ask.

"Any way you choose."

I shrug and get down on my knees, and I place the roller into the paint gently.

Then I look over to her.

"Will you marry me, Lila Chapman?"

"Maybe, Daniel Mangan."

"*Maybe?*"

"Yes. Of course I'll marry you, you goof."

"This is the way I dreamed it would be."

I struggle back up to my feet.

"What about a ring?" she says.

"Wait," I tell her.

I go into the john off our bedroom. I get into a rectangular container, and then I return to her.

I rip off the outer paper of the band-aid, and then I take off the covers of the adhesive, and finally I wrap the flesh-colored bandage about her ring finger.

"It'll have to do until we finish this bedroom. I think we'll have time to make the jewelry store on Harlem Avenue, if you quit screwing around and finish."

Harms' Jewelers is opened until nine. We get there at seven. It takes Lila all of ten minutes to pick out her engagement ring.

"It's too small," I tell her.

"Are you nuts? It's $1200.00!"

I show her one that goes for two grand.

"That's ridiculous!"

"Do you like it?"

"Of course I—"

"Then get it. I'm never doing this marriage thing again, so we're blowing the door off the hinges. Get the one you really want, Lila. Don't go discount on me. Not you. Not this time. I can afford it."

She looks up at me. She reaches up and kisses my cheek.

"How come you never got married? Tell me again," I tell her.

She colors, slightly.

"I told you that fable three times."

"Tell me again."

"We went together through high school. We were going to get engaged when I graduated the Air Force Academy, but my senior year he got tired of waiting, he said."

I look around the jewelry store. No one's in ear shot.

"And when did the interest in the other team begin?"

"Why're you asking me all this *now?*"

I look down at her and take her shoulders.

"Mary's out of my life, gone. I want to know that's the way it is with you, too. Everyone else is out of it, gone."

She looks up at me again, but this time her eyes are filling.

"I love you. And you're all I want. Okay?"

I kiss her before the waterworks commence.

"Perfect. Absolutely outstanding, Lila. That's all I wanted to know. Now go crazy. Put me in hock for twenty years."

She bats my chest with the back of her right hand. I pretend she's knocked the air out of me.

The first thing she does when we get home to the odor of newly painted rooms is to call Kelly at Northern. I can hear Lila squealing and giggling like a teenager, and then Lila puts me on the phone with my daughter.

"I am so happy for you, Daddy!"

It sounds like she's bouncing up and down, even over the phone.

"I'm pretty happy about it, myself."

"When's the wedding?" Kelly asks.

"We haven't set a date, but I figure neither of us wants to put it off very long. We've been doing this mating dance for too long, already."

Lila swats my back, this time.

"I have to marry her soon to start the payments on the setting she picked out. She don't have cheap tastes, let me tell ya."

I get whacked again.

She grabs the phone from me.

"He's the one who went nuts, Kelly. Don't let him give you that crap about my expensive tastes.... Well, I'm happy you're happy. Jesus, everybody is happy. What the hell happened to us?"

She goes on with my daughter for a couple minutes more, asking her how she's doing in the summer session she signed up for. Kelly's determined to get her degree in four years, so she signed up for summer school, and she says she's going in the summer again, next year, too.

I get the receiver, one more time.

"This one's gonna work, Dad," she tells me.

I choke slightly, but then I thank her for saying it.

"No, I mean it. This is your turn. It finally happened for you, and this is your turn. I just know it."

I tell her to take care of herself, and I say Lila and I will come up on Sunday to take her to dinner. And I tell her Lila's wild to show her the ring, too.

Then I say goodbye, and I see my fiancé removing her tank top and her bra and her panties.

I look at Lila. I wish I'd seen her like this when she was eighteen or twenty. It isn't because she's worse for wear because she's in full bloom. A woman at age forty is at her full maturity, at her sexual peak. I read that somewhere, but I can't remember where. I just wish I'd been with her from then until now.

Her breasts are perfect orbs, not too big or little. No sag, which is a testament to the shape she keeps herself in by running and swimming.

She still trains like a cadet at the Air Force Academy. Her sides are sleek and perfect. Her legs, like the rest of her, are lightly tanned—like a doe's skin. Her stomach is flat, and she has a pert inny bellybutton that gives me hours of entertainment. Lila thinks I'm obsessed with her inny, and she's probably correct.

Her butt is tight and only slightly prominent. But it's a really good-looking ass. She wears bikini underwear because she knows it makes me suffer.

"Are you just going to stand there?" she grins.

I take her in my arms before I start throwing off my clothes.

"Is this $2000 ring going to give me anything a little special, tonight?"

"What you get with me is special *every* night. And day, for that matter, bub."

"Damn right, you are."

She starts tearing at my shirt, and then she's working on my pants. And last she's removed my Jockey briefs.

"You have to start wearing boxers."

"Don't start again with that, Lila."

"You have one offspring, but that's not nearly the end of your line—and mine."

"Now we're having babies?"

"Three. At least."

"Do I look like an incubator to you?"

"You're my stallion, big boy."

"You gotta stop watching porn with those Vice guys."

"It shows me new techniques. Our love will never get old, Danny."

"It doesn't need any outside help, Lila."

"There, you're right on the money. Don't stop delivering your pizzas. They're the best in town."

I cover her lips with my own. She takes hold of me and directs me where I should be. Then she jumps up so I can get my arms under her thighs. When we're fully connected, I turn around and find that Sonny the border collie is watching us intently.

38

In my dreams, he's loose. He finds a way through security. He runs over their lawns until he hits the wall. They don't use concertina or barbed wire at Elgin because most of their patients are helpless souls who need special care to give them a reason for waking up and breathing for the next twenty-four hours. Most of their patients are defenseless.

The high-risk inmates are kept in an isolation ward. It's pretty much state of the art, I found out when we dropped Toliver off, there. Everything is done electrically, with cameras covering all the hallways and cells where these dangerous cases are housed. From what I saw, it doesn't seem likely that Franklin is going to bust out like John Dillinger did in the '30s. I can't picture Franklin brandishing a Thompson submachine gun and then Toliver busting guards' heads as he bullies his way free to some moll—like Jennifer O'Brien—waiting for him in an eight cylinder getaway car.

No, in my dreams he weasels his way out with his charm. He simply asks twelve guards to cut him loose, and miraculously, they do. The twelve guards are, of course, the twelve jurors who deemed him crazy and who put him in a hospital instead of on death row, where he belongs.

Steinback told me what I already know: You never know what a jury's going to do, and neither do they until they do it. It's our system of justice, warts and all, but it's ours.

That's where the dream always ends. Then I wake up, just after he's climbed the wall and escaped into the mist of my fantasy. I thrash a lot while it's going on, and it wakes Lila up.

"Danny?" she murmurs.

"I'm sorry, babe."

"Same dream?"

"Same dream."

"Go back to sleep. We have to go on shift in three hours."

It's three-thirteen A.M. on the digital. We're working days, but Lila has made the request that she be assigned a new partner. She explained to the Captain that we were getting married sometime soon, and the commandant said he'd expedite matters to accommodate Lila and me.

After all, I'm the man who shot Liberty Valance—I captured Franklin the Maniac, the Twin Killer, so my shit is very precious right now in the CPD. There were stories in both major newspapers, and I reluctantly gave an interview to the newsbabe on Channel 5 because the Captain made it clear I was to cooperate with the media because the Department needs the good pub, lately. So I talked with her, and Lila forced me to watch it on the evening news, a few nights ago. She loved watching me squirm through the whole eight-minute interview.

"You look *very* sexy," she giggled as we watched.

I glide my hand down my fiancé's left flank. She always sleeps on her right side. She purrs like a feline. Her side becomes slightly rigid, and then it relaxes and softens, and finally she turns over to me.

"We can sleep when we're old and fried," she smiles groggily.

She pulls off the oversized tee shirt that she wears as a nightgown.

"You're killing me," I say as I feign weariness.

"Let's make it permanent. Let's die in each other's arms, Danny."

"I don't want you to die. Ever."

"I won't. I promise."

"Yeah, you say that because you know you'll outlive me. Women have a habit of doing that to men."

She reaches down and touches me through the boxers she bought for me for my enhanced sperm count. She's still on the pill, now, though, and she says she will be until I make her an honest woman and until we're both ready. But she keeps telling me she's already at the far edge of primetime baby-making. We're both around forty, she reminds me.

"I love the morning best. You're always ready. No foreplay necessary."

"It's the nature of the wee fellow," I smile at her as she grips him tighter.

"Easy, Bubba," I urge her.

"He's not so wee, and I don't know any damn body named Bubba."

She yanks the white boxers down, and then I kick them off. She separates my legs so she can squeeze in between them and join us at the same time. It looked as though it would be an awkward position, but Lila has a way of getting us where we want to go.

Her heat is what always surprises me. Not all the women I've slept with are literally hot, the way Lila always is, when we enjoy "sexual congress." I've always liked that term because I get an image of the Senate and the House rolling on the floor of Congress.

Her heat is what makes me want to have orgasm a little too fast, some of the time, but she knows how to back off when I become too intense. She'll slow things down and kiss me. Or she'll help me withdraw just so I don't finish too fast for either of us. We don't always throb together, but we're getting more in sync, now that we're together regularly. When we had those single encounters—twice—I was like the veritable billy goat under a bush. I was out of control.

Now I've become far more patient than I was when I was with Mary or any of the other few women I slept with.

But the flesh is weak, and even though I've tried the best way I know how, the passion and the heat overcome me, actually both of us, and we're straining to somehow merge into one body. It's as though I'm trying to enter Lila *all over*. It's an impossible physical feat, but my mouth covers hers, our tongues are deep inside the other's mouth, my shaft is straining to get deeper into her womb, and we're struggling not to be separate from each other. It's like the reverse of the rib story in Adam and Eve.

Finally, we're spent.

"What time is it?" Lila asks. "My eyes are too fuzzy. Everything's freaking glowing in here."

"It's 3:59," I tell her.

"Shit. It's all your fault. I never should have bought those damn boxers."

She smiles at the ceiling with her eyes shut. I can barely make out her face, but I can see her teeth, even in the dark. I lean over to her and grab a few strands of her long hair. Then I let go of the strands and graze her left cheek with the back of my hand.

"I love you so much that I can't tell you how much I love you."

"You're balmy. Better go back to sleep," Lila tells me. "And stop wasting your rest on that prick in Elgin. I'm going to exorcise the son of a bitch myself. I'm going to throw him out of your dreams. You're only going to dream about me, Danny. Nothing and nobody else but me."

"I like you in the real world better. You feel a lot more like you."

"That doesn't make any damn sense."

"But you know what I'm trying to tell you, right?"

She opens her eyes and rolls toward me again. Then she worms her way down toward my middle, and I feel her starting me up, once more.

She halts, momentarily.

"If we're up, we might as well get some exercise," she proclaims.

Instead of feeling drained and punchless, I feel energized. I take Lila out to an expensive Loop eatery for breakfast, and we both pig out on a trillion-calorie meal of pancakes and animal fat patties of some brand. It's delicious, but it sits like an anvil in my stomach. This joint is open twenty-four hours, but I've never seen it empty. It's called Fazio's, and it's not far from the Art Institute. So we can make it to work by 7:00. We got here at 5:45, and the place was already hopping.

We sit in a booth. It was the last seating available. The booths have windows that look out at the spectacle of Michigan Avenue. This is the hood in Chicago that the photographers visit when they want to capture anything elegant about this town. You don't take pictures of the west side, or most of the hoods north and south—you go to the lakeshore to glimpse at the civility of the city with "the big shoulders." This is close to the Gold Coast. This is where you live if you've embraced the American Dream—You know, the cause we bled for in Vietnam and in every other bloodbath we've engaged in?

I don't know why a $30 breakfast brings out all the above in me, but there it is.

It's 6:45. We need to boogie. The Captain is being a nice guy by assigning Lila to another partner in Homicide. He could've put her in Burglary or Auto/Theft or even Vice. But he knows how good she really is, and, as I said, I'm still Wyatt Earp, for a little while, until everyone forgets Franklin Toliver and Kirk Radley.

July Fourth is our day off. Luckily, Lila has the same day off as I do, even though she's been paired with Ben Bradford, a twenty-five year vet with two ex-wives and thirteen kids to support in his old age. Lila says all he talks about is his bills. He keeps joking that he's worth more dead than he is alive, and I wonder if he's really joking. He might want to talk to Dr. Fernandez, himself. Me? I'm scheduled to see her tomorrow.

We've been talking about my ex, and the shrink knows now that Lila and I are going to be married. She told me it was a smart move to take the air out of the balloon and have Lila get a new partner. She said our relationship didn't need to formally begin with all the pressure of hiding our togetherness with necessary lies.

Now we can at least begin out in the open. It made me think of Lila's former bi-sexuality, but her past hasn't bothered me the way it used to. And Lila insists it *is* all behind her, now, and I believe it.

On this Fourth of July, Kelly has come home, and the three of us are going to Grant Park to watch the fireworks show. The show almost didn't happen because of a gigantic thunderstorm that buffeted the entire top one third of Illinois. It knocked down power lines all over northern Illinois, but we were spared at our house, and the lights in the Loop are mostly back on, by now. It's eight in the evening, and we've got a blanket spread on the grass. There must be a few hundred thousand people here by now, and more will be coming. The park is well lit enough even when the dusk becomes night. But the real show will be over our heads. The Navy's Blue Angels squad of fighter jets has already flown over us several times. I could see the look of awe and the ache of remembrance in Lila's face as they passed over the park with a BOOOM! that startled all of us here below.

Kelly has a new boyfriend. His name is Matt, and he's in pre-med. We'll meet him the next time we go to Northern to visit my daughter. Kelly's got the same happy glow that she had when she was with Michael, and I'm thankful she's found someone to be with, especially since Lila and I have so recently come together. When you're alone, you don't want the people you love to be alone, but when you're a couple, you want those beloved to have someone with them even more than you did when you were flying solo.

I know that eagles don't fly in flocks, but there's something to be said for community, for partnership. I was trained to fight alone in the jungle if I had to, but it was always better to be with a partner—or twelve or twenty or a hundred. There is something about numbers. Which is why I like the feeling of celebrating the Fourth in the middle of a vast mob of humanity. When I was by myself, I never would've come out here. I would've stayed home and read a book or watched a ball game on the tube.

Lila has truly civilized me, at least for the moment. I'm not adverse to being with the herd, with the masses. I'm not political, but I've always been an individualist, in my own head. I have not always been all that rugged an individualist, however. I'm thinking I might even join something associated with the church—maybe get into a softball league or learn to play golf at one of their outings.

I don't really know what's come over me, but it isn't unpleasant.

The show begins at 9:30, on the button. Starshells go up and burst into a multitude of colors. The streamers rip through the sky in every direction. The pops come just before the explosion of light and reds and greens and blues and oranges and golds and every other imaginable hue in the spectrum.

The noise and the fury and the spectacle go on for a half hour, and then we're on our way to battle the traffic and to return home.

It's on the answering machine when I get home and turn the lights on. I see the flashing little red bulb pulsating with the call. It's the Captain. He wants me to call him at home.

I'm thinking perhaps there's a problem with Lila's new assignment—but he would've called her direct.

I dial his number, and he picks up on the third ring.

"There's a problem, Danny."

My heart begins to race.

"Which is?" I ask.

He hesitates, and I wonder if the line's gone dead.

"You remember the big storm early this morning?"

I wait.

"The lights were out everywhere. And I guess it hit the northwest suburbs worst of all. And there was power out everywhere—"

"He got out."

The line goes silent.

"Yes," he finally responds. "The supervisor of his block called a few hours ago. I tried to call you right away, but I kept getting your answering machine, so I left the message."

"He got out."

"It was chaos, this guy said. Their power went out, and their backup generators blew because of the heat and an overload. The doors were opened because everything's electronic—"

"He's loose."

"I'm sorry to have to tell you all this. Especially now, when things—"

"They're certain he's sprung?"

"In all the confusion, I guess he just walked out of the fucking place."

"They lost Franklin."

"What else can I tell you, Danny? What else can I say?"

39

I get a call from the Lieutenant Governor. He's going to be in Chicago, and he wants a sit-down with me. So I arrange to see him at his home in DesPlaines.

The drive takes only forty-five minutes at 10:47 A.M. The rush traffic is history by almost two hours, now, but the Stevenson is always at least partially blocked somewhere by some knucklehead who insists on tailgating another knucklehead, and then you have a gaper's block of clowns all taking in the majesty of a rear-ender.

Today, I'm more fortunate. No accidents en route. I pull up to the house in DesPlaines, and I see three State Trooper vehicles. Two Staties are at the door. I show them my badge, and they open the door for me. I find the Lieutenant Governor in his study, at the direction of an aide who's female and drop dead, salivating bountiful. Must be in her mid-twenties. One of those birds you can't elevate your eyes from her chest type. She's got a stone beautiful face, and now I'm thinking I know why Raymond Toliver rarely came home to DesPlaines from Springfield.

"Please sit," Toliver beckons as the babe closes the study door behind me.

Raymond sits down behind the lavish desk where his wife sat, all those months before when Lila and I interviewed her about Franklin.

I sit in the straight-backed, plush chair opposite him. I'm again fascinated by the number of volumes he owns on those shelves behind him.

"Thank you for taking the time to see me," Toliver smiles.

"You're welcome. No problem. I assume this is about Franklin."

"Regretfully, yes, it is."

His handsome face goes somber. He reminds me of Stewart Granger, the English movie actor. He's got the same distinguished streaks of white beneath a dark brown, full head of hair. The hair has been cut with a razor—it's been styled. But he's in the public eye, so I forgive him.

"Any word at all?" he asks.

"He's done his disappearing act, just like he did when we hunted him, all those months. He's very good at going underground."

"I brought you here because I'm asking you to make Franklin your one and only case until you apprehend him. I've asked the mayor, and he's agreed to have your Commander assign you to Franklin's capture. You know my son best, you and your partner. What was her name?"

"Lila. We're no longer partners. I'm working alone, temporarily."

"I see. Perhaps it's better that way."

I look again at his snow-white side locks. I'm remembering Stewart Granger in *North to Alaska* with John Wayne and Fabian, the heartthrob.

"Why am I being thrust into the breach here? Why has this become political?"

He smiles at me.

"Everything's political, Detective. Everything. You're not being assigned this one case just because of me. The Governor has further political aspirations. We're in the same party, as you know, and if I become a detriment to his Senate bid, then he is also affected by Franklin's remaining at large.

"The Governor wants to have me run for his job in the next election. My winning can't help but aid his run for the Senate, so you see how everything fits together, I assume?"

His grin has replaced the wide, TV smile.

"What if I don't get him?"

"The Federal Bureau of Investigation and the State Police are looking for my son, too, so you'll have plenty of company. But I have a feeling you'll be there when he's found. I know your background. I've read about your decorations, but I see your exploits themselves are classified."

"I had hell catching him the first time. This isn't the jungle."

"There, you're wrong. There's just less foliage. Some jungle creatures, but less shrubbery."

"You might be right, on that one. But I'm not as confident as you seem to be."

He goes sullen in the face, suddenly. His fingers are spread out over the green mat on his desktop.

"You haven't noticed the competitive nature Franklin has? He's always competed, even though he was neither an athlete nor a scholar. He still had to struggle against someone or something for recognition. He just didn't do it the way most people do."

"You mean like killing six prostitutes."

His face goes positively sour at their mention.

"I mean that Franklin will be competing against you again. He reads the newspapers. He knows who you are, and not just because you arrested him. I saw him at Elgin two weeks before he escaped. He talked about you, almost obsessively. He asked me questions about your background, which I didn't know, two weeks ago. They don't allow him access to books or newspapers. Franklin, as you know, was in Elgin's version of solitary confinement, so he asked me question after question about you."

"Are you telling me you think Franklin's coming after me?"

He watches my eyes carefully, as if he's anticipating an attack of some kind.

"He never said that. He also asked me about your partner, Lila. I told him I knew nothing about either of you, personally, but he kept on asking anyway. As I said, he's very—"

"Competitive."

"Yes, Detective."

"So you brought me here to warn me."

"In part. But I wanted to tell you how imperative it is that you find him before he finds you. A lot of lives could be affected by my son. I know six already have been, and beyond all that about politics, he needs to be locked in a real prison where he'll never get out again."

"Who's to say they won't remand him back to Elgin if we find him again?" I ask.

"Can we share something private, you and I?"

He leans toward me as if he's going to whisper something to me.

"If you can kill him, do it. If he gives you just cause, don't hesitate."

"I'm just a policeman."

"I know that answer, Detective, but you know Franklin."

"It seems like enough people have been killed already."

"Self-defense is a moral imperative, Detective Mangan."

"I know. I was in a war, once."

He looks at me, and now his face softens.

"I don't live here, anymore. I'm putting the place up for sale."

"It's a little rich for my blood," I smile at him.

I'm having trouble not liking him. I know what a problem child can be like, but his kid and mine are in two very different ballparks. And my kid is climbing all the way out of her hole and into the sunlight. Franklin is worming his way into the netherworld. I can understand the misery this man has endured. His wife left him a bit differently than Mary left me.

"She's still here, you know."

"Who?" I ask him.

"My wife. She's still here."

"You mean her spirit?"

"The State Policemen won't come in here after dark. One of them saw her as he was checking the place out, a few days after her death."

"Are you yanking my chain?"

"I'm afraid not. I've seen her, too. I spent a weekend here, getting my personal belongings removed, and I saw her in her closet, where she hanged herself. I heard some noise in her room, and I went inside, and there she was. She looked at me as if she wondered why I was home. You see, this was her residence, not mine, really. We hadn't lived together for the better part of three years, but we didn't officially separate because of my career. If I were to win the Governor's job, we would've divorced then."

He looks at me and again smiles warmly.

"I'm not yanking your chain, Detective. I never believed in ghosts, either. Live and become educated, right?"

He stands up, and so do I.

"Please find him and get him back where he belongs, one way or the other. I don't mean to be jerking you around, but he was your case from the beginning, and I truly mean to tell you that I'd be looking for him to make contact with you.

"So please be careful. And tell your former partner to keep her eyes open."

He reaches across the table and takes my hand.

I feel like telling him he's got my vote when he runs for Governor, but I hold back, and I leave.

I tell Lila about my conversation with Raymond Toliver. We're at home, sitting on the new couch that Lila bought with her own coin. It's royal blue, and it's a three-seater with recliners at either end and a setup that you can use as an arm rest and a cup holder in the middle that flips down and then back up—retractable.

"We have loaded weapons in this household, right?" she smiles bravely.

"He's not going to come here, Lila. He was just planting a seed in the old man's head because he knew Raymond would warn us."

"How'd he know he was going to bust out?" she asks.

"He didn't. But he was looking for an opportunity to blow Elgin the minute we dropped him off there."

"How do you know?"

"Intuition. I'm psychic," I grin at her.

"Then let's go to Vegas and make some real money."

But her pretty face has clouded over.

"This had to happen now," she says.

"You mean, about us?"

"Of course I mean about us."

"Too bad your name's not Nora and my name's not Nick."

"I'm saying is this going to postpone our wedding, Danny?"

"Absolutely negative, Detective. Not for a minute, not for a second."

"Then I want to get married soon."

"How about today?" I proffer.

"My parents would murder us both, and then you wouldn't have to worry about Toliver Junior."

"I forgot about your parents, the lawyer and the pediatrician. You don't mess with professional people, no."

"Knock it off, Danny. They both love you."

"They've only met me twice."

We went to brunch once and dinner once with them, and Lila's right. They didn't deserve the wise crack. They're both very nice people. And they made Lila, and I firmly believe in genetics.

"No, we'll get married on the day you pick," I tell her.

She bites her cuticle, deep in thought.

"Christmas Eve?" she asks.

"I don't think Catholics do that day."

"Then how about the Saturday before Christmas Eve?"

"Fine. Done."

She bites that same cuticle again.

"You think we can get another dog so we have one inside and one outside?" she asks.

"You want another dog? Fine. I don't want some fucking beast that's going to get in fights with Sonny."

"You know I love Sonny, dumbass."

"A minute ago we were getting married on Christmas Eve, and the next minute you call me dumbass and want to bring a fucking pit bull into the house."

"No, I do not want that kind of pet. I was thinking maybe another border collie."

"Not a female. No puppies."

"No female. But I'd like it if we had more company around the house."

"Just one. No fleet of pooches, madam."

"Just one.... And a security system."

I laugh out loud.

"Two cops and two dogs and a security system. You want concertina wire and a machine gun nest?"

"It isn't funny, Danny. Toliver was warning us. He brought you all the way to his home to warn you. I think all that might be significant, don't you?"

I hug her. Then I kiss her on the lips and hold the kiss.

"The Feds and the Staties are after him. The Fibbies especially love headlines. They'll catch him within a week. He's got no money. He's got no ride, and he's got a mug that's been spread all over the media. There's no chance he'll ever get here. I already called the FBI and the State Police and told them what Raymond Toliver said to me, so they're going to keep the house under watch, twenty-four-seven, until somebody catches this diseased prick."

"He can't screw us up, Danny. We won't let him."

"You have my word, lady."

I kiss her again.

"But I still want the extra dog and the security system. And you need to give Kelly a heads up."

When she mentions my daughter, a shiver rises up my spine.

"He's capable of anything, Danny."

I look into her eyes, and then I kiss both of her cheeks, one at a time.

"Maybe I ought to charge a bounty on Franklin. Make it worth my while."

"It already is very worth your while."

I embrace her tightly once more, and I feel that same chill snake up my back.

40

It's difficult to get through the end of summer, or any other clump of days, without Lila. She gives me feedback while we work a case. She has sure-fire intuition, and she's exceptionally bright. I depended on her to help me get those redliners off our board.

But now there's only one name on the white board. And I'm getting tired of looking at Franklin's moniker.

Dr. Fernandez told me not to fixate on him or on anything else. She says I'm going to have to look at him as if he's a task and nothing more. If I do obsess over Toliver, she claims, it only serves to give him power over me.

There was a Native American in my platoon in my last hitch in Vietnam. His name was John Glover, but his real name used to be Two-Hides. John Two-Hides. When his father left the res, he legally changed it to Glover because his dad liked an All American halfback from Stanford by that name.

John was pretty tight with me before we both returned to The World alive. He used to tell me on the hump, while we were walking somewhere very frightening, that his ancestors liked to think they assumed another man's power when they killed him. They used to eat the hearts of their enemies, long ago, because it made them feel they were acquiring their foes' energy, their strength. Their power.

So when the Doc tells me not to let Toliver assume my sap by letting myself become hung up on his capture, I try to tell myself to relax and treat his case as though it were any other.

But it's not, of course. I've got the Mayor and the Lieutenant Governor and even my own Captain demanding results. They want this asshole nabbed and bagged *yesterday*. I think my shrink knows I've got enough self-imposed stress on myself without their adding to my burden.

If Franklin were a Viet Cong or an NVA, and if he were hiding in the bush, I'd go out and find him. I tell myself that Vietnam was the fucking rainforest, and my prey out there had a lot more places to burrow in than he does in the Chicagoland area. He has no money, no vehicle, I keep telling myself.

But what *are* his resources? Jennifer O'Brien and the Aryan Nation. That's the extent of his assets, I make it.

I try O'Brien first. I drive out to Orland Park again, and the mother answers the door. I receive a very hostile glare from mommy. She asks what I want, this time. She doesn't invite me inside, and it's a torrid mid-August afternoon.

We stand on her enclosed front porch. It's screened in, but it doesn't keep the humidity and the high heat out. Just the bugs.

"I want you to know that my daughter lost her job at the school because of you and that maniac. Some columnist wrote that my daughter was associated with a hate group, and that writer wondered why any school district would employ anyone of her 'moral caliber.' And then her fiancé broke off the marriage two weeks before the wedding. And you come here and you want to talk to my daughter?"

I wait for the inferno to dwindle down to a blaze.

"It wasn't my intention to hurt your daughter. I'm chasing an escaped lunatic who killed six women, and if you find my coming here distasteful, I gotta tell you, ma'am, I don't much give a damn. Please tell your daughter I'd like her to call me if Toliver tries to make contact with her again."

"Jennifer thinks you've tapped her phone. She says she hears clicking sounds."

"She's been watching too many movies."

I don't feel moved to tell her or her daughter the truth. And the FBI is tapping her phone again, not me and the CPD.

"Do you think my daughter deserves all these terrible things to happen to her?"

"I wasn't alive during World War II. But my father was. He helped liberate some of the death camps. Maybe you ought to take a trip to the library, and bring Jennifer with you when you go."

I turn and walk out of her screened in front porch.

The other asset will be harder to reach. But I do get a chance to talk to their sub-commander, Richard Ellsworth. He operates out of his basement on the southwest side, not far from Marquette Park, where I hauled Franklin in.

Ellsworth is in his early fifties, I'd guess. There's no sign of a wife or girlfriend inside his brick bungalow, here in this working stiff, blue collar hood. The houses on his block are almost replicas of one another. They have tiny front lawns that you could cut with a scissors, and equally dwarfish backyards with chainlink fences and loud dogs within.

He has a shaved head and the requisite teardrops on his cheeks that he makes no attempt to hide by using makeup or bandages. I can't imagine a business hiring him, unless it's something where he doesn't come into contact with the public.

He has the shape of a tree stump. He's maybe five-seven, and I'd guess he tips them at 240 pounds or so. His neck seems to blend into his shoulders so that it appears his melon head is simply resting atop them.

Ellsworth guides me down into his basement. There is a door off from his kitchen.

We hear growling as we descend the steps.

"Herman! Sit!" Ellsworth commands, and the German shepherd meekly obeys, at the bottom of the rungs.

I watch Herman as I pass him, and the dog eyeballs me right back. I have my right hand ready to reach for my weapon in my waistband holster, but the dog whimpers a bit, and I'm beyond him. I assume Herman's a he.

Ellsworth turns on the fluorescent overhead lights, and the room is blaringly light. There are swastikas and German flags from World War II and the obligatory poster of the Fuehrer on the wall, as well. It makes my stomach literally turn, but I needed to talk to this asshole.

He has a desk. There is a chair opposite the desk, so we sit.

"You know what aiding and abetting mean?" I ask.

The tree stump remains mute. I'd like to shoot him and rescue his dog.

"How long you been on probation?" I smile.

That gets his undivided attention.

"You been keeping your distance from the kiddies?" I keep smiling.

"What is it you want?"

"Remember the stuff about aiding and abetting? That's what you'd be doing if you didn't tell me that Franklin Toliver has contacted you and asked for help from you and the Nation."

"Toliver has never called here. He wouldn't. He knows the FBI has our phones tapped."

"Isn't that a bitch. Where's privacy, anymore? Where are all our civil liberties? Oh! I forgot. You lovers don't believe in civil liberties. You're fascists! Shit, I'm sorry. I forgot."

The stump is coloring with rage. I wish he would get physical. Maybe all this stress I've been discussing with Fernandez would be released if I could kick hell out of this piece of flotsam.

"Is there anything else?"

"If you withhold on me, dickhead, I'll be there behind you wherever you go. Yeah, harassment. But you'll never be able to prove it. I made my living shadowing the little people far, far away in an old lost war. I'll make you my personal fucking pincushion, Richard—or do they call you *Dick?*"

"Is there anything else?"

"Are you trying to tell me that you don't want to talk to me anymore? I know your probation officer—Tim McCain? He speaks very highly of you. He knows you liked Menard so well that you'd just love to go back for a lifetime visit. Nice prison, Menard. All kinds of interesting dickwads, there. I've visited a few, put a few there, myself.

"I'll be talking to you, *Dick*."

I rise from my chair, but he stays seated.

"Tell the dog to behave. I'd much rather put a round in your forehead than in his."

He yells out for Herman to stay.

Then I make the ascent from this primeval cave to the surface.

The phone calls start two nights later. Lila is the unfortunate recipient.

"What does he say?" I ask.

"He doesn't say anything. I can just hear him breathing lightly."

"We have an unlisted phone number. Our address isn't published, Lila."

"I know. But he knows where we are," she says.

I ask the FBI to tap my phone at home, and they agree. I ask them how they think he got my number. They respond the only way they can figure it is if someone at CPD is handing out information.

I walk downstairs to Personnel. The supervisor's name is Maryann Dempsey. She's been with us for twenty-two years. We go into her office, and I shut the door behind me.

"I think someone in your office has given out my phone number, and maybe other personal information about me."

She's heavy, but she has a very pretty face with abundant strawberry blonde hair haloing her head. She looks like a PTA mom.

"I don't think that's very likely, Detective. These are all solid people who work in this office."

"Anybody relatively new, in here?"

"There are two girls who were hired two years and three years ago, respectively."

"You do checks on all of them?"

"Sure," she replies.

"I'm not here to assign blame on anyone, Maryann, but you've heard of Franklin Toliver?"

She nods.

"You'd have to be in Tibet not to have heard of him. We were all shocked when they put him in Elgin, Detective Mangan."

This time I nod.

"He's been calling my house."

"He *has?*"

There's nothing feigned about her reply. She sounds sincerely shocked.

"Our federal brethren seem to think the only likely place he could've gained access to that information is here. So, what color are the two newest employees in here?"

"They're both white, but we have a number of Hispanics and African Americans here, too."

"Maryann, I'm not with the NAACP. Relax. I just figure it isn't likely that the Aryan Nation would have a non-white mole working in Personnel. Do you think it'd be likely?"

She shakes her head.

"We're going to see if we can trace any calls from here to the outside. They were probably smart enough not to make any calls from your phones, but maybe we'll get lucky. The storm troopers and their followers have never been known for their intellects, but they'd make good weasels. I just came here to ask you to keep your eye out, for me. The FBI is going to check any of your outgoing calls for the past few weeks. Please keep all this confidential. Okay?"

She nods again, and I can see she's upset. I feel like giving her a hug and buying her some coffee and a doughnut, but I don't have time.

Lila picks up the phone. And ten seconds into the call, she pulls out her police whistle and lets loose into the speaker end of the phone. The blast nearly explodes my own eardrums, and then she slams the thing back into its cradle.

"Jesus, I think you made *me* deaf," I tell her.

"I hope I made Franklin go dumb, I mean really dumb. Or is it deaf?"

"It's deaf. Dumb means you can't speak," I tell her.

"Whatever."

"I hope it was Franklin, not somebody who didn't speak up fast enough."

We now have our second border collie, Snuffy. He's six months old, but he's already granted Sonny the alpha male role that Sonny deserves around our house. The two of them are inseparable, so keeping one inside and one outside isn't going to work. They're like twin brothers, although Sonny is twice as old as Snuffy.

"They'll make plenty of noise if someone approaches the house," I tell Lila.

"I want them both inside at night, okay?"

"They'd be inside no matter what. You know I don't let them stay outside after dark. The bugs would walk away with them."

We had the security system installed last week. The house is wired, top to bottom. And they put movement sensitive lights in the front and the back of the house. Anybody comes near, a blaze of wattage erupts.

I brought two shotgun pumps into the house. They're next to the bed when we go to sleep at night. Lila has her piece on the nightstand, and so do I. Just for good measure, I keep my six-inch switchblade on the nightstand, as well, and I keep the knife in my pocket whenever I go outside. My .38 is always on my waist in its holder.

So it's not like we're unprepared.

But the phone calls spook Lila, even with her police whistle. They disturb me, also.

And I'm thinking real hard about granting Raymond Toliver's request for me to put one right in his son's noggin, if Franklin will just cooperate.

41

The FBI is able to trace the call made to Richard Ellsworth, my buddy, Dick, and the call was made by Susan Parkley. We find out that Parkley has been an employee of the CPD Personnel Division for eighteen months. She has no known connection to the Aryan Nation, but the Feds find out she's the second cousin of that same Richard, *Dick,* Ellsworth.

The FBI guys allow me to bring Parkley in for an interview. I see her alone in the interrogation room down the hall from me, but there are a few witnesses outside, watching and listening through the one-way window/mirror.

Susan is only twenty-eight years old. Her jacket says she just graduated community college, a two-year program, and that she's the single mother of a four- year-old son by a now gone south marriage. I start to feel bad for her, until I remember that she put Lila and me in jeopardy with Franklin Toliver and the Aryan Nation.

We've since changed our phone number, but she gave out our address—which we're not changing.

I look at her, and she drops her eyes to the table in front of her. I'm sitting directly opposite Susan Parkley.

"You know you're going to lose your job," I tell her.

She looks up and the tears well in her eyes.

"Why'd you tell your cousin my information, Susan?"

She begins to bawl. I hand her the box of tissues next to me. She blows her nose.

"You know that your cousin gave that information to Franklin Toliver, don't you? And you know I'm the cop who arrested Toliver. Why would you do it? Did he offer you money?"

"No. He threatened me. He threatened my son. *What could I do?*"

"You could've told me, instead, Susan. I would've helped you. Now he's lost your job for you."

She sobs quietly.

"I read how hard you worked to get where you are. And you're a single parent."

"I'm so sorry, Detective. I didn't mean you any harm, but he said I'd come home one night and Randy, my son, wouldn't be there, and he said that if I told the police, if I told anyone, he'd kill us both. Do you know what kind of animals these people are?"

"Yeah, I do. But I have a daughter and someone else I love very much, Susan. This man, Toliver, wants to do us harm, too."

"I wish I could change what happened, Detective. I'm so very sorry."

"Did Ellsworth mention anything about Toliver when he contacted you?"

"No. He never said why he wanted your personal information. I told him I'd get fired, and then he threatened to kill me."

"Would you testify that he threatened you?"

"He said he'd kill both of us, Detective."

"He can't hurt you if he's in jail, Susan. And the Aryan boys have enough heat on them from the FBI because of a slew of civil rights crimes. They won't want to get into it because Ellsworth was dumb enough to have you call him from Headquarters. Your cousin is too dumb to live, and you can bet the Brotherhood will be happy to get rid of this moron."

"Can I get any protection?"

"If you work with me, I'll make it happen."

She looks at me sadly. She's a single mother, thirty pounds

overweight, and she's about to become unemployed.

"I'm so sorry this all happened," she says.

"You help me with Ellsworth, and I tell them that you were coerced into handing out the information, maybe we can save your job, Susan. I don't know. No promises, but I'll give it a shot."

I'm thinking this bastard Toliver and his friends like Richard Ellsworth have already hurt too many innocents. It's time to contain the body count.

The dog is in the backyard. Luckily he's as dumb as his master, and he goes for the pound of ground chuck I throw him over the fence before he gets the chance to start barking at me and waking up Ellsworth. It takes three minutes for Herman to scarf down the chuck, and it takes about twelve more minutes for three of Lila's sleeping pills, mixed inside the raw meat, to put Herman night-night. He finally slumps down on his side and konks.

It's past three in the A.M., the best time for a raid or an ambush. I was fortunate I was upwind when the German shepherd saw me tossing him his sleep-inducing treat. I'm hoping he won't OD on the sleeping pills, but I'm no vet, and I couldn't have him disturbing Richard.

Once the pooch is out like a light and on his back and snoring, I climb the six-foot chain link fence and walk over to Ellsworth's back door. I take out my pick, and I have his deadbolt opened in under a minute. I learned how to break and enter when I was a Burglary detective, just before I made Homicide. It is of course very illegal to enter anyone's residence this way, with or without a search warrant.

The time to play fair has come and departed. Toliver's fucking with my family, and I include Lila in "family" even though we're not married yet and won't be until the week before Christmas. I could go to jail for this, naturally, but Kelly and Lila and I could get killed by Franklin Toliver, on the other hand, so I figure this is well worth the risk. I won't allow him to threaten my two women. If I could kill enemies in Vietnam, then I can do the same in this country. Again, going by the rulebook has allowed Franklin to go free. The gloves are finally off.

I walk into the kitchen of Ellsworth's bungalow. There are dirty dishes in the sink, and the garbage can is over-stacked, and the can stinks of tuna fish.

I'm wearing my requisite all black, pants and tee shirt. I've also got my black running shoes on. It's a blistering evening in late August, and thankfully he's got central air conditioning, which was why I was able to approach the dog outside. Even if he had begun to bark, Ellsworth might not have heard him for a while because everything is shut up inside his house, and he's got his storm windows secured, as well.

I walk toward the bedroom on the main floor, just outside the kitchen. Actually, there are two bedrooms, here. I can hear Ellsworth snoring in the second bedroom, just down this entry hallway. His door is opened. It would really be nice if he were giving shelter to Franklin, so just in case, I check the first bedroom, the one with the closed door. But there's no one inside, and the double bed is made and doesn't appear as if it's been used, lately.

I walk toward the opened bedroom where the grunting and huffing and snarling are coming from. I enter, and in the dimness from the nightlight he has plugged in out in the hall, I can see him on his back, sawing lumberjack logs with his laborious breathing and snoring. Occasionally, he stops breathing, and I figure he's a candidate for a heart attack soon.

I quietly break out the duct tape I have in my small carryall bag. I've got my .38 in its usual waistband holster on my right flank, but I've got all my goods in the bag. It unsnaps quietly.

He has his arms at his sides. I take the duct tape and gently put an edge under the bed frame, and then I drape the tape across his left arm, then his chest, and finally over his right arm and finally onto the frame on the other side of his bed. I drape six stripes of the duct tape across his upper torso and six more across his lower legs. He has cooperated nicely by remaining asleep. He snores, and then he stops breathing, but he doesn't awaken.

Plan B was to knock him out with a shot or three to his face if he had awakened, but that would make all this take longer, waiting for him to come back to consciousness. And I prefer having all this bloodless, too, but it was always up to Ellsworth.

When I strap his mouth shut, he wakes and tries to lunge himself upright in bed, but the duct tape has him secured.

I let him see it's me. I want him to know who's doing this to him.

"Hello, Richard," I tell him as he settles his square head back onto his pillow. He knows he's bound, by now.

When I take the switchblade out of my back pocket, and when I flip it open, his eyes go wide. He can only just make out the knife because of the dimness of his bedroom, and I haven't turned the light on at his bedside. No need for light. This is black work.

But it's illuminated in here enough for him to see the six-inch blade.

"You remember me, don't you, Richard?"

He blinks. I guess he's trying code on me.

"Sure you do. I was the cop who talked to you about Franklin Toliver. And you were the dumb prick who lied to me that Franklin hadn't contacted you. But I know you're the swinging dickless who gave Franklin my phone number and my address. And you're going to tell me where Toliver is.... Blink if you agree."

He doesn't blink.

"You're telling me you didn't tell Toliver my information that your cousin gave you?"

He moves his head from side to side to tell me he's not saying what I just proposed.

"So which is it?"

He finally decides to blink in affirmation.

"Where is he?"

I tear the duct tape off his mouth, and he winces in pain.

"You make any noise, you know, like crying out for help, I'll cut your throat, Richard. I'll never lose any sleep over it, either, just because you think I'm a cop and that cops don't do things like this. And normally we don't. But you and Franklin are threatening the people I love, and that's when the law of the fucking jungle comes home to roost.

"Are you following all this, Richard?"

"Yes," he breathes hoarsely.

"Where's Toliver?"

"I don't know. Honest to—"

I grab his crotch and squeeze.

"Think before you lie. You have both your balls, I assume?"

"Yeah—Yes."

"If you don't tell me what I want to know, I'll cut a hole through your covers here, and I'll cut open your scrotum. Then, if you still don't want to tell me.... Well, you do see where all this is headed, right?"

He nods because he can't seem to talk. I have the tip of the switchblade resting right over his genitals.

"Where is he?"

"I swear to God I—"

I grab his nuts through the blanket. Then I release as he squeals and I begin to cut a hole around where I figure his manhood must be.

"Stop! Christ, please! I don't know!"

I get the hole torn out, and I can see his boxer shorts, now. I take the knife and I touch the skin inside the flap.

"*No! Please God no! Okay! Okay!*"

"I'm waiting, Richard."

"He's.... He's at the house. His old man's—his mother's house."

"In DesPlaines?"

"Yes."

"How'd he get back in there? Aren't there cops watching it?"

"The State Police stayed for like three weeks after the old lady did herself, but they can't hang there forever. We watched the house. We went by it until we saw the place wasn't being looked at by the cops. It's boarded up, but he got in through the back, somehow. I don't know if he's still there, but he told me that was where I could find him if I needed to."

"You're not lying to me, are you Richard?"

"No. I swear to God it's true."

"Listen carefully. If you try to take this little encounter to the police or the Feds or anybody, I'll come back and kill you. I can play the way your guys play, too, Richard. Your mother and father still alive? Any siblings, girlfriends? Boyfriends?"

His eyes have widened even further.

"I'll kill all of you. I did it for a living in the jungle, and I can do it again. You see, I *can* be provoked. I'm not Pablo."

317

There's a question on his face.

"I see. Not a reader, eh? Well, fuck it. Just remember, you'll be first. I got by that highly trained hound of yours and I got into your fucking bunker here and I'll find you wherever you are and you'll be first. Then I'll eliminate your whole family fucking tree, Richard. Are you understanding all this?

"Then again, I left no prints. Nothing the police could use to establish my presence here tonight, and it'd be my word against yours. And who do you suppose the police would believe? Me, or an Aryan Nation storm trooper?"

His mouth is open. I think the look is called "aghast."

"Any recriminations against your cousin, same deal is in effect. You'll be first, numbnuts. You really need to shower, man. You just unload in your pants?"

The odor is not a joke. There is a stench rising.

"You can wriggle out of the duct tape in maybe a half hour. Remember what I told you, Dicky. Mum's the word. Right?"

He nods.

"You have a great night. What's left of it. You're going to need to do some laundry, but that can wait until tomorrow. Go with God, Richard. Sieg motherfucking heil!"

I snap my stuff back into my carryall, and then I leave the way I came in.

"What if he'd called the police?" Lila asks me at breakfast.

"He won't, I don't think. He had laundry to do, instead."

"What?" Lila asks.

"Nothing. Forget about it."

I eat the rest of the bacon and eggs she's made me.

"Want to go to a haunted house with me tonight when it's real dark and scary out?"

"Halloween isn't until October," she tells me.

"This year it arrived a few months early," I reply.

42

"So why didn't you call the cavalry and go out to DesPlaines right after you, uh, *questioned* that Ellsworth idiot? And I'm still pissed you broke in and pulled all that crap, Danny. You could've gone to jail, and you still might, and where's our wedding then, dummy?"

"By the time I got done with Dicky, the dawn was coming on. This is black work. And I wouldn't worry about him calling the cops on us. I think he got the message."

"Which is thuggery for thuggery."

"I have no defense, Lila. It was wrong. But I'm not going to let Toliver or his friends get close to you or Kelly, and like I told Ellsworth, there ain't no rules when it comes to survival.

"If we'd brought out a legion of cops, I figure Franklin would've boogied by the time everyone got in place. You notice how easily he avoided us when we came at him with standard tactics."

It's 2:27 A.M. We're both supposed to be at work at 7:00, but I'm really not expecting to find Toliver at his father and mother's home. Ellsworth's information was a few weeks old, and Franklin has never roosted anywhere longer than a couple of days. It's a very long shot that he's still there now, but I have to know. And if he is there, I think a small operation stands the best chance of landing him. It's much quieter, just Lila and me, and he won't be expecting me to come without a platoon or company of coppers as backup. If he is there, we just might be able to surprise him.

"What if Ellsworth warned him?"

"I don't know how he'd do that unless Franklin is using a payphone. The house line was cut off two weeks ago. I checked yesterday. He'd have to have prearranged a number to call, and I'm betting that's not how Franklin works. He's got to know what a fucking idiot Ellsworth is, and it's not likely he'd let Richard call him—he'd do the calling.

"But I could be wrong. We'll find out when we get to DesPlaines."

This is the only time traffic is close to reasonable in Chicago. The only people out on a weekday at three in the morning are drunks or lovers. All the midnights shift people are already at work. The rush won't start until six A.M. We float through the Stevenson all the way west to LaGrange Road. Only a few cars flow with us and stream the other way, across the expressway.

I don't play the radio. It grates me, early in the morning, and Lila never turns it on, especially when she's driving, as she is now.

We approach the Lieutenant Governor's residence about 3:17 A.M.

Lila pulls the car to the curb a good half block from the house. We'll approach on foot. No lights, no noise.

This neighborhood embodies "suburbia." There are tall elms and oaks, and there are a few birches and evergreens thrown into the mix. The leaves are preparing to die, but they haven't begun to change hue just yet. It'll be October before the colors turn scarlet and orange and yellow and golden brown. We had a wet summer, so the colors should be riotous. Something to do with the amount of water that comes down from the heavens determines whether it'll be spectacular or dull.

As we walk toward the front of the house, I see the wind powering through the leaves. The branches are heavy with those dying extensions of green. You can hear the gentle fluttering from above us.

There is no birdsong. The light is still not forthcoming—not until about 5:20 A.M. Pretty soon, the days will last fewer hours and the dark will linger, in the morning and at dusk.

I motion for Lila to head around toward the back of the house. We'll look for his point of entry. The front door has been boarded up until they put the house for sale. The publicity of Toliver's wife's death has made this home too attractive to the rubberneckers who like to see a crime scene. So until the suicide's media coverage is over, they'll keep this place nailed shut, pretty much.

There's a four-foot chain link fence in the back, but the gate is not locked. It'd be rather pointless since it's so easy for an adult to hop over. So we open and shut the gate as we pass through, and then I open that same carryall bag I brought to Ellsworth's crib. I have a pen flashlight that gives off enough of a glow to see but doesn't cause enough of a glare for any of the neighbors to notice that Lila and I are creeping the Lieutenant Governor's place.

The windows back here have been boarded-over, also. There is at least a half-acre backyard here, so it would make a convenient entry point to the house for Franklin or anyone else who might want to break in. We check each of the boards—there are four windows and a glass door, back here. They've also boarded the door inside the glass door.

None of the nailed pieces of plywood seems to have been disturbed. So I take my breaker bar out of the carryall, and I begin to remove the rectangular piece of plywood from the inside of the back doorway. The wood creaks as I pry it away, but it's not loud enough to wake the neighbors. Toliver has a wide lot, and his neighbors on either side would have to be already awake to hear the slight moaning sound that my breaker bar is making. The wind is rustling the trees pretty noisily, as well, and I figure that breeze is helping to mask any noise I'm making.

The plywood is gone in less than three minutes, and then it takes another 180 seconds to pick the deadbolt on the back door inside the glass screen door.

It's pitch, inside. They've left no lights on. I don't know if they've also shut the juice off, but I rather doubt it if they're trying to sell this place. I flick the kitchen light on and off quickly, and there is electricity, Lila and I see.

I take my .38 out of its waistband holster, and Lila has her .32 snubnose out, as well. I can barely see her. Only the dim moonlight shines through the kitchen window. It's behind the sink. The kitchen is spacious. There is an "island" in its middle, and pots and pans still dangle from hooks.

There is a holder for kitchen knives on the wall next to the sink, and I see that all the holders still contain cutlery. Nothing's missing.

I motion for Lila to follow me, but she walks alongside me, instead. We've secured the kitchen, but this is a very large house. I have no idea how many rooms there are, but I've seen the inside twice, and I know we've got a lot of ground to explore.

I'm not going to light any fixtures because there is a slight chance Franklin really is here. So we enter the dining room, next. The table and chairs are in place as if someone still lived here. The table was mahogany. I saw it when I visited Mrs. Toliver. It's covered with a cloth, now, however.

We keep moving. The living room on the main floor is in front of us, and the furniture is sheathed in plastic. I use my pen light to sweep the room. There is the upstairs, next. The bedrooms are up there.

I gesture toward the ascending steps. Lila nods.

We walk up the steps, treading on the outside edges of the stairway. The creaks are fewer than walking on the middle of the rungs.

"You said this joint was haunted?" Lila whispers in my ear.

I nod in the affirmative. I stop and whisper in her ear.

"The Staties don't like coming in here. Some of them won't, anymore."

I see her visibly shiver.

"*Cut it out*," she murmurs, almost inaudibly.

We keep going up toward the bedrooms. We arrive at the first— I think this was the son's room. Franklin was an only child.

I slowly turn the handle. I open the door just as slowly. Then I flash my small light all over the room, and we find no one home, as expected. We check the walk-in closet, and nothing hangs from any of the wire and wooden hangers. The place is deserted. I feel as though no one has occupied this room in many years.

The second bedroom is the master. It's where the Lieutenant

Governor and his spouse slept together, when they were still a couple, at least. It's where Mrs. Toliver hanged herself in the closet with a belt.

Lila halts before we enter the second bedroom.

"Is this the one?" she whispers confidentially into my ear.

I smile, and then she socks me on the left arm. Hard. I wince.

"*Shit*, Lila," I protest faintly.

I open the door and we go inside. The bed is made, the pen light shows us. The pillows are fluffed. The room smells as if it were recently cleaned and freshened. Maybe they've been prepping the house for a sale. Who knows?

There's also a faint fragrance of lilac. I'm trying to recall where I smelled lilacs before, and then it returns to me. I think Mrs. Toliver exuded that same scent when I talked to her. I remember the presence of lilac on her. She wore it subtly—not like some older woman who might've doused herself in the perfume. It was faint, that smell, as if she'd just dabbed a finger of it behind each ear. But it was unmistakable and it was there, when I last saw her alive.

Some things linger after people, like memories, I suppose.

"Let's get the hell out of this room," Lila urges me quietly.

I have to look, first. So I open the accordion doors of her large closet.

I see the chain dangling from the light fixture, so I pull the chain, and the bulb illuminates the entire closet and bedroom. Lila grabs my arm.

"Let's get *out* of here, Danny!" she urges me in a hushed voice.

I snap off the light.

We leave the bedroom and head to the last room at the end of the hall. The bed and the furniture are covered with blankets, in here, and I check the closet as well, and then we head back toward the stairs.

There's only one area we've missed. There is a basement in most structures like these. I noticed a door off the kitchen hall, and I'm betting it goes downstairs. The only other place we haven't looked is the large garage, way out by the alley in the back.

We head toward that door in the kitchen, and I find out I was right. As I open the door, I see the stairs that head down into what people used to call the cellar.

She follows me. We still have our weapons in hand, but the presence of Toliver grows fainter and fainter as the minutes inside the house accumulate.

The basement is finished, but there is nothing down here—no furniture, no recreational stuff. There is only a small utility room at the far end that contains a washer and a dryer. There is literally nothing else.

We've wasted our time. We check the basement out thoroughly. Then we decide it's time to check the garage and then get the hell out of here.

Lila heads up the stairs first. As we reach the top, I think I hear something from back below.

"Hang on a minute," I whisper again.

"I'll wait for you in the kitchen," she says.

"No, just wait here."

"Forget it. This basement creeps me completely."

"Then just stay still up at the top, okay?"

"Okay."

She heads up to the main floor, opens the door, and then walks out toward the living room.

I hurry back down the stairs. I find a switch for the overhead fluorescents, and I snap them on. The room comes alive in a wash of illumination.

But there is still nothing here. I quickly check out the rest of the basement, but there is nothing moving.

Maybe they have mice, I figure.

Then I hear Lila scream. And it's no muffled sound. It's a full-throated shriek.

I burst up the stairs, and I race into the living room, where I thought the sound was coming from.

Lila is sitting on the couch, her .32 lying on the seater next to her, and she's sitting straight up, as if a ramrod were holding her erect. I flip on the lamp which is atop the table next to where she's seated.

She's ashen. She's staring straight ahead.

I kneel down by her and touch her cheek with my left hand.

"What happened?"

At first she doesn't answer, but then she slowly turns toward me.

"Forget the garage. You were right. Franklin's not here. But his mother is. I just saw her by the stairs."

Before we left the Toliver house, I took Lila upstairs one last time. I took her with me because she refused to stay in the living room alone. So she stayed as close to my back as she could without grabbing hold of the rear end of my shirt.

There was nothing up there, in any of the bedrooms, including the master.

On the way back home, she couldn't stop shivering. It was in the low eighties outside, and we had the windows opened, and the equatorial heat was making me sweat. But Lila couldn't stop quaking from what she'd seen. Or what she thought she had seen, at least.

"What was it?" I asked her again, just as we were pulling in front of our house.

"I already told you. Don't make me say it again, because if you do *I'll* start to think I'm nuts, too, and I know I'm not, Danny. She was there. It wasn't a mist or a hallucination.

"I don't believe in ghosts. I'm not so sure I believe in the Holy Ghost, for that matter. But I saw Mrs. Toliver standing by those stairs just as sure as I see you sitting next to me right now."

I pull to the curb in front of the house.

I look over to her and I want to ask if what she saw was the form of a real, living person, but I know not to pursue it. I only wonder why I never got to see Mrs. Toliver, why she didn't appear to both of us, why she picked Lila to scare the hell out of.

I could say that she was already frightened about being in that house and that she already heard the story about the Staties' encounter with the recently departed Mrs. Toliver. I could explain to her that the power of suggestion is a mighty influence upon what people *think* they see or observe.

Lila was a Vietnam vet. Decorated multiple times. She's no vulnerable kid who's receptive to illusions. So what did she really see?

I've never heard Lila Chapman scream, let alone hear her belt out the shriek that came from the upstairs at the Toliver place just a few minutes ago.

Odysseus departed the land of the living to visit the land of the dead. I'm no Greek hero. I was a warrior, once, and so was Lila, my beloved wife-to-be. I don't believe in haunted houses and I believe less in spooks and spirits. I don't buy much of anything that's supposed to be supernatural.

It begins to really piss me off that I decided I had to have one more look at that basement. I should have been there with her to see what she saw. I should never have left her alone in that damned place.

43

Lila's going to see Dr. Fernandez, now, too. On her own, of course. She can't reconcile herself to what happened at Raymond Toliver's house in DesPlaines. I can't talk her out of seeing the shrink, and I don't think I really want to.

I'm not sure what Lila saw, but I know she's not insane. She's not even a little nuts, and in fact she's the most down-to-earth, common sense human being I know. And she wasn't the only one who saw Mrs. Toliver after Mrs. Toliver's demise. I'm referring to the State Troopers, and those guys are not known for selling fish stories.

The Toliver house is under constant surveillance. Franklin's photos are in circulation in the tri-state area, and it's not likely he'll be able to remain subterranean much longer.

But that's what I said the first time he went invisible, after the six slayings. The fact that he has no friends, no family (except his father who told me to shoot him if I could) and no fellow warriors from the Aryan Nation who want anything to do with him should help him resurface soon. What he's living on, no one knows. He has no resources. His bank assets have been frozen and his credit cards and checking account have been cancelled. The FBI made certain of the above.

The only place we didn't check was that garage. So I'm going back now to have a look. And I didn't invite Lila to come with me because I don't want her anywhere near that place in DesPlaines.

This time I arrive in full daylight, about 12:19 P.M. I show the State Policeman out front my badge, and he smiles and waves me on through to the backyard. I walk directly to the garage, and I enter through a side entrance that is unlocked. It's not locked because the garage is barren. There is nothing, not even a newspaper.

There is, however, a small pool of oil on top of the cement on the left hand stall side. I touch it. I'm no expert, but I think it may be fresh.

If he's been parking a vehicle in that garage, it's a stolen car, of course. Nothing with wheels was left available for him to drive once he was tossed into Elgin. His father, as I say, is not a resource for him, and the Lieutenant Governor has extra security guards watching him twenty-four-seven in Springfield. I doubt that Franklin wants to wander out of his comfort zone.

So I drive over to the DesPlaines PD and talk with a Lieutenant Gunnerson. He looks as Scandinavian as his last name sounds. He's a light brown-headed giant—he's got to top six feet five. His hands are like huge paws. His right covers my own hand when he shakes with me.

I ask him if he can FAX me any reports of stolen cars in his town over the last month. He says he'd be happy to, and he tells me he's hoping we collar Franklin *yesterday*. I smile and thank him for his cooperation.

How'd he get back to this area without transport? I'm guessing he hitchhiked or he walked. People who allow strangers into their cars on highways aren't the brightest bulbs in the batch. You really don't know who the hell you're picking up on the road, and I hope I don't offend all those Jack Kerouac *On the Road* fanatics, but there's a good reason hitching is illegal in Illinois. Me, I'd rather walk. It's much safer.

Has he been cooping in that garage or inside the house? He always seems to be several paces ahead of me, just when I think I know where he's lighted. Maybe he's psychic. Maybe he's clairvoyant or whatever.

Lila's experience has me thinking spook. The only spooks I used to know were CIA operatives in Vietnam and Laos and Cambodia. They were very human spooks, even though many of them were stone killers. But then, who am I to talk? The only difference that I can see is that I did my trigger time in uniform, straight up. The CIA fellows were chameleons, they blended into the background as well as white guys could, even though not all of them were Caucasians.

I've got a ghost and Franklin and the Aryan Nation working on me all at the same time, not to mention I'm still in conversation with Dr. Fernandez about my fractured previous relationship with Mary, my ex. I've got a wedding coming up at Christmastime, and I've got a rehabilitated daughter going to school sixty miles away from me where I can't keep an eye on her.

I don't think Kelly's location was listed in my personnel file, but Toliver has had some success finding out other things before, so who knows if he knows where my kid is.

I call Kelly late that same afternoon. She has a phone in her dorm room, and luckily I catch her there.

"You okay?" I ask.

"I'm fine. Why?"

"Just checking in. I want to come see you this weekend."

"Can we make it the next weekend, Dad? I've got three tests, next week."

"Oh yeah, no problem. Is it okay if I call you, though?"

She goes quiet for a moment.

"Are you worried about me, Dad?"

"Always."

"You don't have to be. I'm fine."

"How's Matt?"

"He's great.... Dad, c'mon. What is it?"

"Nothing, I just—"

"It's Toliver again. Right?"

"Yeah. You haven't been getting any strange calls, have you?"

"No. Nothing. Really."

"You know what he looks like, right?"

"His picture's been on TV and in the papers so many times, Dad, that it would be impossible *not* to recognize that creep."

"I called the DeKalb police and told them about you, and they said they'd try and keep a lookout for Toliver. They've got his photos, too."

"You really need to quit worrying about me so much."

"Not likely. You been eating?"

"I gained three pounds."

"Good, you could use ten more."

"You want me to get fat?" she laughs.

"I want you to live forever and laugh like hell every single day, Kelly."

She doesn't respond.

"You there?"

"I'm here. I wish you wouldn't get sentimental on me, though."

"I know how tough you are. You're my girl. I got a lot of unused sentiment for you that I never used before, and I'm damn well gonna spread it thick as glue on you."

"I'm fine, Dad. Really."

"I don't want to hold you up, so I'll call you on the weekend. Okay?"

"Of course."

"I love you."

"I love you, too. Talk to you soon."

We end the call.

In early September, I notice that my pants are getting tighter. I don't see any swelling in my face when I look in the mirror as I'm shaving. Lila wants me to grow a mustache, but I'm trying to put her off. She says the mustache would give my face "definition." I think it would give me more hair and a chance at seconds for anything I eat or drink, but she doesn't appreciate my attempt at humor.

But she does agree that I'm putting some poundage on, so we decide to run in the mornings together since we're both working days. We get out of the house at 5:00 A.M. so that we can both clean up and eat breakfast before we go on shift. Lila is very big about breakfast, and she tells me because I skip it so often it could be a contributing factor to the weight gain. She wants me to eat only three meals, no junk food, and she doesn't want either of us to eat later than six at night. She says if we stop at six, it gives our metabolism a shot at burning calories. So I go along with her. All I've got to lose is tonnage.

We do a route down our block and we keep going four more blocks in that direction. Then we take a right and do four more blocks, and then a right again and four more blocks and then another right and then home. I think it's about a mile and a quarter. Lila is starting us out slow. I'm wearing my sweat pants and a sweatshirt and my old White Sox baseball cap. She's wearing running pants and a tank top that makes me want to pick her up and drag her back to the bedroom, but I refrain and we continue running.

I get to see the neighborhood this way, even though it's dark when we begin our route through the southwest side neighborhood. The homes are mostly brick and mostly bungalows and ranches. Most of the yards are much smaller than mine, but just about everyone has a dog inside a fence, and we get a lot of these mutts yapping as we pass by, out on the sidewalk.

I enjoy the jog. It's a jog, Lila explains, because we're both hitting middle age, and neither of us needs shin splints or stress fractures. I tell her I never had anything like that, but she says she's taking precautions.

I have the feeling, occasionally, that somebody's watching us when we run. I know it's probably paranoia or overreaction to Toliver being on the loose, but I get that clammy feeling that he's observing us, somehow. Franklin is hardly omniscient and omnipresent, but I still have the hair stand up on my neck as we run the route, and I still have to jerk looks over my shoulder, from time to time, to make sure someone's not coming up behind me.

Fernandez is concerned about my fears that Franklin is lurking about, watching for an opportunity to strike. She spends more time on this early September late afternoon talking about my unfounded fears than she does about the breakup of my first marriage.

Which is all right by me because I don't look forward to talking about Mary. Long gone Mary.

"How's it going with Lila?" I ask.

Fernandez smiles.

"You know I can't talk about that with you," she says.

"I'll get it from Lila, then."

"Knock yourself out, Danny."

I smile back at the knockout Latina shrink.

"I'm really worried about her."

"I know you are, Detective."

She's wearing a bright red lipstick for the first time since I began seeing her here. Her fingernails are painted the same scarlet shade of red.

"I didn't see anything. By the time I got up there, all I saw was Lila. Christ, I thought she might be in shock."

"Danny, I can't talk about what Lila and I discuss. You know that."

"Well hell, I was there, too."

"Were you disappointed you didn't see anything?"

"I'm pissed I let her go up those stairs without me. It could've just as well been Franklin Toliver up there, with a weapon."

"But he wasn't there, was he."

"No. I didn't see a goddam thing."

She rocks in her leather chair gently. She never lets her gaze stray from mine.

"You religious, Danny?"

"I'm a Catholic."

"I used to be. Not anymore. But I still think of myself as spiritual. And I think there's more in heaven and earth—You ever read *Hamlet*?"

"In high school, I think."

"There's more going on than any of us can comprehend, and

when something comes along we don't understand, the only way we can explain it is to call it supernatural. There's an explanation for what Lila thinks she saw, but it's probably not supernatural."

"So what would you call it? Tremors? Subterranean gasses? What?"

"I don't pretend to know. But without getting too specific, Lila really did see something that disturbed her deeply, so don't blow it off."

"Not happening, Doctor. You don't blow Lila off."

She watches me for a moment, and then her face softens.

"Franklin Toliver has become an obsession."

"He's been one for a long time."

"And we talked about how destructive he can be, just be being out there."

"I plan to alter that situation as soon as possible."

She grins.

"I know. I have confidence you'll do just that. Do you have confidence in yourself, Danny?"

I look over her shoulder and out at the lakeshore. It's a brilliant, clear, crystalline September day. Franklin Toliver has no right to occupy me or anyone else on such a day. I wasted enough days being afraid, in the jungle. But those days are with me still, because of him. And because of the things I did, a decade ago.

"I'll have to, won't I?" I ask her.

I call Kelly on the weekend, on Sunday in the early afternoon. As promised, she's there, in her dorm room, studying Biology. I'm beginning to believe she'll be a medical doctor some day soon. I just want to be there when she gets that degree and goes into practice. I want to be her first patient. I wouldn't trust anyone else with my life, except Lila.

Lila and I have increased our running regimen. We've got it up to around two miles, and the jogging has been replaced by a quicker pace. Lila has us both stretch before we begin our pre-dawn run. The running has left my pants a bit less tight, and she's bought a scale, so we both check our weights on Saturday mornings. My weight is at 183, just five pounds over my Ranger weight. Lila is very pleased with my conditioning, and hers, too, so far.

But I still have that chilled breeze creeping up the back of my neck as we take off down the street in the dark before the morning, occasionally. It still won't leave me.

The third week in September marks the end of summer, and you can feel the change coming on. The humidity lessens, and the air becomes crisp and cool at night, especially. The sky turns a deeper blue, this time of the year, and there is less of a white haze, the way there was back in July and August. The days seem to flee behind us, and Franklin Toliver is still out there, somewhere between DesPlaines and the city. Somewhere out there, still.

44

The Captain and I interceded on behalf of Susan Parkley, the girl who works in Personnel, and since I personally told her Supervisor, Janelle Frampton, that Susan was coerced by a member of a hate group to hand out my information, Frampton decided to suspend Parkley for three days without pay and then Susan would be fully reinstated. I tried to get her Supervisor to dump the suspension, but Frampton said there had to be some discipline because Ms. Parkley could've reported the threat to her boss. So I shut up and let well enough alone. At least Susan got her job back. One less victim for Franklin Toliver.

When I went back to the church with Kelly, all those months ago, I asked the priest there to help me secure an annulment. Since Father Bob is a canonical lawyer, he's been working on it for me all this time, and now, in early October, the annulment comes through. If I hadn't annulled Mary, I couldn't marry Lila in the church. You can't divorce and remarry in Catholicism unless you're widowed or annulled or never married in

335

the first place.

So now we can have the church wedding. It's finally official.

We have to go through the rigors of pre-wedding instructions. Lila and I have to take a test to see if we're compatible. It won't cancel the wedding if we don't pass, but we're supposed to see if there are areas we need to work on before we walk the aisle.

I match up with her pretty well, because, frankly, I'm not real honest with some of my answers. I try to answer the way I think Lila would, and luckily, I do pretty well at putting myself in her place. The results show we're pretty much inside the same mindset.

We're required to go to confession now, and once right before the wedding. The last time I confessed, I told the priest I wanted to murder Franklin Toliver.

Today, though, I confess to Father Bob. His full name is Father Robert Dowling, but everyone calls him Father Bob. He's just over seventy, I was told, and he's been at our church for thirty years, first as Associate Pastor and more recently, for the last fifteen years, as Pastor.

I'm in the traditional confessional with him, but he knows damn well who he's talking to, regardless of the black screen between us.

"Father, forgive me for I have sinned."

He asks me about the last time I confessed, and I tell him, but I don't mention the part about murdering Franklin. One time with that story was enough. I've gotten over it. As I say, I'm not an executioner, even though the Lieutenant Governor would have me become one. On the other hand, if I catch up with Franklin, and it's him or me....

"I've taken the name of the Lord in vain, several times."

"Yes."

"Lila and I have been living in sin for a few months."

"Tell me something I haven't already heard."

"Lila told you that?" I laugh.

"The confessional is confidential, my son."

"Anyway, I love her."

"That doesn't excuse you for living in sin, as you call it."

"Yeah, Father, I know."

"Who am I to turn back the clock and expect that men like you will keep it in their pants?"

"*Father!*"

"Okay, go on."

I try to stop laughing before I continue.

"Sex outside the sacrament of marriage is nothing to laugh about. I was being sarcastic, so you'll have to forgive me."

"I know you were being sarcastic, Father."

"God forgives everything, right? Get on with it."

"You in a hurry, Father?"

"As a matter of fact, I have a dinner engagement at seven."

"I'll try to move it along, then."

"Only kidding, Daniel."

"Were you the neighborhood wiseguy, Father?"

"We're not here to go over ancient history, Daniel."

I hesitate, and suddenly I just have to ask him.

"Do you really believe in ghosts?" I ask the priest.

"Of course. It's integral to the faith."

"No, no. I mean other than Jesus coming back from the dead."

"What do you mean? Like haunted house ghosts? Edgar Allan Poe? That kind of ghost?"

"Yes."

"You've been watching *The Exorcist*, haven't you," he jokes.

"No. Lila thinks…. Lila thinks she saw a dead woman—I mean she thinks she saw the ghost or the spirit of someone who committed suicide, not long ago."

"Lila doesn't seem like the flighty type."

"She sure as shit isn't…. Sorry."

"Go on. What about this apparition or whatever?"

"We were investigating the whereabouts of Franklin Toliver— You know, the man who killed those six prostitutes and then escaped from Elgin."

"Yes, unfortunately I've read about him."

"We were in the family home, looking for Toliver, and while I was in the basement I heard Lila scream, and when I got to her she was nearly in shock. And now she's seeing the Department psychiatrist. So am I, seeing the shrink I mean."

"And your concern is?"

337

"I know this isn't really my confession. I just wanted to know if you think Lila might really have seen Mrs. Toliver. The story is that some State policemen saw her, too, at that house. But that's really just hearsay."

"Do you think they saw her, too?"

"I think they saw something. And I know Lila doesn't lie."

"Lazarus came back from the dead. We believe in eternal life. I myself have never seen someone come back from the dead, but I have faith that we really are reborn, Daniel. No, I don't think it's over when it's over, or even when the fat lady in the opera finally sings. But how about you?"

"I saw a lot of dead people in Vietnam. I work with corpses all the time, here in the city. But I never saw anybody get back up after they were ten-counted. Never. Not once.

"All I saw was death, in Asia. Young, middle-aged and old. Dead bodies all over the vegetation, all over the jungle and the rain forest. No one ever blinked or said another word.

"You ever read Dostoevsky, Father?"

"I think I have, back in college, before I went into the seminary."

"Ever read *Notes from Underground?*"

"Yes, as a matter of fact, I have."

"Sometimes I feel like the guy in the book. I feel as if I'm isolated and all alone. I haven't felt like that as often since my daughter and I started getting along and since Lila told me she'd marry me. But before those two things happened, I felt like one of those tunnel rats back in the War. You know, the guys who searched the VC tunnels with a flashlight and a .45?"

"Yes, I've read about them."

"I've felt as though I were buried alive. I could see the sun and the sky, but the feeling of suffocation, emersion—I don't know how to describe it. I just felt as if I were covered over and planted like a dead body into the ground. Except that I was aware of the world above ground, but it would have no part of me. I was always excluded, somehow. I was always separate.

"The character in the book was always bitching about how society, people, excluded him, how they looked down on him and vilified

338

him. I never felt as extreme as he did, but I always felt as though I knew exactly what he was talking about.

"And his attitudes toward the world were extremely cynical and negative, and I couldn't help seeing things the way he did. I have trouble trusting other people. I spent years being suspicious of everything my daughter did. Only recently have I been able to feel comfortable about what she tells me. I know I had good cause to suspect her when she was doing her addictions, but it was hard to stop mistrusting her, even when she went straight.

"And Lila. I doubted Lila when she rejected me, at first. And when she came back, I kept waiting for her to take off, just like my ex-wife did. And I'm still listening for those footsteps."

"Footsteps?" Father Bob asks. "You mean like in football?"

"Yeah. It's like waiting for someone to come up and blindside you, and I'm still listening for that change in tone in her voice, that little suggestion that she's changed her mind again and that I'll see an empty closet some night when I come back from my shift."

"You know what I'm going to tell you, don't you."

"You're going to tell me that faith is believing without seeing."

"Bingo."

"I don't mean to hold you up, Father."

"Don't be silly. Finish."

"I want to believe that Lila saw Mrs. Toliver. I want to believe that Kelly is really rehabbed and is headed right toward medical school and an MD. I want to believe that Lila really loves me and that she's committed to growing ancient with me and that we'll retire together and buy a beach front house in southern Wisconsin and watch our dogs run in the sand and watch the sun beam off the water and the parasailors floating by over the lake, and everything will end happily ever—"

"After. And why not, Daniel?"

"That's not the way of this world, is it, Father Bob? You've got a few decades on me, so tell me. Do you really believe in happy endings?"

"Not in this world, necessarily. Death is ugly. But so is childbirth. I really think the line points upward, not downward. You're a reader, it sounds like. You read Faulkner?"

"A few of his books."

"Ever read his Nobel acceptance speech?"

"No. Don't think so."

"He said, Daniel, that man will not merely survive. He said that man will *prevail*. How's that grab you?"

"I don't feel like I've prevailed."

"Because of Franklin Toliver?" the priest asks.

"Yeah. And there have been others who've scooted, who've escaped."

"Screw 'em if they can't take a joke, Daniel. Right?"

"Toliver's not very funny."

"Yes, I know. Forgive the jocularity."

"It's all right."

"*Act as if ye had faith*. You know that old bromide?"

"Yes, Father."

"Then, like Emerson said, 'Keep up the comedy.'"

Halloween arrives. The DesPlaines police let me know that four vehicles were stolen on their patch during the last four weeks. Their stolen car numbers are far fewer than ours because DesPlaines is fairly affluent and they're far smaller than the city, of course. I get the makes and the models and the plate numbers, and I circulate them to the tri-county area so that if Franklin is mobile, someone is eventually going to see him.

The house in DesPlaines is no longer under surveillance. The cops in the suburb can no longer justify the manpower hours, and neither can the State Troopers. So Franklin could be cooping back in his old haunts.

The FBI arrests Richard Ellsworth and ten other members of the Aryan Nation. I get a call from Dan Packard, a Chicago special agent with the Feds.

"We found out that Ellsworth was involved in black market weapons. They were selling pieces to gangs in Cook County. Ellsworth wanted to cut a deal with us, and one of the things he sang about was that he gave a piece to your boy."

"My boy?" I ask.

"Franklin Toliver is armed and dangerous. I thought you ought to know."

"Did he tell you where Toliver was?"

"If he had, that would've been the first thing I'd have told you. Sorry. He doesn't seem to know. He gave the gun to Toliver about four weeks ago, at Ellsworth's house. You know, the bunker?" Packard chuckles.

"What kind of weapon?"

"It's an old US Army .45 automatic. Apparently, he wanted something that blows very large holes into things."

We keep up the running in the morning, but I'm beginning to ache in my legs. Lila massages my calves and thighs, but she never gets to finish her therapy because we always wind up getting another form of exercise in the bedroom.

We're lying together, intertwined and perspiring all over each other. It's the night before Halloween—All Souls.

"I missed," she says.

"You missed *what?*"

"Take a wild guess, Danny."

"I thought you were on the pill."

"I told you I had to go off because they were giving me headaches."

"And you said you were going to use something else. I remember, now."

"Yeah. The diaphragm. But if you nudge the little devils, and if just one of your little marauders reaches my beachhead...."

"You think you are?"

"I'm pretty regular, Danny, but it might just be that I got off the pills. We'll need to wait and see."

"But what do you think?"

She takes my face in her hands and kisses me.

"Would it disappoint you if I were pregnant?"

I look deeply into her gaze.

"You know it wouldn't."

"We're both pushing my biological clock, you know."

"You been having morning sickness?"

"No. Not all women do, and not with every baby."

"Well, there is one thing I am disappointed with."

She purses her pink lips and stares down at me.

"And *what* might that be, Danny?"

I touch her lips with my forefinger.

"That I didn't knock you up with this last effort. I think it was my finest work, don't you?"

45

On my visit to Dr. Fernandez in early November, she finally corners me on the issue of Mary.

So I begin, close to the beginning. I met Mary during my senior year at the Catholic high school I graduated from. It was all boys, but Mary went to the public high school not far from where I went. We met at some dance her school was throwing for graduating seniors. The dance was open to the public.

I found Mary O'Hara at the end of the night, sitting alone on the bleachers. She was sitting on the bottom rung, and what possessed me to go right up to her and sit down beside her—I'll never quite understand. But I did, and we began talking about casual things, like where I went to school and if I played any sports. Mary O'Hara was on her high school's volleyball team. She was All City her sophomore and junior and senior years. This dance was in the spring, not long before both of our graduations, so her career as a setter was over. She said she thought she might attend the same downtown college I had my eye on, and we talked about maybe going out the next weekend. She said she would go out with me, and the next Friday we had our first date.

There was no physical stuff the first two or three times we went out over the summer, but on the fourth date or so, we went to a drive in movie. The joke about the drive in was that they didn't sell tickets at the entrance; they sold rubbers. They used to call them passion pits, and they were.

We became rather intense, that night, as I recall, but we didn't have sex. The sex didn't occur until a few more dates were history. But once we started, it was standard. I mean we made love every time we were together—when we were alone, that is. I suppose our relationship wound up being more physical than anything else. I can't remember having any drawn out conversations with Mary. We'd go to a movie or get something to eat. Sometimes when I had money we'd go to a concert. But we always wound up in my mother's beat up Chevy, parked at Donovan's Woods, a nearby forest preserve.

The cops were lazy. The park district cops, I mean, and they didn't much care what anyone did as long as they didn't leave used condoms all over the parking lot. If anyone left scumbags on the pavement, you could expect a big crackdown on nighttime activities at Donovan's Woods. So most of us respected the rules. Sex was okay, just no messy sex.

After all these years, you'd think I wouldn't still ache for Mary O'Hara. It was just a superficial, physical partnership, right? It wasn't based on any mutual interchange of feelings or ideas, was it? We just explored our (then) immature bodies and exhausted our combined energies on sexual congress. There was nothing more to it, right?

I keep asking myself those questions after all this time, but I cannot rid Mary from myself. It should be easy to reason that it was lust and not love and then let go of it, even if our relationship ended in marriage and a child and then Mary's desertion. The ache I feel isn't just about her leaving me, or about the fact that I can never enjoy her physical presence again. I can't join her genitalia with mine, in other words.

All of the above sounds very cold and brutal to me, and it is. I'm wondering if there was any genuine affection in the few years we had together, but I cannot recall any instances of that gentle feeling that lovers are supposed to experience with each other.

I can recall the heat, the animal desire that we shared frequently. I can even remember the night we conceived Kelly. The sex was outrageously passionate, but the times in between bouts in bed were not nearly as memorable.

When we were together we often fought, but our battles were always quiet. She wasn't a yeller and neither was I. We'd both become moody and distant, and only when we made up did the sexual thermostat ascend. It became sort of like a roller coaster, emotionally. I'd come home to her at night, before she took off, and I'd dread the next prolonged bout of silence between us.

Then came the War and the hurried nuptials and the birth of my daughter, and one night I returned to absolute quiet in our apartment. I knew she was gone without even looking around the small two-bedroom flat. I could hear she wasn't there anymore. I couldn't smell her scent, the fragrance of the perfumed soap she bathed with every night. Mary had gone, and she never came back.

Dr. Fernandez wants to know if I'm worried that Lila will desert me, too. I tell her the notion has crossed my mind more than once. Fernandez is very familiar with Lila, by now, because Lila is also her patient. She won't tell me anything that my fiancé tells her in their sessions, of course, but we talk about her as far as I'm concerned, relationship-wise. It's hard to avoid Lila. She's one-third of my life. Kelly is one-third, and my job is the final fraction of the pie. Dr. Fernandez thinks that one-third is too big a piece, regarding my profession. I agree with her, but I don't know how to change anything. I don't think of myself outside of the two women in my life and the job that I perform. I have no hobbies, no other outside life that occupies me when I'm away from Homicide. She thinks maybe I should play softball with the parish team, or take up bowling—any damn thing. Fernandez says obsession is a destructive element in anyone's life, and my particular obsession is, of course, the one case that I'm working.

Franklin Toliver.

My relationship with my ex-wife is an example of my personality. Fernandez claims that I become overbearing about everything I do—personal or professional. She tells me I have to learn to give Lila and Kelly their own space to travel in, or I'll inevitably alienate both of them if I become too protective of them.

345

I remind her that Toliver has my address, and that he used to have our phone number.

"Do you really think this man is going to stalk a Homicide police officer?" she grins.

"Yeah. I think he wants to, and I think he has, already."

"You've seen him around you, Danny?" she asks, her face going solemn.

"No. I've never seen him, but I feel him all the time."

"*Feel* him?"

"It's the gut wrench you get when you know someone is behind you."

"Why don't you have the Department watch your home?" she asks.

"They are, but they can't send someone out there continually since this jerk has gone phantom on me again."

"Don't you think he'd be smarter than to go after two Homicide cops who are both military trained in martial arts and weapons? And you were a member of an elite fighting force—this guy can read, can't he?"

"He has a slight disadvantage, Doctor."

"What's that?"

"He's fucking nuts."

And I really do sense someone out there in the neighborhood at night. Perhaps he's there in broad daylight, as well. I wouldn't put it past Franklin. He really has nothing to lose, at this point. He knows he's going to be apprehended. It's only a matter of when, not if. Too many people know his by now infamous face. He's the Number One Most Wanted Man in America, not just in Illinois. He's made the FBI's very short list. As incompetent as the Feds can be, when they really want someone, they tend to deliver. They put aside the politics, occasionally, and they get their man, like the Mounties.

I just hope someone pops Franklin before he gets an opportunity to hurt Kelly or Lila. I'm really not worried about myself because I've had men become very hostile toward me before. I'm used to it, courtesy of the military. But when it comes to putting your family in the line of fire, it's something altogether different.

Pursuits are much like homicide cases. The longer they drag on, the more difficult they become. It's November, and the fall has definitely changed the weather pattern. Most of the leaves have descended, by now. The drive I take on Lakeshore, the Outer Drive, is noticeably different, lately. The water of Lake Michigan appears brackish, gray and cold-looking. The waves are choppier. It reminds me of the Gulf of Mexico. (I visited Texas to see a cousin, back after I returned from Vietnam.) The lake water has lost its appeal. It seems to offer no relief, now, as it did in the swelter of summer. It appears hostile and frigid, maybe even ominous.

The vitality of spring and summer has been replaced, removed, and the withering chill will become colder and colder as the year fades into the dregs of 1987.

The Challenger tragedy still lingers, after almost a year. There are the usual catastrophes all over the planet. We call it history, and it never reads very happily. Only the people in our personal lives keep us going on, keeping us up with what Father Bob quoted from Emerson: "*It's the pious man's duty to keep up the comedy.*" Or something close to that.

Lila takes the at-home test in mid-November. It comes up positive. What she suspected is true, so I'm going to be a father in about seven months. Her due date, she figures, will be some time in either late June or early July of 1988. Maybe we'll have a firecracker baby, maybe he or she will arrive on the Fourth.

"You're sure?" I ask.

She wrinkles her brow.

"I did the test twice, but we won't get confirmation, honey bunny, until I see the doc."

"*Honey bunny?*"

"I rather like that term of affection, don't you?"

"I can live without it, Lila."

"How 'bout baby cakes?"

"Worse."

"You're right. I'll stop, because then you'll try to get even and call me sweetie pie or honey bun. That'd give me morning sickness for sure."

"Have you had the barfs?" I ask her.

"Have you heard any retching from the bathroom in the morning?"

I shake my head.

"There it is, then. So far, so good, as the man who jumped off the fifty-fifth story kept saying as he passed every window on his way down."

"You're really feeling all right?"

"I'm feeling really pregnant."

"You'll have to translate into male-ese."

"I'm feeling the best I've ever felt in my life."

"Even better than when you got shot?"

"*That* was a highlight, Danny."

I grab hold of her and squeeze.

"Don't never get shot again."

She laughs up at me.

"There, you'll get no argument."

"I think you better stop running in the morning."

"The hell you say. Exercise is good, unless there are complications, and there ain't gonna be, I'll tell you right now. This is not going to be a fat baby and he or she's not going to have a fat momma."

"The more to love."

"Bullshit. Who loves a stroke walking?"

"You're rather harsh on fat people, Lila."

"I'm not harsh on them. I just don't embrace their lifestyle. I'm going to keep running. Get it?"

"Yes, *ma'am*."

"Danny, are you really happy about all this?"

"Ecstatic. Can't you read it all over me?"

She looks at me as if she's a trained clinician.

"I mean I really need you to be happy about this."

"Your needs have been fulfilled, lady."

"Don't call me lady."

"I forgot. It's the eighties."

"Which would you prefer? Boy or girl?"

"I'd like one with all the equipment, and I'd like all their equipment to be highly functional. It doesn't matter. Which would you prefer?"

Lila purses her lips. We're still seated on the bed.

"Boy. You already have one with indoor plumbing."

"That doesn't matter. Just make it like I said, healthy. I'll take what I get."

"We'll both have to. That's the way it always works anyway. Right?"

I bend over toward her and kiss her.

"This isn't going to stop our sex life, is it?" she asks.

"That's up to you, Lila. You're the pilot, remember?"

"I intend to wear you out until my water's ready to break. And then about a month and a half after the birth, we'll start on the second in the batch."

"You don't intend to go back to work?"

"They can't can me for getting knocked up. Remember, this is the eighties. Power to the bitches!"

She kisses me, this time. Then I put my hand on her lower belly, and she bursts out bawling.

We've had sightings on two of the stolen cars from DesPlaines. One of the vehicles was abandoned on the southside of the city, and the other was pulled over with the booster still in the driver's seat. But he wasn't Franklin Toliver, of course. He was a sixteen-year-old white kid who wanted to go on a joy ride, and now his ride has become joyless.

I have dreams of hooded phantoms. I never see Franklin's face, but I know who it is, inside the hooded sweatshirt. It's the object of my search.

He's the sole name on my whiteboard, currently. He's the kernel of my monomania. He's Ahab's white whale and Hester Prynne's scarlet letter and Holden Caulfield's phonies. Franklin is the object of my singular desire.

His face is shrouded in shadow. He comes meandering toward me in my dreams. Walking down my block, he approaches me. I'm standing outside our house, and I'm ready to run with Lila on our usual route, but for some reason, she's not with me on this pre-dawn morning.

And here he comes. He's in no particular rush, but when he gets into range, I reach for my waist, for my gun, and the holster's empty. I don't have a knife or a club or any weapon at all, but Franklin has something dangling from his right hand, which is at his side, right at his right thigh.

I look around frantically for something to defend myself with, but it's hopeless. There is nothing to wield, nothing to swing at him or to hurl at him.

I have only my bare hands and my feet. He has the advantage. He can pull on me and kill me without touching me. But I have to somehow take the offensive. I can't just let him raise that hand and kill me.

So I rush at him.

And his right hand rises.

46

I begin to feel the aches and pain after our run on a Sunday morning in late November. Thanksgiving has passed peacefully, but not entirely so. Franklin is still at large, and the pressure is building downtown for me to deliver and put Toliver away for the last time.

If he returns to Elgin, in other words if I don't kill him, they intend to put him in an ultra maximum security area, and if the lights go out again, they're going to have him in a cage with deadbolts that don't rely on electrical power to keep him inside. Dr. Talbot called me two weeks ago. He was very apologetic, but I reminded him that security was not his responsibility. It didn't seem to make him feel any better. He said he felt personally responsible that Franklin Toliver was on the loose. He also said that Franklin should have been sent to prison because he's just too dangerous to be in any hospital, at least a traditional mental hospital. I didn't argue with him or tell him I told you so. I hung up after telling him that I'd catch up with our hooded monster, sooner or later.

I've had a phone call from Alderman Tony Vronski, also. He wanted an "update" of where I was on the escapee. I tried to be civil to him because I could not be polite. If I made wise with this political wiseguy, our beloved Captain would be the recipient of the doo doo that always flows downhill. I'm just a drone, a cog, so I'm certain my boss would have become the fall guy if I insulted the oily son of a bitch. So I didn't, and the call only lasted about three minutes.

As I say, the aches and owwies have set in. When we get back from our neighborhood trot—it is 37 degrees outside—Lila takes my temperature, and it reads 101. She gives me the two requisite Tylenol, and then she makes me go back to bed. It's our day off, one of the few we share now that we aren't partners on the job, any longer, so I protest and tell her we're going out for breakfast, because even with the elevated temp, I still feel hungry, oddly.

So she concedes, and we head out for Derek's, a nice Greek joint that doesn't flatten your wallet too badly. The owner is Derek Antonopoulos, and he's an ex-cop who went into the restaurant business after he put in his thirty years. Derek is only in his mid-fifties. He became a patrolman when he was around twenty. He knows both of us because we come in here all the time, and he constantly comps us our meals even though we always try to talk him into letting us pay. He makes the other coppers pay full, but I think it's because he's got the hots for Lila. He never flirts with her, but you can see he's taken with my fiancé.

He tries to pick up the check again, this morning, but I'm too fast for him. I snatch it up before he can fist it.

"You're gonna go broke, comping us every time we're in here, and I'm starting to feel guilty about it, Derek," I tell him.

He looks like one of the guys from Crete in *Zorba the Greek*—the movie, I mean. He reminds me of the man who cut Irene Pappas's throat in the flick. He's got the salt and pepper hair and a full head of it, and he's got a gray and white- flecked mustache. I fully expect him to cry out, "*Hoopa!*" every time we get ready to leave his place.

There are Greek landscapes hung on the wall and a picture of the Parthenon. He has spacious booths and long, comfortable tables to sit at. He's in the heart of the Loop, on State Street.

He sits down next to me in the booth. Lila sits across from us. His waiter brings us all coffee. He joins us in a cup.

"You look poorly, Danny. This case making you ill?"

"Yes," Lila tells the restaurant owner.

"You should make him go to bed, Lila," he smiles.

"I've been trying."

"You two are getting married soon?" he asks her.

"Right before Christmas," she answers.

Her face beams when she tells him the date. I can't believe, now, that she's the same woman who kept me at arms' length for so long. But now it's as if we've been together since always. Mary is becoming fainter and fainter, the last few months. I won't forget my ex-wife, but I'm not clinging onto any notions that she's ever coming back into my life, either.

"Beautiful," Derek says. He smiles broadly. He's got the perfect set of teeth, also. The man could've been a Hollywood actor with his good looks. He's probably six two, maybe 200 pounds. No fat, no waste. He must take care of himself. Derek rose to Burglary/Car Theft before he retired, he told me. He's been here for about four years.

"You do look sick, Danny. You eat, then you go home and go to bed. The bad guy will still be there tomorrow or the next day. And don't let the pols make you sick with their bullshit in the papers. You'll get him. I know you will."

Derek Antonopoulos rises and smiles at Lila, and then he excuses himself and goes off to schmooze with some other customers. I remember I'm still clutching the bill so he won't grab it, as usual.

"So I look sick," I say as she prepares to stick the thermometer in my mouth again, once we're home.

I can hear the dogs barking in the backyard, so I try to get up and see what's going on.

"Sit your silly ass back on the bed," Lila commands.

I comply. I haven't got the juice to battle her this morning, anyway.

"You can watch the Bears' game in here on the TV," she tells me.

We've got a 25 inch color set on top of the big chest of drawers, in here.

The Bears are playing in Green Bay. I'm only slightly concerned about professional football—or about anything else extraneous to my singular task at hand, and I don't need Lila or Dr. Fernandez or Derek

Antonopoulos to explain why my resistance is down, right now.

I rarely get colds or the flu. I had the measles, mumps and chicken pox as a child, but that was typical of most kids. I rarely got run down because I was an athlete, and I was in shape all through grade school and thereafter. I never stopped being active. I never ceased exercising, even when I went to college and in my adult years following school. Then the military made sure I didn't get flabby or dormant. We were trained to go on three or four hours sleep, maximum, in the Army Rangers. It was the life. Even when I returned from Vietnam after my tours, I only averaged about five hours sleep a night.

With Lila, for some reason, I've learned to stay in bed longer, but not for additional hours of sleep, of course.

So it has to be my one case that's running me down. It has to be Toliver. Maybe if I crap out here most of the day, I figure, I'll be ready to roll tomorrow. I'm scheduled for days' shift until I catch him, but I usually work far longer than eight hours. My days have spilled over into afternoons, and I've cruised the area of DesPlaines and LaGrange and Lyons and Berwyn and Cicero—all the surrounding suburbs that Franklin Toliver might be hiding out in. I've driven the streets of the western and southwestern edges of Chicago looking for him, as well.

The odds that I'll confront him are very poor. One man in one vehicle is not exactly a dragnet, but I do it for my own peace of mind. Lila has not been amused by the overly long hours I've put in chasing this madman, but she hasn't outright ragged me about it. She probably thinks it's better I'm at least doing something active in pursuing him. She has frequently offered to accompany me in my forays out into the night streets and boulevards and avenues, but I keep on insisting that she needs to stay close to the house when she's not at work. At least she has a partner on the job, so there's always someone there to watch her back. And I know I'd be with her if she were to come along with me, but I want her as far away from this case as I can keep her, and I'll never say as much because I know what she'd say. Lila would tell me she can take care of herself, and I know it's true. But now that the baby is inside her, things are different.

She made that trip to the gynecologist, and the home test was confirmed. She is definitely with child. So I'm trying, in my feeble way, to minimize the amount of time she is out in the field, where, somewhere, Franklin Toliver still remains.

I fall asleep, watching the Bears at Green Bay. When I nod off, I begin to dream again. But this time no hooded phantasm invades my dreamscape. This time I'm newly married to Mary. I'm remembering the heated passion of our time together, before she decided to disappear me from her life.

Then the dream switches to Kelly, Kelly when she was using, Kelly when she was purging and turning into a wisp, a fragment of herself.

Then the dream wanders off again, but this time the backdrop is very unfamiliar. I'm on some kind of a boat. And I'm dressed like some ancient Greek sailor. And Derek Antonopoulos seems to be the captain of our vessel. The ship has sails, and we appear to be out on either a very large lake or an ocean. I can taste salt in the air, so I assume it's an ocean. Maybe it's the Aegean. Perhaps it's the Mediterranean. With my friend the Greek restaurant manager as our captain, I'm leaning toward Greece.

We seem headed toward danger because all the crew members are leaning into their oars. But for some reason, I'm at the front of the ship, standing next to Derek. I don't feel like I'm in command of this crew, of this ship, but I'm standing in a position of prominence.

Finally, I ask Derek:

"Where are we headed?"

"Wherever this foul wind blows us," he replies. His handsome face is lined and furrowed in seriousness. We're running fast toward trouble, but he won't tell me exactly what kind.

"We're all headed for death," he pronounces.

Then he smiles at me as if to cancel his last utterance.

"But then, what is the purpose of life if not to head toward that place from which no one re-emerges?"

He smiles again.

"Death is nothing, Danny. Death is peace. Death is rest."

I want to remonstrate with him, telling him that I have a wife (soon) and a baby (on the way) and that I have no desire to meet that final rest just yet.

He won't turn his glance toward me. He eyes the horizon. And then I see the outline of land. I can smell earth on the salt breeze. We are approaching landfall, and the ship runs fast and true toward a distant beach.

"What is this place?" I ask Derek.

"This place? It's hell, Danny. We're headed straight for that dark coast where dawn never arrives."

He isn't smiling, and he still won't turn and look directly at me.

I want to jump overboard, but as I peer into the deep, somehow the waters seem more forbidding than the coast we're aimed at.

When I look back at Derek, it isn't him, anymore. He's transformed into someone else.

The new master of the ship looks directly into my eyes.

"There is no escape there, my young friend. The water is no longer our home. It hasn't been, for thousands and thousands of years. You and I have been exiled to this vessel, to this voyage, for twenty years. We've encountered gods and goddesses and sirens and one-eyed monsters, and still they will not let us go home. To rest, to be at a final peace. To be one with our brides. The fates have determined our voyage for us, and now we are headed for a land which offers no respite for the weary traveler.

"We are condemned to follow this path, young man. It is pointless to seek refuge when there is none. This is our way, and there is no other."

Suddenly, this unknown commander turns back into Derek Antonopoulos. The ex-cop turned restaurant owner.

"You want some more coffee?" he abruptly asks. "Danny?"

"*Danny? Danny? Danny?*"

I open my eyes and see Lila's beautiful face. She's in the first blush of her pregnancy, and I want to reach up and kiss her, but I don't have the strength to rise toward her. She sits at the side of our bed.

"Here. Drink this."

She's got a large glass of orange juice in her right hand, and the delicate appendage is stretched out toward me.

"What were you doing? Dreaming?"

I nod, woozily.

I take the orange juice and I gulp down a third of the glass.

"Easy! Don't choke yourself."

"I'm so damn thirsty. I dreamed I was on a boat. A ship, I mean. But it had to be two thousand, three thousand years ago."

I see the thermometer. She inserts it, waits, and then removes it.

"One hundred two," she says. "You're going to a doctor, tomorrow. If it goes any higher, we're going into emergency, and no talk about it, either, Buster."

She gives me two more Tylenol, and I put them down with another gulp of the orange juice. My thirst has risen, but I don't feel at all hungry, anymore. There is no nausea. I just feel as if I've been beaten with a bag of phone books.

"I don't like this, Danny. Maybe we better go to emergency, anyway."

"No. I'm better off here, with you. If it goes higher, we'll see, but I'm not that bad."

"I've never seen you ill, so I have nothing to compare this to, and you're scaring me."

"It's just the flu, and you need to keep away from me. No more kissy. No more exchange of bodily fluid," I try to smile.

Even my lips are beginning to ache.

After ten minutes or so passes, I think the Tylenol kicks in, and I'm beginning to feel a little better. She takes my temp again, and it's still 101. But she seems to feel more relaxed about my condition. At least it didn't get worse.

On the other hand, only ten minutes have gone by.

"Tell me about your dream, Danny."

By the time I'm ready to tell her, I doze off. The last thing I see is her watchful face.

This time, though, there are no dreams at all.

47

Dreamless sleep is the other side of the coin for heaven and hell. The great nothingness. Nada. Nihil. It's the stage before conception, I'd guess, but I'm certainly not a philosopher. I was a grunt, then a patrolman, and finally and now, a detective. So you could say I'm sort of an underground detective, seeing that I deal so often with the dead.

The dead are trouble enough, but the living are far more of a pain in the ass. Living creatures like Franklin Toliver, and all the other killers I've dealt with, task me more than those souls gone underground.

When I finally wake up, it's 7:35 A.M. By now we usually are done with our running route around the neighborhood. I look over at the other side of the bed, and I see the covers pulled back and I see Lila's work clothes laid out and her .32 snub nose resting inside its holster and I see her work shoes lying on the floor next to the bed.

She should have left for her shift, by now. So I try to jerk myself up in the bed and instead I'm successful in making myself dizzy. I wait a few beats, and then I try to rise again, and this time I make it upright into a seated position. I wait yet another few moments, and then I seem clear-headed enough to throw my legs over the side of the bed. Something is very wrong.

It's not that Lila left her weapon here because she never takes it when she runs—*I'm* the one who insists on toting a firearm on my waist as we trot the hood. I won't go out on the street without an equalizer, not after hearing that Toliver got hold of a gun from his Aryan friends. But my stubborn fiancé doesn't think Franklin's really out there waiting for us.

I stumble to my feet, and then a wave of nausea hits me. But as soon as it arrives, it vanishes, so I begin to throw on my running gear to search the route for Lila. I finally get my shoes tied and my own pistol cinched onto my waistline, and then I wooze my way toward the front door. I hear the dogs barking in the backyard, so Lila must have let them out before she went running.

When I go out the front door, I feel the chilled drizzle that is misting and falling lightly. It's a dark, rotten morning in late November. The leaves have long since fallen, so the trees are barren and the sky is a dull lead color. I want to turn and go back inside and call for some help, but I'm not sure what's going on, yet, so I stubbornly try to begin jogging the path that we take every morning before we go on shift together.

I'm going to raise hell with her when I find her. Going out alone, without her gun. It's beyond logic, beyond common sense, but it is.

I don't think I can keep going after the first block is behind me, but sheer terror keeps my feet moving in a steady beat onto the sidewalk. No one is out on the concrete with me because of the shivering rain that comes down in fog-like sheets.

I can see the streetlights are lit because it's still so dim out here.

I finally pass the halfway marker for our run, but there's no sign of Lila and there are no passersby to ask if they've seen her. Everyone is either already gone to their jobs or they're nine to fivers, still eating breakfast. The kids have all gone to school a half hour ago. It looks like a scene from some science fiction post-apocalyptic flick. *Everyone* seems gone.

I get to the halfway marker and it's the same. Two more blocks, and no change. I wind up back at the front of our house, and now I'm frantic. I bolt up the stairs, but the effort makes me pause, just inside the door. I almost fall face forward, but I grab hold of the couch in front of me, and the lightheadedness passes.

I want to call for backup, but I don't know where Lila is. If I bring them here, it'll waste even more time. I try to get my head on straight, but I can feel the heat singeing my ears. I must be running a temperature in three digits, but I don't have time to waste taking any Tylenol.

I grab my car keys off the hook in the kitchen, and then I head back out the front door. I have an idea where Lila might be.

I finally call for backup when I'm a half-mile from my destination. The frenzy of looking for Lila has been replaced by something cold and clean in my head. *This is a mission*, I begin to think. The same kind of mission I went on over and over when I was in the War. It's clear who the enemy is, but I'm going strictly on my gut as to his whereabouts.

The picture of the oil puddle in Toliver's garage appeared in my febrile head just before I grabbed the keys and took off. He's at his mother's home. What other safe house has Franklin got to return to? He has no money, unless the Aryans gave him some, but they're not notorious as being moneylenders or banks. Weapons, they might give him. They'd probably enjoy my demise, and Lila's too.

They don't know about the third party involved with Lila and me, but we both know. Franklin is not aware of our unborn child unless he's a psychic—and he's not. The word for him is *psychotic*.

I pull over to the curb about a third of a block before I reach the Lieutenant Governor's one-time residence. It's almost pitch dark outside. There's a pre-winter storm coming, but the temperatures are above freezing, so far, so it's just rain and not ice or snow. I'm wearing a sweatshirt with a hood. It's an old Army hoodie, and it has a few holes in the chest—but the holes came from wear, not bullets or frags. I never wore this heavy thing in the jungle.

I go around the back to check the garage first. No one is outside because the rain is falling harder. There are rumbles of thunder in the distance, and the wind is ripping out of the northeast. It's the Hawk, the bringer of all mothers of bad weather to Chicago.

I know she could be anywhere. Perhaps he doesn't have her at all. Maybe he's not here, either. Toliver could be any number of places. He could have played it smart and stolen another vehicle and disguised himself and headed for Canada or Mexico. He could have funds we don't know about stashed somewhere, and he could've made his way through security onto a plane headed for anywhere. It could be that the Aryans stole him a passport. They know people who're fine forgers, I'm sure.

Anything's possible, but this is what comes up in my head. Franklin won't leave his comfort zone. When he was booted from college, he ran home to mommy. When he was killing the six women, I'm certain he bunked here, in DesPlaines, at least some of the time. He feels safe here. It's his haven. I know the odds are that he wouldn't come back here yet again, but I just have the sure notion that he's taken Lila home to meet his mother.

I open the side door to the garage. It remains as it was, unlocked. The car is here. It's green, it's four door, and it's a Chevy Impala—one of the four rides listed as boosted by the DesPlaines PD.

Franklin is here, so I assume Lila is with him.

I can't expect the troops to arrive for at least ten to fifteen minutes. I called DesPlaines second, so they might arrive sooner, but he could have already slaughtered Lila and the baby by now, so I can't wait. I have to go inside.

I walk out of the garage and head for the back door. This time, I won't have to break in because the door is still wedged slightly open. Someone's made entry, and I'm betting it was recently.

The house is even darker than the outside. The power is probably still on since the place is up for sale. I saw the lock box on the front door handle, and the realtor's sign was planted in the lawn out front.

I don't dare flip any switches. I have to take it as a given that Franklin knows I'm here. He wants me present. He wants to kill Lila in front of me, I'm thinking, and then he wants to finish me, too. So he'll be waiting for me.

It's not like I haven't dealt with this scenario before. The VC and the NVA had excellent intelligence. They frequently knew when we were out looking to engage them in a firefight, and they knew who we'd targeted for assassination. It was their country, their turf, and they were very aware of what was going on in their jungle-hood.

I'm not going to be able to sneak up on Franklin—this is his patch, this is his real backyard. He knows every cranny in this house. I've only been here a few times, and I didn't scope it out for any future encounters on scene. I thought Franklin might just stay a while in Elgin, that Dr. Talbot might be smart enough to never spring him. And if it hadn't been for that whopper blackout storm, he'd probably still be in that electrified little security cubicle, thinking his fevery little thoughts about eliminating anybody he'd like to eliminate.

As I make my way toward the living room, I feel another quick wave of queasiness. I don't think I'm going to puke. I think I just need to sit down. But I can't, of course, so instead I grab hold of a chair in the living room, and I pause until this wave diminishes. It takes a bit, this time. The spells are getting more elongated, each time they occur.

I didn't have time to bring anything other than my piece. I don't have my penlight, and I don't have my switchblade.

So I decide to head back to the kitchen. I stagger there slowly, but I'm still on my feet. I see that the pots and pans haven't been removed, and the knife holder is still in place over the sink, with all the cooking cutlery still intact. I reach for the biggest butcher knife I see. Then I look in several of the drawers until I find tape. They have scotch tape in the second drawer, and even as groggy as I am, I'm able to strap the kitchen knife to the small of my back, horizontally to the waistline of my jogging pants. I haul the waistband over the blade, to help keep it in place, and it feels secure enough. If Franklin is able to take my gun, at least I'll have a little insurance.

But I'm not planning on giving up my weapon. That's the cardinal rule in the cops: you never give up your gun. You do, the hostage gets it in the head and so do you and the bad guy boogies. You're probably better off trying a headshot than you are letting him hide behind the innocent bystander.

Lila is no innocent bystander. He must have had the pistol to get her into the car. I'm sure he used his standby duct tape to bind her hands and feet—otherwise, given the opportunity, Lila would've killed him. She's very lethal, in hand to hand. As I said, I've seen her in action, and I'm never afraid to go into dark places with her.

He had to have tied her up, so I can't rely on Lila for help. I'll have to do this on my own. And it'll have to be very soon because I'm sure he'll shoot her if he hears backup crashing down any doors. I didn't have time to tell them I was going in, here. Time is going to get both of us waxed if I don't move it along right now.

My head seems clearer, now. Perhaps the adrenalin has kicked in, but I'm navigating toward the living room, once more. I search out the main floor, but I don't hear anything and I don't see anything in all this dimness.

I ascend the steps toward the bedrooms, but then I hear something that sounds as if it's emanating from below, in the basement. I retreat toward the kitchen where the basement door is located. I open the door carefully, and it makes no noise.

I hear nothing from downstairs, but I have to check it out anyway. Those cops are likely almost upon us, by now, and if they try to bust in, the party's over, and so is my life, one way or the other. As I walk slowly down the steps, I know I'm through in this life if I lose Lila. I deeply love my daughter, but she's got her own way, now. She's becoming more and more mature as the weeks recede behind us. Lila is my life, outside my daughter, and the baby is our future, and if I lose the baby and Lila....

When I reach the bottom, I stand and listen, with my gun hand stretched out in front of me. Nothing happens. There is no other audible disturbance. The clock is ticking, and if I don't find Franklin and Lila, this house will turn into a fucking shooting gallery.

So I head back upstairs, and only the slight creaks of my footsteps crack the absolute dark and the absolute silence.

I'm back at the stairs heading toward the bedrooms. When I'm halfway up, I hear her.

"*Danny!*"

I begin to rush toward the sound, but when I hit the top step, I hear a thump.

I can't tell which of the bedrooms the sound came from. The doors are all shut. So I'll have to search them, one at a time.

The first bedroom is on the left. It was Franklin's when he was living at home, the mother told me. I bolt inside and sweep the room with my gun, but there's no one here. I wait and I listen, but there is no further voice to call my name.

And then I hear the squeal of rubber from outside. Someone's here, and they're likely to have a lot of company with them. They'll be getting into position soon, and they're likely to be accompanied by special tactical teams, probably SWAT from Chicago. I told them that I thought Franklin had snatched Lila, so they'll be coming with sufficient firepower. All they had to hear was that a police officer had likely been taken hostage. They won't be in a good mood, having heard all that.

I'm leaving Mrs. Toliver's bedroom for last. I don't know why, but it's probably because that's where I'm expecting the two of them to be. So I go to the third bedroom, beyond the master, and I quickly pop open the door and again sweep the room with my gun-holding hand, and I find what I expected, an empty room with sheets covering the bed and all the furniture.

Then I make my way to the only place that thump sound could've come from, Mrs. Raymond Toliver's bed quarters.

My hand is on the knob, and as I turn it, I stop suddenly. I'm sniffing the air as if I'm a bloodhound, but I catch no scent. And I listen before I burst open the entry.

Now I hear more sounds of arriving vehicles outside.

It comes to me that Franklin is calling his own tune, creating his own final scenario. He wants to end it all. That's why he's come here, to such an obvious place to construct his own final death-scene. He expects to be shot. He knew I'd follow him here when he grabbed Lila off the street. I suppose he was hoping to snatch us both on our morning run. He must have been watching us for a long time to establish our routine. We couldn't change the time frame because of the demands of our work, and our regularity and punctuality made it easy for him. Franklin must have delighted at the chance to catch Lila on her own out there and unarmed.

I have my hand still firm on the doorknob.

Then his voice breaks the pause and the silence.

"Come on in, Detective Mangan."

48

I squeeze the doorknob when I hear that voice. I grip the handle of my .38 firmly, and then I fling the door wide open.

He's standing behind Lila. Her feet and her hands are bound together with his usual gray duct tape, and there's a flap of the tape across her lips. Toliver tears the mouth tape away as I point the pistol toward his head.

"Danny!" she cries out.

"Let her loose, Toliver. There's an army about ready to break in, here, and you're going back to your fun palace in Elgin."

His face is obscured from the shade that his hood creates. They are standing to the left of the bed, just in front of the wide walk-in closet where his mother strung herself up.

He's got the Luger pressed against Lila's temple.

"I'm sorry, Danny," she says. Her voice is controlled, but tears stream down onto her cheeks.

"Not your fault. It's his. All of this is *his* goddam fault."

"Is it?" Franklin smiles. I can see his teeth beneath the shadow that covers the upper half of his face.

"Yes. You killed those girls. You escaped from the one place you had a chance to survive. And you don't deserve to live another minute."

I cock the piece and aim for the middle of his forehead.

"You know I'll scatter her brains all over this bedroom."

"Momma wouldn't approve of messing up her room, would she, Franklin?"

"She's dead and she doesn't care anymore."

There's still a glint of white coming from the darkened visage.

"Why the hood all the time, Franklin? You afraid someone might really look at you and see what a fucking coward you really are?"

I tighten my finger on the trigger, just slightly.

"I'll kill her if you shoot. And you don't want to lose her, do you, Detective Mangan."

"Why'd you let her call out to me?"

"I was getting tired of waiting out your thorough search. That's why. And now she can talk all she wants because at least two of us are never getting out of this room."

I have to keep him talking. I'm not a negotiator, but I know that much about hostage situations. One thing is not negotiable: I don't give up my gun. Then he kills Lila and me for sure. He still won't get out of this house alive, though, because SWAT'll be planning a violent entry, about now.

"You want to do murder in your mother's house, Franklin?"

"I would've strangled that bitch myself if she hadn't hung herself for me. You have no idea what that woman was like. I should've killed her a long time ago."

I strain to keep the .38 pointed at him. If I'm going to take my shot at him, it'll have to be soon. I can't keep my arm elevated like this for too much longer, or I'll start to wobble.

Then the nausea returns in a strong, elongated wave. My hand involuntarily begins to descend, and the barrel is now pointed at Lila, instead of Toliver. I release the tension on the trigger, and I have to allow my arm to fall to my side.

Falling is what's going to happen to all of me if this surge doesn't dissipate. I feel as though I'm going to plunge face first at Toliver's feet, and then Lila and I are finished. I don't hear any movement from within the house. They know I'm in here, and perhaps they're waiting for some kind of signal from me to burst in. But they will only wait briefly because they know Franklin Toliver will kill us both, if he can.

"What's the matter, Detective? You feeling poorly?" he says with a mock tone of concern.

"Danny—"

He presses the barrel of the Luger harder against her right temple.

"You shoot her, and I won't kill you fast. I'll bleed you. I'll tell them to stay the hell out, and then I'll skin you, Toliver. Inch by inch."

"Those are big words from a man who's about to topple onto the floor. Then you'll take all the fun away."

The sickly force is lessening, it seems. I'm able to stand straight up, again, and when I straighten, my hand holding the .38 rises, as well. I've got it aimed at the spot between his eyebrows. The only problem is that he might pull his own trigger from the reflex after I've blown his brains against the wall.

The queasiness returns, suddenly, and this time it comes on even stronger, and as it gains in intensity, the .38 drops from my grip, and now I find myself on my knees in front of Lila and Toliver.

The gun lies to my right, and my head is bowed. He's going to kill us both, and I still hear no sound from beneath us that would signal a rescue attempt. They might come through the window after sending tear gas inside, but I don't sense any activity at all, and I'm going to lose Lila and the baby.

And my life.

I feared death. I respected death. I despised death as a competitor when I was in the War. It was always lurking; its stench was omnipresent. And now I smell that vile reek once more. It followed me all the way home to this city, and now it emanates from the floor of this bedroom. It's worse than the stench of road kill. Nothing can equal the putrid odor of a dead human being, and that stink has begun to permeate this room.

I try to lift my head and look at Lila for the last time, before he kills her, and then me. I can only get my chin up slightly because I feel like I'm about to black out.

I can only see their feet in front of me. And then I see a mist

367

gathering around their shoes, and I know I'm beginning to hallucinate. The mist develops into a white fog and it begins to rise up Franklin's and Lila's legs. I can see up to their kneecaps, and I can't pull my head up any higher now.

Then I hear Franklin scream, and the two people in front of me are suddenly separated. I'm thinking they've shot a tear gas canister into the bedroom, but there was no crash from a broken window. And no one's kicked in the closed bedroom door.

Franklin screams again, and I hear him crash into the blinds that cover the bedroom window. I'm on my hands and knees, and I reach wildly behind me and grope for the butcher knife taped to the small of my back. And as Franklin Toliver bellows out in terror one more time, I have the ten inch blade firmly gripped, and somehow I'm scrambling to my feet, and as I'm vertical, I can see the look of mortifying fear on his now unhooded face. He's glaring at something by the closet, but I haven't got time to see what he's staring at. So I summon anything I have left, all the hatred I have for Toliver, the man who'd steal Lila and our child. The man who'd rob me of seeing Kelly reach her dreams in medicine. And I hurl myself at him, and I raise the knife, and Franklin tries to aim the Luger at me, but I lunge at him and stick the sharp point of the knife into his throat and the blade sinks all the way through his soft neck, and my momentum slams me into Toliver and we crash through the blinds and the window—

The next thing I sense is the immense impact of our bodies hitting the front lawn outside, and now it is black and silent and nothing more.

Shapes of gray and cobalt and murky white race across the insides of my eyelids. So this is death. This is the underground. This is where I sent all those souls, dispatched all those soldiers that I killed in the War. They're waiting for me here. They've been waiting since 1972. I'm finally with them.

What will I say to them? That I'm sorry I aborted their lives when they were fully grown but still very young men? Will they apologize to the men they've slain?

The shapes keep shifting inside my eyes. I know I'm somewhere else. I know I'm not on the grass in front of the Lieutenant Governor's home anymore, but I wonder if I'm on a slab in the morgue where we took all the stiffs, all the dead bodies whose murders we investigated.

In the War, we stuffed them in body bags, and the ones who were recovered got to take the funeral flight back to the World. At least they went home.

But I'm in some netherworld, some place in between heaven and hell. Perhaps this is the place Catholics call Purgatory. We got rid of Limbo, I think. But that was our version. Who knows where I've really landed.

Then I hear her voice, summoning me. Telling me to come back. *It's Lila.* I recognize her voice as well as I recognize the voice of my daughter. And I hear Kelly's voice, next to Lila.

I struggle to open my eyes. It seems as if they're seared shut. But I finally flap my right eyelid open, and I see two very fuzzy outlines, which appear to be feminine, after the eye begins to focus a little better.

Then I've finally got the other eye opened, and slowly, slowly, the fuzziness fades, and I see Lila and my daughter standing next to me. I'm lying in a hospital, not the morgue, and when I see Lila alive, and Kelly standing next to her, I can't stop myself from weeping.

"Danny?" Lila says, her own voice overcome with emotion.

She comes up next to me and bends over and kisses me, all over my face.

"*Ouch,*" I groan.

She laughs.

"That's all you can tell me is *ouch?*" she laughs again. I hear Kelly joining in with her, and then my daughter kisses me on the left cheek, and that causes a bit of discomfort, also.

"You're all beat up," Lila explains. "They took all kinds of glass out of your cheeks, but you're lucky you didn't catch any shards in the throat or the eyes. Toliver broke your fall. He was underneath you, sort of like a cushion. He didn't do nearly as well as you."

Lila looks over at Kelly, and then I remembered sticking Toliver with the kitchen knife, and I understand why Lila doesn't continue the details of Franklin's demise.

"You suffered a pretty good concussion, and they put about sixteen stitches in your puss and about twenty in your forearms where the glass cut you. You looked like a porcupine when the paramedics got to you, Danny, with glass quills."

She looks over at Kelly.

"Honey, can I talk to your dad alone for a minute?" Lila asks.

"Sure. I'll be out in the hall."

Kelly walks out the door of my hospital room.

"Do you remember what happened, Danny?"

I look at her and watch her bluer than blue eyes.

"I remember hitting the deck in the bedroom, and then I looked up and things got sort of cloudy. But the clouds were on the floor...."

"Do you remember hearing him scream?"

"Vaguely. Why'd he yell out? What happened?"

"I don't know, Danny. He had the gun pointed at my head, you went down, and I thought we were both dead. And then he turned away from me toward that closet, and he must have thought he saw something, but I didn't see a damn thing. There was no one in that room with the three of us. But he thought he saw something, and he started backing up toward that window, away from the closet, and then you were charging him, and the two of you went through the window, and then the SWAT team burst inside, just about when I heard the two of you thumping onto the lawn. That was when *I* let loose with a few howls of my own, because I thought you were dead, down there, Danny. I thought I lost you."

She bends toward me and kisses my lips gently, once more.

"You didn't see anything?"

"Nothing," she answers. "But I know what Franklin saw."

I lie at St. Mary's Hospital in Evanston for another week before they'll let me out. We're into early December, and every time Lila comes to see me—which is every hour she's not working a shift—she tells me just how our wedding's going to go. Kelly has returned to DeKalb to take her final exams, but she'll be back around the 15th of the month for her Christmas break. Lila and I will get to meet her new young man, Matthew, over break, and it seems as if my daughter has found a keeper, this time.

I know I have. I can't remember the last time I really celebrated the Holidays, but I have a feeling this will be the year.

A number of vets always told me that they never felt more alive than when they almost caught it, out on the battlefield. The nearness of death somehow seems to revitalize the man who gets close enough to smell the rot of hell itself. When Odysseus emerged out of the underground, he was finally allowed to return to Penelope and to his home of Ithaca. It took him twenty years, but he got there.

It's been about sixteen years since I returned from Southeast Asia, almost that same time frame that Odysseus/Ulysses wandered the seas, escaping sirens and Cyclops and assorted other baddies.

But in this hospital bed, at the tail end of my recovery, I feel like land is in sight. After seeing the grave sites in the pauper's cemetery where Cook County buries indigents, after seeing the graves of those six murdered women, it seems finally that I've returned to the land of the living.

Anyway, Lila fills my head with the promises of our oncoming wedding and of Christmas, itself. It'll be our first Christmas as man and wife. I used to have doubts that Lila could settle in with one man or one woman, but I have no such doubts, anymore. I can sense that she has resigned herself to living with another Homicide detective, that we'll go on looking for more killers like Franklin Toliver or like the drug salesman who slaughtered Bill O'Connor's wife.

I can see the stitches in my arms, and I saw the ravages that the glass did on my face, and I'm worried I'll look like Frankenstein's famous creation at our wedding, in a few weeks.

Lila tells me she can do makeup for me if I feel all that self-conscious, but I responded telling her there was no way I was going up the aisle in pancake. They'd have to take me the way I was.

And she insisted that was the way she always wanted me, anyway.

I know what Franklin saw, even though I was the only living person in that bedroom who never got to see Mrs. Toliver. Lila saw her, I'm certain, back when we searched the house for Franklin, together. But I never saw her after she passed. Maybe I wasn't supposed to.

And maybe she was just the power of suggestion to Lila and

Franklin. Perhaps Dr. Fernandez can explain it all away. Something or someone made Toliver let loose of Lila. Something or someone saved my life. He would've killed us both before the cavalry arrived, I'm certain of it. Maybe it's fate. Maybe it's earth tremors or static electricity.

But someone else was in that room with the three of us, and I owe her, big time.

49

My daughter has bloomed like Gregor Samsa's sister in Kafka's story, "The Metamorphosis." She's thrown off the grays and pale colors, and she's come alive in ways I couldn't imagine, only a few months ago.

When they finally let me go from the hospital, it was just ten days until our wedding. The nuptials are on December 22nd. It doesn't leave me much time to heal, but I'm taking all the days I've got accumulated at work, and we're taking the week after Christmas as our honeymoon. We aren't going very far from home, just up to the Lake Geneva, Wisconsin, area. We're going to stay in a very expensive hotel called The Abbey. It's all on Lila's father's tab. He's doing rather well in his legal practice, Lila informs me, and he'll be running for circuit court judge, next fall. And mommy is a big time pediatrician, so it's just penny ante stuff for her folks. Which she tells me so I won't feel like a leech. I could've sprung for the hotel, but Lila insisted it was on the bride's side to take care of it.

Kelly and I have virtually no family except each other. As I said, my parents are dead, and my relatives, such as they are, are scattered on the East and West Coasts. I was never close with any of them, so I don't see any reason to send out invitations to people who have no intention of showing up. And I really don't want gifts, just for sending out the invites. I got all the gifts I want, now that Lila is marrying me and Kelly is a full member of the living, again.

I offered to take us to Florida or to the warmer climes somewhere, but Lila likes Wisconsin, and so do I. We've already talked about retiring up there, once we've done our requisite years on the force. She'll open an aerobics school, up there, and I'll catch up on all the Kafka and Tolstoy and Faulkner I never got to read, to this point. I could see sitting on that beach-front property and just reading novel after novel during the summer and early fall. The dogs would be chasing each other on the sand, though they'd both be getting up in age by then. And in the colder parts of the year, late fall and winter, we could both hole up in front of a fireplace, Lila and I.

I know that my life will never go as smoothly as I pictured it above, but it's a very pretty fantasy.

It doesn't really matter all that much if we don't get beach front property or even that we don't move out of the house we live in now. The "where" doesn't matter nearly as much as the "with whom." In other words, as long as my kid lives forever and Lila does, too, I won't bitch about my fate. She is my Penelope, after all, and it looks like I'm finally going home.

Kelly came home last night from school. She claims she did well on her finals, but she'll know for sure when they post grades right after Christmas, she says. I'm expecting the best because I know how hard she's worked, ever since her last semester in high school.

Lila is out looking for the few invitations we'll need. They're being sent out on very short notice, obviously, but all she needs is about twenty, for her family's side here near town. It's going to be a very small wedding, probably fewer than fifty invitees. The ones she's inviting are very close to her and her folks, so they'll likely all show up.

I don't have many friends, so I ask a guy I know pretty well from Homicide to be my best man. We've known each other since I was a patrolman. He's one of the most respected detectives on the force. His name is Jimmy Parisi, and he's already established a rep among Homicides. He generously accepted his role at such short notice.

Kelly is going to be Lila's matron of honor, and that's the extent of the wedding party. Lila vowed to keep things short and sweet, and she did. We could've waited until spring and then launched a bigger affair, but neither of us wanted to wait another week, let alone all those months.

I suppose we're behaving like a couple of twenty year olds instead of the almost-middle aged couple that we are. And then there's the baby. He or she has to have legitimate parents—Lila's words, not mine. But I agree with her. Kelly has my name, and the new kid will have a name, too. Lila wants to go by her married name, but I never insisted. She is, after all, a feminist in basic philosophy, but she doesn't buy everything from the party line.

"I can think for myself," she tells me.

I'm sitting in the living room watching nothing in particular on the tube. Kelly is sitting next to me. When all this started with Toliver, we never used to occupy the same room, let alone sit this closely. Shit happens, as the bumper stickers proclaim. Things really do change. But she's sitting on the seater next to me on the three-seat sectional.

"Do they hurt?" she asks me.

"Does what hurt?" I reply.

She nods toward the remaining stitches on my forearms.

"They itch, once in a while, but they'll be coming out soon."

"What about all those bruises on your ribs?"

"They only tug at me rarely. I'm lucky I didn't bust any. But then Franklin served one last good purpose. He cushioned my fall real nice."

Kelly doesn't smile.

"You could've been killed, Dad."

"Anybody could be walking into that bus, kid. It's part of the job description."

"You could do something else."

"Could you do something besides medicine, someday?" I ask her.

She smiles and smells the trap.

"They don't throw you out of windows or shoot at you or tie you up and kidnap you like they did Lila."

"That's true. Different sports, different rules. This kind of thing rarely happens, Kelly."

She burrows her head against my left side, and I want to wince, but I don't. I put my arm over her shoulder and I hold her tightly. Then she sits back up, straight.

"I never hated you, you know," she says. "I was just a little bitch wrapped up in her own melodrama."

"You had reason to be pissed. Your mother took off and I wasn't there like I should have been."

"You were there. I just wouldn't let you close. It was my fault."

"Don't play the fault game, Kelly. It goes round and round and eventually it goes no damn place at all. You're here. I'm still here. Let's start from today and screw what's already behind us. It almost seems like it never happened, right now."

She leans back into me, and once again I refrain from groaning. She's tickling my ribs, but this kind of pain never felt so good.

"Do you still love Momma?"

She's talking about Mary, of course.

I look over at her and engage her eyes with mine.

"I never stopped loving your mother, and I never will. And Lila knows it. But she knows I'll never go back with your mom even if she shows up at the door tomorrow. That life is gone. But I don't stop loving people, even when they stop loving me. It's what they call a tragic flaw."

"It's no flaw. Maybe a weakness."

"Maybe you're right. You miss your mother, still?"

"Sometimes I do. I tried hating her, at first, but I couldn't. I just didn't have the energy or the concentration to hate her. I should have. She left me—and you, too. I sometimes think I wouldn't have done what I did if she'd stuck around, but that's bogus, too. I'm the one who purged, and I'm the one who scarfed all that stuff into me. Nobody else."

I look at her again, and I hug her.

"What's that for?" she smiles.

"Just for the hell of it," I tell her.

She settles back against the couch.

"How's Matthew?"

We still haven't met her significant other.

"He's coming over in a half hour."

"Jesus Christ! Why didn't you tell me?"

"You've got time to get dressed. Lila said she'd be back in ten minutes," she says as she looks at the battery clock on the wall over the TV.

I struggle to get up, but I make it, and then I aim myself for the bathroom.

"Why the hell didn't either of you tell me?" I gripe as I head toward our bedroom.

"Just so you wouldn't stress out, just like you are, right now," she laughs.

We go to Marco's in Oak Lawn for a late dinner. I suppose I should've wondered why Lila didn't make dinner before she left, about 4:00 P.M. Now I know. Lila drives the four of us to the restaurant. I can handle the wheel, but she babies me no matter what I say or how I remonstrate.

Matthew is a tall young man, maybe six three. He looks like he might have played basketball, but Kelly has not volunteered all that much information about him, just yet. He's very polite, but he seems natural in his manner, not forced. I'm sure Lila has noticed how good-looking he is, but she never informed me what a stallion my daughter seems to have landed. There's no telling how far these two will go in their college romance, but I'm hoping it works out, if it's really meant to.

We arrive at Marco's about 8:45. This is unusually late for dinner, but my routine has been altered pretty well, the last several months. I'm getting used to changes.

Matthew talks about himself easily, and he appears confident but not cocky. I like the kid and I've only known him for less than an hour. And then Kelly knows him far better than Lila or I do, and I respect Kelly's opinion.

The four of us sit in a booth in this bar and grill, and I look around and see that the place looks new, or it was newly remodeled. When the food arrives, it's very good. We sit and talk for a half hour after the meal. I feel as if I've known everyone here for as long as I've known my daughter.

Something has to disrupt all this good cheer. I'm remembering Dr. Fernandez and our discussions about those "footsteps" that signal something evil is afoot. We worked on my paranoia, if that was what it really was. It could be just cynicism or pessimism about the way things work in life. The literary term is foreboding. You get this sense that something bad is catching up with you, and it's always just about the time your life seems to be at its best.

Like now. I survived a fall from the second floor of the Lieutenant Governor's house. I crashed to the ground on top of a multiple murderer and general psychopath. I avoided getting my jugular sliced by a piece of broken glass. I only bruised several ribs instead of breaking them, and I avoided slicing various arteries in my arms on my plunge to the lawn atop Franklin.

Fortuitous? I don't know if it was luck or fate. I don't know if misery is just around the corner, although I have suspicions that it'll rear its ugly head sooner or later.

But I've got someone to face it with, now. Actually, two someones. Lila and Kelly. I have a family, I think, for real, for the first time since Kelly was born. Mary ran off, and then my daughter and I were never really all that close. Lila seemed to vanish from my horizons, but she was reclaimed to me.

There will be other killers to catch. We never run out of them. We never run out of business, in Homicide, and it's likely our trade will never hit a Recession or a Depression, unfortunately.

But I'm going to forget all that for tonight. I'm going to allow myself to emerge from the underground, and if only for a few minutes or hours, I'm going to let myself be happy.

She wears white. I have the suspicion that she's not a virgin. She might as well be, with her beaming face, coming down the aisle of the church toward me. Her father walks her with the music accompanying them.

Jimmy Parisi, my best man, looks a little uncomfortable wearing the tux we rented for him in a genuine rush job. This whole wedding has been accomplished in a blur. Jimmy's about my height. He looks like Al Pacino, a little. Maybe it's just the Italian in him, and maybe I'm typecasting. His wife is out there in the pews, and so is his partner,

Harold (Doc) Gibron. That's about it from my side, other than Matthew and his mother and father and his younger brother, Dave. The bulk of guests belongs to my bride. There are maybe thirty people on her side of the pews.

Lila arrives at the altar, kisses her distinguished counselor of a father, and then he hands her off to me. We turn around to the cross and we face the priest, and he begins the ceremony.

The roads are all slick on the way up to Wisconsin to The Abbey Hotel. I think the town's name is Fontana. It's only a ninety minute drive in optimum conditions, but tonight, after the fancy, expensive reception that Lila's parents threw for us at a place in the Loop right by the Chicago River, it takes two hours of laboriously slow driving to get where we're headed.

During the last half hour of the drive, conditions improve because the salt trucks cover the highways, and it stops raining with its icy mixture. By the time we hit the hotel, the trees are glistening with ice, but the roads are clear and melted.

When I see the interior of The Abbey, I'm glad her father picked up the bill for the week. This place is far out of my league.

But I could really get used to it. Room service has been included by Lila's dad, as well as all of our meals in the restaurant in the hotel. But we're going to fast food it for everything but our nightly dinner so that we don't soak the Chapmans worse than they're already getting hosed for the cost of this almost-impromptu wedding. Nothing wrong with pancakes at the mighty Mac's. Lila likes their food, too.

We're fairly destroyed by the time we reach our wedding suite. There's a magnum of champagne waiting for us, and we drink just one glass before Lila tears our clothes off. We consummate the marriage with all appropriate brio and enthusiasm.

"I thought it was supposed to be better when we weren't married," she smiles as she kisses me.

"Practice, practice, practice," I reply as I kiss her and move her head back down onto the pillow.

"I'll try to be gentle," I tell her. "I know it's your first time, and I'll try to take it easy on you."

She laughs.

"You're the one who has to be coddled. Look at you! You're a mess, Danny. You look like you met up with the cold cuts slicer at the deli. All those laces in your arms. Those lovely purple welts on your ribcage. I really should be turned off. Hell, I want a refund."

"You're not happy with my efforts?"

She shoots me a very sly grin.

"Happy? No. That doesn't capture it at all."

She starts snaking her way down toward the middle of the bed, toward no man's land. And then my eyes pop open in surprise when she begins.

We take walks around the hotel property. The lake, Lake Geneva, is only a few hundred feet behind the hotel. They have scores of ducks that walk the lake- front, scavenging for food from the guests. The ducks are very domestic—they have no fear of people, probably because their diet relies upon the kindness of strangers.

Lila bought some snacks from the gift shop just for the quackers. She's been here before, with her parents. When she extends her hand with the junk food, the mallards or whatever they are come rushing at us aggressively. I almost want to go for my gun, but we left our pieces back in the room. We're on honeymoon, Lila told me when she saw me putting the holster around my waist. So I dropped it into the drawer where she put her .32. I'm relying on her intuition that they don't allow bad guys at The Abbey.

At night, we go to the movies. We watch some pseudo thriller where I figure out the surprise ending thirty minutes into the two-hour flick.

"I'm not taking you to the movies again," she complains halfheartedly.

I whispered what was going to happen at the end about twenty minutes before it did. She punched me on a non-stitched part of my arm, and she caught me good.

Later at night, we made up for the more than thirty-eight years I never knew Lila Chapman. She's insatiable, but I'm worse. We get almost no sleep. Every time we roll away to try and catch a few, she or I start it up all over again. I never realized I had all this sap and energy. At least I haven't since I was in my twenties.

As the cliché goes, *she makes all things new*. Me, included.

Epilogue

K elly's got a year of college behind her. She nailed a 3.85 GPA, and she's made herself and her old man proud. Not to mention Lila—who Kelly has begun calling "Mom." It startled Lila the first time my daughter called her that, but it's really made my wife happy. So I'm hoping she'll always think of Lila as her new "Mom."

The summer brings out the worst in those who have the worst in them, and we're busy in Homicide. That little respite in The Abbey is over, and it's back to business as usual. No multiples, yet, this summer, but some asshole will have to make up for lost time. Someone has to be heir to the throne that Franklin Toliver sat on. Someone has to make headlines and become high profile.

High or low, I have to chase them all. My job is like the Greek legend of the guy condemned to roll the stone up the hill only to have it roll back down at him every time. His name was Sisyphus. That's my job, sort of. You get things in place, you catch a perp, and a new baddie comes along and starts that stone rolling right back down at you, all over again.

As I said, we'll never have to worry about business, not with all the knuckleheads in this city, in this world.

I picked up a habit I learned from my best man, Detective Jimmy

Parisi. He would always visit the graves of the victims whose murders he investigated, and he would place a single yellow rose on the site, beneath their markers.

I've picked up the habit. I've begun to frequent the cemeteries where my ex-cases rest. I place a single yellow rose on each spot, also.

Yellow roses stand for loyalty, fidelity. Faithfulness.

I figure I owe each of those departed victims the gesture. It isn't much to ask, I guess.

Author's Note

As a work of fiction, this novel acknowledges that women did not fly combat missions until *after* the Vietnam War.

Acknowledgements

To Thomas Palakeel, my *Underground* partner in crime.

Also by Parkgate Press (Dionysus Books)

www.mattfullerty.com

www.dionysusbooks.com
www.parkgateoriginals.com

THE KNIGHT OF NEW ORLEANS
The Pride and the Sorrow of Paul Morphy

A quiet boy is born in New Orleans with a spellbinding gift: he can beat anyone at chess. But what happens when love, desire and ambition intervene?

THE MURDERESS AND THE HANGMAN
A Novel of Criminal Minds

The story of female killer Kate Webster, the man who hanged her and the missing head found 132 years later in Sir David Attenborough's garden.

About the Author

Thomas Laird has published four novels: *Cutter* (2001), *Season of the Assassin* (2003), *Black Dog* (2004) and *Voices of the Dead* (2006). The first three books were co-published in London and New York by Constable & Robinson and by Carroll & Graf (Perseus), the fourth in the Czech Republic by Domino Publishers.

The books received favorable reviews from the *Washington Post*, the *Chicago Sun-Times*, *Publishers Weekly*, *Library Journal*, the *Independent on Sunday* (UK) and *Crime Time* (UK).

Thomas Laird lives in Peoria, Illinois.

This title is also available as an ebook from Parkgate Digital.

Lightning Source UK Ltd.
Milton Keynes UK
UKOW042140250612

195050UK00005B/33/P